ACTS OF BETRAYAL

ACTS OF BETRAYAL

GERALDINE MURPHY

Macdonald & Co
London & Sydney

A Macdonald Book

First published in Great Britain in 1983
by Macdonald & Co (Publishers) Ltd
London & Sydney

ISBN 0 356 09190 2

Printed in Great Britain by
Redwood Burn Limited, Trowbridge, Wiltshire
Bound at the Dorstel Press

Macdonald & Co
Maxwell House
74 Worship Street
London EC2A 2EN

'For nothing can seem foul to those that win.'
Henry IV; *Henry the Fourth, Part One*

ONE

O, the blood more stirs
To rouse a lion than to start a hare!

    – HOTSPUR; *Henry the Fourth*, Part One

The television cameras arrived at noon. Within seconds the foyer was transformed by cables, lighting equipment and the raised voices of technicians.

A man with coal-black curls, tinged here and there with grey, leaned against the reception desk and watched.

It looked like bedlam. Clients and staff mingled confusedly with media people; two commissionaires, ostentatious in their gold-braid uniforms, were trying to take charge; a flustered PR man was searching frantically for the director.

One of the crew paused in the middle of the vast expanse of carpet: he stared at the brilliant array of hothouse plants, the sweep of the great staircase, the long row of discreetly panelled lifts, the sculpture that stood against the pale cream walls. Then he looked at the portrait that hung directly opposite the main doors. It was an excellent and flattering likeness of the present chairman. He shook his head thoughtfully and turned aside, muttering under his breath.

The man by the reception desk ran his hand through his hair; his mouth twitched into a smile.

The confusion was lessening. A security guard was directing people to the furthermost of the lifts and to the staircase. Another was stopping new arrivals at the door, demanding to see credentials before he allowed them in. Three receptionists were on duty, answering questions and giving advice like practised politicians. One of them was almost permanently on the telephone; each time she put it down it would buzz again insistently.

'No, the chairman cannot,' she snapped at the end of a fraught conversation. 'It is impossible . . . All lines to the chairman's office are engaged at the moment . . . They would tell you exactly the same thing. Tomorrow, by all means . . . And the chairman couldn't care less.'

Turning to look at her, the man realized that the last sentence had been directed at him.

'Still in a board meeting, would you believe.' Hopelessly clumsy at trying to flirt, she blushed a little as she spoke. She was a pretty girl, nineteen or twenty at the most, and her brown eyes were sharp as a sparrow's.

'Well you know what these important board meetings are like,' the man grinned, as though entering with her into some complicity over the derisory nature of all such goings-on.

Delighted, she smiled back at him. She'd been watching him, on and off, for the past ten minutes. She'd spotted him the moment he'd walked through the door, with his dark tousle of hair that was almost as attractive as a girl's. Close to, though, she saw that he was older than she'd imagined: his eyes were bright blue and mischievous, but there were faint lines around them, just as there were strands of grey in his lovely hair. His features, too, were less handsome than they'd appeared from a distance. They were strong and rather craggy, and he looked fitter than most men of his age – almost too much so, like the professional bodyguard the chairman had used when there'd been all that worry about a visit to the Middle East.

This man was tough, she decided, and for all his faultlessly tailored suit and easy manner, she didn't know whether she found him attractive or disquieting.

Suddenly nervous, she blurted out the first thing that

came into her head: 'Any normal person would be excited – a whole television programme to themselves.'

'Ah, but we all know the chairman isn't a normal person, don't we?'

He was teasing her, and she felt even more uncomfortable.

'It's on at peak viewing time,' she said, and as she met his gaze wasn't sure whether his eyes were simply mischievous or if there mightn't be a glint of something harder there. 'Sixty minutes, I think. Some people have all the luck.'

'I know,' he said, and as the telephone buzzed again he moved away, towards the chairman's private lift where he had no right to be going.

The programme was called *Success*. This was its second year, and it was still high in the ratings.

The chairman of Borjex's European operations was ideal material. Anyone who, at not yet forty, could run an organization with a turnover in the billions, and so diversified that it included chemical plants, research establishments, opencast mining, engineering works and even soft drinks manufacture, had to be an extraordinary kind of person.

But even the headquarters themselves would provide some first-rate shots. The large Queen Anne mansion in the centre of London was as elegant inside as out. Its use for business had been meticulously planned – computer terminals and information banks tucked neatly away in the sprawling basements, air-conditioning systems hidden from view, cornices and woodwork and marble stairways all carefully preserved.

The octagonal board room, with its sound-proofed windows and mahogany-panelled walls, had double doors that reached almost to the ceiling. Shortly after noon, at the close of the monthly planning meeting, they burst open. Flanked by legal adviser and personal assistant, the chairman was the first to emerge and strode briskly down the long corridor towards the penthouse suite.

Mrs Egerton, the senior secretary, was waiting in the outer office. Deep piles of memoranda and letters were arranged on her desk.

'Good meeting?' It was her habitual greeting, and meant little more than 'good morning'.

'Not bad. Figures for the chemical plant are a bit vague, but there again so is Dr Beloff.'

Mrs Egerton tutted.

'You haven't got long,' she said.

'Hm. Any messages?'

'None that can't wait.'

'Good.'

Going through to the bathroom, the chairman locked the door and sighed deeply with the relief of being alone for a few minutes. Then she opened her handbag and took out her make-up.

Gareth Williams hesitated, then slipped quickly behind one of those absurd sculptures that lined the corridor. He wondered if she was responsible for their presence, or if they were the result of some sort of directive from on high. Not that there was anything very much higher than Katherine Hanson.

She swept towards him and he wished he was wearing a hat; even a bowler would have done, so long as it hid those curls that were a certain giveaway.

Opening his briefcase and pretending to rummage about inside it, he watched her out of the corner of his eye, through one of the triangular holes in the marble. But he needn't have worried, she didn't even glance in his direction. She looked neither to right nor left as she walked, just straight ahead. She held herself very erect, and her hair, he noticed, was still blonde and shining – just as he'd always remembered it, except that it was shorter now and better groomed, with subtle highlights that seemed to change as she moved. Her face looked thinner, but healthy, and from this distance he couldn't tell whether there were lines on it or not. The clothes he wasn't so sure about; they were smart, and doubtless expensive, but too severe for such a woman. Still, they were her working clothes, so he supposed they had to be plain. But the legs below the linen skirt were devastating, superb beyond question.

He felt an overwhelming urge to whistle, suppressed it, and grinned; he might have been right back in his twenties, instead of a respectable millionaire of over forty.

The truth was that he hadn't expected anything quite so awe-inspiring as this. She was an amalgam of beauty and forcefulness; cool, competent power. He wondered if he would still be able to make her shriek and laugh, like before, but her lips were set in a hard, thin line and she looked almost frightening. At any rate, the retinue that was hurrying after her looked suitably on their mettle.

She paused to give some last-minute instructions to a pale-faced boy with a nose like a parrot. The lad seemed to be some form of personal assistant, and was obviously suffering from hypertension. There was a rigidity about his limbs, as though they'd been ever so slightly embalmed, and the bulbous eyes held an expression of intense eagerness. He wondered if this could be Richard Stempel, the bright young graduate who was supposed to be going places.

Taking a sheaf of papers from his briefcase and bending his head over them, he edged nearer to the largest of the holes. He managed to see her legs right down to the ankle: no hint of swelling, he was glad to note; if anything they seemed shapelier than before. All in all, she looked as though she'd kept herself in first-rate trim.

By God, though, her voice wasn't merely clear and resonant, it rang out like the chapel bell.

The pale-faced boy turned grey, but was saved by the

appearance of an elegantly dressed, balding man, with a high-domed forehead and a general air of being both unhurried and in control.

'Hugo—' he heard her say. 'Just the person I wanted to see.'

This, then, must be Hugo Palfreyman, the chief legal adviser. Drawing Katherine aside, he began to talk to her in an undertone. She listened attentively, shook her head once or twice, and finally thanked him. Moreover, she actually smiled. It wasn't much of a smile, more a token curve of the lips, but it was a kindlier dismissal than she'd given the pale-faced boy, and it augured hope for the future.

Any second now she would move on again. He toyed with the idea of changing position, or even strolling out into the corridor in order to catch a glimpse of the back view, but any radical gesture might draw attention to himself, and indeed he had the impression that Palfreyman had already spotted him, just as the lawyer had been retreating from Katherine's considerable presence. The high-domed forehead had turned towards the sculptures, and an expression of recognition followed by shocked disbelief had flitted across those patrician features.

No, the back view would have to wait until another day.

Nodding pleasantly to a middle-aged woman who happened to be passing, Katherine called after her: 'Unobtainable for the rest of the day, don't forget.' Then she strode on, to her private dining room where the first part of the interview was to be shot.

As soon as the important people had gone, he emerged from hiding and descended the staircase to the floor below. There were cushioned benches arranged at intervals along the walls, and he chose one that was more secluded than the rest and sat down. It was surprising what hints you could pick up, if you arrived in a place unannounced and just had a good look round.

He'd called in on the spur of the moment, without giving Katherine even an inkling of his intentions. She would be completely unaware of his presence in the building, and he hadn't the faintest idea what her reaction would be if she should come face to face with him. But he guessed that she would be far from pleased.

It was fifteen years since they'd last met, and in view of the fact that it was she who was now chairman of this company, he wondered if he wasn't pushing his luck to even consider doing business with Borjex. It could be an extremely useful move, but he would be foolish to rush into a situation where there could be all sorts of complications, a situation that might keep him away too much and too long from his own enterprises in the States. He'd fought so hard for his success, and he had no intention of letting even a part of it slip away from him. On the contrary, he wanted more.

He'd worked relentlessly at first to establish his business, and taken all kinds of risks. That was the part he'd enjoyed, the calculated moves followed by gambles that others might never have dared to take. That was where the fun had come in, the thrills and that sweet elation that accompanies success after near-disaster.

New York had been a hostile place when he'd tried to make his mark there, but he'd conquered it, not merely through grinding perseverance but through sheer nerve. He wasn't ashamed of any of the things he'd done, because he'd only done battle with people who were already in the arena and that seemed fair enough to him.

One skirmish, though, had left his opponent so completely defeated that he'd never entered the arena again, which was not what Gareth had intended.

Ellis McKay had been his partner for two years when it happened. Poor, foolish Ellis who wasn't even the business member of the team! Middle-aged, phlegmatic Ellis with his wife and three daughters to provide for! How crazy he'd been to try and cross Gareth – to attempt to outsmart him in the most cowardly and underhand way possible! But he'd learned his lesson. Gareth had all but destroyed him – and nearly lost his own life in the process.

Even now he could remember lying in that hospital bed, and cursing himself for the one basic fact he'd overlooked – the ferocity of a woman's emotions when she's in love. And Ellis's wife had been nothing if not loyal. He could remember her standing in the dock, months later, telling the whole wide world about why – and how gladly – she'd tried to murder Gareth Williams.

The television crew had several hours' work still ahead of them when Gareth retraced his steps, crossed the sumptuous foyer of Borjex, nodded to the commissionaire who held open the door for him, then strolled out into the noise and hurly-burly of Knightsbridge.

There were pros and cons about becoming involved with this mammoth corporation, and there was an excellent chance that Katherine Hanson could make the project a complicated one. Clashes of personality were almost certain, and God alone knew what other events mightn't be provoked by this liaison.

Katherine Hanson! He was starting something, if he got too close to her again. Katherine, with those slanting hazel eyes and that vicious temper.

He smiled to himself, and felt his pulse quicken.

Bill Skerrett's office was directly below the chairman's. Sometimes he imagined he could hear her footsteps, and would look up at the ceiling, as if watching the skies and listening for God.

Today was exceptional in its awfulness. Not only was the woman trampling back and forth on his head, but so were hordes of other people, all come to praise her, to stamp her face and her voice and everything else about her on cellulose.

The fuss they were making reached even the peace of

his sanctum. Board member and director of no less than two major departments, his association with Borjex spanned nearly twenty years, and he saw his importance reaffirmed in his vast, leather-topped desk, in the crystal glasses that stood on his drinks cabinet, in the very atmosphere of this dignified room. It was six square feet bigger than Katherine's. The thought made him chuckle; he quickly put a hand over his mouth, stifling the sound.

He swivelled thoughtfully in his enormous, winged chair, his little legs dangling free and his pointed shoes just skimming the surface of the deep-pile carpet.

His face was wreathed in lines of anxiety and obsequiousness; it looked like a shrivelled nut, and contracted still further as he listened to the sounds of someone else's publicity.

He swivelled faster, and as he did so he trembled – very slightly but all over – and his mind was whirring, too. He felt terrible. Beads of perspiration glistened precariously on his upper lip. A familiar stabbing pain started up, dangerously near his heart. Fishing about in his pockets, he found a phial of tablets, took one, and then tried the deep-breathing exercises his doctor had recommended.

He heard a loud thud, somewhere above him, followed by a burst of laughter.

The pain was in his head now, as if whatever had been dropped had been successfully aimed at him.

Looking up at the ceiling, he reached for the telephone. 'New York office,' he said.

While he waited, the door opened and Tony Rykwert came in.

Rykwert was one of the numerous people Skerrett did not like. As board secretary, Rykwert did his job well but failed to look the part. This irritated Skerrett. Those flamboyant clothes, for instance, looked wrong on that enormous frame. His trousers were always half an inch too short, his collar an eighth of an inch too tight. And that floppy silk handkerchief waving about on his chest could have come straight from some theatrical entrepreneur's pocket.

Nevertheless, he was a greedy misogynist with a particular loathing for Katherine Hanson – characteristics which, on occasion, made Skerrett warm to him.

'Am I interrupting anything?' Rykwert spoke slowly, even with difficulty at times, as if his cumbersome limbs were draining his mind of its strength.

'Ringing the president,' Skerrett put his hand over the mouthpiece. 'I've given it a lot of thought, and I've finally decided it's my duty. I don't know if Irv realizes what's going on here, but if he doesn't he's bloody well going to.'

'Of course he knows all about it.' Rykwert sat down heavily on a small, upright chair.

'Yes, but the way it's being handled . . .'

'It's being handled well. Don't speak to him yet. I'd like us to – uhm – have a chat first.'

'Yeh?' Skerrett screwed his face up.

'About madame. There are better ways of dealing with her than soliciting New York's help.'

'Cancel that call.' Skerrett banged down the receiver. 'It's scandalous!' he hissed. 'Television indeed! It'll be all about *her*, you know. What a nerve – using us to get publicity for herself.'

'It's a debatable point.' Rykwert's bovine brown eyes fixed unblinkingly on Skerrett. 'If she does it well, it'll be good for Borjex.'

'She'll do it her way, won't she? In my opinion, there are several things New York ought to be made aware of. Nicely, of course, and from someone with my kind of experience. Just look at her management style – today's a prime example of this mania for publicity, this all-systems-go kind of—'

'So far, Irv's perfectly satisfied. Other people may not be in the near future.'

'I'm not satisfied now.'

Rykwert ignored him. 'I was chatting to the union secretary of MATEX this morning.'

'Jo Cleary? What were you doing talking to him?'

'Just bumped into him – he's being filmed as well.'

'Yeh?'

'They do some tough jobs, his people – the chemical plants, the opencast sites . . .'

'I know. Industrial Relations is my department, isn't it?'

'Well think about the opencast sites for a minute. Millions of pounds worth of plant would be lying idle if those men pulled out. A few days out of action and half that equipment would be unsafe to use.'

'So?'

'So the sites would be lethal. If children managed to get on them – well, you just can't tell. That's how disasters happen. We've seen it before – public outcry.'

'We all know we don't want a strike in that area.'

Rykwert looked round the room. There was an expression of long-endured contempt on his face. For a moment Skerrett thought he'd finished speaking.

'Jo Cleary,' Rykwert started up again, 'reckons the board will have to give way over the next wage claim.'

Skerrett snorted. 'Madame won't. Not for another year at least. She's planning on reinvesting everything she can lay her hands on.'

'Oh I know that.'

'You didn't tell him, did you?'

As the chauffeur approached Kensington, she opened her bag and took out her latchkeys. A second before he drew up outside her red-brick Georgian house, the key she would need first was between her thumb and forefinger. Opening the car door with the remainder of her fingers – absurd to wait for the cumbersome procedure of his strolling round to let her out – she said 'good night' the moment her Gucci shoes touched the pavement. Five seconds later, portfolio and handbag tucked under her left arm, she opened the heavy, white-painted door of her home. A firm push from her shoulder closed it again behind her.

Halfway down the hall, she paused for ten seconds to deposit portfolio and bag on the Chippendale table, and to peel off her jacket which she hung neatly in the cupboard. Then six quick strides and she was in the kitchen.

A note was lying on the table. It was from Mrs Thake, the housekeeper, and contained a list of items of food bought that day. At the bottom was an intricate calculation, and the words 'GRAND TOTAL' written in huge letters and heavily underlined.

Katherine pursed her lips, though she agreed with the sentiment. It was an astronomical amount to spend on dinner for four, but cooking was the only hobby she allowed herself and she rarely had time even for that.

Picking up the internal phone, she buzzed the housekeeper. While she waited, she could imagine her scurrying across her basement flat, prim and proper and slightly out of breath, like a harassed mole.

'Mrs Thake? I got your note, thanks very much. The bill's fine. There was no need for you to have gone to all that trouble – working the details out.'

'I like to keep things right. Just in case.' The last two words were uttered on a note of deep gloom.

Katherine smiled to herself. 'As you please. I shan't be needing anything for the next few nights . . .'

'I thought you wouldn't.' She sounded more cheerful. 'There'll be enough there to see you through for a good long while.'

'. . . because I'll be eating out. So you'll be able to take a few hours off.'

'I don't know about that,' she sighed. Then as an afterthought: 'I've seen to your wine and vegetables.'

'I never doubted it. Bye.' She replaced the receiver.

A quick glance in the fridge assured her that the wine really was chilling; a longer glance at a row of basins, followed by a poke at their contents, and she left the room satisfied.

As she passed the hall clock, it chimed the half-hour. She yelped with temper. Six-thirty already, and fifteen minutes wasted in a traffic jam, plus a further three or four minutes with a shopping list. She'd left the office an hour early, and still she mightn't be ready on time.

She ran lightly up the spiral staircase and into the main bedroom. Scarcely faltering in her stride, she stepped out of her shoes and walked over to the long row of wardrobes, undoing her dress as she went. Slipping it off and shaking out the creases, she hung it up, took off her underwear and flung it into a wickerwork basket, collected her shoes on the way back across the room and put them on the shoe rack. They took their place amongst three perfectly symmetrical rows of spotless footwear. Two more strides and she was in the bathroom.

Opening the glass-fronted cabinet, she selected two jars from a neat arrangement of prettily packaged cosmetics. She cleansed her face briskly, then smeared on a face pack.

Gathering speed, she flicked the switch that locked the bath plug, turned on the taps and began a two-minute exercise routine – bending and stretching, touching her toes and finally running on the spot. She made the most of the time to think about this quarter's figures for the hydraulic-powered supports. They'd reached an all-time high, and there must be no let-up in the sales drive.

Lord Arlingham drove his veteran Rolls Royce slowly down the tree-lined road. It seemed to him that half his time in London was spent looking for parking spaces. About once a week he contemplated getting rid of the car, buying a Volkswagen, perhaps, or even a Mini. It was a depressing thought, like opting for euthanasia or becoming teetotal.

Katherine looked out of her sitting room window and saw him cruising up and down. He spotted her, played a couple of notes on the hooter, and drove on.

Two Minis, parked nose to tail, pulled away within seconds of each other. Lord Arlingham pulled in, deposited the Rolls with fastidious precision about one inch from the pavement, switched off the engine and inspected his reflection in the mirror. Not at all bad, he thought, for a man of fifty-two. His hair was very thin and completely silver, but it offset his tan splendidly. His grey eyes stared back at him, kindly and rather wise, with just a hint of good humour. The whites were very white, without any trace of alcoholic redness – but there again he did take care of himself, what with saunas and exercise and one thing and another; even out of the shooting season, he spent as many hours as possible in the open air. Tonight he felt so fit that he saw no reason why he shouldn't start hunting again, come November; nothing like a day in the saddle for shaking up the liver.

He climbed out of the car humming a little tune to himself. It had been a very minor coincidence, those two Minis pulling away like that, but it had cheered him. He patted the boot of the Rolls fondly as he walked away from it.

'Edward!' Katherine exclaimed as she opened the front door to him. 'How long have you been driving up and down?'

'Hello, darling.' He kissed her lightly on the cheek. 'About five minutes.'

'You lazy man! Why didn't you park in the next street and walk? It's only . . .'

He put his arm round her shoulders and stopped her with a long, gentle kiss. With his other hand he closed the door behind them.

'That's how I'd silence you at meetings,' he said, 'if I

worked for Borjex. "Now, Lord Arlingham", you'd be saying, a frown starting up between your eyebrows and your voice bellowing out like a fog horn . . .'

'I have an excellent speaking voice,' she prodded him in the ribs.

'All right, then, your voice ringing out like a school-house bell. "Now, Lord Arlingham, in my opinion you have given insufficient thought to these proposals. Might I suggest" – and here you'd do your frowning and smiling at the same time bit – "might I suggest that a committee of, say" – and at that point I'd leap to my feet, rush round the board table, grab you by the hair, wrench back your head and press my mouth over yours. Gasps of astonishment would go up from committee members – others, slumbering quietly, would be awakened. "What's happening? What? What? Somebody brought the drinks in? No by God – chairman's collapsed – old Arlingham's giving her mouth-to-mouth resuscitation." Parrot-faced Stempel would make a careful note of it for the minutes, and at least two others would be grovelling on the floor – fighting to snatch your chair from beneath your thrashing limbs.'

'You fool!' she shrieked with laughter. 'Come and have a drink. And will you see to the wine for me? The white's chilling, but two bottles of Rhône need opening. Boeuf Wellington for the main course.'

'Aha. Just what I needed.' He followed her into the kitchen.

'To keep your strength up for the House?'

'I've been sitting on a Select Committee today.'

'And you have the cheek to make fun of me.'

'This committee is very serious business.'

'Nothing you do can be *very* serious business.' Only half listening to him, she opened the oven door and inspected the beef. 'Because you don't have to *earn* your living.'

'How dare you,' he said, not in the least offended. 'If I

didn't work as hard as I do the estate would soon be bankrupt – mortgaged even. And what I do for politics is because of my deep concern for this country and for our allies around the world. I work hard at that, too – selflessly and with dedication. As a matter of fact I think it's jolly decent of me. Never you forget, Ms Hanson, that the House of Lords has a vital rôle to play in international affairs nowadays. Any hors d'œuvres?'

'Coquilles St Jacques. And before you ask, there's nothing but cheese afterwards.'

His face fell.

'But the Boeuf . . .?'

'I mean after the beef. I didn't have enough time.'

'Marry me and you'll have all the time in the world.'

'I think that's what your third wife found,' Katherine said, 'when you disappeared for a couple of months.'

'She jumped to hasty conclusions,' he replied. 'As, I am afraid, you have a tendency to do. I've often noticed that small flaw in your character, Katherine, especially where relationships are concerned. I happened to be an extremely busy man at the time my third wife and I went our different ways.'

Pouring dressing over the salad, she tossed it vigorously.

'You don't really want to marry again, do you?' she asked.

'I'm thinking of you, Katherine. At thirty-nine it's high time you settled down.'

She snorted.

'Katherine—' he cajoled. 'Wouldn't you like to be married to me?'

'No.'

'Do you want to marry me at all?'

'Not at the moment.'

'Then I'll say it again – marry me.'

She laughed.

'I'm an extremely busy woman.' Putting down the salad, she turned to face him. Her smile disappeared.

'Wouldn't you get a shock if after all this time I suddenly said "yes"? What if I decided I'd achieved all I wanted to achieve – in my career – and wanted a proper home? What if I was suddenly bored with being what I am?'

'You're not, are you?'

'Don't worry.'

'Seriously,' he said, picking up a wine bottle and starting to uncork it, 'we could be happy. We always have been happy together, haven't we? If we were married, that probably wouldn't change anything.'

The cork slid out with a pop.

'We're all right as we are. We see each other whenever we want to. We're free to come and go as we please.'

'You're not very free. Borjex owns you.'

'Rubbish.' Wielding a large carving knife, she chopped a courgette into two precise halves.

'Oh dear,' he said. 'Have a drink. Come to think of it, I haven't had one myself yet. Where've you put the scotch?'

'You don't want a scotch before dinner.'

'Of course not. Sorry. Forgot what I wanted for a minute.'

He poured two glasses of wine and handed her one.

'To us,' he said. 'To good friends and happy times.'

'To us.' She raised her glass.

They smiled at each other, ignoring for a minute the chiming of the doorbell and the ringing of the telephone.

Mrs Thake emerged from her basement to clear away the dishes. She did it swiftly and efficiently, but with much sighing.

The four of them – Katherine and Edward, and Barbara and David – sat round the table long after she had gone, sipping coffee and talking.

Barbara looked well. Strict dieting kept her full figure curvaceous rather than fat, and her button-like dark eyes were bright with mischief. David was much slighter, with a round face and soft, babyish fair hair. With little to say for himself, and only pleasant things at that, he resembled nothing so closely as a middle-aged cherub. His main aim in life, apart from running his dental practice, was to take care of his wife.

Tonight he was being especially devoted. When she got to her feet, he rushed to move her chair back; when she returned to the room, he jumped up again, watching her steps with deep concern, as though her muscular legs might falter and her stalwart frame crash to the floor.

Barbara took no notice of any of this.

'I had some headline news today,' she announced, reaching across him to help herself to yet another chocolate mint.

'It's not that I'm mean with the mints,' Katherine said, 'but you'll ruin your diet.'

'More of Barbara would always be welcome,' Edward interjected.

'Flattery will get you everywhere. Speaking of which, the beef was delicious. Its succulent juices are still lingering on my palate. I could eat it all over again.'

'Delicious,' David shook his head at the memory, and chuckled. 'Really delicious. And the Stilton.'

'So what's this news?'

'Guess, Katherine. Guess.'

'David's capped a royal tooth.'

'See how your mind works?' Barbara munched steadily. 'I'm having another baby.'

'Oh!' It was a genuine gasp of surprise. Katherine's coffee cup nearly dropped from her fingers.

Edward raised his eyebrows.

'It's the time of year,' he said cheerfully.

'That's not just headline news,' Katherine whispered, 'it is wonderful news. Marvellous.'

She wasn't sure what it was that pulled so at her heart. It wasn't that she wanted a baby – at least, it sometimes seemed like a pleasant idea, but she felt no great longing.

Ten years from now, maybe, she'd be sorry that she had no offspring, but at the moment a baby would be an impossible inconvenience, it would ruin everything – all the things she'd worked so hard for, and for so long. If she had one by mistake she knew she would love it too much afterwards, it would make up for all the loneliness in the past and she would put it before all else. How easy it would be to spoil a child, especially the child of the man you loved. But there was nobody that she loved that much, nor had there been for many years. It was all those images that a baby conjured up, she decided, that reminded her of her own insecurities. False images, without a doubt, but so reassuring from a distance: a man who loved you, a home that would protect you, the warmth of a family, knowing you'd never be alone or frightened again.

Everyone said how strong she was, how calm; one man had even called her courageous; another had said, maliciously, how hard she was, totally uninfluenced by sentiment. It was a good thing they didn't know her too well, or they'd have destroyed her long ago; but she'd built herself a fortress in her own particular style, and it was far more secure than marriage.

The image of who she was, and all that she'd achieved, flashed across her mind. She held it there, because it was comforting, and knew that it was neither marriage nor a baby that she craved, it was simply that Barbara's announcement had sparked off half-forgotten memories. She tried to think of the endless babies conceived without passion, the tedium of nappies and washing and cleaning . . . but on a night like tonight, when the air was warm and the darkness beyond the windows was the soft, purple darkness of early May, you thought of sweet lilting songs and laughter, trees all swollen with blossom and a hand on yours; you thought of lovers.

Looking round the table, she realized that the three of them were staring at her. She had no idea what her expression had been like, but presumed it to have been wistful and stupid. It was rare that she let her concentration wander, and the slip annoyed her. Flashing them a quick, bright smile, she cleared her throat and cast about for something sensible to say.

Edward beat her to it.

'Come on, David,' he said smoothly. 'Cause for celebration, if ever there was one. Let's get stuck into the brandy. Generous one for you, Katherine?'

The opencast mining site covered seven acres. It was bleak and grey, all vegetation gone except for one withered tree, standing gaunt against the east perimeter where a barren hillock converged suddenly with undulating green fields.

Earth-moving equipment roared deafeningly; it was cutting deep tracks into the grim landscape, upturning boulders and heaving them effortlessly aside. Around the outskirts of the site the occupants of a few desolate houses were fighting a daily but losing battle against dust. A mile or more distant, its turrets just visible above a thick belt of trees, stood Tylowe Castle. Neither noise nor dust reached even the boundaries of its well-tended park.

Jo Cleary had positioned himself on a rise fifty yards from the main entrance to the site, where he could see as much as possible without having to move. He was leaning against a stationary machine; its wheel alone dwarfed him.

Skerrett and Rykwert were plodding slowly across hardening tracks. Jo's spectacles glinted in the daylight as he watched them.

'What can I do for you two boys?' he yelled as they approached.

'Hi, Jo,' Rykwert managed to pant.

Skerrett was too exhausted to do more than nod.

'Well? What d'you want?'

'Thought we'd pay you a visit,' Rykwert said.

'I'd already worked that one out. And this one—' he jabbed a finger at Skerrett – 'should be bloody ashamed of himself. Supposed to be head of industrial relations and hasn't been seen on a site for over three months.'

'Come on, Jo – that's not fair. I never have any time. You know how it is for a board member . . .'

Jo burst into a spasm of laughter, which turned immediately into a violent coughing fit. He pulled out a packet of cigarettes and lit one. The coughing subsided into a painful wheeze.

'Well, I'm here now, Jo,' Skerrett added.

'An' I'm none too keen on that, either, poking about without giving anybody warning. Who told you where to find me?'

'One of your friends at the union headquarters,' Skerrett smiled. 'We're only paying a friendly call. As you say, I probably don't keep in close enough touch with the – the grass roots.'

Jo wheezed again, and looked across the site to where a skip was loading rubble. A few yards from it a man stripped to his vest was drilling at a solid wall of stone. He was damp with sweat and streaked with mud.

Boxes of explosives stood at a safe distance.

'In fact,' Skerrett broadened his smile still further, 'there are one or two things I need to talk to you about.'

'Such as?'

'We can't talk here. Why not come and get changed and have a bite of lunch with us?'

'Oh-ho,' Cleary said, and stubbed out his cigarette. 'It's a good long while since you've given me lunch. Where are we going? Back to Borjex?'

'I've booked a table in a restaurant.'

'A provisional booking, I hope.'

'Come on, Jo, you'll enjoy it – far more relaxing than the board members' dining room. Nice and secluded with excellent wines and discreet waiters – an ideal place for discussing the chairman's new investment plans.'

'*New* investment plans?' Jo said. 'I didn't know she'd got any.'

'Didn't you, Jo?' Skerrett frowned at him.

'Unless you're talking about last month's report, but there was nothing very new in that.'

Skerrett said nothing.

'All right,' Jo went on, 'how quiet is this restaurant?'

'It's perfect,' Skerrett's face wrinkled into lines of conceit at his own cleverness as he led the way towards the makeshift car park. Then he froze; tramping towards him was a familiar figure, wearing overalls and carrying a yellow tin helmet. Her hair swung freely about her face as she turned to speak to the man by her side, then she looked directly at Skerrett and waved to him in greeting; a terrible pain stabbed at his diaphragm.

'Talk of the devil,' Jo laughed, and hurried towards her, bellowing at the top of his voice: 'Aren't I the lucky one? A visit from the chairman.'

But as he drew closer to her he thought how stern she looked today, and plain. She could look lovely at times, but at the moment her face was scrubbed clean of make-up and her mouth was set in a harsh, determined line. And despite her friendly greeting there was no smile in her eyes.

He wasn't sure what Skerrett and Rykwert were up to, but whatever it was he hoped he wouldn't get caught in the middle.

TWO

Yet the first bringer of unwelcome news
Hath but a losing office

– NORTHUMBERLAND; *Henry the Fourth*, Part Two

Dropping into second gear, Katherine turned right between high stone gate-posts and into a meandering coach road. She was in an excellent mood and ravenously hungry after five hours in the fresh air. The morning had passed quickly enough, with the signing of a few documents followed by a leisurely drive to what had become known, because of its proximity to the famous castle, as the Tylowe site. Opportunities for such visits had become all too infrequent since she'd been made chairman, and she found herself having to make all manner of excuses to ensure even one a month, whether it was to a chemical plant, a research establishment or to workings like Tylowe. Today, however, lunch with a major client had been cancelled at the last minute and, since it was a Friday and she was due to spend the week-end with Edward – and Arlingham Hall was only a few miles further on – she had ignored the stack of papers on her desk and driven over.

Seeing Skerrett and Rykwert there had been a surprise. The latter, being company secretary, had little or no need to pay such visits, and Skerrett hardly ever did even though he ought to. She'd wondered why Skerrett had had to drag Rykwert along with him today, but a board member's business was more or less his own and she had no wish to interfere, especially as he seemed to be getting along happily with the union leader. At the thought of Jo

Clearly she smiled: in the early days he'd tried to provoke her, but she'd been more than a match for his pushiness and, despite their sometimes vitriolic arguments, they now had enormous respect for one another. Nothing, she hoped, would ever change that.

Skerrett worried her a bit: it was becoming increasingly obvious that there were vital areas of his job he didn't take care of to the full, but his position on the board made him virtually unassailable – always provided he did nothing radically wrong. She'd have to talk to the president about him, especially about the fact that he didn't look well. Perhaps they could find grounds for an early ill-health retirement, though she doubted it: Skerrett was the type who would cling to his position for years. She'd give him until autumn, she decided, see how he went and then maybe drop a few gentle hints.

Rykwert, as always, remained an enigma. What a delight it would be to have one glimpse at the thoughts behind those opaque brown eyes.

She decelerated to bump over a cattle grid, then rounded a bend in the driveway. A hundred yards ahead stood Arlingham Hall. Just beyond it, next to a summer-house with 'Cafe' painted in Tudor lettering on its roof, was a small amusement park – swings and roundabouts, and a few gaudy plastic horses. Its entrance was marked by a souvenir shop.

Signs telling you the cost of admittance were posted outside the main gates of the hall. A hefty figure, in gum boots, scruffy trousers and a tweed jacket, was peering at the entry prices.

Katherine slowed down and braked only inches from the figure.

'Good morrow, my lord!' she called, getting out of the car and slamming the door behind her.

'Just what I was hoping for – a damsel in distress. Incidentally, far from it being good morrow, it's six o'clock and you're late.'

'Incidentally, I am not a damsel in distress, but a powerful châtelaine.'

'Ah – if only you were châtelaine of my estates. Tell me, d'you think the new entry prices are too high?'

'Too low. Put them up another twenty per cent.'

'What a brilliant woman you are.'

He opened his arms to embrace her, and she froze.

The tweed jacket had fallen open, revealing the heraldic family crest emblazoned on a too-tight sweatshirt.

'Ugh – Edward – you've got rampant cotton lions prancing across your middle-aged spread.'

'It's my crest and I'll put it where I like. I helped myself to it in the souvenir shop. I thought it looked rather good, actually.' He glanced down at it and stroked it proudly. 'And since we're talking of clothes, I feel I ought to point out to you that you're wearing overalls – filthy ones, at that. Is this some trifling oversight or a new trend in fashion? But please feel free to wear whatever you like. We're not hidebound by convention here.'

'I've been working.'

'I see.'

'Visiting the Tylowe site.'

'That reminds me,' he said. 'My mother's invited us over for dinner, and if you want to go riding tomorrow we might as well stay the night.'

'Suits me. I love being at Tylowe. I drove past it on the way to the site today – I noticed she was having repairs done to the west wing battlements.'

'A facelift for the stonework,' Edward shook his head sadly. 'She spends a fortune on that place and still doesn't bother with essentials like rewiring, just because it doesn't show. I don't know why she can't go and get her own bloody face lifted instead, like most women.'

'She doesn't need it at the moment,' Katherine said. 'She's already had it done twice, and her stomach and her bust.'

'*What?* I didn't know that. How much will that have cost, then?'

'You're getting forgetful,' Katherine said, delighting in the look of horror that suffused Edward's face. 'She told you all about it, I was there at the time – at Barbara's party last year.'

'Really? I must have got confused, thought she was talking about the battlements or something. But anyway, how much would it have cost?'

'I don't know,' Katherine laughed. 'But she was telling me she wants a complete overhaul next year.'

'She needn't come to me for the money,' he said. 'I shall tell her she must learn to grow old gracefully,' and he strode over to Katherine's car to remove her case from the boot. 'Shall I put this straight into the Rolls or d'you want to get changed first?'

'I'll just take a couple of things out thén you can have it.' Taking the case from his hand, she laid it on the gravel, unzipped it and removed an immaculate linen outfit, low heeled shoes and a leather sponge bag. 'I think a quick change wouldn't be a bad idea. We don't want your mother to die of fright.'

'Don't we?' he said.

Refastening the case with a flourish, she handed it back to him. 'I'm getting worried about you, Edward!'

'Katherine, you must realize that Helen spends money like water on the most absurd things. I know rewiring a place like Tylowe would involve a tremendous outlay, but when she goes and spends thousands on facelifts for herself and the battlements . . .'

Still grumbling, he set off towards the Rolls, case in hand. Katherine stood looking at the new amusement park, the immobile plastic animals oiled and ready for action now that the summer season had begun.

'All right,' Edward said, rejoining her, 'so they look out of place, but have you any idea how much it costs to keep Arlingham going?'

'Only a rough idea, but in fact that's something I'd like to talk to you about.'

'Oh?'

'I'll tell you all about it when we get to Tylowe – I'd like to hear Helen's views as much as yours. You're ideal people to supply me with a few tips.'

'Curiouser and curiouser.'

'You'll have to wait, I'm not going through the whole thing twice . . . And don't fret about the amusement park, it blends in quite well.'

'Just too bad if it doesn't. Now why can't Helen do something like this? Everybody else does. I don't understand her, this absolute refusal to open Tylowe to the public.'

'She loves the place, doesn't she?'

'So do we all, but that's not the point. I only wish she'd let me run it for her, or at least give me some idea of her financial affairs. She's far too secretive.'

'But since Tylowe was her first husband's and not your father's, it isn't really any of your business, is it? And she's inherited two fortunes, hasn't she?'

'What about death duties, and taxes . . .'

'Come on,' she headed towards the house. 'I want a bath.'

'It's ridiculous,' he said, falling into step beside her. 'An elderly widow living in a place like that. It's at least three times the size of Arlingham. She could move into a very pleasant cottage.'

'Helen? In a cottage? That'll be the day.'

'Or she could move into the hall . . . Inland bloody Revenue,' he muttered, pausing beneath the stone porch to cast a vicious backward glance at the Rolls. 'And I can never find a parking space for that thing.'

'I'm glad it's all the craze again.' Helen, dowager Lady Arlingham, was mixing exotic-looking cocktails. She was doing it with all the skill of a professional barman; there was a faint smile on her lips, and a tiny frown of concentration on her otherwise flawless forehead. 'Though personally I never entirely abandoned the habit. Here you are.'

Dropping slices of cucumber into the three glasses, she handed them round.

'Lovely,' Edward said with a grimace. 'Beats scotch any day.'

'You don't want scotch before dinner. Does he, Katherine?'

'That's what I'm always telling him. Cocktails are a good habit. You get plenty of vitamins with your alcohol.'

'Exactly. So tell us more about this plan of yours.' Sitting down in her favourite armchair, Helen crossed her silk-stockinged legs, leaned back against a pile of cushions and waited.

'It's scarcely even a plan as yet,' Katherine said. 'I've mentioned it to a few board members and had mixed reactions. The thing is, Borjex is making a healthy profit and I want to reinvest – and diversify – still further. And I want to use historic houses – or what the magazines might call 'stately homes'. Basically, I'd take a stately home and turn it into the most well-equipped business centre imaginable, and at the same time it would be a luxury hotel – the grandest of country clubs – and a businessman's retreat.'

'Business*person's* retreat,' Helen corrected her with a smile.

'Quite. Everything the wealthy businessperson needed would be there in one beautiful place. You see, even the best hotels aren't entirely suitable for commercial needs – large-scale commercial needs. Certain stately homes could be. I'd have one near each important capital across Western Europe, starting with England where we'd have the "pilot run". Of the kind of thing I'm planning, there'd be no need for more than one in each country – because the scale would be so lavish.'

Helen arched her softly plucked eyebrows; her violet blue eyes opened a fraction wider.

'For want of a better word, I'm calling them "statels". Each "statel" would have to be near a motorway, on a major railway line and near an airport. It would also have to be no more than an hour by car or rail from the capital. It would have to be a large stately home, suitable for conversion and with its basic structures still sound. That shouldn't be a problem, though – most of England's old houses are structurally fit to last another few centuries, so long as repairs and restorations are carried out.'

'And what would you do with them exactly?' Edward said.

'I'd install conference theatres with all the latest equipment, studios and interview rooms with closed-circuit television, audio-visual aids and so on. Small private meeting rooms – and private dining rooms, Edward, as well as a first-class restaurant. Libraries, computer facilities – and lots of things to make life more pleasant. Good wine cellars, delightful food – fresh dairy produce and vegetables from the home farm – saunas to work it all off in, squash courts, gymnasia . . . You name it.' She shrugged. 'The bedrooms wouldn't be like ordinary hotel bedrooms, either. I'd have them fitted with all the amenities, but each would have a character of its own. Outside there'd be the gardens, and the park – riding, fishing, all the country sports.'

'So compared to a normal hotel . . .' Edward interposed.

'Equally convenient – or more so – but a much more attractive and interesting place to be. The best of historic interest and modern amenities. Your average busy chairman is fed up to here—' she gestured at her chin – 'with hotels. This would be a country club on an international scale; businesspeople would know who they'd be likely to meet there, and who they wouldn't. But the great advantage,' Katherine said, 'is that it takes so long to travel across towns nowadays – the thing you're always moaning about, Edward – that you might as well have everything you need in one place, within easy reach of the town should you want to go there. Fly into the nearby airport, land your helicopter in the park – and everything's laid on for you without any further upheaval.'

'What an extraordinary idea.' Helen patted her immaculately groomed grey hair into place. 'Though I do believe it could work.'

'Of course it could,' Katherine agreed. 'I know *I'd* prefer it to some modern hotel in the centre of a town – they just can't provide what the "statel" could provide. But if you don't believe me, ask any businesspeople what their problems are.'

'And financially,' Edward asked. 'How would it work out?'

'To buy a stately home would be no more expensive than building a hotel. What's more, it would be an investment. If we wanted to – when the market was right – we could sell off the farmlands and just keep a section of the park, sell off the most valuable of the antiques and paintings and retain the rest to keep the right sort of atmosphere . . . for anyone who could afford it, and Borjex can, the investment is obvious. Particularly if we bought the place complete with art collections and all contents, as we probably would.'

'And the service?' Helen said, a note of concern in her voice.

'The best,' Katherine laughed. 'Dorchester standard. Don't you see what I'm trying to do, Edward? Not only am I going to invest in a stately home, I'm actually going to make it earn money for me. A lot of money.'

Edward smiled ruefully. 'Not just entry prices.'

Katherine reached across the sofa and took hold of his hand.

'Don't look so miserable. It's only because Borjex can

afford the outlay. But we'll make sure the tariffs are high – only the very rich will be booking into "statels".'

'How vulgar,' Helen said. 'I intend to have another cocktail before dinner. I feel I deserve one.'

It was a chilly night. Katherine pulled a coat round her shoulders before she set off for her after-dinner walk.

The three of them had gone their separate ways when the meal was over. Edward was relaxing in the library with his favourite book on veteran cars, and Helen was in the drawing room, playing a repopularized 1920's tune on the grand piano.

Katherine left by a side door which led into the courtyard: the floodlit fountain was still spraying its jets towards the sky, and the scent of honeysuckle, growing wild on the ancient grey walls, hung heavy in the air. Crossing the cobblestones, she emerged on the lawn in front of the castle.

On either side of her was a row of majestic oaks, the furthermost tips of their branches reaching out towards each other, almost meeting but just falling short, high above her head. The moonlight caught them, touching the buds here and there so that they gleamed like jewels. Stars glittered and twinkled; rattling its chain, a dog from the stable yard howled and bayed at them, then fell silent.

From an open first floor window came the faint, sentimental strains of Helen's tune: Katherine recognized it as 'Blue Moon', and smiled to herself. 'Pennies from Heaven' might have been more appropriate, she thought, as she paused and looked back at the castle. It was so vast that she would have had to stand at least a hundred yards away from it to see its entire frontage: what a lucky person Helen had been – but not just lucky, shrewd as well. Never allowing her romantic nature to cloud her judgement, each of her husbands had been both rich and devoted. Even on his deathbed Edward's father had been

signing cheques for her, convinced till the end that she
was too sensitive to cope with money.

Katherine strode briskly on, down the archway of trees,
her gaze on the firm earth and her head full of yesterday's
meetings: amendments and decisions and fresh investment plans.

The 'statels' would work, she was sure of it. Right
across Western Europe there were people who would be
only too glad to be rid of enormous old houses, especially
if offered an apartment in them for the rest of their
lifetimes, and a generous lump sum.

It was a pity that the English one couldn't have been
Tylowe – the place was ideal.

By the gates into the park, she paused and looked back
at the castle. Its buttresses and turrets were etched against
the dark blue sky; the round tower at its east wing was of
majestic proportions, in itself big enough to hold half a
dozen cinemas or lecture theatres. It was a perfect
structure.

In the rolling parkland, the shadowy forms of deer
moved amongst the trees. The moonlight shone full on
the lake, turning it to silver-shot glass, and one tiny
rowing boat was moored by the landing stage.

Katherine sighed and pursed her lips.

To extend a lake of this size by fifty per cent, and equip
it with half a dozen small boats would cost, she calculated
– then she stopped.

For a second she closed her eyes. When she opened
them, she looked again at the castle, at the black gleam
of its mullioned windows, at the honeysuckle clinging to
its walls. And she looked again at the silver-shot lake,
and thought – as she had done so often over the past few
weeks – of a boy with dark curly hair and laughing blue
eyes. But of course he wouldn't be a boy any longer, he
would be a man of over forty. She wondered what he
looked like now, perhaps he was white-haired or bald, fat
or wizened, grown ugly with the passing years . . . It was

impossible to imagine him care-worn and staid, and she would not have wanted to see it: she remembered him only as young and healthy, swimming in the sea, his brown limbs glistening in the sunlight, his eyes shadowy in the starlight, his hands holding her, as though they would never let go – and she began to tremble, as she stood there alone in the night.

The strains of Helen's tune were going through her head; she hummed it, very softly, as the tears coursed down her cheeks.

When Katherine glanced across her office, checking that the bags were all there for her six-weekly trip to the New York headquarters, it never crossed her mind that this was going to be anything other than a routine visit.

The president, Irv McKenzie, wanted to hear more about her ideas for reinvestment – in particular the 'statel' scheme – and then to discuss plans for reorganizing the European board. Important matters, both of them, but they didn't worry her unduly, and when Mrs Egerton buzzed through on the intercom to let her know the chauffeur was waiting to drive her to Heathrow, she replied with unexpected cheerfulness.

But after all, it was a spring morning – the sun was shining, the clouds were only wisps of whiteness and she didn't have a problem in the world that she couldn't handle. Or so it seemed on such a day – the kind of day when you ached to be out in the bright fresh air, when you had to pull your thoughts back time and again to investment proposals and retirement offers, and time and again they'd sneak away to a lonely beach, where you'd met your lover for the first time and the sun was dazzling . . .

The intercom buzzed again; with a sigh Katherine pushed away the signed letters that were lying in front of her, picked up her handbag, collected her cases and headed for the outer office and the lift. Sixty minutes later she was in the VIP Lounge at Heathrow Airport, drinking mineral water and waiting for her flight to be called.

By her side was Richard Stempel. He wouldn't be accompanying her on the trip, but it was useful to have him at hand until the last possible moment – just in case. She'd already made the most of his presence to run through the publicity handouts for next year, or at least she was trying to: irritatingly, they'd been interrupted twice by airport staff, asking her if there was anything else she might need.

'And don't forget, Richard,' she told him, when it was finally time to board the plane, 'I want the regional directors' recruitment budgets telexed out to me.'

'If they're through to London before you get back.'

'They'll be through by tomorrow. If not, chase them up.'

'Oh . . . me personally?'

'You're my personal assistant, aren't you?'

He nodded, and looked unhappy.

'Just get on with it,' she suggested. 'I'll call you from New York as soon as I've dumped my bags.'

'I'll be – I shan't be going out this evening, so I'll be waiting for your call. I shouldn't think anything will have happened between now and then though.'

A crisply attired hostess was trying to usher Katherine politely towards the boarding gate.

'Yes, I'm just coming. Good luck with the regional directors, Richard.'

'And have a good trip,' he muttered.

She hurried down the long, perspex tunnel towards the waiting plane and, comfortably settled and strapped in, waited patiently for the craft to be airborne.

The seat belts warning sign was still lit up when she opened her briefcase, took out a thick wad of correspondence, and once more dismissed all irrelevant thoughts from her mind. At the top of her reading list was the financial director's paper on property development in

Britain. She read it now, in preparation for a hectic three days in New York, and catastrophe was the last thing on her mind.

The cacophony of noises in New York always delighted her. There was something thrilling about the blaring yellow cabs, the scream of rubber when brakes were applied with needless energy, the extrovert shouts of the street vendors – and all the other city sounds that, in London, were so much tamer. She loved the hot, dirty, dusty smells, too, and the smells that wafted out of restaurants into the scorching air – smells of oregano and garlic and olive oil that would change just a block away to spices and oriental aromas. You could have been walking from one country to the next in the space of minutes.

The people, too, never ceased to surprise her – the shopkeepers who forgot their manners, or had never had them, who never seemed to consider that they were supposed to be providing a service . . . the ultra English courtesy of the staff in the great stores, and in the big hotels . . . the unexpected humour of a cab driver, or the impudence of a New Yorker who'd suddenly decided he fancied you.

She loved it all, even the tall buildings that could look so ephemeral from an aeroplane – most of all at sunset, when the sky was pink and hazy in the heat. And yet, she always declared that New York was most certainly not her kind of city. And it was true – but like so many things or people that were wrong for you, you could find yourself bewitched by them for ever . . .

The first evening was fun, as always. Katherine, Irv and his wife and an old friend of Katherine's went for a Mexican meal, then on to a club.

Irv made it a rule on such occasions that no business was to be discussed. Jonathan, Katherine's companion, related a few amusing anecdotes about his work as a

cosmetic surgeon, and that was the nearest they came to
mentioning work – apart from Irv's whispered, 'Got some
interesting news for you tomorrow, Katherine.'

'Great!' she said, and thought no more about it. At two
a.m. she returned to her apartment with Jonathan, gave
him a quick coffee and bade him goodnight. She still felt
wide-awake – New York invariably had that effect on her
– and yet within minutes of taking off her make-up and
climbing into bed, she fell into a deep, untroubled sleep.

At seven next morning she was up and about and
looking forward to the day. She brewed herself a pot of
coffee and glanced out of the window at the New York
traffic that was already speeding up. There seemed to be
a lot of noise and confusion out there, but the apartment
was peaceful. It was an excellent arrangement, having this
place set aside for the European chairman – much better
than booking into a hotel. Not only was it private and
quiet, with the bonus of having a spare bedroom, but it
was available whenever she needed it. If anybody else
from Borjex wanted to use the apartment they would
inform Mrs Egerton or Richard Stempel, and vacate it as
soon as instructed by London that Katherine's schedule
included a visit to New York.

She made the most of the privacy now by doing half an
hour's work. There were some complex financial discussions ahead of her, and she wanted to be certain that she
was thoroughly prepared. Reinvestment was the major
issue: Borjex had a great deal of money at its disposal and
did not always – or so it had appeared from Katherine's
investigations – put it to best use. Apart from a healthy
profit which, if projected figures for the next five years
proved correct, would increase substantially, there was a
proportion of invested money which was not working to
the full and ought to be transferred. The possibility of
moving into the property field, in particular the purchase
of historic houses to develop as business centres, had been
at the back of Katherine's mind for nearly a year. Since

her appointment as chairman only two months ago, she had used all the resources available to her: she and the head of the finance department, along with a small team of specialists, had spent hours examining the potential drawbacks and assets, and when she had finally put the 'statel' suggestion to the full-time members of the European board they had, on the whole, greeted it with optimistic caution. Irv's initial reaction and that of the New York board had been less cautious. If she made more exhaustive investigations and came up with detailed proposals, followed – perhaps – by a pilot run in England, there was a good chance that the scheme could go ahead.

A lot would depend on today's meeting with Irv.

Filling herself another coffee, Katherine read through her notes once again. The 'statels' would be a mammoth project, one which could make or break her as chairman, and she intended that it would make her . . . The idea of combining lavish business centres with some of the finest architecture Europe had ever produced was enthralling. International country clubs for the business élite, not merely preserving but putting historic houses to good use once more, and at the same time having an excellent long-term investment for Borjex's funds, to say nothing of the prestige the scheme could bring to the company . . . the potential was almost unlimited.

Katherine was in a calm, determined mood when she left the apartment at 8 a.m., and quite prepared for a wearing, difficult day ahead. In the event, the general progress meeting with the headquarters board took little more than an hour, then she and Irv went off alone to Irv's office.

'As chairman,' he said, 'one problem that you're always going to have to tackle is your own board.'

'I know that,' she said, and caught a hint of something she knew only too well in Irv's lazy, Deep South drawl.

He was scheming; his voice was always warmer than ever when he was trying to manipulate.

'Well,' he continued, 'you're new to this job and ah would be failing you if ah didn't give you all the help ah could.'

'I haven't been chairman very long,' she retorted, 'but let's not forget that I was a board member for a considerable time before this appointment.'

'True,' he said, and smiled at her, his black eyes hard but not unkind – only determined, just as Katherine was.

'Oh come on, Irv,' she said. 'What do you want? What are you up to?'

He tried to look as though he hadn't the faintest idea what she was talking about.

'Irv—'

'It's just that your board isn't up to full strength yet,' he shrugged. 'And it's time it was.'

'We were going to talk about that, anyway, weren't we? After we'd talked about the "statels".'

'The way ah see it, –' he sighed and shook his head – 'the statels and the structure of your board are inseparable.'

'To a certain extent,' she agreed. 'Obviously.'

'No, more specifically than that.'

She was suddenly very much on the alert. Her board members, separately as well as together, wielded enormous power. They were the barons of the European operations and could, if they chose, destroy a chairman. Katherine would have like to have limited their influence, but limiting it depended not only on her own astuteness and strength but on the individuals who made up the board – and she would not accept any newcomers without being absolutely certain of their loyalty to her.

'How's Jim Beloff getting on?' Irv asked.

'Fine. Much better since I made him deputy. A bit vague on occasion but I couldn't wish for a better number two.'

Appointing Dr Beloff to this key post had been an excellent move. He was one of the people who had protested when Katherine was made chairman, but he was not a committed enough opponent to be a serious threat – he was far too cautious to take the necessary risks with his career – and his new rôle had boosted his ego while putting him in a position where it would be difficult to cross Katherine without letting himself down. Moreover, though a poor leader, he was a good 'number two', having many of the characteristics Katherine was too busy to develop. He was academically inclined, would think round problems and invariably came up with well-reasoned answers.

Irv grunted, then said: 'But you're going to have to replace Max Holman.'

Max, who had been the most serious contender for the chairmanship apart from Katherine, had resigned immediately the news had broken of her appointment.

'Sure, Irv – when I find the right person.'

'We can't put it off any longer. Remember ah told you last night that ah had some interesting news for you? Well here it is – ah've found you the ideal guy.'

'I've got my own ideas about the kind of person I want, and how I want to organize my board.'

Irv gave her a quick and rather cold smile.

'If you're to go ahead with your "statel" plans,' he said, 'you've got to convince me and the headquarters people here in New York that you can handle it. In other words, that you have at least one person on your board who has the right background to take primary responsibility.'

'And who is this ideal person that you've found for me?'

'His name's Williams – Gareth Williams.'

She froze. For a split second she thought she'd mis-heard, or that she was imagining things. Fifteen years! Fifteen long, tortuous years since she'd seen him, and of late he'd crossed her mind again – but it couldn't be true, it was too unfair . . .

Clearing her throat and running a hand through her

hair she said, in a voice that sounded too dubious to be her own, 'He's not an American by any chance?'

'As a matter of fact he comes from Wales, near that town where you had your first job. Abertawe, wasn't it? But he's been living in the States for years.'

She felt ill, or imagined she did: she saw him so clearly – coal-black curls that fell untidily over his collar, eyes bright and blue and smiling . . . 'Kate, little Kate' – she could hear his voice, that lovely voice with the soft Welsh lilt . . . Honeyed words . . . And there was the ticking of a clock, the roar of the waves on cliffs far below, gulls screaming in a grey Celtic dawn:

LIAR   HYPOCRITE   BETRAYER

'Under no circumstances,' she said, 'will I have Gareth Williams on my board.'

'Why the hell not?'

'I know him – our paths crossed many years ago. He's a totally unsuitable character and I won't have him meddling in the European operations.'

Irv watched her with interest for what seemed like a minute or more, then he flashed her another smile and said: 'Oh yes you will – unless you can give me some very substantial reasons why not.' Seeing her hesitate, he went on: 'Apart from the fact that Gareth Williams is a friend of mine and my opinion of him couldn't be higher, he happens to be an outstandingly successful man in the property field – we're lucky he's agreed to join us.'

'You mean you've already asked him?' The words came out slowly, a mixture of disbelief and amazement.

Irv looked momentarily embarrassed.

'I mentioned it to him – unofficially, of course. He didn't say he knew you . . . Well, what's the matter with you?'

'You've put me in an impossible situation, that's what's the matter with me.'

Edward's voice on the telephone was reassuring, but this

was something she couldn't confide even to him. She wished she'd told him about the Gareth Williams saga before, but it was too late now, so she merely said that Irv was trying to persuade her to take on a new board member, someone she'd known a long time ago and whom she'd disliked – a devious person who was quite capable of causing trouble.

'Tell Irv to take a running jump,' Edward said breezily. 'Argue with him, refuse to accept this creature.'

'It's not as simple as that. The New York board agrees with Irv, and unless I go along with them the "statel" scheme is going to be postponed indefinitely.'

'Tricky,' he agreed. 'I'd be inclined to accept him, get agreement on the scheme, then try to get rid of him.'

'But Edward, you can't get rid of board members – short of criminal prosecution or something similar.'

'Bad luck, then – you're just going to have to put up with him. Perhaps he's changed since you last saw him?'

As she replaced the receiver, Katherine thought it unlikely that Gareth had changed. He might have altered physically, or mellowed a little, but he would still be the same underneath. Not that she thought about him all that often, and when he did cross her mind it was usually only the good things she remembered, but now that they were destined to meet again she was horrified by the strength of her own reactions: shock, curiosity, and the dread that he might yet again be capable of causing catastrophe in her life. But another part of her longed to see him again, and that was worse by far.

The next morning was disastrous. She and Irv disagreed violently, she trying every way she knew to object to Gareth Williams's presence in the company, while Irv continued to sing his praises. Nothing but the truth would be any use, and she couldn't tell him that; even if she did it mightn't be sufficient in the circumstances, so she stuck to her argument that she considered Gareth an unsuitable character.

Irv maintained that he was ideal: he was the right age, only forty-one, and in Irv's opinion his personality was a distinct asset – he was astute, sympathetic, had a tremendous way with people.

Katherine snorted contemptuously.

Moreover, Irv went on, there was his professional training as an architect, his career in property and property development, and then his own – highly successful – business in the same field. He was English, more or less, had spent years in America and also knew his way round Europe. He'd do the job on a short-term contract and on a part-time basis, and so be able to keep his own business going, too.

He should stick to that, Katherine said, instead of trying to muscle in on Borjex.

Irv said that wasn't fair, a couple of her present part-time members had, or had had, their own businesses as well as other outside interests. It worked fine, as she knew only too well. They brought their experience and outside knowledge to Borjex, and they themselves benefited by keeping in touch with a wider circle of business – and had the opportunity to make fresh contacts. Why, one of her part-time people had three companies of his own.

'Nevertheless,' she insisted, 'Gareth might be difficult to handle. You know how the part-time people tend to consider themselves independent, and Gareth always was headstrong, pushy.'

'Are you trying to tell me there are elements of your own board that you can't handle?'

'I – no. I'm just saying that he might cause extra problems.'

'That just isn't true, Katherine. Ah've known him for some time now – he's a great guy and a first-rate businessman. He's already made his million, you've nothing to bother about. Just be glad of his superior experience – you're very fortunate to have the chance of it.'

She flushed with temper.

'Why,' she asked, 'do you think he failed to tell you that he knew me?'

'Who knows?' Irv shrugged. 'He did say he'd heard of you, but that was all . . . Look, what *is* this thing between you and Gareth Williams?'

'I've told you, I don't trust him.'

'But there's more to it than that. Why it's crazy – you fly into a rage when ah mention his name, he's so cool he might have forgotten you completely.'

For a moment she was silent, then she said 'You're quite certain he knows it's me he'll be reporting to?'

'Personally ah wouldn't use the word *reporting* in this context, Katherine. Not with a board member, and a part-time member at that. But if you mean, as ah presume you do, is he quite clear that Katherine Hanson is head of our European operations, well of course he is.'

'Did he know before or after he agreed to the board membership?'

'Well—' Irv considered for a minute. 'After. You could say it was after. At least, after his unofficial acceptance. We were having dinner together – you know how it is – and ah broached the subject of his joining us, and he liked the sound of it. Then ah said to him you know the new chairman's a woman, don't you? And he said he'd heard as much, and was she a – er, was she a – an *American*.' Irv smiled triumphantly. 'And ah said no, she's an English lady and her name's Katherine Hanson.'

'And he gave no indication whatsoever that he knew me?'

'Well – not exactly.'

'But he had some reaction?'

'Ye – es.'

'And what was it?'

'Well—' Irv was beginning to find the afternoon gruesome. It was dawning on him what treacherous ground he'd wandered on to, simply and in good faith, and because he would never understand anything about women, even women with titles like this one's. He opted for tact. 'Different to yours,' he said, and nodded solemnly, as if to convey the seriousness of Gareth's outlook on receipt of Irv's information.

'But what exactly?' she persisted.

'Does it matter?'

'Naturally, if I'm to work closely with this man.'

'Well—' since whatever he said caused trouble, he decided to take a risk and switch to the truth. It might work, might lighten her intense mood and make her look forward to Gareth's arrival. 'He laughed,' he said, and tried to force his own lips into some semblance of a smile.

Katherine took a deep breath, then glanced down at her hands and saw that they were no longer simply folded together, but clenched so tightly that the knuckles showed white.

'You're dishonest,' she said. 'Gareth's a friend of yours and it's unthinkable in the circumstances that he wouldn't have said something about me.'

'He said *nothing*.'

'I don't believe you for one minute, but never mind. Keep it to yourself – whatever he said – and much good may it do you . . . OK then, I appear to be stuck with this bastard friend of yours, so he'd better come over to England and have a look round the headquarters.'

'He's already been – called in the day you were doing your television interview and spoke to one of your board members. Bill Skerrett, I think it was.'

'For God's sake, Irv—'

'You were tied up! He happened to be in England and just called in on the off-chance. Now don't over-react – anyway after that he decided he definitely wanted to join us.'

Katherine smiled, such an icy movement of the lips that

Irv wondered if, after all, he hadn't made a mistake in crossing swords with this lady.

'He'll bring trouble, Irv, I promise you – and when it happens remember it was your doing.'

The first morning back in the London office was bad. Due to her absence, brief though it had been, there was a thicker than usual stack of papers on her desk and it looked as though it was going to be impossible to see Edward tonight. It was disappointing; she'd missed him and there was a lot that she wanted to talk to him about – and also, when she was with Edward, thoughts of Gareth Williams disturbed her less.

That fraught conversation with Irv had brought home to her a terrible realization: Gareth Williams stood out in her mind as no other individual had ever done, and at the very mention of his name the time and the people that had come between them faded away like shadows.

Work was the only way to deal with it, hard work and concentration, because she certainly had enough problems without allowing Gareth to add to them. There was a bonus scheme to be finalized with one of the more militant unions, then there was the television interview that would be broadcast later this month, and tomorrow she would have to go to the studios and discuss all sorts of important things.

There was no time and certainly no point in thinking of a man who was now approaching middle age, who had probably grown dull and unattractive with the passing years; no point in wondering if she, too, might have lost her looks, even just a little bit; no point in worrying about it because anyway she didn't care what Gareth Williams would think of her when he saw her again. And it would be foolhardy to think of those features that she'd loved so well, and that soft voice . . . 'I wouldn't have hurt you for the world.'

*

The air-conditioning in the studios was perfectly adequate, yet Katherine felt hot. The weather at the weekend had been heavy, followed by a sultry-warm Monday, and she tried to put her reaction down to the temperature outside. But she'd been in the cool building for over a quarter of an hour, and would soon have to admit to herself that she was apprehensive.

When the television company had invited her to look at the rushes, she'd jumped at the chance. Except for the interview sequence she'd enjoyed making the film, but the interview was important and she'd been tense at first, so that she couldn't remember with absolute certainly some of the points she'd made.

A couple of months ago – soon after her appointment as chairman – she'd taken part in a glamorous chat show, but that was a long way removed from this serious programme where she was responsible for the way Borjex was presented to millions of viewers. Hugo Palfreyman's team had briefed her well, and Hugo himself had given her sound last-minute advice, but the interviewer was a man celebrated for his redoubtable tactics and now, as the film was about to start, she felt a definite twinge of anxiety.

The early shots were the out-of-doors' ones, and she was pleased with them. Seeing herself on film was still a novel experience, and the first glimpse of a tall, blonde woman with a voice she recognized brought her up with a jolt. It was like seeing the ghost of someone she knew – and she began to relax, to get caught up in it all, and let the worries about what she had or had not said fade into the category of the irretrievable.

She saw herself looking tough and competent, in overalls and a yellow tin helmet, talking to a foreman in an engineering works; striding mannishly across an open-cast site, her feet clad in heavyweight Wellingtons and the interviewer trailing hesitantly behind; then there were shots of her looking almost sexy, in a cream, tight-fitting suit and high-heeled shoes, walking round Borjex House, describing everything from the Queen Anne stairway to the latest information banks.

A lot of people would be interested in the information banks, the television company had assured her. She supposed she'd have been interested herself, not so long ago.

The twenty-minute interview began, as she had been warned it would, with personal questions.

'— that was an unusual choice of subject for a woman, wasn't it?'

'No, I don't think so. Chemical engineering is a discipline like any other. Women study law, medicine, psychology, so why not engineering if it interests them?'

How sad, that she had nothing better to say after all these years.

'I don't see that being able to balance an equation stops me from being feminine.'

There was no doubt about her femininity: softly waved hair swept back from a sun-tanned face, bright hazel eyes slightly slanting at the corners, wide mouth and pleasantly proportioned features. She would have been truly beautiful, except that the lips were too thin and the jaw line too harsh for a woman. Occasionally it looked aggressive: on the screen, she might have been a star. She could have hugged the cameraman.

And to hell with vanity, she thought. I have as much right to enjoy being attractive as any other woman.

'I tried research for a year, but had too little interest to continue. I've found business a challenge . . . Yes, I am one of the most highly paid females . . .'

True, in return for years of determination and even pain, to say nothing of lost weekends and tired evenings. She'd sworn to herself, not once, but a hundred times, 'Nothing's going to stop me now' – and nothing did, and now she'd got what she wanted she was glad of it. But how she'd had to squeeze in the moments of fun, rearrange whole schedules to ensure even a few hours to herself.

'– but why not just say "people" instead of "females"? It reminds me of an argument I had a few years ago—'

From a distance they'd been glittering years, the last half dozen. The ones before seemed formidable, even in retrospect.

'There is nothing else I want to do at the moment . . . No, I've never been married, and have no plans to do other than continue with Borjex. I was appointed vice president and chairman of the European operations in—'

What a battle it had been – getting there! And yet she thought that that was what she'd enjoyed most of all, what had given her most satisfaction – the hazardous moments when success or failure depended on nerve and daring. The fiercer the battle, the sweeter the prize. She could remember struggles that even now made her heart beat a little faster, not with fear but with excitement. There were other moments, too, just as exciting in their way – thrilling to the sound of a name, the touch of a hand on your body in the warmth of the night, being woken by the sun when you were not alone; and earlier times, a first encounter that was to rock your world – but for all its consequences you'd live it again, if you could.

'We're basically an American company, but we've expanded throughout Western Europe as well as Australia—'

The camera had panned in again for a close-up. It was a misplaced shot, following on such words, and would almost certainly be cut. But while it lasted she loved it: she could fool herself that, just as the face seemed to have altered so little, so too had the person behind it remained unchanged, and the chasm of more than fifteen years closed up. She would have liked to have stopped the film right there, to have jammed the delicate mechanism that caught her in some glorious morning, heading carefree towards the mountains of Wales . . .

The countryside was glistening in the sun after a light September shower. Katherine drove through it slowly, past the little villages with their timbered cottages and carefully tended greens, their antique shops and pubs and rich farmland. Her battered five-year-old Mini was laden with cases, boxes of books and stacks of papers. It laboured up the first of the steep mountains that divided England from Wales, where the earth was already growing poorer and sheep wandered over the bracken and between the grey stony outcrops.

Slipping into third gear, she negotiated the twisting road that took her into the first valley of South Wales: in the distance was the headgear of a mine and the shapeless mound of a coal tip; beyond, clustered at the foot of the mountain, were the terraced houses of the village. Then she was climbing again, towards a high ridge that overlooked hills and valleys. She stopped the car and got out to look at the bleak, magnificent scenery. Far away on the horizon, at the summit of a table-top mountain, were the ruins of a castle, black and jagged against the clear blue sky. The rest was desolate and uncultivated – dry, poverty-stricken acres dotted here and there with grey stone hamlets. The only colour was the crimson of the rhododendrons, running wild in the valley below.

A chill wind was blowing at this altitude, chasing clouds across the face of the sun so that the land was a kaleidoscope of light and shadow, constantly changing. It was an awe-inspiring land, splendid and savage and poor.

Shivering, Katherine climbed back into the car and decided not to stop again until she reached the university. It was an hour later when she drove through Abertawe town centre and out again at the far side, and then she felt her spirits lift again.

There was the sea, a blue-grey Celtic sea sparkling in

the midday sun, and there were golden, empty beaches, white-fronted Edwardian houses and spacious, elegant promenades. Abertawe Bay was a huge, gentle curve; at one end was a busy port and on the far side a fishing village and yachting harbour. In the centre of the curve, overlooking the sea and surrounded on three sides by green parkland, was the sprawling university campus. Sheltered by mountains, Abertawe was warm and fertile, and the driveway that led to the central college buildings was bordered by lawns, exotic vegetation and even palm trees.

Katherine was humming a tune to herself as she drove through the bright sunshine towards the administrative block and her faculty offices. The campus was almost deserted so long before the beginning of the autumn term, but standing on the flight of stone steps that went up to the library was a boy dressed in denims and an open-necked shirt. He was looking down the driveway, as if awaiting her arrival.

As she drew closer, she saw that he was looking beyond her, to the wide main road and the sea. Then for a second he lowered his gaze and looked directly at her.

He grinned.

Caught unaware, she smiled back automatically, half registered his dark good looks, then turned sharp right to follow a sign saying 'Department of Chemical Engineering'.

Glancing in her driving mirror, she saw that he had run down the library steps and was blowing kisses after her receding brake lights.

'Fool!' she shouted at the mirror, and laughed as she accelerated out of sight.

It was a month before she saw him again, and by that time she'd forgotten him completely.

The last few weeks had been unusually busy with beginning-of-term meetings as well as her teaching schedule and research work, and she had few hours to herself. Every now and then she would escape to one of the more deserted beaches to walk and be alone for a while. The tourists were long gone from Abertawe, so if she chose a remote enough cove she could be almost certain of solitude.

There was an early autumn freshness in the air as she set off for a stroll one Friday evening. She scrambled over sand dunes and onto the shingle; it crunched underfoot as she made her way towards the expanse of golden beach. The sand was soft, but only a few yards ahead the evening tide was coming in. She walked towards it: it was a gentle sea today, and it frothed at her feet. In the west the sun was a flaming red, casting its last, brilliant rays across the cool water.

Katherine was happy, as she had been ever since she'd arrived in this place. She no longer missed Cambridge where she'd spent the last three years, and New York – where she'd spent the summer – seemed like a different world. Looking up at the mountains that encircled Abertawe, she was reminded of her home, the small industrial town near the Scottish border, except that here there was a clean, salty tang in the air, and there were cheerful things to look at – the boats bobbing in the bay, a sailing dinghy tacking towards harbour, and a mile or so away was the wharf and then the white-washed cottages of the old fishing village.

Walking slowly by the water's edge, she paused to take off her sandals and roll her jeans up to her knees. Carrying the sandals in one hand, she splashed through the thin waves that foamed round her ankles. The sun was sinking fast now, dazzling her eyes and lighting up the yachts at anchor before it slipped into the sea.

'The last of the sun,' said a voice behind her.

It was a lovely voice – strong and clear, yet soft – and there was a faint Welsh lilt to it. For a second she scarcely believed she'd heard it, for it mingled with the sound of the waves and the light, gusting breeze whipped it quickly out to sea.

Pausing, she looked back over her shoulder.

A few yards behind her, clad in a pair of rough old denims, was a boy she vaguely recognized. He had strong features that would have been handsome had they been a fraction less pronounced; his eyes were bright and smiling, and his hair was thick, dark and rather curly. A few tendrils fell untidily down his neck.

Her immediate assumption was that he was a student, but he looked older than most of the undergraduates and might have been in his mid or late twenties. There was nothing adolescent about his body, either; he was taller than average and his muscles looked hard as well as sun-tanned. He could have been an athlete or a coastguard or a labourer – or anything at all that needed physical strength.

For a second she looked at him impassively, liked what she saw, and then changed her mind. He'd taken a couple of steps towards her so that they were standing only about a foot apart. She edged back a pace.

'I'm sorry,' he said, 'I didn't mean to startle you.'

'Oh – you didn't,' she lied, and was about to turn and walk inland when she caught sight of a figure slithering down the sand dunes. It was wearing a flapping overcoat and woollen muffler, and she recognized it as the professor of anthropology. The man was striding out towards the sea now, his hands clasped behind his back and his head bowed. He looked bent on a watery suicide.

Katherine smiled wryly.

'Evan Griffiths won't rush to your rescue,' the boy grinned. 'He wouldn't even notice if the harbour was filled with warships.'

'You know Evan?' Katherine asked. 'Are you from the university?'

'Miss Hanson!' There was mock dismay in his voice.

Katherine gave a guilty start.

'Of course – you're one of my students, aren't you? You must excuse me – I've only just started here and there are so many faces to remember—'

'Don't worry.'

'I'm afraid I've also forgotten your name.'

'Williams,' he said. 'Gareth Williams.'

Katherine tried to place him. She had three or maybe four Williamses on her list.

'I was at your seminar the other week.' His smile was polite as well as friendly. 'I enjoyed it – you lecture with plenty of confidence.'

'Thank you, though officially I'm not a lecturer, you know. I give the occasional seminar but in fact I'm just a tutor, and I do research. I only graduated myself last year – this is my first job.'

'You must be very bright.'

'Hard working,' she said.

He grimaced. 'You shouldn't work too hard – it'll stoop your shoulders and put lines on your face . . . Mind if I walk along with you?'

'Well—'

But he'd already touched her arm as though he were chaperoning her through a crowded restaurant, and was walking by her side in the direction of the wharf.

He asked her questions, prompted her to talk about her work, then they were chatting about this and that, anything that came into their heads . . . her summer in New York, a visit he'd once made to India, the fishing fleet coming in on the evening tide . . . and she found she was enjoying herself. He was light and easy to talk to, and they were even laughing together, about Evan Griffiths and his appalling forgetfulness, about stupid things they'd both done in the past.

When she glanced at her watch and saw that it was nearly seven o'clock, she was surprised. Then she suddenly noticed how chilly it was, and she shivered in her light shirt.

'Cold?' he said.

'Not as cold as you must be,' she replied, glancing at his body clad only in the rough demins.

'I'm too thick-skinned to mind. But my car's parked just up there by the wharf. Let me give you a lift back to the university – it's much too far to walk.'

'That's all right, thanks. I like walking.'

'Rubbish,' he said. 'It's a half-hour walk and only five minutes in the car. Come on – I'll race you to the sand dunes!'

Grabbing hold of her hand, he broke into a run. Short of flinging herself to the ground she had no choice but to run along with him.

'Would you mind . . .' she tried to shout.

'Very much!' he laughed. By the time they'd clambered over the dunes she was laughing, too, and breathless.

Just ahead of them she saw a new-looking jeep with its top down. It had been parked on a flat stretch of sand next to a sign saying 'No Parking'.

He went towards it and with unexpected courtesy opened the passenger door for her.

'Bit late for that kind of gesture, isn't it?'

'Exactly the right moment,' he said, going round to the other side and climbing in.

He pulled on a tee-shirt, then produced a sweater and put it round her shoulders.

'Here – this'll keep you warm. Right, let's go.' He started the engine. 'Do you live on the campus?'

'Hm-mm. I'm lucky – the university supplies me with a flat. Where do you live?'

'Oh – I have a place not far away.'

Within minutes they were on the campus and passing the central library. It was then that she remembered where she'd first seen him, standing at the top of the steps on the day she arrived.

'You came down a long time before the start of term, didn't you?'

He grinned, and dropped into second gear.

'Which is your block?'

It was the grin that did it, of course. He wiped it from his face almost as soon as it had appeared, but it was irrepressible and came back immediately in his eyes.

'Which is your block?' he repeated, and held the car stationary on the clutch while he waited for her answer.

'First right, second left, the last block before the park.'

He drove on, then pulled up again outside the entrance.

'I forgot to ask you,' she said, with a smile, 'are you in your first year or second year? I know I ought to remember with such an extraordinary character as you, but . . .' she shrugged.

'Third year,' he said.

'Then you wouldn't be coming to my tutorials. You'd be with the Professor.'

'I don't go to your tutorials,' he said. 'I wandered in to one of your seminars the other week – I told you.'

'Ah, of course. Then that must have been the one on thermal balances.'

'Don't worry about work right now,' he advised.

'I just wondered if, in your opinion, I was right to touch on fluid flow and heat transfer in the same talk. It was nothing more than a broad, introductory discussion, I grant you, primarily for first-year people, but should I have stuck to thermal balances?'

'Well – maybe.'

She shook her head thoughtfully.

'Not material *and* thermal balances, then?'

He looked marginally distressed, then screwed up his face to indicate that he was giving the matter serious consideration.

'Possibly,' he said at last.

'Or should I have saved thermal balances for seminar number two?'

'Yeh, you should have saved it.' He revved up the engine. 'Now then, dinner.' He flashed her a smile. 'I was going to ask you if I could pick you up in, say, an hour's time? If you'd like to have dinner with me, that is.'

She sighed.

'What a lovely idea.' She looked him right in the eye. 'But I've got to go through your essay.'

He looked shocked.

'My essay?'

'Yours and about a dozen other people's. The Professor's still at the conference – he's handed me some final-year papers to have a look at.'

'Do it tomorrow.'

'I can't. And I particularly want to give yours plenty of thought: I shall go through it with a fine tooth comb.'

'Ah.'

'I want to put you on the straight and narrow, help you. I should hate to have to fail you.'

He looked intensely irritated, then smiled.

'Maybe tomorrow night?'

'I'm sorry,' she said. 'I think we'd better leave it. Since I'm so closely involved with supervising your work, I'm beginning to think that it would be a mistake to get to know one another too well. Besides, you shouldn't be buying me dinner.'

'Why not?'

Trying to look concerned, she said: 'As a student, I'm sure you must be—'

'Broke? Is that what you're trying to say?' He opened his mouth as if about to say something, then changed his mind.

She got out of the jeep, closed the door and flung his sweater into the back.

'Work hard,' she said, and turned aside and headed for the foyer.

'As a chemical engineer,' he called after her, 'your hips are a disgrace!'

She froze.

'You put a man off his thermal balances!' His voice was

so loud he might have been speaking through a mega-
phone. A couple of passing Welsh lecturers, deep in some
grim conversation, looked up bewildered.

He gave a great bellow of laughter.

'I'll be back,' she heard him say, as he revved up the
engine and roared away.

And he did come back, and she wished he never had.
Even at that first innocent meeting he'd had to lie – had
proved himself a cheat and a charlatan as if just for the
hell of it. But though she was nearly forty now she
remembered his laughter, and the touch of his fingers on
her arm and the sun that was dazzling in her eyes.

THREE

Come, Kate, thou art perfect in lying down:
come, quick, quick, that I may lay my head in thy lap.

– HOTSPUR; *Henry the Fourth*, Part One

'This is completely unfair!'

Edward got to his feet, snapped off the reading lamp that stood on his desk, strode across the room and took hold of Katherine's hands.

His last gesture had caused the papers that were lying on her lap to slither to the floor, and she howled with irritation.

'You've been back from New York for two days,' he complained. 'This is the first time I see you and yet you say you have work to finish before we can go out for the evening. And as if that isn't bad enough you suggest I follow your example – and *I*, a grown man and presumably with a will of my own, am foolish enough to listen to you.'

'I'm sorry,' she laughed. 'Here, help me sort these papers out—'

He stooped and picked up three or four, then held them at arm's length.

'You can have them back,' he said, 'if you promise not to touch another scrap of Borjex rubbish till tomorrow morning.'

'All right, then, it's a promise. In any case,' she added, 'I'd already finished.'

'As I said, this is completely unfair.' He kissed her slowly on the lips.

'But nice kind of unfair,' she muttered, as he drew her

to her feet and held her close. 'Perhaps we shouldn't go out till much, much later?'

'Oh.' He sounded disappointed. 'As a matter of fact . . .'

'Yes?'

He let her go, went over to the drinks cabinet and poured a gin and tonic, then a scotch and water.

'Well?'

'I'm afraid I'm rather—' he handed her the gin and tonic – 'a bit *hungry*, as a matter of fact.'

'Edward – you really are incredible! I thought it was something important for a minute.'

'It is in a way, isn't it? While it lasts . . . By the way what's happening with this Williams fellow?'

'Oh – *him*!' She waved a hand dismissively, sat down again on the sofa and sipped her drink.

'But is he going to be on the board?' he prompted, joining her and slipping an arm round her shoulders.

'Unfortunately, yes. Irv's rushed into this feet first – he's so tactless. D'you know what he said to me finally, the other afternoon?'

'Tell me.'

'He told me not to worry about anything, to give Gareth Williams as free a hand as possible with the "statels" – just leave it to him and take his advice . . . Honestly, Edward, it's my project and I'm chairman.'

'Naturally you'll still be in charge, but there's no reason why you shouldn't take Williams's advice. Why should you resent that if he's as good as Irv makes him out to be?'

She tutted, got to her feet again and glanced at her reflection in the square Georgian mirror that hung above the fireplace.

'It's not that I *resent* it, it's just that I hope nothing goes wrong.'

'What could go wrong?' He watched her searching for

the right words, then added: 'Just what's so special about this character?'

'He's devious – totally immoral and completely selfish. Greedy, too, and unscrupulous.'

'So are ninety per cent of Borjex's senior management – and you haven't done so badly yourself in the past.'

'Thanks.'

He was silent for a moment, then said, too casually: 'Were you very much in love with him?'

She smiled. 'It wouldn't matter after all this time, would it?'

'Not in itself, no . . . Now what could he have done to you to make you single him out for such hatred after all these years?'

Over the next few days Katherine began to notice a change in Edward. Attentive and well mannered even at the worst of times, he now became the very epitome of courtesy. He took her to their favourite restaurants, spent ages choosing the wines and even longer trying to ensure that Katherine was kept amused and happy. It was as if he was trying to seduce her all over again. But he did it so smoothly, so subtly, that it was almost imperceptible – totally unlike the way Gareth had chased after her in those early days at Abertawe, when the attraction she'd felt at their first meeting had passed and she didn't even want to know him.

It was Gareth who'd won in the end, though, for she'd agreed to see him again and eventually found out more about him.

He wasn't a student at all, but an architect who was working for some property company in London. He had to come to South Wales each week on business, and his family lived there, too – in fact he'd been brought up near Abertawe. An old schoolfriend of his was a lecturer at the university, and Gareth had been looking him up when he'd first laid eyes on Katherine, driving across the campus in her battered old Mini. And the next time he'd seen her he'd had the cheek to follow her onto the beach, and make up that story about being one of her students – just to have an excuse for chatting her up.

Gareth Williams, she'd decided, was nothing but a likeable rogue, and the stories he told her about his misspent youth only confirmed her opinion of him. He'd been sacked from one job for punching his boss on the nose – to defend some girl, according to Gareth – had been unable to get a proper reference for months and had done everything from working on building sites to farm-labouring. That, she supposed, was why his hands were so calloused – but they were good hands, strong and decisive, and they managed to touch her gently. He'd been in all sorts of other trouble, too – even hitchhiked to India and then – for reasons not specified – been deported. Finally, this property company in London had taken the crazy decision to allow him – a failed or disillusioned architect – to join them. And at last he was doing well, but in a business rather than professional capacity: the technicalities of designing buildings no longer interested him, but money did. Katherine thought he would always either fail at everything or do resoundingly well. There were no happy mediums with Gareth, and perhaps that was why he was so exciting. He didn't really gave a damn about anything – seemed so full of life that his love of it was irresistible. Just as he was.

Never, ever, she promised herself, would she get involved with such a man – and when he next tried his honey-tongued charms on her, she told him so.

'Yes you will,' was Gareth's retort.

They were standing in the sitting room of her flat in Abertawe. It was a restless, October night, with the wind whistling through the trees in the park outside, and the distant swell of the sea only just audible.

'I think you should leave soon,' she said. 'It's after midnight and I have to be up early in the morning.'

Then she realized how silent he'd become, and that he was watching her, his eyes enigmatic and his expression sealed and disturbing.

She hesitated, then said quickly: 'I really would prefer you to go—' and turned away.

But he caught her lightly by the wrist and pulled her back again.

They stood facing each other, only inches apart, and the force of their attraction slammed against her like the shock of lightning on a summer's night.

The breath might have been knocked from her body; her legs trembled, her pulse leapt, and as he put out a hand to touch her hair she saw such unexpected tenderness in his face that for a second the world stood still.

He undressed her slowly, there in the lamplit sitting room, as though to have hurried would have broken some undreamed-of bond.

She wanted to speak his name but could not; he said hers softly, like a whisper, when his mouth found hers. And then his lips were on her body, calling her again and again as he went down on his knees before her and she held him to her. He hid his face against her stomach, her thighs, and she ran her fingers through his hair, the thick, black curls that fell so wildly down his neck – and outside the autumn wind was screaming through the trees and far away on the nightswept beach the waves were bursting, tearing apart in the starlit air.

They rented a cottage on the Abertawe peninsula, and moved in immediately. Gareth's work was still based in London but he managed to get down to Wales for at least three days out of every seven.

How happy they were! Gareth loved to tease her and call her 'Kate', which she loathed, or even 'little Kate', which was worse. They always seemed to be enjoying themselves and laughing, as if they didn't have a care in the world. They were together at every possible opportunity, greedy for each other and insatiable: the company of their friends seemed like an intrusion, and whether they were indoors or outdoors they tried to be alone. The ridge of mountains that sheltered that part of Wales ensured mild weather until late in the year, and they made the most of the sunny weekends to drive across the moors, then walk along hardened tracks where foliage was dying slowly, turning late to the yellows and browns of autumn. They would hold hands like children, kicking through the banks of fallen leaves, or racing to the sandy beach to watch the sea foam thick and white in a blustering wind.

Some nights they'd go to the Mill House Restaurant that overlooked the salt marshes. While they ate and talked they could watch the wild birds coming swiftly homewards, flying in low over the reeds, and the grey strip of the estuary as it swelled with the evening tide – and sometimes, on nights such as that, there was a pathos about their love that she could not understand.

Gladness and optimism were her usual feelings in those days. She fancied that she and Gareth were the perfect couple and that nothing could ever come between them. They were both ambitious, but there was nothing what-soever to stop them realizing their ambitions together. She could see no flaw on the horizon, and everything about the present delighted her – from the feel of Gareth's hands on her body, to the pleasure of seeing him in Gwilym Cottage.

They'd christened it 'Gwilym' in honour – or so Gareth told her – of a famous Welsh bard. Katherine lavished attention on the place – but then it was the first time she'd had a home that was hers as opposed to somebody else's.

When Katherine Hanson was ten and her brother Daniel was twelve, their small family had hit disaster. Paul, their father, was a solicitor: he was struck off for malpractice and he and his wife Miriam, finding themselves without an income, had turned against each other and argued violently. He'd left home without a word and Miriam had been obliged to seek help where she could.

The possibility of remaining in their large house in Kent was out of the question and Miriam, virtually destitute, had moved with her two children into her sister Joan's house in Langston, in the North of England.

Langston was a small industrial town and Joan, who ran a dress shop there, lived in a tiny modern house on the edge of a council estate. She was kind enough to offer the Hansons a home, but it was always an unhappy place for Katherine and Daniel. It seemed grey and lonely after the Kent countryside where they'd been brought up, and where all their friends were. It was a harsh place, too, where they could no longer afford the things that other children had, and where they had to do odd jobs in the evenings and at weekends to help make ends meet.

There was never a word from their father, and night after night Katherine would fight back the tears – or comfort Daniel who used to cry himself to sleep. He was a boy and older than she, but she was much the better at hiding her emotions, and it was she who helped him through the worst times. The worst phase of all was when their mother started drinking, and when she finally decided on a cure she chose the very moment Joan was about to go into hospital for a major operation.

Katherine and Daniel were taken into care by social workers, and afterwards – though their mother wept and said she hadn't meant to let them down – it seemed hard to forgive her disloyalty. It wasn't just for herself that Katherine felt the pain – but for the sight of Daniel at the age of thirteen, yelling and fighting against the horror of being impounded in some institution.

When Miriam's 'cure' was as complete as it would ever be, things seemed to pick up a little. Katherine, encouraged by her headmistress and Aunt Joan, did well with her studies and won a scholarship to a girls' public school.

She worked even harder there, because success was one thing she could aim for and might attain: normality appeared lost to her forever. Her friends all seemed to come from typical family backgrounds where there was plenty of love and affection and security, while she was continually the odd one out. Every time she passed an exam with flying colours, or did especially well in some competition, it was as if the triumph ensured she was no longer a loner but someone special; she achieved things – she was successful and respected and, if not loved, then smiled on warmly.

At the same time she developed a reputation for being kind to the most improbable people, girls who were homesick or somehow misfits, and nobody realized why she felt such sympathy towards them. One such girl, a shy, pale little creature called Melanie Charles, became her closest friend, and Katherine would protect her in the same way that she used to protect her timid brother Daniel.

It was during holiday visits to Melanie's parents' home that Katherine's ambitions began to form themselves. The house was a rambling, mellow old farmhouse with uneven, stone-flagged floors and gleaming mahogany furniture. It was surrounded by woods and fields that reminded her of her old home in Kent, the place where she and Daniel and their mother and father had once been so happy; there were dogs, and a pony that she learned to ride on, and above all there was security and laughter.

One day, Katherine promised herself, one day she would be so successful that she would have all the security and good things she needed – and she made the promise like a vow.

Cambridge was different. There was such a mix of people there that it would have been impossible to feel exceptional in any way – and Katherine enjoyed herself thoroughly.

Only two things spoiled her time at Cambridge. The first was that Daniel emigrated to Canada as soon as he was twenty-one, and the other was that she saw her father again.

He'd remarried and gone to live in South Africa, and on a holiday visit to England had decided to trace his ex-wife and children.

For years Katherine had kept some fragments of her love for him alive – and yet, when she finally saw him again, she hated him. She wished he'd never come back. He was a big, fair-haired, powerful man, and Katherine took after him in looks and personality as much as Daniel took after Miriam. But after their reunion in Cambridge she prayed that there was nothing of him in her.

He'd been successful in South Africa, that was true, but was so blatantly insensitive that Katherine could do nothing but think of Miriam and Daniel – the years of hardship, her mother's pinched face and Daniel's tears – and contrast them with this tough, cheerful man who'd been oblivious to all that. This man who simply hadn't wanted to know.

'Traitor,' was her final word to him.

The year she graduated from Cambridge she was offered the post at Abertawe – and met Gareth. And the happiness she knew with him seemed to make up for all the past heartbreaks.

They lived like man and wife – slept, ate, cooked and occasionally even worked together, Gareth poring over contracts for the property company and Katherine trying to plan seminars or write notes for her thesis. Sometimes she would want him so much that she couldn't concentrate for more than half an hour at a time; she would glance across at him, then he too would look up from his papers, smile, hold out his hand to her and everything else would be forgotten.

He still went back to London for a day or two each week, and though her work at the university usually prevented her from going with him, she did manage the odd visit. He had a small flat in Bayswater – just one large room and a kitchen and bathroom. Since it was only used as a place to sleep in a couple of nights a week, it looked cold and unlived-in and Katherine never cared for it much.

When the pressure of her own work increased and she found it impossible to make even the occasional journey to London, it didn't matter to her at all. She loved Gwilym Cottage, looked on it as her first real home, and the nights when Gareth wasn't there she would tidy and polish and clean it till everything was spotless. She bought pots and pans and all sorts of odds and ends for the kitchen, and when she was cooking there would think how lucky she was, to have a home of her own, to be sharing it with Gareth and to have a successful future ahead of her. Because even then she was determined that she would be successful, come what may.

One morning, when she was preparing breakfast and he was complaining that he was late, she offered to iron a shirt for him. She realized it was the first time she'd ever made such a gesture, and laughed and said: 'Now I really feel like your wife!'

She hadn't meant it seriously; they'd never discussed marriage and the idea meant little to her, but for a moment he neither moved nor spoke, and if she could have retracted the words she would have done.

'I've already been married,' he said, and his voice was brisk, as though she were simply a passing acquaintance who needed to be made aware of some tiresome fact.

She was shocked. It was simply that she couldn't imagine Gareth – charming, ambitious Gareth, Gareth the rebel – doing anything so solemn as getting married.

He smiled.

'It lasted seven months,' he said.

She was curiously jealous, too – because somehow the vows of matrimony were so intimate, so private and special, that they linked people in a way that nobody else could ever share.

'We were just infatuated with one another,' he shrugged. 'Like fools we rushed off to a registry office and got married. We had one very happy month together – just one – then six months of hell before we split up.'

'My God.' She moved away from the ironing board and stared at him. 'Why didn't you tell me before? Something as important as that . . . You even told me you'd lived with somebody . . .'

'Well I was married to her. In any case it all happened ages ago – before I'd even qualified as an architect – when I was twenty-one and even less cautious than I am now. Don't let's make an issue out of it.'

'An issue? Really, Gareth, I do think you might have mentioned it!'

'I was going to,' he protested, 'but at first I was just trying to pull you, wasn't I? And I thought it might sound a bit heavy, or put you off. Then later on . . .' he smiled his winning smile, came and stood in front of her, put his hands on her shoulders – 'when I grew so fond of you, it became more difficult. The time was never right and I wished I'd done it earlier. I'm glad I've said it this morning, and now it's over and done with.'

'Over and done with?'

'In every sense. I don't want to talk about it because it's an incident in my life that's closed. It wasn't a happy incident, except for the first few weeks, and I can't see the point in discussing it. What would you want to know, anyway?'

'Where did you meet? Where did she come from? What was she like?'

'I knew this would happen,' he said irritably, then

turned aside and picked up his shirt. 'Typical. Tell a woman one fact and she can't let go of it. Like a dog with a bone.'

'How rude!' she retorted. 'And you'd better finish off that shirt because I'm not doing it and it's still creased.'

'Oh.'

'Though you might at least tell me what her name was.'

'Miranda,' he said without interest, and made a clumsy attempt to iron the shirt.

'Was she pretty?'

He looked surprised at the question, then laughed.

'I suppose so. Anyway we fancied each other and that was it. All, in fact. A short interlude that took place over four years ago and I haven't laid eyes on her since. She hardly ever even crosses my mind.'

He glanced at his watch and announced that he was now hopelessly late.

'But I am glad that I've told you about her,' he went on, and his eyes as they met Katherine's were very blue and clear. 'You know – leaving aside our first encounter – I've always tried to be truthful and open with you, and I believe you have with me.'

'Yes,' she said. 'I have.'

'Let's keep it that way.'

'Let's.'

He had another go at ironing his shirt, and after a minute or two she pulled it out of his hands and did it for him.

'I'm only doing this as a special treat,' she warned him. 'O.K.?'

'O.K.'

He watched her, then said: 'I'm afraid I wouldn't want to get married again, or not for some time.'

'Don't apologize to me!'

'When we're successful, then there'll be time for things like that. Maybe kids, too – proper marriage and a proper family. Miranda and I never had that – it was just two people living together for a while, legalized by a registrar. I don't know why we did it really. I think it was just that it seemed exciting at the time. Everyone else was against it and that made it even more of a provocation. How stupid—'

'Mm.'

'Within the next couple of years,' he said, 'I want to start my own business. Perhaps in the States, if I can – or start it here and move over there later. That would be a challenge, wouldn't it? You and me—'

'You and me? In business together?'

'Why not? We've got a tremendous future ahead of us, Kate!'

FOUR

This evening must I leave you, gentle Kate.

– HOTSPUR; *Henry the Fourth*, Part One

They had less than a year together.

The cruelty, the injustice, the sheer betrayal of the events that parted them combined with her loneliness to almost – but not quite – break her.

'I wouldn't have hurt you for the world,' was what he'd said, but in her early days in London – when she'd left Abertawe and covered her tracks so well that he'd had no means of tracing her – there'd been nothing but pain.

To add to her distress she'd arrived in London broke, without even the deposit for a room in a flat or a bed-sitter.

A British company were employing her, and they gave her a small advance on her salary. For a month she lived in a shabby and rather dirty bed-and-breakfast place in Hammersmith; she bought cheap, cold food – bread, cheese, fruit, pre-packed ham and milk, and ate in her room. She knew no one, and saw no one outside work. All her colleagues were middle aged and commuted from as far away as Brighton, so she remained alone. How stark those solitary suppers were compared to the happy times with Gareth!

The contrast depressed her beyond belief: one minute she'd been in that cottage at Abertawe with the person who meant more to her than anyone else in the world, and the next she was in a shabby little hotel. But she didn't stay long. As soon as she received her next month's salary she moved to a rented room. There were cooking facilities – a gas ring and a fridge – in one corner, and a washbasin and a shower in the other. In between was a bed, a cupboard, two chairs and a table with stains on the top.

She neither expected nor received any sudden stroke of good fortune; she had no regrets about leaving academic life – it had never been her intention to stay in research for more than a year, anyway – and she was prepared to work hard and to fight for what she wanted, possibly with little reward at first. But then again she had no choice, since it was work or slip back into the way of life her mother and Aunt Joan had grown accustomed to. The very thought was enough to make the muscles of her stomach contract, to make her waver on the brink of panic.

Those months were amongst the worst in her life, because the difficulties she had were trivial next to what she felt for Gareth. It wasn't only anger, it was that even her hatred couldn't cancel out what she had once felt for him. She ached for him – long, long after he had disappeared into that grey Celtic dawn.

Flinging herself wholeheartedly into her work brought some relief, and some success.

The following spring she was able to move her few belongings to a much smarter flat in a prettier area of London; six months after that she applied for, and got, a junior line management post with Melco, one of Britain's largest employers of chemical engineers.

It took her three years to establish herself as a practical engineer, but far less time to win a sideways promotion into general management. She was put in charge of Group Six, one of Melco's smallest and most inefficient units – for although the company employed other women in senior positions, Katherine was one of the youngest and they were wary of her.

Within a month she was loathed by the entire group, and finally she was respected.

She arranged for the ageing group administrator to be made redundant, his clerk to be sacked for stealing office equipment, persuaded two bored secretaries to hand in their notices, switched the line-of-command for the scientists and marketeers from their functional bosses to herself, then fought tooth and nail with her own bosses to increase the salaries of all who remained in Group Six.

The group's figures, each quarter, crept up and up until in the end Group Six was a profitable as well as highly efficient unit.

As a British company Melco's salaries were not high, but Katherine could afford to buy and furnish a two-roomed flat, run a decent car and whenever her schedule wasn't too busy have a pleasant social life.

Gareth Williams was by now only a shadow from the past, and he rarely even crossed her mind. Once, though, in the ice-cold January of her second year in London, she'd imagined she'd seen him again. It was on the Underground of all places, during the evening rush hour. She'd been waiting in the throng of passengers for a train to arrive, and when it had finally hurtled into the station and ground to a halt with a scream of metal, Katherine had stepped back from the surge of people spilling out – and then nearly fainted.

He'd been about twenty yards away, his head raised above the crowds as he'd alighted. It was the hair she'd recognized first – that rich, dark, curly hair – and then she'd caught a glimpse, a fleeting precious glimpse of that profile, those features that had once had the power to turn her limbs to water.

She'd called his name and yelled and yelled – forgetting all the wrongs that had been done, aware only of a terrible need to get to him. She'd fought her way through the crowd, yelled again – and for a second, beneath the 'Exit' sign, he'd hesitated, tilted his head to one side in a way that was heartbreakingly familiar – and then he was gone.

That night she'd gone home, sat down in an easy chair,

rested her arms on her knees and her forehead on her arms – and wept.

Katherine learned a great deal during her time with Melco, and not only about business. She learned to cultivate a cool façade that never came naturally: her true personality was more like her father's, quick tempered in the extreme – fiery and emotional and highly combustible. But she taught herself to conceal all these traits, to become a paragon of level-headedness and chilling reserve.

When she broke away from Melco to form her own engineering consultancy, she knew money would be scarce for a while but she was prepared for that. She had enough set aside to maintain her flat, to send small amounts to Miriam and Joan in Langston – and had just about enough left over to send useful gifts to Daniel, who was now married and finding life hard in Canada.

She worked day and night to get her business under way: she herself was no longer a practising engineer, but one of her partners was, and the other, Ray Gifford, provided the financial backing. She organized, cultivated clients, did everything from filing letters to inspecting opencast mining sites, did every conceivable task to ensure the venture would be a success.

It was a disaster. Ray Gifford's financial dealings were to blame, but it was futile to allot guilt and the company was simply too young to survive a major setback. Katherine closed it down before they reached the bankruptcy courts, paid off a proportion of the debts, and at the age of thirty-two found herself right back where she'd started – no income, and alone. She sold her car and put her flat on the market.

It was then, through her depression and despair, that her mind went back again and again to Gareth Williams. And somehow the memories were comforting, as if they proved that life wasn't all hard work and no pleasure. She would look back on those carefree times and remember only the finest fragments, like a dream you try to recapture but cannot. Lovely moments like driving over the snow-capped mountains that encircled Abertawe . . . a holiday Gareth had taken her on to Italy . . . lying with him in the big double bed in Gwilym Cottage – listening to the pounding of the waves on the rocks below, and Gareth's deep, steady breathing. She could remember how she would move up close to him, and sometimes in his sleep he would turn and put an arm round her, and the next thing she would be aware of was that it was morning.

Neither of them knew then that their days together were drawing to an end, a bitter end with neither forgiveness nor compassion.

But it wasn't the saddest moments that she needed to remember now – it was the happiest. Her present problems gave her more than enough heartache: in the same week that she found a buyer for her flat, and was wondering how she could possibly – with debts still outstanding, even after the sale – start up in business again, she received yet another blow.

Miriam telephoned her to inform her that Joan had had a massive thrombosis, and had been found to be dead on arrival at hospital.

Miriam looked a tired old woman at the funeral, far older than her sixty years; standing next to her, an arm protectively linked with hers, Katherine too felt old. She was bowed with grief, thinner from the pain of the last few days and the strain and disappointments of the months that had gone before.

When the harrowing ceremony was over and Katherine and her mother were alone, there were more decisions to be made. Miriam begged Katherine to stay and Katherine, not wanting to but having no business to attend to in London, compromised. She said she would stay for a week, then go back and finalize the arrangements about her flat and its contents and look for a job.

The night before she was due to leave, in an attempt to distract both herself and Miriam, she drew more than she ought to have done out of the bank, booked a taxi and reserved a table for two at The Huntsman.

Situated in the bleak countryside some five miles from the town, the restaurant was the smartest in the locality. That meant that it overcharged and was frequented by a number of small business men, solicitors and other professional people who considered it a sign of their success that they could eat once a week at The Huntsman. Nevertheless, the food was good and it was somewhere to go on that depressing evening. It was the first time Katherine had been anywhere for weeks, and still longer since her mother had eaten out.

The bar was busy. A quarter of its limited space was taken up by a party of noisy contractors – the super-rich of the area, the men who made the most of the industry and mineral deposits round about and would buy, sell and generally trade in anything from scrap metal to coal.

One of the loudest members of the party, an arrogant, florid-complexioned man called Jack Bartley, spotted Katherine in the crowded bar and fancied her. He fancied her a lot, decided immediately that he would have her and presumed without a second thought that it would be easy, because even if she wasn't impressed by him – unlikely, in his opinion – she would undoubtedly be impressed by his money, for he was one of the richest contractors within a twenty-mile radius.

He saw her sitting quietly at a table, leaving her drink untouched and inclining her head every now and then to listen to the whispered words of the frail-looking woman sitting next to her. The mother, he guessed, and shrewdly directed his opening conversational gambits at her.

Katherine was irritated, and became increasingly annoyed when Miriam chatted politely and the man, encouraged, persisted and even drew up a chair next to Katherine's. Her gaze flicked over him with such chilling and insulting hostility that for a full thirty seconds he appeared nonplussed, then became excited rather than dismayed by her tight-lipped aloofness.

He pestered them at dinner, too, till in the end Katherine told him that her mother was recovering from the shock of her sister's recent death, and that she herself was leaving for London the next day. Tonight, she emphasized, she and her mother would be glad of a peaceful evening.

He became profuse in his expressions of sympathy; within ten minutes he had won Miriam over completely and she had revealed, with touching pride, that her daughter was a chemical engineer and an experienced business manager.

Jack had looked suitably astonished and exclaimed: 'What wouldn't I give to have someone like you in my business!' Then he gave Katherine his card and said that if she ever wanted to work in the North, she must contact him immediately.

'I will,' she said, and put the card in her handbag, paid the bill and prepared to leave.

'I mean it,' he added. 'I do need a person like you.'

He telephoned her at nine o'clock the next morning, and because she had nothing whatsoever to lose she agreed to see him before she left for London.

They met at The Huntsman, where he bought her lunch and talked a lot. He talked of his business – a world she was already familiar with – of money to be made and of possible partnerships.

By the end of that afternoon she'd agreed to join him on a three-month trial basis, and she knew that he was dishonest and that he would always underestimate her. She loathed him, even as she gave him a warm smile brimful of admiration and told him how much she was looking forward to joining him.

She knew, moreover, that there would never be any

question of a partnership. His was strictly a one-man business run from a grimy little office, where a girl typed his letters and, when she remembered to, did some filing. The most Katherine could hope for from Jack would be a third-rate job doing the odds and ends he himself had no time for. But it would be a foot in the door, and that was what she really wanted.

It was obvious he thought her experience in management was a huge joke, and despite the fuss he made about her qualifications the truth was that he was completely unimpressed: to him she was an attractive woman, she spoke better and had had a better education than any other female he had ever known, and even if he couldn't persuade her into bed he could show her off to his rivals. She was a status symbol, a highly original one – much more novel than having a telephone installed in the car.

Most important of all, he regarded her as a person to be humoured and not taken too seriously – which was exactly the way Katherine wanted it.

She decided to give it six months, and if she hadn't opened the door wide in that time then she'd return to London. Jack, she thought, would be prepared to pay for an expensive status symbol for maybe six months, but no longer, because she had no intention whatsoever of going to bed with him.

It took several weeks to convince him that she would never, come what may, respond to his blundering and often drunken advances, but finally he accepted the situation and even appeared to enjoy it.

'This is my new assistant—' he would introduce her, the partnership idea having been forgotten ever since the day she'd joined him. 'She's a chemical engineer – got a degree from Cambridge,' and then he would chuckle.

Katherine was delighted by all this. She'd told him about her job with Melco, but contrived to give the impression that she'd spent most of her time there doing theoretical planning work. She talked about Cambridge

at length, and skipped as lightly as possible over the
details of her own business. He never bothered to check;
in any case, the kind of work he'd given her to do could
have been done quite adequately by a half-wit. All in all,
he looked on her in exactly the way she'd hoped he
would: as a pretty woman full of theories and too much
education, but with a smattering of business acumen that
he could probably put to some use.

He trusted her absolutely.

The salary he paid her at first was derisory, and part of
it had to go towards paying off her personal debts and to
settling the solicitor's fees for her London flat. When the
money from the sale came through, that too was swallowed up by debts, but then she was free of them and if
she had nothing then at least she owed nothing either.

It was an appalling autumn, and the only thing that
kept her going was the thought that she had her foot well
and truly in the door – in a business that she knew
something about and where there was a lot of money to
be made. And if you were sharp enough, you could make
it quickly.

Every morning she caught the seven o'clock bus to
work, through the sprawling council estate, across the
centre of the town where red-brick Victorian buildings
stood deformed and monstrous round the grubby market
square; then the bus would groan and lurch up Jubilee
Hill, and Katherine would peer through its dirt-flecked
windows, stare at the derelict buildings and crumbling
tenements that made up this suburb of Langston. At last
she would stagger to her feet, ring the bell and the bus
would grind to a halt just a hundred yards from the
prefabricated hut that Jack Bartley used as an office.

The building was adequate: three partitioned-off rooms
plus a lavatory. He didn't need anything smarter because
all his deals were done while entertaining, or else on the
sites themselves. This was merely a base, somewhere to
store papers and where telephone messages could be left.

Maureen, the typist, couldn't have cared less about her job and scarcely even noticed what was going on around her, so she would present no threat to Katherine's plans. In fact her disinterest was helpful at first, because Katherine began by sorting out all the backlog of paper work and inspecting the two sets of books so that within a fortnight it was Katherine, rather than Jack, who knew precisely and in absolute detail what had gone on in this business over the past five years, and what was going on at the moment.

'I'm going to up your salary,' Jack announced, late one afternoon at the very end of that dreary autumn. 'Another twenty quid a month. How about that, then? You've done wonders here in no time at all – better than I'd expected, I don't mind telling you.'

He glanced about the office as though unable to believe the transformation that had taken place there, then flicked his cigar ash on to the floor and departed.

Katherine leaned against the filing cabinet and watched his black Mercedes pull away. She looked out at the rain-soaked street, at the glistening pavements and sodden leaves, at the dull November mist fretting damply at the window. She could feel its chill in her bones even now, and she shivered.

Lights came on across the street, in a terraced house whose front door had been newly painted and where a mongrel pup was whining to be let in. The lights were warm and yellow, and Katherine stared at them for a long time, remembering the lamplight in that cottage at Abertawe, those early days with Gareth in that long, glorious autumn when the sea frothed white like lace and the leaves faded slowly to gold.

Jack Bartley gradually changed his mind about Katherine. He began taking her to sites with him, let her sit in on his deals and sought her opinion constantly. By February she was virtually running his business for him: he'd bought her a car, doubled her salary, given her an expense account and declared she was one of the best investments he'd ever made.

The more responsibility he entrusted her with, the lazier he became. Some days he wouldn't even bother to look in at the office, and often he would allow her to do a few of the smaller deals on his behalf.

Katherine enjoyed it. The men she did business with were tough, but she had one major advantage – they thought that Jack Bartley had become soft in the head to allow a woman to act for him, and that she would be easy to push around. It was an attitude that helped her to win several minor battles before her reputation was established: Katherine Hanson was harder to deal with than Jack Bartley had ever been, and she did it so shrewdly that if you weren't careful you didn't realize she was doing it at all.

She won the respect, too, of local government officials and the men from the nationalized industries, the people who vetted tenders for sites and who had to be cultivated so carefully. Most of all she was liked by Jack's freelance people, the two lorry drivers, the surveyor and the engineer he used whenever he was working a site.

The drivers would often drop into the office for a chat with her, and she would supervise them at the weighbridge, mark their time sheets and do all the other tasks that led them to call her – half-jokingly at first – 'boss' or 'gaffer' or whatever else took their fancy. Pete, the young surveyor, and Tony, the civil engineer who supervised excavation work, became close friends. They were essential to Jack's business because he had no qualifications at all and the law demanded that he employ qualified people at his workings. But although both Peter and Tony were pleased enough to accept payments and various perks from Jack, they had little respect and certainly no liking for him. He tended to sneer at the studying they'd done, and his arrogance over the money he'd made was insufferable. Pete, who had constant financial problems with his young children, wife and heavy mortgage repayments, resented Jack most of all.

Katherine didn't care. She was edging nearer and nearer to the position she needed to be in, and was prepared to put up with just about anything to get there. The fact that she had little time for any kind of private life didn't bother her either. She'd had a variety of boyfriends while she was living in London, some of whom she'd found attractive, but the majority had elicited no greater response from her than affection or vague interest. There were men who asked her out while she was working for Jack, but nearly all were driven by a curiosity to discover more about the redoubtable Katherine Hanson.

These men meant nothing to her. She resigned herself to the fact that she'd grown cold and disinterested over the past few years, and was glad of it. It was one problem the less, and the only pleasure she wanted now was the pleasure of success.

When the chance she had been waiting for came at last, she had no time to think of anything except keeping her wits about her, because success or failure hinged on one thing only – on destroying Jack Bartley before he even knew what was happening.

'Drive up to Fareham with me,' he told her during one of his unexpected visits to the office. 'There's three acres of slurry to be shifted, and once we've got the overburden off—'

'Fareham?' she smiled. 'Don't waste your time, Jack.'

'How d'you mean?'

'A couple of other people are putting tenders in, and more fool them. Pete and I have already checked it out – there are some third-rate deposits there but they're so inferior they're not fit for anything.'

He grunted, thought for a minute, then scowled.

'You checked that out pretty quickly,' he commented.
'Don't I always?'
'I only heard about it myself the other day.'
'It wasn't so long ago that I heard about it, either. In fact I've only just got the results back from the lab.'
'You've already done a bore, then? And taken samples?'
'Of course.'
'You didn't tell me.'
'It was when you were on holiday in Spain with your friends. I'd have told you as soon as you got back if there'd been anything worth following up . . . Spain—' she grinned. 'You lucky bugger. While I'm stuck here in Langston with bore-hole samples and putty-coloured faces all around me.'
'Yeah, well—' Holidays no longer interested him. 'Never mind about Spain for the minute. Who tipped you off about Fareham?'
'The grapevine I hear everything from. Not that it's much use to us as far as this site's concerned.'
He sat down in the chair facing her desk, stared at her, then said: 'Let's drive over there anyway.'
She sighed.
'Do you really need me to come with you? I've got a lot on at the moment.'
'Perhaps you'd better take a second look. Or else Pete can come with me on his own.'
'I've told you, he's already checked it out.'
'Then he can bloody well do it again.'
Pete made a second survey of the Fareham site. He gave his brief report to Katherine that same evening, and she summarized it for Jack's benefit: there was a heavy overburden to be removed, the deposits underneath were of such poor quality that they were useless for the domestic fuel market and even a suitable industrial market would be difficult to find; both the quality and quantity of the deposits indicated an unviably low profit margin if the site were to be excavated, possibly two to three

thousand pounds after the cost of plant hire, wages, etc. had been deducted.

To this summary Katherine attached a laboratory report. It came from Hertman's, the consultants Jack always used for such explorative and geological investigations. As usual, it did not name the site: contractors tended to christen sites as the fancy took them, more often than not using the name of the nearest town or village. The report was headed, for both reference and confidentiality, C/24 – the code designated to the minerals under investigation. Only Hertman's and Katherine could have identified the minerals from that code, and only Katherine could have identified the site from which those minerals had come. The report detailed results from an analysis of samples C/24. Katherine again made a précis:

'The analysis received from the core extracted from the bore hole,' she wrote, 'showed high sulphur content and a high inherent ash; i.e., the calorific value of the site is low, only 3–4,000 BTUs (British Thermal Units). Such a low calorific value, as you know, is virtually worthless from a marketing point of view.'

She took care that neither her own notes nor Pete's mentioned Fareham by name: any future legal action had to be forestalled now.

'You're sure Hertman's haven't made a mistake?' Jack, the following morning, looked puzzled. 'And you're sure Pete's right?'

'It seems unlikely that they could *both* have made a mistake. Hertman's is a sizeable organization, of course, and they might have made a balls-up of it. Errors do occur with companies that size. And Pete could be wrong,' she admitted. 'But Tony agrees with him, and he should know.'

'I was given to understand that there was a chance of some decent domestic fuel at Fareham. At least one other company's considering it.'

Katherine grimaced.

'There are small – *minute* – quantities of what could be used in the domestic market. And d'you know who's already put in a tender?'

'Who?'

'That guy who's just starting up on his own . . . What's his name? Don something-or-other, the fellow who used to work for the Coal Board.'

'That idiot! . . . I don't know, though.' Jack shook his head, paced across the office, stood still for a moment with his head cocked to one side, as if to listen for some warning sound. 'First Hertman's, then Pete. Pete's never been wrong before, but . . .' he shrugged.

'Why not have a fresh analysis done? And since they'll charge you again, why not use a different laboratory this time?'

'Another bore hole? Bloody hell, what d'you think I am? The bloody Bank of England? I'm not a fucking oil company, I'm just a contractor.'

'Well then,' she suggested pleasantly, 'you could always get in a different surveyor, and an engineer, come to that.'

Katherine waited for his response, and as the seconds dragged by she could hear her own heart beating, very slow and steady.

'Nah! For one paltry site? Let them in on my business and have Pete and Tony upset? And when do the tenders have to be in by?'

'Next week.'

'Christ, well there's no time then, is there?'

'Not much.'

'I don't know why the hell you didn't hear about this before. But I should have been keeping my ears open, too . . . What if we—' He hesitated.

'Yes?'

'Say we used my plant and didn't bother to hire any big equipment?'

'You'd have to hire, Jack. Your plant couldn't cope with that overburden.'

'Ah forget it,' he grumbled. 'I'm not wasting my time for a couple of thousand. And if one thing went wrong we'd lose even that and maybe more.'

'OK,' she said, and the following week put in a tender under her own name.

Over the past few months she'd come to know the land within a fifty-mile radius of Langston in extraordinary detail. She'd seen and studied geologists' reports, surveyors' reports, maps and plans and everything else she could lay her hands on. Her knowledge, coupled with Pete's and Tony's expertise, meant she could estimate the profits from the Fareham site to within a thousand pounds, and she estimated those profits at eighty thousand. The reserves of fuel beneath that overburden were of high-grade domestic quality.

Hertman's had acted in good faith: the samples sent to them, from a site covering an almost equal acreage near Birmingham, had indicated a calorific value of no more than 4,000 BTUs. Pete and Tony were not so honest, but they were also scared.

They had been reluctant to join forces with Katherine, and their hesitation had been due mainly to their fear of Jack Bartley – because very soon the profitability of the Fareham site would be public knowledge, and if Katherine had failed to win the contract then not only she, but Pete and Tony as well, would have lost their livelihoods and have Jack's considerable wrath to face. If, on the other hand, her tender was accepted, then she would be in a position to form her own company with the two of them as partners and herself as managing director.

First Pete, then Tony, had decided to take the risk.

The chances of the tender being accepted were high: she was prepared to work Fareham on a comparatively low profit margin, and knew from the information she already had that this would be possible. The overburden, as Jack had seen for himself, could present difficulties but was by no means as great a problem as Katherine had inferred. She knew at least one plant-hire firm who would let her use their equipment for a percentage of the profits from the site rather than a straight payment; Pete and Tony would also take nothing but a share of the profits, and Jack's drivers would work for her for a low wage provided she would guarantee them a much better one plus full-time work in the future when her company was established. The drivers, anyway, didn't care too much one way or the other about Jack Bartley.

Katherine had known about the Fareham site for weeks, and had spent every minute of her spare time in working out the details of a tender whose success had to be watertight, not days but weeks in advance.

At night she dreamed about that dirty layer of earth, the slurry and the black, rich minerals beneath it, about all this ravaged, scarred and desolate land that she'd learned to understand and respect and even love. She'd trudged across acres of it in the past months, and its yield had come to fascinate her as crops might fascinate a farmer: he could curse and moan and begrudge the strength his land took from him, but nothing would part him from it.

Yet when the official-looking letter arrived at her home address, she was terrified. She knew exactly what it was because she received so few business letters away from the office, and she held it in her hands for a full minute before opening it. So much depended on the outcome of this tender, and when she finally slit open the envelope and read the contents – not once but three times – her reaction was numbness. Then she thought: Jack Bartley will try to kill me, literally try to kill me.

Miriam stood in a corner of the kitchen, her shoulders hunched pathetically and her eyes darting back and forth from Jack to Katherine. Then she slipped quietly away, gently closing the door behind her and leaving the two of them to face each other across the table. The breakfast things were still there, a jar of marmalade, the remnants of bacon and eggs, empty coffee cups.

They remained standing, Jack and Katherine, he breathing heavily and she very still and pale.

'You've taken my engineer, my surveyor, my drivers and done me out of eighty thousand quid.'

Katherine said nothing, indeed she hadn't said a word since he'd burst through the door, banging it to behind him with such strength that it rattled in its ill-fitting frame.

'Haven't you?'

'Yes.' To her amazement her voice sounded clear and steady.

Then he let out a torrent of abuse; it went on and on till the words meant nothing to her and she found it easy to go on standing there, motionless and silent, watching the grotesque movements of his mouth and the fleshiness of his cheeks, the crimson flush that suffused his neck, face and even the whites of his eyes.

At last he stopped, gazed at her as though seeing her for the first time, then laughed.

'You'll never make it,' he told her. 'You might have brought off one deal, but you'll go no further. And if you try to you'll have me to contend with.'

'But I've already had you to contend with,' she said, 'and look what happened.'

FIVE

thou variest no more from
the picking of purses than giving direction doth
from labouring; thou layest the plot how.

– GADSHILL; *Henry the Fourth*, Part One

The story of Katherine Hanson's success, of how she had outwitted Jack Bartley and established her own company in this harsh male stronghold, spread like wildfire and then became legend. All sorts of anecdotes, most of them exaggerated or false, sprang up about her until she was regarded as some sort of oddity. Such tales did her no harm, if anything they helped her and at the very least they amused her. By the time she was thirty-six she was wealthy by local standards, and although it was impossible to compete with the huge corporations who were well established in the North, taking the biggest and ripest of the pickings in the opencast field, she more than held her own amongst the smaller businessmen.

She did all the things she'd wanted to do for a long time – bought her mother a house, sent money occasionally to Daniel in Canada, and managed to lead a comfortable, if busy, life herself. It cheered her to see Miriam looking more sprightly at last; one of her neighbours, a widow called Hettie Morton, was a light-hearted chatterbox of a woman and the perfect friend for Miriam who seemed to be gradually taking on a new lease of life. Katherine too had a small circle of friends in Langston, including a shy local landowner called Giles Wills who became fascinated by her. Whenever he could pluck up sufficient courage he would tentatively suggest marriage, and she – as kindly as she could – would refuse, and then their relationship would slip back into its familiar and pleasant old pattern of friendship and companionship.

It was a reasonable enough way of living, but there was an emptiness about it that disturbed her, made her restless and sometimes discontented. In her early twenties pleasures had been heightened, there'd been a sweetness about life that was missing now – and the sweetest things of all had been at Gwilym Cottage.

The cottage in itself had been romantic – in fact it had been an absurdly romantic idea of Gareth's, to christen a house after a poet. But then he had been romantic in his own way, with his reckless gestures and his unexpected acts of gallantry. Happy days.

They'd argued sometimes, but he'd always been able to tease her out of her bad moods. Once they'd argued about ambition; she'd been cooking supper at the time, stirring a casserole with one hand, sipping a glass of wine with the other and talking, loudly and vehemently.

'I know exactly what I want,' she'd said, 'and I don't need advice.'

'All right, then, don't listen to me.'

'Let's not argue.' She'd paused, and raised her glass. 'You're just as ambitious as I am, so let's drink to success.'

'I'll drink to us,' he'd said quietly, and there'd been a long moment of silence before he'd added, in a different tone of voice: 'How long will supper be?'

'About half an hour.'

'Not long, but long enough.'

'I'll bet,' she'd gone on, not listening to him, 'that I shall be buying my place in Belgravia while you're still peddling songs to the Welsh.'

'Office space, not songs.'

'When I come to you for my office space, just make sure it's good and roomy.'

'You've got a long way to go, baby,' he'd said, and lunged forward and swept her up in his arms.

She'd yelped with laughter, the wine glass slipping from her fingers, smashing on the stone-tiled floor as she'd flung her arms round his neck and he'd headed for the stairs.

Happy days indeed, but in the end there'd been that grey dawn, the gulls wheeling and screaming long before the sun was up, and she'd screamed as well – but it was too late by then.

She presumed her life would carry on much as it had been doing over the past couple of years; her business, though, was a different matter. She'd bought her partners out at the end of the last year and they had since formed their own company and were prospering. The time had come to decide in which direction she would expand: she had enemies in the North, in particular Jack Bartley, but she knew she could cope with such people and what she really wanted was a fresh challenge.

'I gather we've got new competitors,' her old partner Tony informed her one morning over the telephone. 'An American company called Borjex are trying to move in up here.'

'That means trouble, then,' she said. 'I know of them, but I hadn't realized they were interested in our part of the world.'

It didn't take her long to discover that, although Borjex had been established in England for several years and in a variety of fields, they had no foothold whatsoever in the opencast industry of the North. They had sites in other parts of the country, but the mineral-rich area around Langston was going to be an essential conquest if they were to be at the forefront of this particular market.

They used buying tactics: they swallowed up Tony's and Pete's business, plus a handful of other contractors', and even put in a bid for one of the major corporations. At the same time they put in a generous offer for Katherine's company, and she was delighted. She could see exactly where her new challenge was going to come from, and how her life was going to change.

To Borjex's amazement, she turned their offer down.

They tried again, and she agreed on condition that she could have a seat on their London board. It was their second most important nucleus, reporting to the headquarters in New York but still powerful in its own right since it controlled their European operations, and this included regional boards in a number of countries.

Her conditions were rejected out of hand, and for a while they left her alone, despite the fact that she was in the very centre of their planned expansion area. Then they had difficulties with local government officials, their tenders were slow to be considered and, on two occasions, rejected. Their far-flung, London-based industrial relations department was floundering: its efforts to control the local, tightly knit labour forces were based on faulty assumptions better suited to large manufacturing units in the South of England or to American-style unions that had little in common with the drivers and manual workers of the Northern contracting business.

When Borjex asked Katherine to reconsider their offer, she agreed to meet them provided she could discuss the matter with the chairman of their European operations, Irv McKenzie, and their industrial relations director.

They were willing.

'I gather you're having teething problems in Langston,' she said pleasantly. They were having a buffet lunch at Borjex's European headquarters, in the penthouse suite that was the chairman's own domain – offices and private dining room overlooking Hyde Park, rooms that so reeked of success that Katherine felt the cold, hard thrust of ambition, an urge such as she hadn't experienced since the day she'd crossed Jack Bartley. The determination that had driven her on over the past year or two was as nothing compared to what she felt now.

'We certainly are,' Irv asserted, and met her gaze with

his piercing black eyes. 'But I daresay we'll sort it out over the next few months.'

He was an extraordinary man, his shock of prematurely white hair contrasting so sharply with his ink-black eyes, and his lazy drawl belying a steel-hard mind. A man to be handled with kid gloves, she thought, and yet instinctively she both liked and respected him.

'I may be wrong,' she said, 'but it strikes me that you can't have sufficient inside knowledge of what you're dealing with around Langston. It's possible that you've approached this expansion plan from the wrong angle. You should have had at least one person in a senior position who could have advised you – worked for you – from within rather than without.'

At that moment she glanced at Bill Skerrett, and saw that he detested her.

Success.

That was the word that rang in her ears when they offered her a seat on the board. Success pure and simple. She was thrilled, nervous, excited, rejuvenated – on the road to even greater conquests and her life was starting all over again.

Langston had been the deciding factor: it would have been far from easy for Borjex to find a person skilled in senior management, with inside knowledge of that particular part of the North of England plus a willingness to leave it and take up a board membership with an American company. But it wasn't only because of their Langston problems that they had offered her a seat on their board. They had begun to take her very seriously after that lunch in the penthouse suite, looked into her background from Cambridge to her triumphs at Melco, decided they were both impressed by her and needed her, and despite protests from Bill Skerrett they made up their minds to have her.

Her brief when she joined them was wide and gave her

exactly the challenge she'd been craving. Bill Skerrett was to remain board member for industrial relations, but Katherine was to advise him over the Langston expansion while getting to know other areas of Borjex's activities. By the time Dr Peter Grettrix – one of the oldest of the board members – retired in three months' time, she should be ready to take over from him.

What a Christmas she and her mother and their friends had that year! Katherine was bubbling over with energy, enthusing about the house she'd bought in South Kensington, the elegant Georgian house she'd been able to afford from the sale of her business. She felt generous from the elation of having won through so far in such circumstances, believed she was entering a new period of prosperity and better fortune. She offered to refurbish her mother's house in Langston, sent Daniel and his family in Canada extravagant gifts, booked a holiday in Switzerland for the New Year celebrations and finally became nostalgic. There was only one other Christmas that had been as good as this, and it had been so simple in comparison – just she and Gareth, setting out together on Christmas Eve, heading towards the grey-stone Welsh village where all his family lived.

She remembered it so well and with such fondness. They'd driven along the high, winding mountain road beneath chilly skies that promised snow, and stopped only once to buy last-minute presents in a bustling market town. Katherine had peered through the window of an antique shop and her attention had been caught by a small, intricately carved wooden clock. A sun and a moon were painted delicately on its porcelain face, and it was so unusual and so pretty that she would willingly have spent her very last penny on it. The time was twelve noon and its hands were pointing precisely to the hour; she fancied she could hear its clear chimes even through the thick glass of the shop front. Gareth laughed and called her romantic, said the clock was over-priced and would probably fall apart as soon as it was rewound, then pulled her away in the direction of a department store.

Half an hour later, in the crush of shoppers, she lost him and after searching uselessly for a while stormed back to the car.

He was sitting in the driving seat.

'Where've you been?' she demanded. 'I've been looking for you everywhere. The crowds in that shop are unbeliev-able. You might have . . .'

She was gesticulating, emphasizing her frustration at having lost him when he snatched hold of her hands, held them both together in one of his, wound a skein of her hair between his fingers and kissed her long and hard.

'See what trouble you get yourself into,' he said, 'when you don't stay close to me?'

Then he reached across to the back seat and produced a brown paper parcel.

'Open it,' he told her.

It was the clock.

'A present for Gwilym Cottage,' he announced with mock solemnity, and when he saw the delight on her face, saw that she was touched by his gesture and couldn't find words to say 'thank you', he added: 'Once I make up my mind—'

'I know,' she murmured. 'Nothing stops you.'

'Remember that, Katherine Hanson.' He ruffled her hair, and they smiled at each other, a slow smile that took a long while to come to fruition.

Then she looked down, at the fragile little clock held so precariously in her hands; she could hear its quiet ticking, hear it pause to chime, and wished like a prayer this moment could last forever.

'Time to go, Kate,' he said, and that was when the first snowflakes began to fall, tumbling soundlessly to earth from the lead-grey skies.

Gareth's was the biggest family Katherine had ever

encountered: aunts, uncles, two grandmothers – and a grandfather who appeared to belong to neither – plus a whole army of children ranging in ages from six to seventeen. They all converged on Gareth's parents' house, and one or two even stayed the night. Katherine shared a room with Gareth's youngest sister, Nina, while Gareth himself was allocated a sleeping bag in his brothers' room.

It was Christmas for children, but everyone became infused with the goodwill spirit and celebrated as though they didn't have a care in the world. The two downstairs rooms were filled with holly and decorations, and in a corner of the dining room was a fat tree sparkling with tinsel and baubles. Presents were heaped around it after the children had gone to bed, then the older members of the family set out for midnight mass.

The snow had stopped falling; the night was cold, clear and frosty – but the chapel on the mountainside was warm, packed with men and women full of good cheer and each and every one of them singing carols at the tops of their voices.

Halfway through the service a boy from the choir stepped forward; a hush fell as he began the traditional piece and sang 'O Little Town of Bethlehem', all alone in front of the vast congregation. Gareth slipped his arm through Katherine's, just as the words 'the hopes and fears of all the years' rang clear towards the ancient rafters.

Christmas! In her thirty-odd years Katherine had experienced all kinds of them: happy ones, sad ones, unforgettable ones – like the one so long ago with Gareth and his family – and extra special Christmases, like the latest one.

It had coincided so closely with her new appointment that it had been a double celebration, but the festivities were soon forgotten. Her rôle as member of Borjex's European board was fraught with problems from the outset.

Katherine found herself at odds with Bill Skerrett over the handling of Langston, at odds with Dr Grettrix over research and development policies – she believing expenditure should be increased and he committed to cutting back – and at odds with the company secretary, Tony Rykwert, for no reason she could fathom except that he appeared to resent her appointment.

'Take it easy,' Irv advised her. 'You're not in any rush to prove yourself. Bill's feeling touchy, and wouldn't you if you were in his position? It wasn't his fault that he didn't have inside knowledge of Langston. Peter Grettrix is over sixty and about to retire, and doesn't take kindly to forcibly expressed opinions from new board members. Tony Rykwert's been company secretary for some time while you've come straight in as board member. Just cool your enthusiasm. You must have had to tread carefully with those contractors in Langston – well Borjex is no different. Civilized veneer, same problems underneath.'

She pulled back immediately, ashamed that she'd let her ambition show through so plainly. She should have known better at her age and with her experience, and she certainly knew she could handle her new job without the need to shout about it. One thing in her favour was that she needed little sleep, five hours a night was sufficient, and then she was disciplined and – most important of all – Irv went out of his way to advise and help her. For a while there was a flurry of rumours about the two of them, but Irv's blatantly happy family life coupled with his fierce treatment of gossipmongers squashed any scandal. It was a momentary bad patch, and Katherine came out of it more guarded than before. People thought her unfriendly and hard; even Jo Cleary, with whom she'd started off on the best of terms, lost his temper during one union meeting and accused her of being as tough as old boots.

'It's just pretence, isn't it?' he yelled at her and leaped

to his feet. 'These warm smiles and back-slapping friendly chats . . .'

'Jo Cleary,' she said, 'the last back in the world I would want to touch, let alone slap, is yours.'

In the face of laughter, he sat down again.

'But you're fair,' he conceded. 'I'll say that about you. And you stick to your word which is more than can be said for most women. Tell you what, take me to Marbella for a week and I'll drop the claim by five per cent. Can't say fairer than that, can I?'

It was her turn to be the butt for laughter, but the tension had eased and they were back to talking business again.

That particular day, with its frictions and conflicts, stood out in her mind because the following morning she met the person who was to change her life.

Borjex were working an opencast mining site on part of the Arlingham family estate, and wanted to buy the large and lucrative drift mine that belonged to the estate and which Lord Arlingham operated as one of his business ventures. Apart from the fact that it was profitable, it was so near their own workings that the convenience element was an added appeal.

Lord Arlingham, however, had been hesitating for weeks. He was primarily a politician, not a businessman, but when the size of Borjex's offer increased he became still more reluctant to sell – and finally began talking of investing in new equipment for the mine.

Irv McKenzie sent Katherine to visit him at Tylowe Castle, in one last attempt to persuade him to change his mind.

She loved Tylowe on sight, its solid mediaeval walls and its mellow old brickwork, and, seeing the admiration in her face, Lord Arlingham offered to show her round.

'It's my mother's place, not mine,' he explained to her as they strolled down the long gallery. 'The Arlingham seat is about five miles away; it's not so fine as this, but still a very attractive Elizabethan house. Tylowe's older and much bigger. More beautiful too. The Lady Helen – my mother – was quite put out when the opencast workings came so close.

'But you can't see them from the castle.'

'Thank goodness. And in any case they happen to be on my land, not hers. Our territories converge, you see. She might have been foolish enough to fling herself in front of a bulldozer rather than let it touch one shrub of Tylowe property.'

They had paused in front of one of the great windows, and stood together looking out at the rolling parkland.

'All sheltered by a belt of trees, you see,' he continued. 'But anyway she'd have had no choice in the end when the government realized what we were sitting on – no ordinary family seat but a rich, unworked seam of coal so near to the surface. Personally I see nothing to complain about – the country gets badly needed energy, your organization wins a lucrative contract, and I get my bit. And very welcome it is, too, I might add. Finally, Parliament obliges you to return the land to its original condition. Stupid demand, that one, isn't it? How on earth can you return the land to its original condition when so many trees are gone?'

'We grass it over,' she said, 'and plant new trees. Five years from now you'll never know the land's been touched.'

'I most certainly will, young lady.'

She smiled; it was the first time anyone had called her that for years, and in any case he was not so terribly old himself – forty-nine or fifty, perhaps.

'Still,' he added, 'the kind of money you get from coal of that quality isn't to be sneered at, not by anybody, and certainly not by a politician with sprawling estates to maintain.'

'Talking of fuel and money,' she said, 'the anthracite in your mine—'

'It is not my mine. It belongs to Tylowe, and is the only part of this mammoth feudal throwback that Helen will let me administer for her. More's the pity. I'd fill this long gallery with tourists seven days a week – double-stacked on Sundays.'

Katherine laughed.

'If it's profitability you're thinking of,' she said, 'there's plenty to be made from the anthracite in Tylowe Drift.'

'I'm fully aware of that.'

'The power stations – the Electricity Board – they're crying out for it.'

'But I know that. It's first-rate stuff, and this is one of the biggest drifts in the country. Thank God it doesn't need deep mining, praise all the right-wing saints in heaven for a lovely great wedge of it so near the soil. I don't think I could bear it if that nationalized bunch of heroes got hold of it.'

'They'd have paid you a good price for it, just as we're willing to. At the current market price,' she added, 'anthracite is worth five times more per ton than ordinary domestic coal.'

'Yes,' he said, and a glimmer of a smile crossed his features.

'However,' she went on, playing her trump card, 'when you were considering selling more seriously, our engineers and surveyors inspected the mine very thoroughly. So much money is going to have to be spent on it to make it a viable long-term proposition that it just wouldn't be worth it as a business venture for an individual. For a company like Borjex, of course, it's a different matter.'

'I'm about to install new machinery.'

Katherine shook her head.

'It isn't just a case of new machinery,' she said. 'There's a serious water hazard – the natural lake in the park gives you some idea about the problems of the land round here.

And on top of that it's an old mine, the roof's cracked more than once. All right, I admit that new hydraulic-powered supports would help enormously, but not entirely. To get at the best of the coal you're soon going to have to drive a new face; amongst other things there'll be drainage problems, and even if you manage to cope you're going to have to cut your losses to a certain extent – a considerable proportion of the anthracite is too near to the castle to be mined. It's virtually unworkable – and possibly for legal and safety reasons as much as for geological ones.'

Lord Arlingham's expression betrayed nothing more than polite interest.

'Your outlay,' she added, 'would be colossal. Why not let us buy it from you – or advise the Lady Helen to sell, if the final word is hers; you'd be assured of your money and we'd run the risks. We can afford short-term losses.'

'Miss Hanson,' he said, 'have you any idea how much has already been invested in the Tylowe Drift?'

'No,' she lied.

'Or the kind of business arrangement I have with the Lady Helen over the mine? She doesn't want to sell because she dislikes parting with Tylowe possessions. But I'm the one who ploughs the money into that mine. I'm the one, therefore, who makes the profit. Have you any idea of the extent of my personal wealth?'

'No.'

'Or the extent to which I am prepared to invest it in anthracite?'

'Of course not,' she said, and knew that this was one deal she'd lost.

'There's an end to it, then,' he said. 'You'll stay for a spot of dinner, won't you?'

They ate in a high, panelled dining room overlooking the park, and afterwards sat in a library where everything seemed faded but beautiful: faded blue curtains at the windows, faded Indian rugs on the broad, polished floorboards, faded books on the long rows of shelves, and Edward's faded grey eyes watching her with admiration.

He was rather like the castle: handsome, well-preserved and in perfect working order, but with the fascination of possessing a long and perhaps colourful history.

The dowager Lady Helen, on the other hand, had a contemporary air about her. She must have been about seventy, Katherine thought, but she was as light and bright as a woman in her prime, and gorgeous to look at: her sweeping hairstyle suited her perfectly, her violet-blue eyes were lively with interest, and her clothes were a mixture of elegance and modern fashion. Despite the difference in their ages, she and Katherine struck up an immediate friendship, and when she retired to bed at eleven the room suddenly seemed empty.

'I must be going, too,' Katherine said. 'It's an hour's drive back to town.'

'You're not going to drive back at this time of night, are you?' Edward asked, horrified.

'I'd like to be in the office by eight tomorrow morning. There's a union meeting lined up for nine, and I have a lot of preparatory work to do, then I'm expecting a call from the States at—'

'Heavens,' he said, 'if anybody had told me yesterday that I was about to fall for a board member of some international conglomerate, and a chemical engineer at that, I'd have called the fellow out.'

For a second she was speechless, but when she saw the genuine respect in his eyes she said, and meant it: 'If anybody had told me yesterday that I was going to visit the Tylowe Drift and discover one of the most likeable men I'd encountered for years, I'd have told them to take more water with their whisky.'

He looked disappointed.

' "Likeable" sounds a bit tame.'

'It sounds marvellous,' she retorted. 'It's rarer than anthracite.'

'Will you let me drive you back to town? I can get someone to bring your car in tomorrow morning.'

'There's no need, thank you. I'm perfectly happy to drive myself.'

'You are independent, aren't you?'

'I don't know. I never think about it nowadays. I've been like this for too long.'

He looked at her thoughtfully for a moment, then said: 'I'm having a dinner party in town on Friday night. I'd be delighted if you could come. Let me give you a telephone number where you can contact me during the day, and then the address of my flat.'

The telephone number was for the House of Lords; his London address was in Mayfair.

'You'll give me a ring, won't you?'

'I'd love to come to dinner,' she said, 'but I can't. I have a long-standing engagement for Friday night.'

'Perhaps we could have dinner together another night, then? I'll ring you. If you can manage to cancel your engagement for Friday – if you want to, that is – then you'll let me know, won't you?'

'I will.'

'There again,' he said, 'perhaps you might find it a little tedious. Just a few old friends of mine, and I daresay they'll all start talking politics. I've had to invite Henry Bentinck, as well, though he's a good fellow underneath.'

'Henry Bentinck?' she repeated.

'The Secretary of State for Industry, you know.'

'I know,' she said, and knew beyond any shadow of doubt that she would cancel that long-standing engagement.

Edward and Katherine slipped easily into an affair. It was the first time she'd gone to bed with a man simply because she definitely liked him but only more or less fancied him.

Yet she found him a good lover, and as a friend he was kind, charming, courteous and endlessly interesting. His political career and estate duties coupled with her business life meant that neither of them had much free time, but when they did they found they could exploit it to the full: their tastes coincided, and there was never any argument about going shooting or riding round the Arlingham estate, spending time with Helen who rapidly became a good – and amusing – friend to Katherine; having a hasty weekend's skiing in Switzerland, or – Edward's favourite pastime – eating. He was the perfect tutor for sport and good living.

After they'd known each other for a year or so, Katherine began to believe that she loved him. At any rate this, she decided, was by far the most pleasant form of love, and if there was any other she didn't want to know about it. After two years with Edward, she had no doubts about her love for him.

Occasionally she felt twinges of guilt about the political connections she was cultivating so tirelessly. Despite the fact that she'd liked Edward from the first time she'd met him, her original intention had been to put him to the fullest possible use. She assuaged her slight but discomforting guilt by telling herself that, political connections or no, she would still have gone on seeing him – and so far, at any rate, the political aspects had done no more than to raise her standing at Borjex. Besides, it would never cross Edward's mind that she would use him.

Henry Bentinck, as Secretary of State for Industry, was potentially her most profitable ally, and it helped that he appeared to like her. She still hadn't decided exactly what she was going to do with him, but she certainly wasn't going to let him go. He had a tremendous amount of influence with the Prime Minister – who didn't hesitate to show his respect for Henry – had been in four Cabinets and, during the present one, had been instrumental in bringing about constitutional reforms that greatly eased the way for growth in the private sector of industry in Britain. One of the moves he'd been most applauded for was his encouragement of foreign investments in the deprived areas of the British Isles which, though relatively poor, had a combination of ideal sites for industrial expansion and large numbers of unemployed. His timing was perfect, right in the middle of the last serious recession, when men were needing jobs rather than strikes. He'd ignored the Conservative policy of trying to persuade the workforce to move to where the work was – both because people were reluctant to uproot and leave their homes and families, and also because it was an expensive policy – and looked to overseas instead. He worked indefatigably at his scheme, with a diplomatic brilliance nurtured during his early years in the Foreign Office. Amongst the grateful was Borjex.

The call came through at two a.m. That, in itself, did not imply that the matter was unduly serious: it might have been a problem at one of the chemical plants – always cause for extra-special concern, especially in view of recent public outcries – or simply a bigger-than-usual union dispute at one of the soft drinks manufacturing plants. Both the chemical plants and the soft drinks production were Katherine's prime areas of responsibility as a board member, and it was not unusual for them to keep her on call twenty-four hours a day. Struggling through the outer layers of sleep, she picked up the receiver. Edward was snoring quietly by her side.

'Katherine.' Typically, it was a statement rather than a question.

'Irv?' she said. 'I thought you were in the States.'

'I am,' he said. 'I have news for you.'

'I should hope you do. There'd be all hell to pay if you woke me at two a.m. to have a friendly chat.'

'Forget about the time. I've got the top job.'

'You've had it for years.' She propped herself up on one elbow and yawned. 'Come on – what gives?'

'I've got *the* top job. Overall president of Borjex. The old man announced his retirement and at the same time nominated me. The New York board upheld the nomination.'

'Christ – Irv – what a shock. I mean, congratulations. I'm delighted for you . . . How sudden.'

'No it's not, it's been on the cards for at least three months.'

'I didn't know.'

'You weren't in a position to be told. Which brings us to the next point: the chairmanship of Borjex's European operations is now vacant, and my nomination will be for you. It'll carry a lot of weight, but not enough on its own. After I've done my bit, you'll have to fend for yourself. All the best.'

And he hung up.

'I gather,' Edward said, pushing himself into a sitting position beside her, 'that your boss has been promoted.'

'He has.'

Neither spoke for a minute.

'How much of a chance have you got?' Edward said at last.

She shrugged.

'Max Holman – an American – is the prime candidate. He's been on the European board for five years, he's highly thought of but a rather cautious operator. The old man was very fond of him, used to look on him as something of a protégé. There are a couple of others who are less likely, and Bill Skerrett probably considers himself a rank outsider but he's not even that. He can be too awkward, and he's a bit on the old side. He's been letting things slip just lately, too. There again, he does have years of experience behind him . . . Oh I don't know. You just can't tell, can you? And there's always the possibility that they might bring someone over from the States, or even appoint an outsider.'

'Hm,' Edward grunted.

'The American bit doesn't count against me,' she said. 'Borjex has a policy of preferring, whenever possible, to use native talent. For all the obvious reasons – they know the country and its ways, it makes for better international relations, and so on. Irv and Max are the only two Americans on the European board. There's a German, too – Hans Neudecker – but he's not in the running. And it's unthinkable, having got this far, that being a woman will count against me. After all, I've been with Borjex nearly three years now and my reputation for getting results is well and truly established, isn't it? Apart from Max, I must be the best contender . . . However,' she cleared her throat, 'Max is a good friend of mine. He's also powerful. He has influential friends in the States – though I'm not so sure about in England.'

'He's Irv's deputy at the moment, isn't he?'

'Ye-es, but that doesn't necessarily mean he's right for leading the board. A good deputy can make a poor number one.'

'But would *he* make a poor number one?'

There was no answer; Edward looked at her face, already setting itself into severe lines of determination.

'All in all,' he prompted, 'how good would you say were your chances?'

She ran her hands through her hair.

'About fifty-fifty.'

'Then we'd better telephone Henry Bentinck,' Edward said, 'and invite him down to Tylowe for the weekend.'

Rain was spattering at the window panes and the afternoon was grey and misty. The panelled dining room looked cosy despite its size and the poor weather outside. Cobden, the butler, had stoked the fire and lit the lamps, then retreated. The five of them were alone now.

Katherine was still reeling under the double blow: the surprise and subsequent tense hopes that had come from Irv's announcement, and the realization that Edward knew she'd been planning to put Henry Bentinck to some use. She wondered how long he'd been aware of the latter, and thought that, although she'd tried to treat all his friends with equal cordiality, he might well have known for months. And he'd never before said one word about it. At least, she thought, he'll never know that I'd once wanted to use him, too.

'What a wretched afternoon,' Helen said. 'I'm beginning to think the spring will never come.'

'It's scheduled for next month,' Judith Bentinck said, then laughed in her rather nervous manner at her own joke.

Katherine, Edward and Helen smiled politely. Her husband ignored her.

Sunday lunch – the only part of the weekend Henry had had free – was over, and the port was on the table. Edward topped up his glass then pushed the decanter to Katherine; she topped up hers and pushed it on to Henry.

'I still prefer to leave the gentlemen at this point,' Helen lied tactfully and pushed back her chair. 'I'm old enough to perpetuate civilized manners; no one dare laugh at me at my age if I take the ladies with me when I withdraw. Come along, Judith,' she smiled at Mrs Bentinck, 'this is a perfect opportunity to escape hearing about politics yet again, and for me to show you those pictures we were discussing.'

Judith Bentinck looked delighted to escape.

'Of course,' Helen added lightly from the doorway. 'I don't count Katherine as a lady. She's a *business* person.'

Henry twitched an eyebrow at Katherine, the nearest he ever came to expressing amusement.

'You've excelled yourself yet again, Edward,' he said as he leaned back in his chair and lit his cigar. 'Excellent lunch.'

'Glad you enjoyed it, Henry.'

'I always enjoy myself at Tylowe. Who wouldn't? So, Katherine,' he puffed out a cloud of pale blue smoke. Wisps of it lingered long over the ancient oak table. 'I gather there are a few changes taking place at Borjex?'

'Yes, Irv goes back to New York next month.'

'Sound man, Irv McKenzie; I'll be sorry to see him go. We did one or two very sensible deals together.' He drew again on his cigar. 'I trust they'll put someone just as good in his place. I'd consider it a bitter blow if they appointed some headstrong character who didn't find himself in agreement with my schemes for industry.'

'One can never tell,' Katherine said, 'who they'll appoint.'

'Or,' Henry challenged, 'which way a person will turn once in office.'

'Some,' Katherine replied, 'are safer bets than others. Some are known factors.'

'Hm. With a company as vital to our economy as Borjex, the likelihood of the unknown in power could be disconcerting. There again, it's equally important to have the best possible man in control . . . This Max Holman chap – would you say he's as sound as Irv?'

'Different. But—' she hesitated, 'yes, in his own way probably as sound. He's a highly regarded member of the board.'

Henry inspected the tip of his cigar, stared at it for what seemed like minutes without speaking, then nodded, as if in answer to a private question.

'Of course I don't know him,' he said at last, and his hooded eyes, bland and almost fishlike in their conceal-ment of his thoughts, met Katherine's and held them.

'He tends,' Katherine said, 'to be cautious in his outlook. He disregards risk areas that I, personally, would exploit to the full.'

'Such as?'

'Irv and myself, for instance, had hoped to benefit more from your encouragement of foreign investments.'

'But surely Max would, too?'

'He'd think twice about investing heavily in the deprived areas. He's uneasy about labour relations there – his background's marketing, you know, and mainly in the States. Irv, had he stayed, would have made fuller use of your policies.'

'He was already starting to.'

'If I had sufficient pull, I'd like to go much further.'

Out of the corner of her eye, she saw a glimmer of a smile touch Edward's lips, then his face became a mask again while she outlined her aims to Henry. It was the rough outline of a long-term plan for Borjex, a plan that could begin in eighteen months' time with the government's scheduled land clearance schemes in the poorest parts of the British Isles.

If Borjex could win the contracts for the clearances and build factories on the sites, they would take on a percentage of the unemployed youth of the localities – untrained and at the moment demoralized people, living on expensive state aid and with little or no chance of finding work. Borjex would train them at their own expense, without government grants and – unlike government retraining bodies – would guarantee them jobs at the end.

'You mean you wouldn't just take on local labour, which expanding companies – including Borjex – are doing already under my scheme in Tyneside and the Clyde, but you'd actually take on school-leavers – teach them a trade and guarantee them a job?'

'I mean exactly that. We'd have to work out the percentages nearer the time, but for every – say – five skilled and fully trained people we employed, we'd promise to take on one teenager.'

Henry ground out his cigar.

'The only way that could be profitable to you,' he

reflected, 'is if you won more than one contract. Having trained these people and guaranteed them jobs, you'd have to be clearing more and more land and building more and more factories to put them in. Also, they'd be trained primarily in Borjex's methods.'

'True,' she agreed.

He snorted; it was perhaps a half laugh or a signal of commendation.

'The government couldn't guarantee you'd win every contract. What about other firms that would be competing? There'd be terrible protests – shouts of corruption.'

'I think,' she said, 'that the government might be obliged to consider our tenders favourably if rejection would put newly trained youth out of work.'

'So finally Borjex would benefit at least as much as the government?'

'We're in business, not politics. But there's no reason why government and industry shouldn't work hand in hand. They should do so far more in my opinion.'

Henry reached for the port, but his hand stayed on the decanter as if to help him formulate his thoughts.

'Why,' he asked, 'haven't you mentioned all this before?' And as he waited for her answer the light of understanding dawned in his eyes. 'Sorry, stupid question. You were saving it till it could be of some use to you personally. Not that I blame you.'

'Irv had hoped to expand more in the deprived areas, but the youth development scheme is mine. I'll mention it to him now—'

'Now that he's no longer in a position to gain any glory from it? But at the same time he's in the most powerful position of all now, isn't he? And if he thinks you can ensure the lion's share of the clearance contracts, because of your personal influence with me, he'll push hard for you to be the next chairman, won't he?'

'Possibly.'

'And if it goes wrong it'll be your fault and not his?'

'Irv may well reason like that. He's more likely to back the youth development plan if he's not directly in the firing line. But there's no rush over all this, it's not for another eighteen months at least. You might have changed your own mind about industrial growth by then.'

He blinked his heavily hooded eyes; it was like two shutters coming down then opening again to reveal a cold stare.

'Of course,' he muttered, lighting another cigar and drawing on it very slowly, 'as Secretary of State I have no right to try to influence an appointment in the private sector.'

'No, of course not,' Katherine agreed.

SIX

These promises are fair, the parties sure,
And our induction full of prosperous hope.

– MORTIMER; *Henry the Fourth*, Part One

The announcement that Katherine Hanson had been made chairman of Borjex's European operations caused an uproar. On the one hand she had the full support of the New York board and the regional boards, and approximately seventy-five per cent support from her own board. She'd expected this, since the prime contenders – and hence, subsequently, the most disgruntled – for the job obviously came from amongst her closest colleagues. On the other hand, Max Holman resigned immediately, and the press had a heyday.

The protests, apart from Max's resignation, came from the most unexpected quarters: one was from the academically inclined Dr Jim Beloff, a board member who'd never seriously been in the running, and the other from a long-serving board member who could never have done more than act as a 'caretaker' chairman in a crisis.

Tony Rykwert and Bill Skerrett were ominously silent.

Henry Bentinck sent his formal congratulations, but declined an invitation to the official celebrations. This was particularly remarked on at regional board level as well as amongst the lower echelons of Katherine's staff, whose goodwill was going to be essential but who were so far removed from the hub of matters that, all too frequently, they had to base their judgements on second-hand impressions. The rumour spread like wildfire that the new chairman, despite earlier gossip to the contrary,

119

was no longer on the best of terms with the Secretary of State.

At Katherine's unofficial party – held, by courtesy of Helen, at Tylowe – Henry Bentinck was one of the most popular guests.

Congratulations poured in by the dozen, but the thing that had delighted Katherine most of all was the upholding by New York of her nomination. With the strength of the main board behind her, she would take office with virtually all the power she needed.

For the first time in her life television cameras were aimed at her, and she knew that that evening sixty seconds of newstime would be devoted to Borjex's new chairman. The newspapers and magazines loved it, too, the former blowing up the implications of Max's resignation and the latter, as expected, making much of the fact that she was a woman. Within two weeks she'd given a string of private interviews and agreed to appear on a television chat show.

The party that Helen and Edward organized was sumptuous: they opened up the ballroom at Tylowe, hired a leading jazz artist as well as a more traditional band to cater for all tastes, had the kitchen staff working for days beforehand to prepare the buffet, brought in a team of waiters to help Cobden, then let the champagne flow.

The setting for the party was exquisite: the ballroom, which ran parallel to the long gallery, had been renovated in the eighteenth century and kept in perfect condition ever since; the upholstery and drapes were dull rose, the walls white with the cornices picked out in gold, and in the centre of the ceiling was a fresco twenty feet in diameter, depicting the gods and goddesses at play.

Katherine danced again and again, went out hand in hand with Edward onto the balcony to breathe in the clear, cool air of the park, then returned refreshed to dance yet again, to talk and laugh and savour her triumph beneath the glittering chandeliers.

Tonight marked the moment, more strongly than the

official announcement had done, but the exact turning point was uncertain. It might have been when she crossed Jack Bartley and won the Fareham contract, or when she first joined Borjex and knew that her career was soaring. It might have been when Henry Bentinck drew on his cigar.

All her friends were here tonight, including her mother and her neighbour from Langston, the lighthearted chatterbox Hettie Morton. It was strange to see Miriam dancing with Irv, she looked suddenly young and carefree; Hettie was dancing with Richard Stempel, the pair of them moving clumsily round the floor while Hettie talked and Richard nodded in agreement. Even her brother Daniel was there with his wife: Katherine had paid for their return fare to England – their first visit to the country in five years – and paid off Daniel's overdraft so that he could share somehow in her success. Her closest friend, Barbara Spencer, was there, putting away vast quantities of smoked salmon while her dentist husband was looking flushed on champagne, glancing none too discreetly at mouths gaping with laughter, as if hoping to find yet another rich client. Tony Rykwert was looking rather the worse for wear, too, and was now standing rigid as a tree trunk against the far wall. He looked as though he might never move again.

Sober or not, everyone seemed to be enjoying themselves; it was extraordinary, she reflected, how she could ever feel lonely when apparently she had close on a hundred friends. Off-hand, she couldn't name more than ten or eleven, even if you counted people like Irv and Henry as friends. There was an army of acquaintances and hangers-on here tonight, as well as business colleagues, including the entire European board – even its part-time members, from old Dr Grettrix who'd emerged from retirement for the evening, to current part-timers whose outside interests were so extensive that she might only see them at the monthly general meeting.

She was glancing across the room, half listening to the conversation of the group she had joined a few minutes earlier, when the chandeliers dimmed and coloured lights started flashing. The band were taking their half-hour rest and had put disco records onto a turntable. Someone touched her arm: it was Hugo Palfreyman.

'Hello,' she smiled at him. 'I didn't know you liked this sort of music.'

'It appeals to a rarely flaunted side of my character,' he said, and added, with one of the most sincere smiles she had ever seen: 'I don't know if you realize this, but no one could be more pleased than I about your appointment. Shall we dance?'

While they moved about to the music, Katherine was aware of a mild sense of elation. Hugo – in normal circumstances a personification of dignity and tact – had been one of Irv's right-hand men. It looked as though he was going to be just as loyal to her, too, and she could have wished for no finer legal adviser. His brief compliment to her this evening was made doubly flattering by virtue of the fact that he would never, no matter how sorely pressed, be drawn into faction fighting or culling favour with those in power. His dogged impartiality, his reputation for being incorruptible, his staunch refusal to judge people except on merit, all made him revered by everyone from the president to the most junior administrator.

The music was so loud that it was impossible to talk, but when the record came to an end he said 'Thank you' with unlooked-for formality, gave a funny little bow and departed, just as Edward seized hold of Katherine's hand and led her further into the crowd of dancers.

When the disco music finally ended and the band came back, Katherine took a glass of champagne from a passing waiter and looked about her for Helen, with whom she had not as yet had an opportunity to chat. Helen had been occupied all evening – moving graciously from one group to another, exchanging a few words with this one and nodding in greeting to that one, keeping an eye on the waiters and going into protracted discussions every now and then with the butler.

Katherine spotted her now by the buffet. She was inspecting the table, still laden with fish, cold meats, quiches, salads, trifles and iced cakes. Then her eye fell on the suckling pig, so beautifully decorated that no one, apparently, had wished to be the first to ask for a slice. It was standing intact as the centrepiece of the table, and Helen licked her lips.

She spoke to the chef who began to sharpen his knife, glanced towards one of the nearby empty tables for four, then caught Katherine's eye and smiled.

Making her way towards the dowager Katherine was waylaid by a group of board members and their wives. As she paused to talk, she saw that Helen, too, had been accosted.

Skerrett's shoulders were hunched forward and he was clasping and unclasping his hands; he kept himself about a yard away from Helen as he talked, as though to come any closer might contaminate her, and there was a grimace on his face that could have been taken for a smile.

Katherine realized with a slight shock that what she saw on his face was snobbery – a pastime which was unlikely to do Borjex any harm, but it was an element of Skerrett's personality she'd never witnessed before. A vague sense of dismay accompanied her next thought – that she herself probably had the same weakness that she'd had at Abertawe and right through her career, a weakness that Edward had told her about more than once: she jumped to conclusions about people. She certainly had a tendency to analyse then categorize them, as she might have done with some unknown fluid in a laboratory, and after having come to a conclusion would continue to act upon it, as though no other factors would have any bearing on her first proven theories.

She'd thought a variety of things about Skerrett in the past, and thought them with neither liking nor loathing, just cool equanimity tempered with mild distaste. She'd decided what he was and what he was not, and that had been that. Because she'd never seen him in an environment where he could demonstrate his snobbery, she'd never credited him with any, just as she'd never credited Hugo with lightheartedness.

It was frightening, an essential part of her make-up was missing, some vital warning signal that most people – and certainly most women – possessed, but which would never flash in her brain.

As she listened to Mrs Beloff chattering on, she watched Skerrett out of the corner of her eye. There were people with titles more grand than Helen's here tonight, but perhaps he'd already worked his way through those. At any rate, he wasn't going to let Helen get away, and in fact was beginning to handle the situation rather well. He had pulled himself up to his normal height, replaced the grimace with a venerable expression better suited to his years, and was apparently suggesting food she might like to sample from the buffet. When her plate was full he carried it across to a vacant table, pulled back a chair for her, then sat down next to her and started talking.

Despite his wiry build he seemed almost dignified tonight, with his silvery hair and crisply tailored black dinner jacket. His face was terribly lined, but in these shimmering crystal lights the leathery quality of his skin contrived to give him an air of callousness and resilience. Not totally unattractive, perhaps, in its own way.

For once he looked impressive – if one dismissed his earlier gestures of risible obsequiousness. Katherine smiled to herself, but then Henry Bentinck was by her side and a moment later they were dancing.

'You're looking fabulous tonight,' Henry said.

'Thank you,' she smiled, and glanced automatically towards one of the tall mirrors that hung against the wall. It caught their reflection as they swept past: Henry was looking imperturbable, as always, but she was looking unusually glamorous. For once she'd been lavish in her choice of hairstyle, and had it swept up on top of her head and full at the sides – a sophisticated and almost regal style that flattered her clear-cut features and showed off her long, smooth neck. The heavy material of her richly coloured dress almost touched the floor behind her, and her jewels sparkled in the bright lights. She was wearing a pearl and diamond clasp round her neck and matching ear-rings, the whole set a part of the Arlingham family collection and given to her by Edward as a present. On one finger she wore a large, square-cut diamond ring, which she'd bought herself.

She and Henry talked of trivia as they danced, about the jazz artist who was to make his second appearance of the evening shortly after midnight, about blues singers and 'white' jazz, and about a club that had opened recently in London. Their very clothes might have been spiked with microphones. She knew that this would be Henry's one statutory dance with her, for appearances' sake, then he would leave early and they would never – not tonight nor at any other time – so much as mention the circumstances of her appointment.

At the end of the dance he handed her over to Edward, who was talking to Judith Bentinck and beginning to look rather bored.

'Can we sit down, Edward?' she said, when the Bentincks had departed. 'I've been dancing for hours.'

'Of course. There are some chairs over there, near the buffet.'

As she headed across the room, Rykwert crossed her path. He too was leaving early, and grunted something at her which might have been 'Goodnight' or 'Damn you'. From the scowl on his face, she favoured the latter.

'What a night!' Edward exclaimed as he pulled back a chair for her and beckoned to a waiter. 'There'll be more champagne along in a minute.'

'Exactly what I was dreaming of. It's thirsty work, having a good time.'

'You've danced a lot, haven't you? I seem to have done more than my fair share, too. Oh look—!'

Katherine followed his gaze. Skerrett was dancing with Helen, guiding her across the floor with confidence and just a fraction too much intimacy: Helen's face was frozen into a polite smile; she might have been wearing a mask.

'Rescue her, Edward, do.'

Edward laughed.

'In a minute,' he said.

'He's been monopolizing her all evening.'

'She won't come to any harm. She's a tough old bat. Ah, the champagne.'

The bottle made a cool, crunching sound in its bed of ice.

Edward filled the two glasses that had been placed on the table, then said, saluting Katherine: 'Congratulations again. Here's to your first term in office, and long may you reign.'

'And here's to you,' she saluted him in return. 'And thank you for all you've done to help – and for this party.'

'There's no need to thank me. I've done little enough, if anything. And as for the party – well, I'm enjoying it as much as I hope you are.'

She sipped her drink.

'By the way,' she said, 'did you happen to hear what Tony Rykwert said to me as he left?'

'No, should I have done?'

'I suppose not, but you were right beside me. It's just that he looked so angry.'

'Yes, he did look a bit off, didn't he?'

'I presume he's jealous, and disgruntled.'

'I should have thought so, yes. But he was never in the running, was he?'

'Not this time round, no. He doesn't have a wide enough experience, as yet . . . He and I have never been over-fond of one another, but some people are apparently impressed by his unshakable calm in the face of crisis.'

'He's not a bad company secretary then?'

'Not bad at all. Dull, but effective.'

'You said "not this time round" – ?'

'I meant that he and I are more or less the same age group. I'm unlikely, in my late thirties, to leave Borjex in the forseeable future. At the same time I can't go up, because Irv's only just got the top job and he's still in his forties, so he could be there for the rest of his working life unless he moves to another company.'

'In fact Tony Rykwert could be just that bit too old next time round?'

'Precisely. He'd have been much better off if someone of, say, Skerrett's age group had been made chairman. Also, he knows I'll never be a "godmother" to him, whereas one or two other people do seem to favour him. Skerrett gets on quite well with him – at least, as well as he can get on with anybody.'

'Hm,' Edward topped up their glasses. 'Have you crossed swords with Rykwert over anything in particular?'

She shrugged.

'He was unhappy when I was made a board member.'

'What was he doing then?'

'Still company secretary.'

'He's been in that job quite a while then?'

'In a sense, but of course I've moved up quickly. And I was brought in at a slightly higher level than him to start with.'

Skerrett swirled past them again, this time with a hefty, red-haired woman in his arms.

Katherine and Edward chuckled simultaneously.

'He's promoted himself,' Katherine commented. 'That was the ageing Marchioness of Renbeigh.'

'Snob, is he?'

'I think so.'

'D'you know,' Edward said, 'I went to bed with the Marchioness of Renbeigh when her name was Susan Waters. First-class lay.'

'Edward! Really!' and she snorted with laughter.

He looked wistful.

'Is she really ageing?' he asked, as an after-thought.

'No, not at all. I just meant—'

'That she looks as though she's ageing. And she does. Don't worry,' he took hold of her hand, 'I'm aware of the fact that I've aged much better. Besides, she's older than I am. Ah-hah, I see your friend Skerrett has abandoned the Marchioness in favour of a drink. Wise man. Doesn't do to fritter away one's energies . . . What an extraordinary assortment of people we have here tonight.' He leaned back in his chair and surveyed the room. 'Looks like well over a hundred to me. Would you believe McKenzie's dancing with his wife at long last? And there's Helen, dancing with a most handsome young chap.'

Katherine looked up, and for a second thought she was seeing a ghost.

She must have gone white, or started, for she heard Edward's voice say: 'Anything wrong?'

'N-no,' she replied after a moment. 'Nothing. Just – someone I thought I knew. Someone I haven't seen for a while, hadn't invited.'

Helen was in the arms of a tall, broad-shouldered boy whose dark hair fell thick and curly over his collar. For an instant Katherine was convinced – almost called out his name involuntarily – but then the illusion was gone, as soon as she remembered that Gareth, too, must have changed with the years.

'What's he doing here?' Edward said. 'He's only a boy!'

'So he is,' Katherine agreed, and as he and Helen drew closer she saw that even that might be exaggeration, for despite his height and well-developed physique he seemed scarcely more than a child. Though she couldn't make out his features precisely from this distance, she could see a fresh-faced, unsophisticated quality about him that bespoke extreme youth. It was refreshing, in this sultry ballroom.

'Nice-looking boy,' Edward remarked. 'Being perfectly charming to Helen.'

'*I* know who he is!' Katherine exclaimed. 'His name's Marius. He's with Irv – related to friends of the family, or something. He's staying with the McKenzies for a few days and Irv asked if he could bring him along. I've only had the chance to talk to Irv for a few minutes tonight, otherwise I'd have met the boy earlier. He's at a public school near here and on holiday at the moment – I forget the exact arrangements but I gather they're all going back to the States within the next couple of days. And here's Irv now, and Deborah.'

But the McKenzies paused for only a moment to say goodbye, shake hands and wish Katherine well, then set off to collect their young charge. Edward followed them to fetch his mother over to the table, and while he was gone Katherine stared at Marius, at the tilt of his head as he turned to say farewell to Helen.

After the fuss had died down and she'd moved officially into the penthouse suite, she launched herself immediately into a round of meetings with the regional boards, the streamlining of production and bonus schemes and – the scheme that would make or break her – the statels, now a word to be reckoned with in the company. If the getting of minerals had fascinated her through her mid-thirties, then by comparison the statels enthralled her. The plans were adventurous, a challenge like no other: if anybody else had been aware of the potential that she was about to tap, then they hadn't dared risk their money in it – but she was going to make it work, turn ancient houses right across Europe into magnificent centres that would carry the Borjex name and hallmark.

Then just as she was poised on the brink of success, just as it looked as though her plans would go ahead, Irv presented her with that crushing blow: without Gareth Williams on the board, she could shelve her plans indefinitely.

As the date of his arrival drew closer, she grew distinctly anxious. She began to wish that she'd misjudged him, that someone would prove all her opinions of him were wrong – over-emotional and unfair. And perhaps, she reflected, even if her views weren't unbiased, Gareth might have changed. It was that hope that prompted her to make a few inquiries about him.

Irv was the obvious person to try and pump for information, and she contacted him under the pretext of wanting to know more about what Gareth had been up to during his highly successful career. She found out little. Next she rang a notoriously indiscreet colleague of hers in the New York office, and found out nothing. Finally, on the off-chance, she contacted an American acquaintance of hers – a Manhattan-based businessman who was involved in real estate. After a long, hypocritical preamble about how delighted she was that one of his own fraternity was joining her company, she struck lucky.

It was a passing comment, nothing more, but it was all she needed.

She contacted Irv yet again.

'Before your friend takes up his appointment with us,' she said, 'you'd better explain something to me of the McKay–Williams affair.'

There was a stunned silence at the other end of the telephone line.

'Who told you about that?' Irv's voice was guarded.

'Apparently it was common knowledge at one time in New York – so common that it was in all the newspapers.'

'It happened some time ago. It's best forgotten.'

'Oh no, Irv,' she answered him. 'If Gareth is going to be a member of the European board, then we'd better get the facts clear right now about his supposed double-dealing.'

'Gareth wasn't the one who was double-dealing! Just what have you been told? You know ah can't stand gossip—'

'Well you'd better tell me the truth, then, hadn't you?'

Irv might be tactless, he might conceal things when he thought it wiser to do so, but once he promised to give you the truth, then you knew that that – whether you liked it or not – was what you were getting.

And by the time he'd run through the details of the McKay–Williams scandal, Katherine frankly didn't know whether it was despicable or high-minded: it was just typically Gareth.

Irv began by saying he'd call Katherine back on their direct line so that no one from Borjex could listen in; reconnected, he hesitated again, saying it was better not to discuss the matter at all until they next met. And Katherine, more curious than ever, was obliged to wait until Irv paid a brief unscheduled visit to London. Even then, in the sound-proofed privacy of Katherine's office, it was only her threats to make her own inquiries – and perhaps, statels or no statels, object to Gareth's board membership – that persuaded him to talk.

He began by warning her that Gareth himself never, under any circumstances, discussed his ex-partner – and Katherine was not to raise the subject with him. And yet, he declared, Gareth was the person who'd come out of the whole sordid business in an excellent light: Irv admired him all the more for the way he'd dealt with a treacherous, no-good coward.

Ellis McKay, apparently, had been Gareth's partner for

a couple of years when it happened. Ellis, like Gareth, was an architect, but was still practising his profession whereas Gareth was purely the business member of the team. Their New York development company was growing, but too slowly in Gareth's opinion, whereas Ellis – a middle-aged man with a wife and teenage daughters to provide for – baulked at the idea of quick expansion. Gareth tried to buy him out but Ellis wouldn't hear of it, and then – perhaps through greed or financial problems or simply because he considered Gareth young and easy to fool – he made his first and last mistake. He crossed Gareth. In the most cowardly and underhand manner he brought off a major deal on the side, then falsified the records to defraud him of nearly a hundred thousand dollars. At that time, such an act had been enough to set back Gareth's progress by years and, even more deplorable, Ellis had been his friend.

Gareth discovered the deception by accident, weeks later, then nearly killed Ellis – hit him so hard that he was laid up for days. Then – and this was the part that wasn't public knowledge, the details that Gareth had confided to Irv, and which Irv seemed to applaud – Gareth determined to have his revenge.

Ellis' behaviour helped him: as soon as the man was capable, he begged Gareth's understanding and forgiveness, became grovelling in his apologies. And Gareth accepted them. He agreed that they both needed each other, and that they ought to try to sort out the mess and keep the partnership going as best they could. Then he shook him by the hand.

A minute later he went to the bathroom and scrubbed his hands in running water.

For a few months he let things go on just as they were, until Ellis was relaxed and confident again. Then his chance came. It was over a contract for an annex to a school – precisely the kind of opportunity Gareth had been waiting for.

He drew up a set of blueprints, then had them copied professionally so that no individual's hand could be detected in the designs – for they were full of gross miscalculations. As soon as he'd hidden them in Ellis's office, he ordered – under his partner's name – a consignment of deficient materials, then bribed a disreputable acquaintance to tip off the authorities.

'Christ,' Katherine interrupted. 'He set the poor guy up.'

'Hell, Katherine – McKay was no "poor guy". He'd just tried to ruin Gareth, a friend of his.'

'And Gareth did it back to him, or tried to.'

'He tried.'

'Did he win?'

'Kind of. Though in fact he treated McKay better than he deserved in the end.'

The authorities, Irv said, taking no chances about a property company that was intending to cut corners and infringe regulations, launched an inquiry.

Ellis insisted, as Gareth had guessed he would, that the company files and everything else in the offices be searched – and of course the faulty blueprints were unearthed. Gareth's defence was that he was not the practising architect of the team, and that the structural plans Ellis had shown him were perfectly satisfactory. He also pointed out that only a few months ago Ellis had tried to defraud him – so could only conclude that his partner was under strain due to money problems, and had lost his head over this school contract.

'Huh!' Katherine commented. 'What a shit!'

'D'you really think so, Katherine? Ah don't.'

'In any case he was taking a colossal risk, wasn't he? The odds against the plan backfiring must have been prohibitive – at least for any normal person.'

'Well – it did backfire in a way, and that's how Gareth ended up – in my eyes – as a fellow with a real sense of honour.'

'No comment.'

'Be fair, Katherine – listen to the good bits about him as well as the bad.'

'Go on, then.'

'Ellis McKay,' Irv said, 'went completely to pieces. Now ah know Gareth hadn't intended that – but it happened.'

'He'd just meant to destroy him.'

'Not totally – just pay him back a little. Anyway, Ellis did go to pieces, couldn't practise again, and Gareth bought him out – for a far higher price than he need have paid. In fact ah advised him against it – but he insisted. And then – ah Christ, Ellis's wife tried to kill him.'

'Tried to kill Gareth?'

'Uh-huh. And she nearly succeeded. It was a year or so later, at an architects' convention. Greta McKay was either fanatically loyal, or off her head with worry about Ellis – ah don't know which. Gareth had been speaking at the convention, and they'd all broken for lunch and were just strolling out into the hotel lobby – and there she was, waiting for him.'

'What happened?'

'It was weird. He told me afterwards that he knew, the second he saw her, what she was going to do. She was just standing there, on her own, with her hands in the pockets of her coat – and the look on her face said everything. Cold as ice with her hatred. He said there was no cover in that lobby, nothing whatsoever he could do. She took a step or two towards him, stopped, told him in the most incredibly calm voice that he was a cruel bastard – then shot him.'

'Had a pretty poor aim, didn't she?'

Irv went quiet, then said: 'It was a good thing for her sake that she did.'

'OK Irv, sorry. I know Gareth's a friend of yours.'

'He turned out to be a friend to Greta McKay as well. He spent a week in intensive care and another two months in hospital before he was allowed home – but for all that he didn't want to prosecute. In fact he'd have done nothing at all if it hadn't been for police involvement. At the trial he managed to save both himself and Greta – and ah know, because ah was in court. He spoke up for her – talked of her misplaced loyalty for her husband, and her integrity. You just should have heard him speak . . .'

'I can imagine.'

'Anyway, he was believed, and Greta McKay ended up with a suspended sentence, probation and psychiatric care.'

'And the true facts about the McKay–Williams affair were never proved?'

'They weren't proved in court – but some wild tales got around about Gareth afterwards. But you know the real facts now, so no matter what anyone else tells you about Gareth Williams – you can forget it. You've got a man joining your board who's got a sense of honour.'

Katherine did not necessarily share Irv's views about Gareth's sense of decency; she gave her word, though, that she would never, under any circumstances, break Irv's confidence. In any case the McKay–Williams débâcle was a dead and buried issue now, and it was Gareth's future behaviour that concerned her.

Come what may, though, she and Gareth were going to have to try and work together – and she was going to have to be sensible. After all, she was nearly forty now, a well-balanced, efficient businesswoman who couldn't afford to let private opinions and emotions endanger the organization she was running.

By the twenty-fourth, the day before his arrival, she'd convinced herself that it would be child's play for a woman like herself to keep Gareth Williams – or any other dubious character – firmly in his place.

She sat down at her desk and inspected her morning correspondence. At the top of the pile was a lengthy communiqué from the health and safety executive, and the one attached to it was from the advisory committee on environmental pollution. She groaned, read them through quickly, then marked the whole lot for Dr Beloff's attention.

Tomorrow, after so long a separation, she and Gareth would come face to face again. She would have to be tolerably pleasant to him, if it helped business to run more smoothly; she would have to do a lot of things . . . though Irv's bulldozing attitude, the way he'd forced Gareth on her, hadn't exactly improved her temper.

Tomorrow! Tomorrow was a disquieting prospect – unnerving, almost. And – though she was loathe to admit it – just a little exhilarating.

She remembered her parting with Gareth, and the cruel events that led up to it. She remembered, too, when they'd first come face to face and the sun was dying, turning that cold Celtic sea to flame . . .

Gareth was annoyed. Not very but enough to put him on his mettle. Katherine had agreed to see him this morning, the twenty-fifth, and at the last minute she'd sent a message saying she was 'unavoidably detained'.

Unavoidably detained. The words rankled him even now. How unimaginative of her, and how rude.

In the end it was her legal adviser, Hugo Palfreyman, with whom he'd had to have the meeting. Hugo, presumably at Katherine's behest, had spent a full three hours with him, explaining in meticulous detail the structure, the inner workings and the problems that made up the European operations. He'd told him who to contact for this piece of information, and who to contact for that, who to avoid and who to depend on. It was all very useful, but Gareth had already had a more sweeping outline – resulting in a somewhat different overall picture – from Irv, and finally his own intuition and common sense were going to serve him far better than a mass of facts. The basic problems were always the same, no matter what the company. At least, that's what he had always found.

Hugo had finally shown him the office he would have use of for the duration of his two-year – renewable – contract. It was on the board members' floor, and was large, beautifully appointed and overlooked Hyde Park. They'd provided him with a good secretary, too, a woman of about his own age called Mrs Rodgers. She looked perfectly capable of supplying him with any secretarial service he might need, which pleased him because he wanted to leave his own PA – who was a shrewd, level-headed young man with lots of promise – in the States where he could help keep an eye on Gareth's property business.

Hugo's departure was swathed in courteous excuses for Katherine's failure to appear: these excuses ranged from an unexpectedly protracted board meeting to some minor problems over publicity from a television programme. She should not, he reflected, have agreed to see him in the first place, though the television excuse was probably true: the programme was being shot when he'd paid his unscheduled visit to Borjex earlier in the year, and he'd made sure he caught a glimpse of her.

He was glad he'd called in on the off-chance, it meant that he had the advantage over her: he'd had the opportunity to see her before she saw him. He'd seen her on the screen, too, a few days later, and thought she looked terrific, in great form and not very much different from the way she'd looked fifteen years earlier. But when the camera had panned in for a close-up he'd realized that the years had taken their toll, just as they had with him.

It had been a slow pan, and he'd noticed the breasts first of all – fuller and heavier than they used to be – yet her face was thinner and there was a hardening of that mouth that he had once kissed and loved.

Her hair, though, was still thick and blonde and

gorgeous. How he used to love to bury his face in it, so long ago . . .

He used to dream of it when they'd first split up, and imagined touching her skin again, the warm skin of her thighs and the dampness that was for him. He remembered her firm young breasts, closing his mouth over the taut pink flesh of her nipple, sucking gently, forcing his tongue to linger – longing for her and holding back . . . moving above her at last, moving inside her, till she answered him and the night had exploded and their bodies were drenched.

Never could people have loved as he and Kate had loved, that was how it used to seem to him. He'd loved her gestures and her smile, her impulsiveness and everything about her. She'd been candid then, even naïve, and all his instincts had been to protect her while they'd lived together at Abertawe.

But what a disaster it had been in the end, and what a bitch she could be, too, with that icy temper of hers that could flare up to annihilate you. He'd had reason to curse her finally, as well as to thank her.

Perhaps, he thought with a sudden wave of sympathy, she was as apprehensive about their meeting as he was. For he was apprehensive, as well as exhilarated by the prospect. He hoped Irv hadn't put his foot in it – he did have a tendency to at times. He should have briefed Irv about how to put ideas across to Katherine, told him a little of what had happened fifteen years ago, but it was too late to bother about such things now. At the time he'd been stunned when Irv had told him that the new chairman was Katherine Hanson, of all people; then, a minute later when he'd recovered himself, the thought had amused him.

Doubtless Katherine, too, would have baulked at taking Irv even partially into her confidence, greeted the news of Gareth Williams's arrival with cold disdain and vicious protests – that would be typical of her.

This time he would approach Katherine Hanson with sound strategies and plenty of forethought, because his own business interests must not suffer and, in fact, should prosper still further. A seat on this powerful board was of course very useful, but if feuds got out of hand he might be unable to spend as much time as he needed to in the States.

Then there was Marius to consider, as well. He'd seen little enough of him as it was over the past year, ever since the decision to educate him abroad at an English public school. Strange to think that he'd already seen Katherine – and while she was celebrating her success! He wondered if she'd spotted the family likeness, and if she'd thought him handsome. Such thoughts were almost incestuous. It was during the boy's last half-term holiday that the McKenzies had looked after him and taken him to Katherine's party in some grand country house. Like most young boys Marius hadn't bothered to find out more than the briefest details about his hosts, and it was only recently that Gareth had put two and two together.

Marius had been enchanted above all by the house, by the weapons and suits of armour in the hall and the acre upon acre of grounds that held promise of unbelievable excitement for an energetic schoolboy. But he had described an attractive blonde woman – old*ish*, he'd called her – who'd been at the centre of things. He'd mentioned her two or three times, as though she'd somehow fascinated him, and then Gareth had asked him what her name was.

'Oh, I don't know,' he'd tried to sound casual, but blushed. 'Not that I was all that interested – she really was quite old. About your age.'

'Mind your manners,' he'd reproached him, and kept his face stern though he was longing to smile.

If he'd known then who that blonde woman was, he'd have staggered from the shock of Marius's reaction.

Besides, in Gareth's opinion the boy was far too young

to be weighing up the pros and cons of females. On the other hand, he reflected, he himself had been casting lustful eyes at girls even when he was wearing short trousers and going to his first little school in Wales. In fact he couldn't remember a time when he hadn't been interested. And the one who'd rocked his world more than any other was the one he was going to confront tomorrow.

Like her or loathe her, she did at least make the blood stir a little faster.

'Mr Williams to see you,' Mrs Egerton's voice came politely through the intercom.

Katherine had been perfectly all right until then. She'd been signing letters with a flourish and keeping her mind firmly on her work. She was damned if she'd let this meeting perturb her in the least. But then there was another dread – unimportant, of course, and best ignored. It was certainly nothing to be nervous about. It was simply that, after all these years, she couldn't bear to see disappointment on his face.

Taking a deep breath to restore equilibrium, she said: 'Show him in, Mrs Egerton.'

It seemed like a major speech.

She took a few more deep breaths, picked up her pen and signed another letter. The characters in her signature seemed spiky, and perhaps smaller than usual. Too bad, because she was going to go on signing letters even after he'd come into the room. After a moment or so she would look up, surprised, as though the announcement of his arrival had been such a trivial thing that it had slipped her mind immediately.

'Ah – Gareth,' she would say, and give him an official greeting – a movement of the lips accompanied by a warm handshake. 'How lovely to see you after so long.'

And then she would give him a bit of blurb about how she hoped they would be able to work well together, and didn't the reinvestment scheme have excellent potential, and then he would go away again and she'd return to her letter-signing.

He didn't appear. At least three minutes had already gone by and the doors were still firmly shut.

She signed two more letters, then got to her feet. Then she hesitated, undecided as to whether she should sit down again and simply wait, or fling open the doors and see what was happening.

On the one hand she couldn't sit there waiting indefinitely, but going out to look for him was really beyond the pale.

She was still standing there, in the middle of that huge office that took eight aggressive strides to traverse, when one of the double doors opened slowly.

Intrigued, she looked out but could see only Mrs Egerton, laughing and chatting happily to someone who was evidently standing behind the door, with a hand on the handle.

Then she heard his voice.

For a second she thought she was imagining it, because of the distance between them and the thickness of the door that was shielding him. But then it came to her quite clearly, and caught her unawares: she'd half expected his voice to have altered, to be American or harder or somehow different, but it was frighteningly unchanged. Strong, while the accent itself was soft with just the faintest Welsh lilt to it.

It was evidently being put to good use at present, in the chatting-up and charming of Mrs Egerton who, in her turn, was clearly forgetting to get about her business. Or perhaps Gareth's company was such that she just didn't give a damn anymore.

Katherine was about to go out and join them, with the best Saxon charm she could muster, when he appeared round the door.

His parting shots to Mrs Egerton meant that his face

was turned away from Katherine, until the last possible moment when he closed the door behind him.

She hadn't expected him to be nervous, nothing stupid like that, but she certainly wasn't prepared for this sort of nonchalance. It had obviously had no effect on him whatsoever, the prospect of meeting her again after all these years. To him it was just a commonplace occurrence, like coming across any other lover or enemy from the long-gone past. He'd probably scarcely even thought of her since those days in Abertawe.

'Hello, Gareth.'

'Hello, Kate.'

And then his mouth flickered into a smile, a slow smile that trembled nervously for a second then widened so joyfully that it touched her heart with its warmth.

SEVEN

What sayst thou, Kate? what wouldst thou have with me?

– HOTSPUR; *Henry the Fourth*, Part One

The entire European board was assembled. It was the monthly general meeting and, apart from the usual items on the agenda, there was a last-minute addition about the health and safety committee, followed by the issue they all felt so strongly about: the statel proposals. Today, the board's final agreement would be sought.

Katherine opened by officially introducing Gareth, although most people had met him informally already. Then she dealt briskly with item one, a review of last month's figures, and handed item two – implications of an operational research paper – over to the German, Hans Neudecker. Leaning back in her chair she surveyed the table: one thing that had become apparent since she'd introduced a round board table was that people tended to glance every now and then at the chairman, even when somebody else was speaking. It was curious: whenever a remark had a doubtful interpretation, or was of special importance, at least half those present would glance automatically towards Katherine, as if trying to gauge her reaction or draw silent advice. It happened again and again, so that wherever she sat became the head of the table. This meant she had to be constantly on the alert in case of betraying some untoward response, and to allow herself a respite she would employ an old knack of hers acquired during unduly prolonged union meetings: she would draw her eyebrows together in a slight frown, set her lips into a line that could be diagnosed as anything from concern to stunned admiration, fix her eyes on the papers before her – this last movement in the sequence having the added recommendation of distracting the union side, lest she should be contemplating some fatal piece of information in her brief – then let her thoughts wander where they chose. She used the technique now, keeping one ear on what Hans was saying so that she could come in again when necessary. Richard Stempel was taking copious notes, so should she happen to miss anything important – doubtful, because she never had done up to now – there would always be records to refer back to.

What she wanted to savour this morning were the repercussions of Gareth's arrival on Borjex, and on her own life. From a company point of view his obvious business acumen was going to be useful, as was his flair for getting on with people. It pleased her that the arrogant side of his nature seemed to have disappeared, either knocked out of him over the years or kept under firm control. He hadn't asked for a free hand with the statels, though doubtless Irv had led him to believe he could have one, and was willing to do an awful lot of listening. It was as awkward for him as it was for her, she thought, and she admired the way he was handling it. If they both remained as polite and cautious with each other as they had done up to now, there should be no problems.

From a personal point of view, they were both being circumspect in the extreme, apart from the first day. It had been so good to see him again, despite all her doubts, that they'd put aside both loves and hates and talked quite normally – like old acquaintances who were going to have to do business together. In the end they'd had lunch and chatted about this and that, nothing intimate or contentious, of course – simply about the statels and Borjex. Then they'd inquired about each other's relatives, talked of mutual friends at Abertawe and even reminisced about that happy Christmas in Wales.

The minutes had flown by and she'd returned to the office in great spirits. He was as interesting to be with as he always used to be – and was apparently still fit and healthy, too. His solid frame was the type that might run to fat, but he looked surprisingly lean and hard, as though the years had toughened him still further.

But he was older: there were lines round those eyes that had once bewitched her, and a strand or two of grey in that untidy dark hair. Otherwise time had been kind to him, physically at least. He was a little more measured in his speech, perhaps, but that was a good thing. If both he and she continued to be cautious with one another, there should be no problems.

She looked up, just as Hans came to the end of his talk, then dealt with the next two items herself. The three after that were dealt with by the appropriate board members, then it was Dr Beloff's turn to talk about the health and safety executive. Katherine gave this her complete attention, because years of experience led her to believe that she hadn't been put fully in the picture – either deliberately or by chance – and the safety section of the executive was going to cause trouble in the very near future.

The problem was the opencast sites, and the Tylowe workings in particular. Beloff was rambling on about health hazards, and a communiqué that both the executive and Borjex had received from the advisory committee on environmental pollution. Serious an issue though pollution was, it was being kept in check at Borjex's sites and, where regulations were not being adequately met, she would make sure procedures were tightened up. More than that – she would make absolutely certain that Borjex went way beyond the basic requirements for pollution control. They'd done it with the chemical plants and they'd damn well do it with the mining sites: protecting the environment was an issue she felt very strongly about. But this could be dealt with, and with infinitely less difficulty than the chemical plants had caused.

As far as Katherine was concerned, the problem was an engineering one. She was, as she had always been, uneasy about the lie of the land around Tylowe. Apart from the natural lakes – and the one in the grounds of Tylowe was an unusually deep one, even for that area – the earth's strata for miles around was a mining engineer's nightmare. There were faults – places where a stratum had split, sometimes badly, and was no longer horizontally intact. Just as serious was the fact that Tylowe was built on sandstone, a highly porous rock. It could look attractive and mellow on buildings, but below ground it could be lethal. With the combination of sandstone and faults, the threat of flooding was a permanent and serious headache.

She wished, as she had done a hundred times, that Edward had sold the Tylowe Drift to Borjex, where there was a wealth of engineering talent to cope with the ever-present dangers. As it was, she could only trust in Edward's assurances that he was continuing to make the best possible professional arrangements, that the men he employed knew their job thoroughly and that the regular – but in Katherine's opinion too infrequent – visits from the government's mines inspectorate would prove adequate, and ensure that potential catastrophes were averted long before so much as one life was put at risk.

But she couldn't dwell too long on the hazards of the drift: Borjex's problem was the adjacent opencast site, the working of which seemed to be hitting snag after snag. Before long Jo Cleary would be demanding a bigger than usual pay rise for his men, or threatening to pull them out, and that would be a disaster.

Jo Cleary himself disturbed her. They'd always been the best of sparring partners, but the last time she'd seen him had been at the Tylowe workings, and there had been an element of strain in his manner. Skerrett and Rykwert had been there, too, and she thought that perhaps they were to blame. In fact the more she thought about it, the more convinced she became that Cleary was dissatisfied with Skerrett as Borjex's head of industrial relations. She remembered her own surprise at actually coming across Skerrett 'at the grass roots', as he would call it, and decided that the only logical answer to Cleary's behaviour lay in his lack of faith in the present industrial relations management. While doing nothing obviously wrong, Skerrett never went out of his way to do more than the absolute minimum, and Katherine herself had to intervene in areas that Skerrett should have dealt with himself.

If he'd been just one rung lower than a board member, she'd have got rid of him. She'd already had to talk to him on several occasions – an almost unheard-of event with a board member – but he remained mediocre, which wasn't good enough. And yet in the past he'd done his job so well, and he had so much experience. Six more months, that's all she'd give him, and if there was no improvement she would make moves to ease him out. Exactly how she had no idea, but she'd think of something. Perhaps his health would worsen . . .

Skerrett spoke now, in reply to Beloff's points. He talked sensibly, she was glad to note, and she only hoped she'd misjudged him.

She scribbled a note and passed it to Richard. It was a request for further technical details about the site, but she knew they would tell her little more than she was aware of already. Her feeling of unease, of not knowing enough, was suddenly so strong that it was like a premonition. If the fuel from Tylowe hadn't been of first-rate quality, she'd have found any pretext she could to close down that problematic site.

Skerrett finished speaking and now they'd come to the last item on the agenda: the statels.

Katherine introduced the proposals, then handed over to Gareth.

Within thirty seconds he had the absolute attention of the entire board. He made his points one after the other with superb clarity, then backed them up with the kind of detail that could only have come from long years of experience. His delivery was masterful: relaxed, inspired and totally persuasive.

The board gave their unanimous agreement, with the provisos that a "statel team" should be established comprising appropriate specialists plus at least one full-time and permanent board member; and that the pilot run should be in England but that no time should be lost in launching stage two: the inspection of suitable European property.

It was a busy period, and Katherine found it increasingly difficult to see Edward at all. He too was preoccupied, both with his political commitments and the management of his estate, and had little time to spare. They did manage one weekend together at Arlingham Hall, but the peace of the Elizabethan house was soon broken by an influx of summer tourists. The amusement park was noisy and crowded – the raucous music of a hurdy-gurdy machine drifted across the lawns and through the open windows, there were shouts and shrieks of laughter, and when Edward slipped his arms round Katherine and nuzzled gently at her ear, he was startled by a slow creaking noise.

'Katherine?'

'What was that? . . . Oh, hello.'

The door had opened stealthily and a family of four stood just beyond the threshold, crammed together and straining to get a better look.

'You're in the wrong place!' Edward bellowed. 'It says "private" outside – these are my private apartments.'

When they'd gone, Katherine said, 'You can understand Helen's reluctance to open up Tylowe, especially at her age.'

'It's not reluctance,' Edward replied. 'It's sheer obstinacy. She doesn't want the inconvenience. But I really feel you could do more to persuade her.'

'How can I? If she won't listen to you, she's certainly not going to listen to me. Anyway I have tried in the past, on several occasions.'

'Well try again, can't you? I'm starting to have nightmares about her finances – she's getting in one hell of a mess.'

'But you're her son. There's a limit to the extent to which a woman's son's girlfriend can interfere. She's hardly likely to let me look at her bank statements, is she? Besides, I've already offered her financial advice and she's refused it.'

Within minutes an argument had broken out, starting with Helen's taxes and culminating in personal slights. Edward accused Katherine of behaving oddly of late, of being distant and even resenting his presence. She retorted that she hadn't the faintest idea what he meant by such reproaches, and that he himself begrudged spending even a weekend in her company. After an hour or more of half-hearted bickering, they both blamed the tourists and the soaring temperatures, and departed to the quiet of Tylowe.

The weather was indeed hot for an English June, and Edward went to sit in the shade near the boating lake while Katherine escaped to the pool which – due to the fact that the climate was normally poor for at least nine months of the year – had been built indoors.

The cellars at Tylowe were an extraordinary mixture of old and new: one steep flight of stone steps led down from the kitchens to wine and game cellars, while another led deep below ground to the old dungeons. Yet a third, which was approached from the central hall and lay on a level with the dungeons, was Helen's own creation. Her work there had started when her first husband – the industrialist Sir Howard Cleave – was alive, and the entire concoction was typical of Helen: she wouldn't bother with vital matters like rewiring, but she would spend a fortune on beautiful luxuries. The main chamber consisted of a swimming pool, to which a wave-making machine had been added the previous year. Through an archway at one end of the room was a gymnasium and sauna, and through an identical archway at the other end was a huge bowl known as a jacuzzi. Helen had tried out the device during her last visit to Los Angeles, and immediately on her return to England had had one installed at Tylowe: this version was sunk firmly into the ground and was big enough for half the European board.

All three chambers had originally been decorated in art noveau style, touched up over the years and completely refurbished when Helen became a widow for the second time and art noveau was once more fashionable. They were a fine example of the rather chilling culture of the earlier part of the twentieth century, and the central chamber was made still more awesome by its ceramic-tiled, vaulted ceiling.

Today, Katherine went straight through to the jacuzzi, switched the control panel to 'cool' then stripped off and climbed in.

The bubbles and ripples were delightful: refreshing and so relaxing that within a quarter of an hour she felt as though she didn't have a care in the world.

There was no harm, she decided, in seeing as much of Gareth as she had been doing – in fact it was vital to see more of him during the early stages of the statel work. The two of them had already welded together a small but effective team, most of whom did not work for Borjex and were employed on a part-time or consultative basis, but who were experts in their fields. All that remained was for Katherine, as chairman, to decide which permanent board member to move across for the next twelve months or so. She couldn't spare anyone who was too busy or important, nor did she want anyone who was so enthusiastic that he would try to interfere. Then suddenly, while she wallowed in the frothing water of the tub, she realized how she could kill two birds with one stone: she would use Skerrett.

While he was tied up with the statels – nominally, for in effect she would allow him only the minimum participation – she would give the bulk of the industrial relations and personnel responsibilities to his number two, an ambitious director with a razor-sharp mind. By the time the early work on the statels was complete, Skerrett's 'deputy' would be doing Skerrett's own job so well that he would be putting him publicly to shame. Also, by that time, even Skerrett's nominal presence on the statel team would no longer be required. He would have nowhere to go, and Katherine would have a ready-trained board member to replace him. What was more, although she couldn't sack a board member she had every right to reallocate responsibilities, and that was exactly what she was going to do first thing on Monday morning.

Diving amongst the bubbles, then resurfacing to lean against the tub's slippery side, she reflected that now that Gareth was proving himself to be useful as well as easy to handle, and Jim Beloff had settled into his rôle as deputy, her senior management was looking very sound. After only this short span in office, she – a woman – was contriving to limit the power of the barons on the board, and without sacrificing any operational efficiency. In fact she had increased it considerably. She was totally in control now, and making progress by leaps and bounds.

There was one other comparatively minor problem to be sorted out on Monday: Sarah Jacobs, Mrs Egerton's assistant, had broken her leg. Katherine had sent flowers and visited her in hospital, and told her not to worry because her job would be kept open for her, even if her recovery meant several months away from work. Sarah's family, however, wanted her to leave Borjex and have an extended holiday abroad once her fractures were completely healed.

Mrs Egerton already had a replacement in mind – a girl who had been working in the reception area for the past six months, but who had secretarial training and experience. She was only nineteen or twenty, a pretty girl with pert features, black hair and brown eyes that were as sharp as a sparrow's. Her name, as far as Katherine could remember, was Jennie Corrin. Apparently she had taken any job she could get at Borjex, just as a means of having a foothold in the company, which was exactly the sort of determination Katherine admired.

Well this was one problem that she could leave to Mrs Egerton and Richard. They could interview her, and if she was as good as she sounded she could move into the chairman's office immediately.

Katherine closed her eyes, let her thoughts wander deliciously to the weeks ahead, to the plans she and Gareth had that would take them from the English countryside to Rome, and from Rome to Paris . . . working together, at long last.

The week was going as planned. Jennie Corrin had moved into Katherine's suite and looked delighted, while Skerrett had moved nowhere but had lost three-quarters of his department overnight, and looked murderous. At least he had until today, but now seemed to have had a change of heart. He was creeping about the place with a smug grimace on his face and could almost have been described as happy. Perhaps – Katherine hoped – he was already dreaming of golden handshakes, or ill-health retirements.

Katherine herself was dreaming a little as she headed homewards. The sun was still shining with a soft evening light and the air was close from the heat of the day. After six unbroken hours of meetings the greenery of Hyde Park was soothing, and she was glad she'd decided to take a walk on her way back to Kensington instead of letting the chauffeur drive her there directly.

'Katherine!'

She paused and turned around; Gareth was striding towards her across the grass.

'Hello,' she said. 'I thought you'd gone home hours ago.'

'I got side-tracked by one of the architects, and finally felt like a breath of air . . . D'you fancy a drink?'

'I'd love one; just let's make sure we go somewhere air-conditioned.'

They veered to the left and as soon as the Kensington Road was in sight Gareth hurried ahead and hailed a passing taxi.

Within minutes they were at the Hilton, and went downstairs to Trader Vic's where the air was beautifully cool. A Malayan girl in a flowered sarong took their order, and when the cocktails were placed in front of them Gareth suggested that they have just the one then go on to the Connaught for dinner.

'I can't.' Katherine shook her head. 'I'd half promised to have dinner with Edward.'

'Would he mind very much if you didn't make it? The thing is, I'd like your clearance this evening on some architect's plans. They're only projected plans for the type of conference theatre we were discussing, but the man's going to Munich tomorrow and won't be back till next week, so—'

She knew full well it could wait till next week, or even longer.

'I'd better ring Edward,' she said. 'If he hasn't booked anything – and if he's as busy as he has been just lately – he probably won't mind.'

When she dialled his number he took a long while to answer. She had the distinct impression, while they were talking, that there was somebody else in the room.

'So you're actually going to be . . .' then his voice cut off for a moment. 'Sorry about that,' he said. 'What were you saying?'

'It was you who was talking, Edward.'

'Oh yes. Yes, I was about to ask you if I'd understood you correctly. You say you're actually going to be working this evening?'

'Most of the evening.'

'Do try and have a spot of dinner,' he urged, but his tone was as courteous as ever so that she couldn't even accuse him of sarcasm.

'I'll try,' she replied.

'And who did you say you'd be working with?'

'I didn't,' she said. 'But as a matter of fact it's one of the statel people.'

'I see. Well don't work too hard and send my regards to Mr Williams.'

At the Connaught, they did discuss work for the first hour. The architect's plans took twenty minutes, then they talked of their forthcoming trips. They already had a list of possible property in England, as well as in four Western European countries. Katherine and Gareth were going to inspect two of the houses on the English list, as well as those in France and Italy. Two other senior members of the team – neither of which was the forgotten Skerrett – would inspect the remainder, and then, if the buildings still promised to be ideal sites in general terms, surveyors and other specialists would examine them before a final offer was made.

'As chairman,' Katherine said, 'I suppose I shouldn't really be doing this sort of trip.'

'Why ever not?' Gareth frowned. 'Just because it might be enjoyable? . . . If these visits were going to entail dull discussions with your regional directors, you wouldn't feel guilty then, would you?'

'Perhaps not,' Katherine agreed.

'Anyway,' Gareth added, 'I totally disagree with your outlook. The statel scheme is probably the most expensive project you'll ever undertake during your term as chairman. You wouldn't baulk at visiting a mining site, would you?'

'Never.'

'Yet that's a drop in the ocean compared to the money that will be tied up in the statels. It would be nothing short of disaster for both you and Borjex if anything went wrong with them. And remember, they were your brain child in the first place.'

'I do remember, and they're very important to me.'

'Well then,' he said, 'not only is it right for you to do at least a few of the initial inspections yourself, but it would be criminally negligent of you not to.'

'Do you know—' she wrinkled her nose in a puckish expression that made Gareth want to laugh and ruffle her hair – 'you were right when you said I might be afraid of enjoying these visits. I mean, enjoying them too much.'

'Good God, woman,' he said, suddenly making his accent very Welsh. 'I don't know what's been happening to you since you left Abertawe. What have they done to you then? Look you now, I shall have to be teaching you all over again.'

'Teaching me what?'

'Teaching you to be happy. What else?'

Darkness had fallen by the time they left; cars had their headlamps lit and the town seemed to be a blaze of electric whiteness.

Katherine felt warm, tingling through and through. She was a little lightheaded from the wine, and a little lighthearted – from the prettiness of the London evening, from his closeness, from his voice, and from the expectation of a long, glorious summer.

'Shall we go to a club?' he said.

'To dance?'

'Well, not to work.'

'This is very bad,' she said, 'we two cavorting round London when we're supposed to be business colleagues. What a marvellous idea.'

She didn't notice the roar of the traffic, nor the petrol

fumes, nor the taxi that drew up just behind the one they were climbing in to.

Opening the door for Katherine and speaking to the driver, Gareth didn't notice it either.

In it were Skerrett, Rykwert and Jo Cleary.

She saw Edward three times on consecutive evenings, and each time it was worse.

On the last occasion Helen was there, too, as if playing the rôle of intermediary. She did manage to act as a distraction, with her absurd questions to Katherine about the latest cosmetic surgery techniques in America, and she wanted to know so much detail about who to contact and how much they charged that even Edward had to smile.

Katherine took her turn at trying to lighten the conversation, but both she and Edward were finding the evening distressing. When he took her home and they were finally alone together, he said, 'You once told me that you didn't like Gareth Williams – that you were indignant over Irv's behaviour in foisting him on you and that you'd only put up with him because you were obliged to. You said he was devious.'

'Gareth Williams?' she frowned and gave the merest of shrugs, but felt uncomfortable. 'Why do you even bother to mention him?'

'Because you do. His name crops up again and again nowadays.'

'Edward,' she said, and put a hand on his, 'that's because we're working so closely together at the moment. I'm so busy with this reinvestment scheme that I can't help but mention his name. And tonight, as soon as Helen had finished quizzing me about America, she wanted to know all about the statels. I can understand her curiosity since she lives in an historic house herself, but it was that curiosity that obliged me to mention Gareth.'

'But you see him outside work, too.'

'Sometimes, but only—'

'No,' he said, and put a finger to her lips. 'Don't make excuses to me. We know each other too well.'

When he'd left, she poured herself a drink and sat brooding. Then she became angry: sitting up at night brooding, losing her concentration, being uncomfortable with Edward . . . these were things she most certainly did not need in her life. This friendship with Gareth would have to be curtailed – kept on a businesslike footing with no more than the necessary minimum of fraternizing. These lunches and dinners and long chats together had been fun – but not strictly necessary.

They took up too much time, for one thing – and time was always at a premium. Not only was Gareth beginning to distract her from her work, but he had the lion's share of her attention when away from Borjex, too. And apart from the fact that she was seeing less of Edward, she hardly saw her other friends at all now – people like Barbara Spencer, who she normally liked to meet up with at least once a week. In fact Gareth was monopolizing not only her time but her thoughts – and Katherine wasn't the only one to be swayed by his charms.

She'd seen Jennie Corrin making eyes at him, offering to do little jobs for him, girlish infatuation written all over her features. Gareth hadn't seemed to either respond or even notice, but still – Katherine didn't want any disruptions at the office.

Jennie's stupidity, of course, could be excused on the grounds of her youth and inexperience, but Katherine's couldn't. And stupidity was the only way to describe the feelings Gareth aroused in her: for the truth of the matter – and the truth had to be faced when you were sitting on your own in the early hours of the morning – the truth of the matter wasn't that Katherine merely enjoyed Gareth's company, or that she found him attractive, but that she wanted him. There was so much about him that was likeable, and so much that was irresistible.

'A cruel bastard' – that was what Greta McKay had called him, just before she'd shot him. 'Honourable' was what Irv had called him. And Katherine thought that maybe, in his own odd way, he was both. She'd already suffered once in her life from those two extremes of his personality, and didn't want to run the risk again. Under no circumstances could she afford to.

How good and stable, in comparison, was her relationship with Edward. How many happy hours they'd spent together, what excellent companions they were and, above all, they were lovers. The passion in their relationship had never been an all-consuming one, and if anything it had dwindled over the past eighteen months – but a great deal remained. They were well-matched lovers, and with all Edward's other attributes it would be difficult – if not impossible – to find such an ideal relationship.

And nothing, she promised herself, was going to destroy that relationship. She'd had too many hard years, too many lonely years, to let everything she'd built up with such care be destroyed by a passing fancy.

She and Edward, they could continue for years – perhaps for the rest of their lives. The thought was a comforting one, and possible alternatives merely alarming.

No excitement, no reckless involvement with a man like Gareth could ever replace Edward. Not that she and Gareth could seriously be attracted to one another again, not that either of them would even contemplate such a foolish step.

Putting down her glass, she decided to go to bed and read. She would have taken a novel except that she rarely bought any nowadays, because she never had time to finish them. Just as she got to the good bits, something would happen and she would have to abandon the book for perhaps a week. It was too irritating, and best not to start.

She took a volume of poetry instead and, as she passed

the bureau, her spectacles case. This she discarded about five seconds later, flinging it on to the hall table with considerable force.

He arrived to collect her at seven-fifteen. She'd cooked dinner for him the week before, and it had inspired him: he now had the ideal excuse for getting her on her own and within easy reach of a bedroom. He merely returned the compliment and invited her back.

Of course, he himself couldn't do more than grill a chop or boil a few strands of spaghetti, so he'd had caterers in to see to the food. And very well they'd done it, too; it had all been waiting for him when he'd returned from the office, and his only worry would be heating up the right dishes at the right time. Most of it was cold, though, as he'd specified. It would give him more leeway – he couldn't be rushing back and forth to the kitchen all night. He hoped they'd be in the bedroom by – estimating the thing sensibly – ten to ten-thirty.

Not that he'd originally planned to go to bed with her again – far from it – and he only hoped he wasn't making a mistake. He'd planned to manage her quite differently, but within days all his wise resolutions had gone by the wayside and tonight, when he pressed the doorbell, his imagination fired immediately. He could picture her walking down the hall towards him, hips and legs and breasts all moving to a greater or lesser extent, wide mouth parting for a second as she licked her lips, wide-set hazel eyes a bit troubled, in case he should realize she fancied him.

'Hi, Katherine.'

'Hello, Gareth.'

He noticed that she greeted him with a friendly but rather cool smile, just in case.

'You look well.' He gave her a brotherly kiss on the cheek – this always reassured them, and Katherine had never been an exception in this field – and then it struck

him that he had just uttered a colossal understatement.
She didn't merely look well, she looked devastating. Yet
again he was bowled over by her sheer desirability: she
wasn't perfectly beautiful – not by any means – but she
did something terrible to him. 'What a pretty dress you're
wearing.'

Again, an understatement, and in any case rather a
pathetic remark. But he was already itching to get hold of
that flimsy material, slip his fingers into the low-cut
bodice – if that was that they called it; anyway, the bit
that revealed a tantalizing segment of breast – get his
fingers round the material, and pull it firmly down. He
certainly wasn't in the mood to think of clever turns of
phrase.

'I shan't be a second, Gareth,' she said. 'I'll just fetch
something to put round my shoulders – it might turn cool
later.'

'Good idea,' he said.

Yet another image flashed across his mind, even as she
turned to open some cupboard door.

Christ, and it was only seven-eighteen. There could
well be hundreds of long, frustrating minutes stretching
out ahead of him . . . It might have been better, all
things considered, not to have got so close to Katherine
Hanson.

'I'm going upstairs for a moment. Help yourself to a
drink – you know where it is.'

'Not just now, thanks. I'll wait for you here.'

Then his glance fell on the hall table, took in a bowl of
flowers, a couple of ornaments and – lying there pathetically battered – a spectacles case.

He felt the muscles of his heart contract. The sight of
that much-used old case touched him, moved him far
more than words or tears would ever have done. A fresh
image of Katherine came to mind, a picture of her
working till even her eyes were tired – as doubtless she
must have done, thousands of times – then returning

home to sit alone in some easy chair, then working again, or reading a novel – or perhaps poetry, like she used to sometimes at Gwilym Cottage . . . He was filled with a tremendous urge to protect and look after her, and even felt sorry for her vanities, because he tried to remember if he'd seen her wearing spectacles in public and was sure he hadn't: he would definitely have remembered such an extreme change in her appearance. With the urge to protect came a rush of sympathy, for the difficulties she must have struggled through, and because she'd had nobody to help her – unless you counted this Edward fellow, who sounded a decent enough sort but hadn't been around all that long, only for the past two or three years. Then he felt a wave of respect, because she'd made it despite everything, despite the disruptive start when she was a child and despite the lack of family to lend a helping hand. And despite people who had let her down so badly – and whether it had been willingly or unwillingly was beside the point.

He understood what had driven her on and what kept her going. The more he thought about it, the more the past drew them together rather than separating them. Their childhoods had been similarly poor – though his had contained much more love and affection – their early twenties had been rich with good times, and the best years had been largely a struggle. Culminating, thank goodness, in some measure of success. Not a complete success, however, because neither of them had either a proper family life or even someone they were in love with. At least, there was nobody special in his life, and he hoped there wasn't in hers. He didn't think there could be, because if she was in love with Edward, she wouldn't be spending the evening with Gareth Williams.

'Katherine!' he called. 'What are you doing?'

'Shan't be a second – I can't find the jacket I was looking for.'

'I thought you were a paragon of tidiness?'

'Got it!' she called back, and a moment later was running down the spiral staircase, and crossing the hall towards him.

Then he knew beyond all doubt that there was nobody else, because her eyes were shining, and the love in them lit up his world.

'What a marvellous meal you've prepared, Gareth. You may not believe this, but I just can't imagine you in the kitchen.'

He looked at her to see if she was teasing him; he thought she was, but she was keeping a straight face.

'I find cooking – relaxing,' he said, and smiled candidly.

He should never have planned to seduce her like this, not Kate. It wasn't the kind of strategy he normally used – in fact normally he didn't use strategies at all, there was no need. But Katherine Hanson was a different matter entirely, she required premeditated actions. His tactics, however, had rebounded on him: whatever fond sentiments and lust she might have provoked in him only days ago had multiplied crazily tonight, from the moment he'd arrived at her home.

'More wine?'

'I'd love some, thank you.'

He didn't know what could have possessed him, letting his libido run riot like that. He was usually a controlled person, but there he'd been less than an hour ago, reacting as if all he'd ever wanted in life was to hold her in his arms, make love to her until they died of it.

She glanced at him, looked as if she was about to say something important, then altered it at the last possible moment.

'We ought,' she said, 'to take Richard Stempel with us to Rome.'

He was genuinely speechless.

'What the hell for?' he managed to say at last.

'It would be good experience for him, and we'll need somebody to take notes.'

'Notes? Odd jottings, perhaps – or a letter or two at the most. I shall dictate mine into a machine. If you really feel the need for a retinue, then of course you must do as you please.'

'One PA is hardly a retinue. Besides, it's not just notes – Richard will be invaluable in all sorts of ways . . .'

She began enumerating the seemingly endless uses to which Richard Stempel could be put. Gareth could think of no use for him whatsoever, except possibly for carrying the bags, and he looked on the frail side even for that.

Topping up his own glass, Gareth relaxed and prepared to wait until she'd finished. He felt suddenly more content than he'd felt all evening. Katherine was sitting next to him, he had good food and wine in front of him, and all around him were nice things: a comfortable two-floor apartment in Hampstead, with French windows open on to a walled garden, the scent of flowers and the touch of a faint evening breeze. And on the mantelpiece was the clock, that funny old timepiece he'd bought fifteen years ago in Wales, and given to Katherine as a Christmas present for Gwilym Cottage. She'd left it behind when she'd gone, but he'd kept it, and the fact that it was on display tonight was not due to preconceived designs on his part – it was simply that he always had it around. It had been in each of his homes in America and he'd had it overhauled regularly so that it still kept time, more or less. Lost an hour or two occasionally, but never stopped.

How Katherine's face had paled, as though she'd seen a ghost, when she'd walked into the room tonight and noticed that clock. She'd gone over to it, stared at it, looked at its porcelain face and the tiny sun and moon that were painted there, and then her expression had changed. It had become soft, almost puzzled, as if she were in the process of amending her views entirely on Gareth Williams. He hoped she was.

'Richard's very good at organizing,' she was saying. 'Apart from anything else, he'll be able to see to the hotel bookings and the airline tickets.'

And outside the sun was melting into the garden, lengthening shadows and touching the leaves with gold.

'I'll be relying on him later on in the year, when I go on holiday.'

'You aren't having a holiday this summer?'

'I can't – not before autumn at the earliest. What about you?'

'I haven't planned anything yet.'

Through the French windows, the breeze was stirring more definitely now, and the room was growing shadowy. Gareth lit the candles.

'It's turning cool,' he said. 'Shall I close the windows?'

'It's a beautiful evening. Do you mind if we leave them open?'

Sparrows and blackbirds were singing out there, and above it all was the insistent note of a thrush.

'How often will you have to go back to America?'

'Every few weeks, but I can stay in touch by phone and do some business from my office at Borjex. Part of the company is here in Britain, and I'm in the throes of trying to expand it. I do quite a lot of work in South Wales, you know.'

'I didn't know that. No wonder there's still a hint of Welsh in your voice.'

'Is there? I didn't think there was.'

He touched her hand, then took it in his. She let it rest there.

As they walked out into the garden after dinner, he slipped his arm round her waist. When they reached the end of the little lawn, and there was nowhere else to go, she turned to face him. She was so close he could smell her perfume, and felt the warmth from her body.

He kissed her, more slowly and searchingly than he'd kissed any woman for years. He must even have closed his eyes – getting drunk on the touch of her limbs – because for a moment he saw nothing, then he was aware of candles flickering in the distance.

When he looked at her, her eyes were lowered and her features were obscured by the gathering darkness.

'Would you drive me home, Gareth?' she said.

Then he saw that she was crying.

He was about to put his arms round her again, comfort her and hold her, when he realized with absolute clarity that if he did he would lose her for ever.

Instead, he said in a matter-of-fact voice: 'I'll go and fetch your jacket. You were sensible to bring one, it is turning chilly now.'

And he determined that he would have her in Rome, and after that he would keep her and things would be very different in the future.

EIGHT

Come, Kate, I'll have your song too.

– HOTSPUR; *Henry the Fourth*, Part One

'I won't let you go,' Edward said.

She could scarcely look him in the eye. He knew her so well that if their glances met he would see it all – the terrible, physical longing she had for Gareth, and more besides.

'It's not a case of letting me go,' she replied. 'I just think we ought to admit what our relationship has grown into – a friendship.'

'That as well,' he agreed.

If she could have liked Gareth less it would have been easy, but despite everything she believed that she was beginning to understand him. And they could discuss almost anything now without embarrassment: they'd certainly discussed things like her attachment to Edward and women Gareth had been involved with while he was in the States; he'd asked her opinion about English schools and Marius's education, and she'd even teased him about the family likeness. For a second he'd looked as pleased as punch, then his face had clouded over, he'd told her he was concerned about Marius, about the boy dividing his time between an English boarding school and two separate homes to visit in the States. Marius didn't get on too well with his stepfather either – but then Gareth had stopped abruptly, almost in mid-sentence as if suddenly thinking he had no right to bother Katherine with such matters. He'd taken her hand in his, held it for a moment, then turned it over and kissed the palm and – oh! a flame had leaped inside her . . .

'Edward,' Katherine said, 'you and I are very fond of each other . . .'

'Fond?' he repeated. 'I remember you saying something similarly insulting when we first met. I think you might even have said I was "nice".'

Edward never came to see her in the office: in fact today was only the fourth or fifth occasion he'd set foot inside this building in the three years she'd known him, but the argument they'd had last night had been their worst ever. Not that they normally argued . . . Three years . . . it seemed much longer. She looked up at him, and suddenly felt irrevocably tied to him, to the way of life they'd shared and to the friends they had, even to Helen whose company she enjoyed so much.

'You've been rather strange just lately, too,' she said.

'In what way?'

She shrugged.

'Perhaps you've been busier than usual.'

'I have.'

He got to his feet and paced across the room, then returned and took hold of her hand.

'We have so much in common,' he said, and squeezed her hand tightly. 'Please think carefully before you make any rash decisions – don't do anything on mere whim. You've had a lot on your mind since you were made chairman, and then this Williams chap turned up again. It was bound to be disturbing.'

'I do love you,' she said, and in a way she meant it; then for the second time in two days felt her eyes prick with tears. 'I should hate to spoil all the happiness we've had. Please believe me.'

'I do believe you, Katherine. What you must do is go to Rome as you planned, but try and take a day or two off while you're there – have a bit of a holiday. You need one badly, then later in the year we'll have a month somewhere or other. Everything will seem different when you get back from Italy.'

'Oh God, I don't know—'

'What don't you know? Come along, Katherine, this isn't like you. Do as I say and have a change of scene.'

'Yes,' she agreed. 'I think perhaps you're right. I'm getting things out of proportion.'

'Exactly. Draw on that celebrated logic of yours and nothing can go wrong.'

She smiled at him.

'Of course it can't; I'll make sure it doesn't.'

'That's my girl . . . You weren't by any chance planning on taking anyone with you to Rome, were you?'

She would have told him the truth, but there seemed to be no need. It would only distress him, and with a little will-power and common sense she would soon have her life under control again. She'd been letting her imagination run riot, that was the trouble.

'Only Richard Stempel,' she said.

'Ah – parrot-faced Stempel. Well good luck to you.'

'Don't be so cruel, Edward – he's a nice person.'

'Another one? Lord . . .'

Jo Cleary lit a cigarette, coughed, then took a large gulp of his gin and tonic.

He'd always had a lot of fun from his private meetings with the various chairmen of Borjex, and Katherine had proved the best yet. But today's working lunch would be the first step in ruining all that, and he was sorry.

Drawing in a lungful of smoke, he reminded himself to go as carefully as possible, because he still wasn't totally convinced that she was crossing him, and in any case it might suit his purpose to change sides later in the year – switch back to Katherine and drop the other two. Whatever happened, it was essential to keep all his options open for as long as possible.

'When are you off to Rome, then, Katherine?'

'The day after tomorrow. We've got four houses to go over.'

'I don't know—' he shook his head ruefully – 'gadding about with young Stempel. What will people be thinking?'

'More or less what they think about you and me having three-hour lunches together behind closed doors.'

He laughed.

If only he could have been certain that Skerrett and Rykwert were wrong – lying or mistaken about everything they accused her of – then he would have tipped her off to take care. How delighted they'd been that night when they'd seen her leaving the Connaught with Gareth Williams; Skerrett had crowed out loud and Rykwert had made some humourless comment about easy ammunition. What shits they were, but if their information was right, then she was an even bigger shit.

'It's going well then, is it, this statel business?'

'Mediocre. Neither of the two places we've seen in England has proved suitable. There was one I liked the look of near Oxford – it was the kind of size I'm after and the grounds were perfect, but I was told it had major architectural drawbacks, that it wasn't suitable for conversion.'

'Oh? Got some decent advisers, have you?'

'That particular one used to be an architect. He's a part-time member of our board now – Gareth Williams. I don't know if you've met him?'

'Not yet,' he said. 'You'll have to hurry up with the English side of it, won't you? Or you'll be getting your knuckles rapped.'

'Who told you there was any rush with the English side? Because whoever it was got it wrong. We don't want to waste time, and the pilot run will be here, but we're not going to invest large sums of money in a panic.'

This was exactly the lead-in he'd wanted.

'How much do you estimate the whole scheme is going to cost, then?'

She stared at him, and he wasn't sure whether it was to collect her thoughts or to devise the best means of prevarication.

'I can't say, Jo, can I? The whole thing's going to take years. I could only speculate in the most approximate way. Prices will change, our profits will fluctuate, we can do no more than make plans and modify them as need be.'

'But you know how much you've ear-marked for the first –' he shrugged – 'let's say eighteen months.'

'Naturally.'

'And you wouldn't like to tell me how much that is?'

'I'm surprised you even ask, because it's none of your business. You and the other unions know how much profit we've made and how much we're setting aside for investment, but I have no intention of breaking down our internal facts and figures for you.'

The conversation gradually became strained, with Jo complaining of the difficulties some of his men had to contend with on the mining side, particularly at workings like Tylowe, which had surface dust in this weather only to become waterlogged after the first downpour. Then he mentioned his annual claim, talking in terms of an absurdly high figure, as she'd feared he would.

He had the impression, it seemed to her, that all profits were going to be ploughed into the statel scheme, leaving nothing for anybody else. She couldn't refute him absolutely because she still didn't know how much there would be available to spend, nor had she agreed with the board on what sort of figure she could settle with Jo. Whatever happened, his union, MATEX, would not come off the worse through reinvestments, but even if she'd had an approved settlement in mind she could not disclose it at this early stage – so long before the official negotiations.

'Jo,' she said, 'I'm telling you quite frankly that we will spend a lot on reinvestments – not only on the statel scheme but on other relatively minor ones, too. For example, I'm considering the purchase of a small company to add to our soft drinks sector, and we're spending more on research and development. But all that is as it should be – we're making a healthy profit and it must be used wisely or the whole organization will be choked – and MATEX will be amongst the first to suffer. You know that as well as I do.'

'But you won't even name a rough figure for the pay rise? Even now, behind closed doors?'

'I don't have a rough figure yet, but the rise will be a fair one. It always has been, hasn't it? No higher than is right, or I'll have the rest of the organization out on strike, but as generous as it can possibly be.'

'We went along with you and your redundancies, in the spring.'

'And you're getting an improved bonus scheme out of it.'

'My men do dangerous jobs—'

'Some do – but that's a different argument, isn't it? I'm as concerned as you are about safety and mining conditions, and you can't say otherwise.'

'True, but I'm far from happy about your reinvestments.'

She looked at him in perplexity, rather than irritation, then said quietly, 'Just what the hell are you getting at, Jo?'

When he said nothing, she went on: 'Even if you had X-ray vision or some contact who'd show you confidential board papers, you wouldn't be much wiser – because our projected spend figures have got to be offset against taxes, overheads and inevitable losses in certain areas – as you well know. What I'm saying is that even if you *knew* – and I promise you I'm far from certain myself – how much I'm planning on ear-marking for reinvestment, you'd still only have half the picture.'

'I'm all for investment,' he said. 'Within reason. But

even if the statels create new jobs, they won't be for MATEX members, will they?'

'That's true, but investment creates money in other areas – income to be spent in fields outside the investment area.'

'But after how long?'

'I've given you my word,' she said, 'that MATEX won't lose. You and I have been working together ever since I joined Borjex, and we've never let each other down yet. We're not going to start now, are we?'

Rome was unbearably hot and incredibly noisy. Richard looked touched by sunstroke already, and was staggering under the weight of his one small case.

'Richard,' Katherine said to him, as they stepped into the hotel foyer, 'the porter will help you. Leave it.'

'Oh thanks, thanks,' he muttered, as though she'd offered to carry his baggage herself.

Gareth grinned and she flashed him a warning frown.

'All right, Richard?' he said, taking no notice of her.

'He's perfectly all right. Aren't you, Richard?'

'Actually,' he began, 'since you mention it . . .'

'Right,' she interrupted. 'Let's go and look at our rooms, shall we? A cool shower and a change of clothing and we'll all revert to our usual brisk selves.'

The hotel they were staying in was near the centre of Rome: not one of the grandest establishments but Gareth had suggested it because of its typically Roman atmosphere, from the architecture of its seventeenth-century walls to its antique furnishings.

Richard had a room on the third floor at the front of the building, while Katherine and Gareth were sharing a suite on the first floor at the back, overlooking the gardens. Katherine had told Richard to ask for a private sitting room that could be used as an office, but the nearest the hotel could come to her requirements was to provide a *salotto*, with a large bedroom and bathroom off

one end and a smaller bedroom and shower off the other
– evidently a family suite.

The arrangement was adequate, because she and
Gareth were separated by the *salotto* and were more
private than if they had had adjacent rooms.

Tomorrow, work would start in earnest, but tonight the
three of them were going to enjoy Rome.

Katherine soaked in a bath and began to feel refreshed,
but Gareth's choice of hotel had been a wise one because
the rooms themselves had a restorative atmosphere. They
were high-ceilinged and white-walled, and the thickness
of the stonework would have kept the heat at bay even
without the air-conditioning. Both the outer and inner
shutters had been closed during the afternoon, and the
suite was dim as well as cool; it had a deliciously
Renaissance quality to it, especially with the ornate but
uncluttered furnishings and the faint, unmistakable smell
of Italy. When Katherine climbed out of the bath,
wrapped herself in a light robe and opened the shutters
of her bedroom, the smell came to her more strongly: it
was a mixture of flowers from the garden, along with
something musty and old and, perhaps, something that
meant dirt or bad drainage but added nevertheless to that
intoxicating compound – Rome and sultry-hot weather.

Dusk was falling quickly when the three of them set
out for the evening, and by the time they had meandered
through the crowded streets for half an hour or so, it was
almost dark. They became jolly, as if on some school
outing, because they knew no one and no one knew them,
and they had no car and – for the next twelve hours or so
– they could pretend they had no responsibilities.

The restaurant Gareth took them to was on a steep
incline, part of one of the seven hills across which Rome
was straggled: it was little more than a *trattoria*, and few
tourists knew of its well-deserved reputation for good
food. Its dozen or so tables were on a roof garden,
sprinkled like white-clothed oases amongst pots of

greenery; Gareth had reserved one by the balustrade so that they could look out at the great vista of Rome while they dined.

Acres of rooftops sloped away into the darkening night, roofs of all shapes and sizes and even colours; some of those near at hand looked old and unsafe, and some of the flat ones had washing strung across them, hanging like grey spectres and still drying in the heat of the night. But soaring out of the squalor were domes and towers and fountains, and lights glittered like fairy lights amongst the shadowy splendour.

'It's too beautiful,' Katherine said. 'I think I'll just look at the view and forget about eating.'

'You'll regret it,' Gareth told her, 'once you've had a glimpse of what this restaurant's capable of.'

In the end all three of them tried several different dishes, exchanging morsels from each other's plates whenever they spotted something that looked interesting. Richard began to undergo a personality change, relaxing and regaling them with stories, and by the time they descended into the street to look for a taxi, he was in charge of the party.

On Gareth's instructions he managed to explain to the driver where they wanted to go, and they careered at break-neck speed past the Trevi fountain and the Spanish steps towards an open-air night club.

They were shown to a quiet table set well distant from the band, and Katherine danced first with Richard and then with Gareth. Everything seemed slower and more deliberate tonight, even the rhythm of a familiar tune, and the heaviness of the air created the strange illusion of weighting their limbs.

Yet when they returned to the hotel and bade each other goodnight, Katherine realized that her senses – though slower than in England – were twice as powerful once stimulated. What was more, England seemed further away than it ever did when she was in New York: it seemed insignificant and trite.

She took off her clothes and opened the inner shutters: slatted moonlight and distant city lights streamed into the room, fell across the cool marble floor, the huge double bed and her naked body. She sat on the edge of the mattress and waited for him, listening to the chirp of a cricket in the garden below.

The door opened almost soundlessly, then the latch clicked to behind him.

He stood there for a moment, watching her, then he was beside her, putting his fingers beneath her chin and tilting her face so that she must look at him.

She told herself that it wouldn't matter, that afterwards things could go on just as before with old sins well buried and the present intact. He was only a man she liked and found attractive, someone whose closeness she would enjoy before she returned to Edward. Nothing more, because nothing could disrupt her life.

He touched her lightly on the lips as he stood over her.

The earth might have moved.

They awoke to brilliant sunshine and blue skies.

Breakfast of coffee, hot bread and apricot jam was served to them on the balcony, and they ate ravenously. Then Katherine rang through to Richard's room and asked him to put back the day's schedule by two hours. To her surprise he agreed without sounding in the least perturbed by the prospect, which would entail a long and complicated series of telephone calls.

'Italy seems to be doing something wonderful to Richard,' she said, as she rejoined Gareth on the balcony.

He looked up at her, and she was struck again as she had been last night by the terrifying power of their attraction. She felt that if she moved now, took one more step towards him and touched him, their flesh would burn in the current that passed between them.

They might have been burning now, just by holding each other's gaze in the fresh early morning.

Last night, while they were still in the *trattoria* overlooking Rome, she'd known that nothing would keep him away from her now. And she'd also known, as she'd waited for him in the hotel bedroom, that it was going to be wonderful. But her memories of fifteen years earlier must have grown dim, or their love or passion or whatever it was must have grown a hundredfold, because she'd expected nothing like the magic of the past few hours. From the second his lips had touched hers she was lost, and he was undoubtedly lost with her.

He'd kissed her face, her neck, her breasts, her thighs, letting his mouth linger as he called her name. And she'd answered him, aware of nothing except that he spun the world on its axis, fired the darkness to blind her with light.

All her thoughts had vanished, from the grandest to the most petty, and with them had gone every last shred of logic. That she could ever have dreamed of merely going to bed with him, and of somehow continuing with Edward afterwards, seemed the most absurd illusion she had ever nurtured. For anybody but Gareth to touch her now would be an affront worse than rape, and she would rather have died by Gareth's hand than been unfaithful to him.

Pushing aside the breakfast things, he got to his feet and opened his arms to her, and she stepped forward.

The *palazzo* outside Rome was a vast, grim fortress that had been added to at irregular intervals since the fourteenth century – most of all in the baroque style. Once the property of a warmongering Pope, it had passed through the hands of a variety of families until acquired by a Roman merchant during Garibaldi's struggles to unify Italy. For the past decade it had been rarely used or even visited, and its present owners could scarcely believe their luck that a buyer might be found for this edifice that was – to them – nothing but a white elephant.

The building showed signs of falling into disrepair: parts of its façade were crumbling, but the reports that Borjex had received indicated that its basic structure was sound.

Signor Galeotti, the owners' legal representative, greeted the English trio and showed them round. The tour through the dozens of rooms took up the entire afternoon: Katherine was enthralled, and everything she saw became heightened by Gareth's presence – by even the accidental brushing of his hand against hers. Colours were brighter, sounds were sharper, and voices whispered of music – not of deals and contracts and facts and figures.

A caretaker and his wife trotted along in front of the party, flinging open high, thin shutters and letting sunshine stream into the long-closed building. Dust particles hovered everywhere, dancing in the clear, Italian light and settling on the visitors.

The rooms were all bare of furnishings, except for an apartment on the ground floor where a few nondescript pieces were shrouded in dust sheets, but the paintings could have filled a gallery. Here and there one had been removed, leaving a pale square on the wall, but those that remained included what looked to be excellent examples of Italian art – though whether good copies or originals remained to be judged by an expert.

Katherine began to hope that the building would prove as suitable for conversion as it seemed at first glance. While Signor Galeotti was engrossed for a moment in conversation with the caretaker, she drew Gareth aside and asked his opinion; he sounded optimistic, and she asked Richard to contact the specialists at Borjex as soon as he returned to the hotel: the *palazzo* was definitely going to be worth a closer inspection.

It was built round a series of porticoed courtyards, where acacia and cypress trees gave added shade, and there were fountains – silent at the moment and in need of repair, but whose moss-covered statues reminded you of coolness despite the red-hot day.

Guided by the lawyer, the group trailed up and down sweeping staircases, looking at ceilings whose frescoes would have put Tylowe to shame, then they wandered down long passages and into rooms where the remnants of splendour still remained: plasterwork picked out in gold, crystal chandeliers tinkling in an unexpected breeze as heavy carved doors were opened, revealing the magnificence of a ballroom, or the stillness of a long-forgotten bedchamber.

Their footsteps echoed eerily as they descended to the central hall; they thanked the caretaker and his wife, then returned with Signor Galeotti to his office in Rome. On the way there he confirmed what Borjex had already been led to believe: that the *palazzo* was to be sold with whatever contents remained, including the paintings.

The next three days were business disappointments: the buildings they saw were either unsafe or of the wrong proportions for conversion, and Gareth suggested they recommend only the *palazzo* of Signor Galeotti's clients.

Both Katherine and Gareth dispatched their work at top speed: phone calls were completed in seconds rather than minutes, and letters were dictated at a frenetic pace. They couldn't wait to be alone and, once alone, couldn't get enough of each other.

Meals were still taken with Richard, but he had developed the habit of going out alone after dinner, and appeared so happy and self-contained that there wasn't even a need to think of excuses for leaving him.

The only excuses they did need were for not returning to England on the fourth day. Discussions with Signor Galeotti were good enough reason for Borjex, particularly as everyone sympathized with the complexity of doing business with an Italian – though in point of fact the lawyer couldn't have been more helpful. On receipt of Katherine's telegram announcing her delayed return, Edward sent a telegram back saying he was delighted she had taken his advice and was having a holiday – but that she ought to have extended it to a week rather than just a long weekend.

Gareth, as far as Katherine knew, had no one to make personal excuses to.

Richard left on the Friday morning, shaking them both by the hand and thanking them.

'You've nothing to say "thank you" for,' Katherine said. 'But if you've enjoyed it so much, then it's a good thing you came.'

'It is,' he agreed, and signalled to a porter with unexpected confidence.

Telephone calls took up the rest of the morning. Although booked in advance, infuriating hold-ups still occurred, and Gareth showed an unprecedented display of anger – talking rapidly and rather heatedly in Italian to the hotel switchboard, so that Katherine couldn't understand a word of what was going on.

Her call to London came through without any problems, but his link-up with America was disconnected twice. He fared no better with his call to Cardiff – where, he said, some property deal hung in the balance – since even when he was connected he couldn't make himself heard properly. Finally he swore, and she walked out of the room and left him to it.

It was half an hour later when he joined her on the hotel terrace, and after they'd ordered themselves a *negroni* each and the drinks had been served, he looked more relaxed.

'What was the matter?' she asked.

'Not as serious as I'd thought,' he said. 'Luckily . . . I told you I was expanding my company in Wales, didn't I?'

'Mm,' she nodded.

'Well it was to do with that,' he shrugged. 'Property in Cardiff.'

'What sort of property?'

'You don't want to hear all about my business problems, do you?'

'I only asked you what sort of property.'

'The difficult to get hold of sort,' he brushed her question aside. 'I've spent too long in America – my contacts in England aren't as good as I thought they were.'

'Perhaps I could help—'

'No,' he said, 'but thanks for the offer. I'm already doing all that needs to be done.'

'It's not a serious problem, is it?'

'I've just told you it's not. Now enough of all that – let's have an early lunch or there won't be time for a siesta. The flight to Pisa is at five.'

They took a taxi from the airport at Pisa to Florence, and as soon as they had been ushered into their hotel room and were alone, Gareth locked the door, swept her up in his arms and dropped her onto the bed.

He unfastened her dress and slipped it down as she lay there, then undressed himself slowly, his eyes on her face before he stretched out next to her, pulling away what was left of her clothing and touching her in a way he'd never touched her before. His movements were as assured as ever, but firm to the point of brutality. He twisted her this way and that, turned her suddenly onto her back again and moved above her. Then as he held her gaze his expression hardened: he thrust forward, made love to her with a violence that made her cry out, first in surprise then in dizzying euphoria.

Afterwards, he caressed her limbs and made love to her tenderly, so that she half closed her eyes and saw him only as a blur – thick, dark curls and powerful muscle. Then he took her into his arms and they lay pressed up close against each other, listening to the sounds of the busy street below.

It had been dark for some hours by the time they bathed and went out for a late supper. From now on until Tuesday, they had nothing to do except make the most of Florence, and of the chance to be together.

After a light meal in a restaurant off the Piazza della Repubblica they walked along narrow, cobbled side streets to the banks of the Arno.

The Florentine night was close and humid, the heat of the day trapped by the surrounding Tuscan hills, yet Katherine and Gareth were loath to return to the cool of the hotel. Instead, they crossed the Ponte Vecchio, with its little shops huddled against the parapets, and paused to look at the jewellery that was being sold even at this late hour. Lamps strung from post to post lit up the open-fronted stalls, gleamed on the slow-moving waters of the Arno so that their reflections floated there, fragile as midnight flowers.

'Shall I buy you something?' Gareth said. 'A bit of nonsense from one of the stalls?'

'No,' she said. 'Don't waste your money – they're thieves, these stall-holders.'

'Tell me what you want,' he insisted, and pulled her towards a display of gold- and silver-work.

'All right, then – let's see, that bracelet's pretty—'

He bargained with the shopkeeper till it was reduced to half its original price, and when he finally fastened it round Katherine's wrist he looked as pleased as a schoolboy who'd won a prize.

Putting an arm across her shoulders, he steered a way through the crowded bridge and onto the Via Guicciardini. They walked as far as the Palazzo Pitti, then stopped at a café and sat down at one of the awning-covered tables; music was playing, and in the sense of contentment that sprang up between them, neither Katherine nor Gareth felt the slightest need to talk.

They returned to the hotel in silence, and made love in silence, and the mood was only broken next morning with the noise from the bustling streets.

At nine o'clock they set off to hire a car, and Gareth drove them out to the Piazza Michelangelo from where they could look down on the city with its network of twisting streets, and see the Duomo of Brunelleschi as it glittered in the sunlight. Then they drove to the heights of Fiesole for lunch, and there was a welcome breeze up there, brushing through the olive groves and cooling the midday sun.

'I shan't be a moment,' Gareth said, when a carafe of wine had been placed on the table and they were waiting for the first course to be served. 'I have to make a phone call.'

'Now? Who to?'

'As it happens,' he said, 'to the hotel. I'm expecting a telegram.'

'What about?'

'Do you always question your men so closely?' he said. 'Do you ask for a detailed account of every move they make?'

'I'm sorry,' she replied. 'I didn't mean to give the impression that I was interrogating you. But just for the record, don't refer to "my men" again, it's insulting.'

He grinned and ruffled her hair; she slapped his hand away and he laughed, turned on his heel and disappeared into the interior of the restaurant.

Sunday was a day of half-deserted streets, empty pavements where market stalls had stood only hours previously and shuttered windows of shops. Peal after peal of bells rang out across the city, and on impulse Gareth suggested they go to the Church of Santa Croce.

As they approached the steps leading up to the basilica, Katherine was chatting about visiting the Boboli Gardens that afternoon, then perhaps going either to Sienna or to the coast for the last day of their holiday. Gareth was quiet, and she too fell silent as they walked down the nave towards the chapel where mass was being said. They looked at Ghiberti's stained-glass windows, at the sculptings and carved tombs, and at the scaffolding standing like some skeleton in the shadow of an archway: traces of the 1966 flood disaster would remain for generations, and repair work would take years to complete. The delicate task of restoration was being carried out continuously, and as a gentle reminder to tourists there was a plaque on one wall which read: 'ON NOVEMBER 4, 1966, THE WATERS OF THE ARNO REACHED THIS HEIGHT.'

Katherine shivered and turned towards Gareth, but the pool of light in which she was standing dazzled her: it was red and yellow and blue from a stained-glass window, and for a second she felt alone. She could hear the choir in the chapel intoning words she could not understand, and a sense of foreboding swept over her – like the unease she had felt in a board meeting weeks before, but much stronger.

'Gareth?' The word echoed, reverberated from the stone and marble and the crumbling frescoes all around.

'I'm here,' he said, and emerged from the dimness of the baptistry to take hold of her hand.

But the sensation lasted all day, even in Sienna where they sat side by side on the terrace of a café, watching the sun die in the Tuscan hills, and watching the clusters of trees, still and hushed in the breathless air. One of them was laden with white flowers, and it stood out high above the rest, framed like a wedge of delicate ivory against the darkening sky.

'How was Italy?'

'Interesting,' she said. Then hesitated before going on: 'Edward – I must talk to you.'

'That sounds sinister. There's nothing wrong, is there?'

'I'll tell you when we meet.'

When she told him, his eyes narrowed perceptibly and he immediately accused her of lying.

'You said you were only taking Richard Stempel with you.'

'I didn't want to distress you – I hadn't meant to get involved with Gareth again. I thought . . .'

'I don't believe you thought at all,' he said. 'I believe you simply did what you felt like doing on the spur of the moment, and without any thought for the consequences or the pain you might cause others.'

'That's not true, Edward. I'd thought about it for weeks – and it was only because of you that I didn't go to bed with him before.'

'That's another lie,' he retorted, and stood stock-still in front of the cold, empty fireplace of her sitting room. 'You didn't go to bed with him before because you were afraid – afraid of what he would do to you and afraid that your life would be disturbed. If I entered your thoughts at all, it was only because I'm part of the pattern of your life at the moment.'

'Edward, I loved you.' She too stood up but the distance between might have been carpeted with barbed wire. 'And I still love you in a way . . .'

'How dare you say that to me,' and the chill in his voice was ominous. 'When you've been to bed with that man.'

'I love you differently,' she said, 'and you love me in the same way. That's the truth, and if it was you leaving me instead of the other way around, you'd be saying the same thing. We're fond of each other, good friends.'

His grey eyes softened, and misted over.

'I've been a good friend to you,' he said.

A lesser man would have said: 'I've helped you', but Edward didn't.

'But you've been a good friend to me, too,' he added, very quietly. 'I wouldn't have missed it for the world.'

'Nor would I,' she said, and felt a constriction in her throat as the tears choked her.

'Do you remember the very beginning?' he said. 'When you first came to Tylowe – and I invited you to a dinner party that Friday night?'

'Very clearly.'

He smiled, pulled out a handkerchief and blew his nose.

'I hadn't planned that dinner party – let alone invited Henry Bentinck; I had to ring him the next morning and persuade him to come.'

A chill swept over her.

'Oh Edward—'

'I didn't mind that you wanted to use me – I just wanted to win you. I know that you've loved me since then.'

'So much . . .' She put a hand to her mouth, rummaged clumsily in her handbag for a tissue. 'You must believe that. Please – otherwise it would take away everything.'

'I do believe it.'

'Nothing must destroy what we've shared.'

'Sh,' he said. 'Nothing can . . . Keep the jewels I gave you.'

'No – but thank you. I'll return them.'

'I'd like you to keep them.'

She shook her head.

He was silent for a moment, then suddenly, and very calmly, he said: 'You're stupid in a way, aren't you?'

She looked up at him sharply.

'You expect me – good old Edward – to accept this and do nothing about it. What are you waiting for? For me to wish you luck and smile on you benignly? Behave terribly properly as usual, walk out of the door and not bother you again? After all that's passed between us? Well I'll tell you something that will surprise you – I should like to kill this man, and I should like to see you begging me to take you back. And then I should walk out of the door and not bother you again.'

'Don't talk like that, Edward, please, it isn't . . .' she paused.

'It isn't what?' he said, and took a step towards her.

Instinctively she stepped back. His eyes had hardened again; they were no longer faded and grey, but flashing like steel. 'It isn't like me, was that what you were about to say?'

'It *isn't* like you. There's no reason for us to part on these terms.'

'No reason? You imagine yourself in love with this Gareth Williams and you have the effrontery to tell me so, then you say there's no reason to part on bad terms.'

'I am in love with him,' she glared back at Edward, half defensive and half embarrassed.

'You foolish woman.' His voice was thick with contempt. 'I'll tell you a few home truths about yourself, shall I?'

'No, thank you – I don't want to hear.'

'Oh, but you will hear,' and he came even closer to her, as though in proximity he could somehow mesmerize her. But there was no need, because she stood her ground and met his gaze, listening to his words like a challenge.

'You're a selfish, insecure, frightened woman who's as near as dammit past childbearing age and full of nothing but regrets.'

'That is quite untrue!' As soon as she'd spoken her mouth set into a hard, thin line and her eyes were cold with resentment.

'You pretend not to be bothered about children – and what else can you say since it's too late now, anyway? You regret your own childhood and the loyalty you wasted on your father, you regret most of your twenties and the best part of your thirties when you did nothing – it seems to me – except drive yourself like some workhorse in the most dismal of surroundings. Stop to smell the roses on the way? You'd have trampled a rose underfoot if it dared to grow between you and your goal. And what was this all-important goal? Nothing but some sterile image of security that you, wrongly, imagined came out of success.'

'You're so mistaken! Of course I have a few regrets, but how can *you* understand how I had to work? You who were born with so many advantages – you who have never had to worry where the next penny was coming from, you who . . .'

'And,' he cut across her, 'you can think of nothing but money – how you, independent, wonderful you can make it and prove how singularly—' he paused, and smiled in such a way that she felt the blood drain from her cheeks – 'boring you are. Asexual and totally unfeminine. When I think about it more carefully, I'm glad you're going. And you can take with you your last regret – the fact that you're growing older. Because that's the real reason you've rushed headlong into this stupid affair, isn't it?'

'No.'

She said that one word so firmly, so completely without emotion that for a second he wavered.

'But that, Katherine, is what Gareth Williams believes. D'you think I haven't made my inquiries about this man? I've heard more than enough about his unscrupulous character. Your earlier attitude towards him was the right one.'

'You know nothing about Gareth Williams!'

'My dear Katherine, I can tell you now that he's making the most of your fears and insecurities. You've walked straight into his trap – walked in with open arms, apparently,' he pointed out with stinging sarcasm, 'but eyes tight shut. Whereas he's walked in with his eyes wide open. He's as hard as you normally are, so maybe you are well matched, in a way. He's using you . . . misguided, besotted Katherine Hanson.'

She looked down at the floor, struggled to curb her anger.

'Just get out of here, will you, Edward?' And when he didn't move but she saw the dejection on his face, she added: 'You envious, spiteful man. You're not in love with me and you haven't been for a long time, you just can't bear the thought of me and Gareth Williams together. You and I, Edward, we've been *friends* – other things, too, but that most of all. However, I appear to have overestimated the finer sides of your character. I'm sorry we can't remain friends, very sad you couldn't control your vindictiveness and had to say all these cruel and terrible things. But I understand, and still have a great deal of love for you. At least I will have if I can dismiss what you've said.'

His face crumpled; he turned aside, put one hand on the mantelpiece and the other to his eyes.

'God Almighty,' he muttered.

'Perhaps in a few months,' she said, 'when we both start to feel detached about it all—'

'Yes of course. Dear God—' he shook his head. 'Besides, you might need me.'

'Perhaps.'

'I'm sorry but—' he shook his head more slowly – 'I am afraid he'll hurt you.'

Katherine went over to him, put a hand on his shoulder and he took it almost gingerly in his.

'We mustn't see each other again yet,' he said. 'Next year, maybe.'

'Yes.'

He loosed her hand, and as he moved towards the door his shoulders sagged and he looked every one of his fifty-two years.

'I'm quite convinced,' he paused and glanced back at her, stared at her as if for the very last time, 'that Gareth Williams will try to manipulate you. Watch out for yourself.'

And when he'd gone she broke down, cried as though her heart would break, trying to sort out truth from untruth in his words; but the sharpest pain of all came from his final warning – 'Watch out for yourself.'

They were perfectly happy: there seemed to be no flaw in

their lives, and the nearest they ever came to an argument was about where they should live.

Katherine wanted them to live together, but Gareth refused on the grounds that it would mean moving into her house, which he would not do.

'I'll buy a house,' he said, 'then you can sell yours and move in with me.'

'That's ridiculous,' she said. 'If your flat's too small for us both, all you have to do is give it up and move in with me.'

'No,' he insisted. 'I'll buy a house which will be ours – not a place where you've entertained Edward and God knows how many other men.'

'That's the second time you've made that kind of remark, and I've warned you before that I don't like it.'

'How do you mean, "warned" me? You get out of hand at times with this dictatorial bit – you're not at Borjex now, you're with me.'

'What's the matter with you?' she laughed. 'I believe you're jealous – jealous of my job, and jealous of any other man I might have been to bed with.'

'Not jealous,' he replied. 'Just starting as I mean to go on.'

'Oh Gareth – we're in the 1980s. This attitude is crazy, and I wouldn't have expected it from you.'

'1980s or 1890s, fundamentals don't change. And that's the end of the discussion.'

'It most certainly is not. Why don't you move in here temporarily? We can sell it and buy something together if this house displeases you so much.'

'I'm already looking round for a house for us, and until then I'm keeping my own flat.'

'Please yourself,' she said. 'You always seem to anyway.'

He looked as though he was about to add some cutting rejoinder, then changed his mind.

Katherine decided not to raise the subject again, and in any case they were too busy to bother about disagreements: they spent as much time together as they possibly could, occasionally with friends of Katherine – hers rather than Edward's – occasionally with the few friends Gareth had in England, but mostly alone. They still saw each other at work, but less than before: now the statel scheme was progressing, Katherine had to turn her attention to other matters, and Gareth also had to give time to his own business. He was away from Borjex for up to two or three days a week, and apart from keeping an eye on the business of his own company, he took Marius away on a two-week fishing holiday before the boy had to return to school for the autumn term.

Katherine had met Marius several times during August and liked him. He had spent a few weeks with his mother in Florida when the summer vacation started, then came to London to spend ten days with his father before the two of them went on holiday. It was inevitable that Katherine should meet him since he was staying in Gareth's flat, yet she found herself to be nervous about the encounter.

She remembered him from the party at Tylowe, but wondered what he'd look like close to – whether his features really would resemble Gareth's, and if his personality would be like his father's or if it would have developed along lines that were alien to her.

Their first meeting was a success, as all the subsequent ones proved to be. He was strikingly like his father, even to the blueness of his eyes – and whether it was school or Gareth that had influenced him, his character, too, had that touch of Celtic charm that won people over.

He would get to his feet when a woman came into the room, open doors for her without making a fuss about it, and his handshake was friendly and strong.

Gareth told her he'd been difficult when he was younger, after he'd spent too much time in his mother's and stepfather's company, but the way he behaved now made that hard to believe. He was interested in all sorts of things, from sport to politics, and his enthusiasm as soon as he started to discuss a subject made him a delightful companion. Katherine noticed that Gareth would glance at him sometimes with pride, and she felt a twinge of envy, that he couldn't have been hers and Gareth's rather than Gareth's and someone else's. No matter how well she came to know Marius, she would always be the outsider, and when she saw him standing next to his father and mentioning a name or an event that meant nothing to her, she felt almost childishly hurt and excluded. She would long for this little family to be hers, and if it had been she could think of nothing else on earth that she would ask for.

Sometimes, when Marius didn't know he was being watched, a fleeting expression of sadness or loneliness would cross his face. Gareth might have been able to come to terms with the fraught relationship that had produced his son, but the boy was still living with the consequences. Marius was the one who would have suffered most because of his parents' unhappiness – handsome, sensitive Marius who'd been brought up amongst so much discord. Katherine knew exactly what he had been through and what he was still going through, and her heart ached for him – just as it had ached for her brother Daniel all those years ago. It was worse for a boy than it was for a girl, because boys were expected to control their emotions more closely, and she wished she could have more time with him to try and help him.

As it was, they struck up a brief but happy friendship, and he loved nothing better than hearing her stories about what life was like in the countryside of England, and what it was like to go down pits and visit mining sites, and what machinery they used and why. She promised him that on his next half-term holiday she would take him round a site, and Gareth promised him that the three of them would go for a weekend in the country, perhaps to Wales.

Katherine missed them both when they went to Scot-

land for their fortnight's fishing, but try as she would
there was no way of escaping her exacting work schedule.
Only days after their return, Marius had to get ready to
leave for school, and on the night before his departure
Gareth took him and Katherine out for a farewell dinner.
When they returned to the flat, a call came through for
Gareth from America; he switched it through to the
bedroom, leaving Katherine on her own with Marius for
nearly a quarter of an hour.

He was in the middle of telling her some involved story
about his school rugby team, when she noticed that his
voice shook. Glancing at him sharply, she saw that his
eyes were glistening with tears.

'Marius,' she said softly. 'What's the matter? Don't you
want to go back to school?'

'It's not that,' he said, and coughed and brushed at his
eyes, as if hoping to disguise his tears. 'I like school,
but . . .'

'But what? Tell me.'

'As soon as things are all right, something comes along
to spoil them.'

'You've enjoyed this holiday, haven't you?'

'The best ever,' he said, suddenly looking and sounding
terribly young. Katherine was reminded that he was still
little more than a child, despite the breadth of his
shoulders and his pleasant manners.

'There'll be lots more good holidays,' she answered
him.

'Will there? I don't know. Why is it that when you're
happy it all has to stop?'

'I don't know, Marius. But even if it does stop, it comes
back again later.'

'Always?'

'Not always, and not in exactly the same way, but you
can't be either happy or miserable all the time. It's like
swings and roundabouts – now you're up, now you're
down. But the older you get, the more your life settles

onto an even keel. You don't have depths of despair, and you don't have such heights of – of fun, either.'

'Is that true?' he asked suspiciously. 'Is that what you've found?'

She hesitated.

'No,' she said at last. 'I'm still going up and down.'

And then they both laughed, and he blinked away his tears.

'You're honest,' he said. 'You say things directly – that's much better than what most people tell you – any old lie just to fob you off. How can you find out anything that way?'

'I don't think you can. But I'm sure your father doesn't fob you off.'

'No,' he thought for a moment. 'No he doesn't. But my mother does . . . I hate being with her,' he added, with boyish vehemence.

'Marius!'

'But it's true. Did he tell you she'd married again? She's got other kids, she's not bothered about me. And she drinks too much as well. It's awful.'

'You're going to have to try and be really strong. It's not easy, I know. When we have more time, I'll tell you about my mother.'

There was the noise of a door opening in the hall.

'Don't tell my father I – that I was upset, will you?'

'He wouldn't be angry – he'd be sorry, he'd understand.'

'But don't tell him, anyway. He'll think I'm wet. Promise you won't tell him?'

'Promise.'

'Shall I write to you from school?'

'That would be lovely.'

'What's all this?'

Gareth was back in the room again, and had caught the end of the conversation.

'Katherine and I,' Marius told him, 'are going to write to each other.'

'Are you now?' Gareth said, and his eyes crinkled into a smile. 'Then I'm very pleased.'

The telephone call from Helen came as no surprise. She and Katherine had been close enough friends to keep in touch despite all that had happened, and Katherine had been considering contacting her soon to try and find out how Edward was.

Apparently he was very well, and when Katherine probed further she discovered that he already had another female 'friend', as Helen called it.

'Goodness,' Katherine said, 'that was quick work. He must have been seeing her while he was still seeing me.'

'Oh no, dear,' Helen sounded shocked. 'I'm sure he wouldn't do a thing like that.'

'It doesn't matter,' Katherine laughed. 'I'm equally bad, aren't I? Anyway, I'm relieved that he's happy.'

'Not all that happy, dear. He does miss you, and I really feel it would be better if you didn't see each other for a while.'

'We'd already decided that, Helen.'

'And quite right, too. Now, how is the wicked Mr Williams, and is he taking proper care of you? Oh and of course – how is your important job coming along? You were terribly engrossed with buying up country houses last time I saw you.'

'The wicked Mr Williams is well, and causing no problems. As for my important job – and by the way, when are you going to stop making fun of women who actually have a job to do? – my important job is also under control. I saw some perfect property when I was in Rome, so I'm pleased about that, too.'

'No ideal English property as yet?'

'Some near misses, but nothing that's ideal.'

'What a busy life you have. I wasn't making fun of it, you know, not entirely. In fact I'm rather envious – I get so bored nowadays, stuck here at Tylowe and hardly seeing a soul. Sometimes I devise plans for making things happen, I even do little things like rearranging furniture or having flower beds dug up – just so that I can feel the day's been eventful.'

'Helen, I'm sorry – I hadn't realized you were so bored.'

'I suppose my life's over now, or at least it will be if I carry on sitting in this castle, fiddling about with my hair like some wrinkled Lady of Shalott.'

'You mustn't say things like that, you're a most attractive woman. Listen, why don't you come up to town once in a while, have lunch with me or something?'

'I'd love to. Would you be free tomorrow?'

Helen could be amusing and Katherine enjoyed their get-togethers, but they soon became too frequent and Helen even started popping into the office. On one occasion Katherine was entertaining the statel team to an afterwork drink to celebrate the conclusion of the Rome deal: the intercom buzzed and Jennie's voice announced Helen's arrival.

Katherine was irritated, and determined to make it quite clear to Helen that this must not happen any more – it was to be prearranged meetings only. On the other hand, business was finished for the day and everyone was relaxing over a glass of champagne, so if Helen wanted company so badly she was welcome to join them.

The dowager made a grand late entrance, looking immaculately groomed and graciously dignified in a blue silk dress and coat, matching pill box hat and high-heeled shoes. Gareth raised his eyebrows at Katherine: she gave an indecipherable little shrug then smiled.

'Come on in, Helen, and have some champagne . . . I think you already know a few of the people here, but you haven't met Gareth Williams.'

After introducing them, Katherine said: 'Let's see now, who else is there that you might like to meet . . .'

'Oh look,' Helen said, glancing across the room. 'There's dear Mr Ferrett, mouldering away in a corner.'

'*Skerrett*,' Katherine whispered in her ear.

'Scarcely his fault, though, is it?' Helen said. 'I must go and have a word with him, try and cheer him up. He *does* look miserable, doesn't he?'

After Helen had swept away in Skerrett's direction, Katherine turned back to Gareth.

'Honestly,' she said. 'Helen really is the limit. What's more, I distinctly remember telling her I was going to be busy this evening with the statel people.'

'She lives at Tylowe, doesn't she?'

'Yes, she's Edward's mother.'

'Oh I see . . . What's it like, this Tylowe place?'

'Fabulous,' Katherine said. 'But I'm afraid it's not on the market.'

Helen's visits and telephone calls came to a halt after that evening, chiefly – Katherine thought – because she had overstayed her welcome and felt embarrassed.

She'd monopolized Skerrett for over half an hour, and when finally she'd said goodbye, Katherine had asked her if she had the chauffeur waiting, and if not could she or Gareth give her a lift to the station.

'Bill has offered to give me a lift,' she said. 'So there's no need for you to bother at all.'

'Bill?' Katherine said incredulously. 'You mean Bill Skerrett?'

'Yes, dear,' she said. 'Why not?'

When, after a day or two, she heard nothing more from her, Katherine decided to leave her alone for a few weeks, then perhaps pick up the threads of the friendship on a different and less time-consuming basis. Besides, board meetings and union negotiations, to say nothing of design plans for the Rome *palazzo*, meant she had no time to think of anything but work.

She and Gareth were also going to be temporarily separated: he had to go to New York, then to Wales for a few days, and Katherine also had to go to New York but at a slightly later date than Gareth, so that she would be arriving just after he had left for Cardiff.

Her regular transatlantic journey for discussions with Irv and the New York board went badly: the flight was delayed, her luggage was lost and took two hours to find, and when she finally arrived at the apartment off Fifth Avenue, she discovered that some of her most important notes relating to the statel scheme were missing. She put a call through immediately to Richard in London, and after a brief search he called her back to say they'd turned up in her office. She was certain she'd given instructions for them to be included in her folio, and Richard was equally adamant that he'd enclosed everything she'd told him to enclose.

Annoyed, but unable to prove anything one way or the other about the incident, she set off to meet Irv.

While they dined in a quiet restaurant, sitting in a secluded alcove where they could not be overheard, he broke his golden rule of not discussing business during her first evening in New York.

The first thing he told her, directly but with a hint of concern in his voice, was that her relationship with Gareth was the subject of unpleasant gossip.

'What kind of unpleasant gossip?' She felt her colour rise, but more from surprise and anger than embarrassment.

'The chairman of Borjex's European operations – ' he shrugged – 'and a board member whose private business interests happen to be in property – you know the kind of thing people say. Especially since we're in the middle of the statel plans.'

'How ridiculous.'

'And they say you're spending less time than you should at Borjex – that you're obsessed by Gareth.'

'Lies!' she hissed. 'Evil minds who want to cast doubts on my reputation.'

'But these lies,' he prompted, 'they have a basis in fact, don't they?'

'We're not having some thoughtless, indiscreet affair. Gareth and I are—'

'Are what?'

'That's our business.'

'Not entirely. You can't hold a job like yours and give free rein to every whim that takes your fancy.'

'I am not giving free rein as you call it to some whim. Nor is Gareth.'

Irv looked unconvinced.

'When we first talked about Gareth joining you—' he began.

'No, Irv,' she said. 'When you insisted he join me.'

'OK, then, when ah insisted he join you, you said that your paths had already crossed and you considered him an unsuitable character, that you didn't even want him on the board. You said – if ah remember correctly – that he'd bring trouble.'

'I did, but I changed my mind.'

'Ah can expect some more, then, can ah? . . . What *did* happen between you and Gareth Williams? And what apart from sex is going on now?'

'Nothing! For goodness' sake! If you don't believe me, ask him. He's a friend of yours, isn't he?'

'Ah did ask him, only last week when he passed through New York.'

'And what did he say?'

Irv snorted.

'More or less what you've just said. Nothing.'

'I suppose he also asked who the person was who started this rumour?'

'But it's not just a rumour, is it?' he snapped.

'We're having an affair! So what?'

'Apparently,' Irv looked momentarily uncomfortable, 'you also had a holiday in Florence on company money.'

Katherine stared at him, then laughed.

'If you seriously think I'd risk my career for a thing like that, then I'll ask Gareth to show you the cleared cheques from his account. If he still has them, and I'm sure he must. But you didn't believe that allegation, did you, Irv?'

'No, only ah've never liked gossip as you well know, and ah don't see the point in giving people the chance to talk.'

'This is all crazy, especially the nonsense about Florence.'

'Maybe. Ah know you and ah know Gareth and ah like you both, but it's the gossip ah object to.'

'Will you tell me who started all this trouble?'

'You know better than to ask me a question like that. Ah wouldn't tell Gareth and ah won't tell you . . . One thing ah will tell you, though, is that the person who made that sickening phone call has sunk very low in my estimation.'

'It was Richard Stempel, wasn't it?'

'Because he was the one who was with you in Italy? Fast and easy, that's the way you make your mind up, isn't it? Poor old Richard.'

Then he signalled the waiter and the conversation was closed.

The meeting the following day revolved around property discussions: the New York board was pleased about the Rome deal, but concerned that the 'pilot run' in England was no further forward. All the houses that had originally been thought suitable had, on closer inspection, been shown to have some major flaw, and a fresh list of possibilities would now have to be drawn up. It was agreed that the European board should not be panicked into buying property that was less than ideal, but that Katherine should aim to have the 'pilot run' under way by next spring at the latest, that in the meantime she should continue the European searches and start the renovation work on the *palazzo*.

Since business had been dispatched more rapidly than anticipated, and since Katherine had no desire to see Irv socially at the moment, she cut short her visit and returned to London.

One of the first things she did on her return was to telephone Barbara Spencer to see if she would be free for lunch the next day. Barbara said Katherine had given her a marvellous excuse for cancelling an appointment with her son's headmaster, and the two women arranged to meet at one o'clock in the bar of the nearby Borgia Restaurant.

When Katherine arrived at five past one, Barbara was already perched on a stool, nibbling crisps and sipping fruit juice.

'What have you got to tell me?' she said, as Katherine joined her. 'Lots of exciting things about Gareth, or still better things about New York? I've got nothing whatsoever to tell you, except that my eldest son seems to be growing into some kind of delinquent – or maybe the school's too strict. The headmaster's dreadful, all mean and nasty.'

'Talking of mean and nasty things,' Katherine said, 'what's the telephone equivalent of a poison pen letter? Because somebody's made a very unpleasant accusation to Irv about me and Gareth.'

'Who?'

'I don't know, Irv won't say. I'll tell you about it later,' she added, with one eye on the barman, 'while we're eating.'

A waiter showed them to a table set against a wall; Barbara wanted as much room as possible so Katherine sat facing the other diners. She glanced at the menu but didn't feel at all hungry, and was half deciding on which omelette to opt for when Barbara said:

'What sort of accusation did this person make?'

'That Gareth and I have been enjoying ourselves on company money, that I'm obsessed with him and all sorts of other rubbish.'

'Oh some people are so sick. You wonder what on earth can be going on in their minds. What was Gareth's reaction?'

'I don't know yet. He's not due back till tomorrow, and I don't want to discuss it over the telephone.'

The waiter reappeared to take their order. Katherine asked for a plain omelette, but Barbara hesitated; while she talked to the waiter, Katherine let her gaze wander over the rest of the room. In a recess, seated alone at a table for two, was Jennie Corrin.

Katherine was surprised to see her there: the restaurant was expensive and rarely frequented by people of Jennie's age.

'What are you pulling faces for?' Barbara said.

'Jennie Corrin – Mrs Egerton's assistant – is over there.'

'Oh?' Barbara said without interest. 'I'm having lamb cutlets. When did you say Gareth was due back? . . . Oh I say, you've gone white.'

'Don't look round,' Katherine said. 'Whatever you do, do not look round.'

'Oh my God – whatever have you seen?'

'That girl, Jennie, she's one of my secretaries.'

'So?'

'She's with Gareth.'

The reason Katherine hadn't been able to catch Jennie's eye was that the girl had half turned her face in the direction of the cloakroom; suddenly, and evidently at the reappearance of some person, her expression had lit up. Then Gareth had stepped into full view, looking straight ahead of him and smiling at Jennie.

He joined her at the table, said something to her, and she bent her head towards him. In turn, he bent his head a little closer to hers. He looked happy. Her fresh young face looked ecstatic. Katherine felt her own head whirling.

Next, he took Jennie's hand in his, and squeezed it. She said something else and he ruffled her hair, just like he used to with Katherine.

They were so close their bodies were touching. Neither of them looked up; both were totally engrossed in each other, and in their intimate conversation.

'Do you want to go?' Barbara said, and her tone was a mixture of commiseration and concern.

'I want to kill him. I swear I want to kill him. If I move now I shall do.'

'Take a deep breath, then let's get out of here and we'll talk later . . . go on, I'll see to the bill and follow you out.'

Katherine got to her feet and stumbled from the restaurant, drunk with jealousy. She had to lean against the wall outside for support.

A moment or two later, Barbara joined her; she, too, looked grim.

'It *was* him, wasn't it?' Katherine asked.

'I'm afraid it was,' Barbara said.

NINE

In faith, I'll break thy little finger, Harry,
An if thou wilt not tell me all things true.

   – LADY PERCY (KATE); *Henry the Fourth*, Part One

'Good morning, Miss Hanson.' Mrs Egerton's face beamed cheerfully, like a well-polished apple. 'I'm sorry you were unwell yesterday – your friend Mrs Spencer said you were taken ill in the restaurant. Nothing serious, I hope? It's not like you to be ill.'

'Just some kind of bug, I think. I had to hurry straight home.'

'You still look very pale.'

'I didn't sleep too well.'

In fact she hadn't slept for more than an hour. At first she'd felt genuinely ill: everything had seemed far away, as though she was fainting or suffering from some minor brain disturbance. Later, when Barbara had gone, she'd raged and cursed and finally wept. At one point she'd yelled and smashed an ornament at the same time, so that the housekeeper, Mrs Thake, had rung through on the internal phone to see if it really was Katherine who was making the noise, rather than a burglar.

After that, Katherine went to bed, then got up again and paced the house, then cried until she fell into an exhausted sleep just before dawn.

It had taken two hours of eye pads and careful applications of make-up before she was presentable for work.

Before she'd left the house she'd felt indescribably hurt and defeated; she kept wanting to cry again, or – worse still – beg him to love her. Now, however, she was ice-cold.

'Where's Jennie?' she asked Mrs Egerton pleasantly.

'She's not in yet. Strange, because she's usually so punctual. I don't know what can have happened to her.'

'Perhaps we're all a little out of sorts this morning.'

Mrs Egerton laughed politely, and began typing.

The door opened, and Jennie breezed in. She did look pale, as though she, too, hadn't slept much, and there were dark lines beneath her eyes. But her face was alight with happiness.

'Morning, everybody,' she chirruped.

'Could I have a word with you, Jennie?' Katherine said. 'In my office. . . . And would you mind closing the doors behind you.'

Five minutes later the doors burst open again; Jennie ran out, snatched up her handbag and fled into the corridor. Mrs Egerton stopped typing, and Richard and Hugo Palfreyman chose that precise moment to saunter into the office.

'What on earth's going on?' Hugo said. 'Jennie nearly ran smack into me just now.'

'I've told her she can expect to be moved in the near future, possibly back to the reception area.'

Richard looked appalled; Hugo looked surprised.

'What for?' he said.

'Gross negligence, Hugo. She's made one terrible mistake after another. She's nothing but a liability in a chairman's office.'

'I've always found her most efficient,' Mrs Egerton cut in. 'Pleasant and helpful and—'

'Well I haven't.'

'But you never said anything to me . . .'

'I'm saying it now,' Katherine rejoined. 'Am I right, Richard, in saying that she was the one who helped you get together the folio for my last trip to New York?'

'Ye-es,' he said hesitantly. 'But I was the one who . . .'

'Documents were missing, important and highly confidential documents relating to the statels. Those documents did finally come to light, but I – for reasons I do not wish to divulge to you at this moment – am most uneasy about who saw them in the meantime. I'm not blaming you, Richard, so don't start to splutter like that, but the matter is serious. Then there've been one or two other incidents, and last night I found these—' she waved a handful of papers at them – 'in my home. They are my notes for a union negotiation, and should have been filed here under lock and key, not been stuffed into my briefcase. No, you can't see them, Hugo, nor do you have any reason to. Why were they stuffed hurriedly into my briefcase? Vital and confidential notes like these. It's nothing to do with you, is it, Mrs Egerton?'

'No!' Mrs Egerton expostulated. 'It most certainly is not.'

'Quite. Anyway, I think you're starting to get the picture. I could outline several other equally worrying occurrences, but I don't think that would serve any useful purpose. Richard, ring personnel, will you? Tell them to get Jennie's papers together and have a look at their own files – see who could be promoted so that Jennie can be moved back to the kind of job she's suited for. And tell them to get a temporary for Mrs Egerton.'

Katherine then walked slowly back to her office, pausing to add to Mrs Egerton: 'And get Mr Williams on the phone, would you?'

'Mr Williams is in Cardiff.'

'I believe he has already returned. If he's not in the building, try his home number.'

'Miss Hanson, he is definitely in Cardiff. He paid us a fleeting visit yesterday, but went back to Wales this morning.'

'Tell his secretary to let you know the minute he returns.'

Then she closed the double doors of her office, and

went and stood by the window; she stared out at Hyde Park for a long time.

But it wasn't the trees or the grass or the tourists that she saw; she was merely horrified by her own stupidity, picking over the thoughts that had plagued her last night, furious that she'd needed such a pathetic reminder of Gareth's character to bring her to her senses: he was as unscrupulous as he was charming.

How worried he'd looked during those last weeks in Abertawe. And small wonder, she reflected. He seemed to be working almost continuously; he was away in London for the greater part of every week, and when he did come back to the cottage he would seem distracted and uneasy. There were dark lines around his eyes and Katherine became concerned about him. He had enough stamina to do two jobs, let alone one, and she began to think there was some serious problem that he was keeping from her. He denied it, but he would return from his days in London looking more and more strained, and once rang her with some patently untrue story and she saw no more of him for two whole weeks.

She was frantic. She could understand nothing of his behaviour, and it was the first time for months that she'd had cause to doubt him. He'd spun her fanciful yarns at the very beginning, but those had been so exaggerated that a child could have seen through them. They weren't serious lies – but this was different. Besides, they were in love now, and living just like any other couple: they shared the same house and the same bed, and a thousand little things made up everyday life. And it was he who had insisted that they always be entirely honest with each other. She had been, and she would have staked her life on the fact that he had, too. Until these last weeks.

All the old terrors of insecurity flooded back, but it was the busiest time of the year for her at the university – examination time and her thesis was due to be presented

– so she flung herself into her work and concentrated on the future.

Gareth wanted to start his own business and they'd planned, long ago, to live together in London as soon as Katherine's commitments at the university were finished, then maybe move to the States within the following year or two. It was a subject rarely discussed now but still quite definite in Katherine's mind. She was determined to work in industry, and Gareth had finally said how delighted he was that she was leaving academic life, and that they'd make a great team together, one way or another.

Her competence as a theoretical engineer was not a problem, but she'd recently read up all she could on industrial applications and wider management issues until she'd acquired a fair smattering of knowledge. One of the companies she'd most wanted to join had been impressed by her apparent understanding of business as much as by her qualifications; they'd offered her a job – not very well paid, but it was a start – and the future looked as rosy as it possibly could: she was going to stay in Wales until August, then she and Gareth would go to Greece together for a holiday before moving to the new flat, the flat he was in the process of looking for.

Then it happened again. He rang her to say he would not be coming home that Thursday as planned. There were too many problems to sort out in London; he'd be back next Thursday, if he could. And no, he hadn't had time to do anything more about looking for a flat.

He'd sounded unhappy, tense, and vaguely irritated. Her hands were shaking as she put down the receiver, and the premonition of loneliness was so strong that she wept.

Then she started behaving irrationally. She got some investigation agency to follow him around London, but they couldn't have been much good or else there was little to see at that time, because after a week they'd come up with no more than she knew already about his life. By then she'd spent more than half her meagre savings – but of course it would be all right when she started work in London because there would be Gareth, and if he had to support her for a few weeks it wouldn't matter. Surely not. Next she panicked, thought she was definitely going to lose him and that she bored him, was unattractive and not sophisticated enough.

She bought new make-up and perfume, had her hair re-styled and purchased the most stunning clothes she could find in Abertawe.

It was a childish gesture, she realized afterwards, but at the time it had seemed the only thing to do. At least her confidence was running high: she'd never worn such expensive outfits before, and felt sophisticated and ready to fight to keep him. Whatever the matter was they would talk about it together. They knew each other only too well by now, so whatever was wrong could be overcome. Nothing, she thought naïvely, could be more important than the fact that they loved each other, hence nothing could destroy them.

But something did, and she came face to face with the unkind reality on a gentle summer's evening, when the great arc of Abertawe Bay was at its most lovely, and a salt breeze rolled in from the sea – stirred the grass on the lawn of Gwilym Cottage.

Katherine walked down the path, pushed open the door, then paused on the threshold: she saw his briefcase lying open on the table, saw the two figures seated there with an untidy pile of papers between them, their dark heads bent so close together that their hair seemed intertwined.

The woman saw her first, and got to her feet. Then Gareth looked up – how strained his face was – and he too rose.

'Hello,' it was the woman who spoke. She looked poised and confident, hypnotic in her beauty. She was tall –

almost the same height as Gareth – yet there was a delicacy in her fine bones that gave the impression of extreme vulnerability. And there was an air of true sophistication about her: as she made the slightest of movements, glancing in Gareth's direction, Katherine's gaze took in the tasteful simplicity of her dress, and her own new clothes seemed garish – ill-fitting and cheap.

Katherine was mesmerized by the entire scene, as though it were of paramount importance; she moved further into the room, but was suddenly self-conscious and unsure of herself.

'Katherine . . .' Gareth stepped forward, put a hand on her shoulder and for an instant she remembered the day they'd met, on the beach on a sunshiny day like today. 'This is Miranda—'

Then he hesitated.

'Well, go on,' the woman urged him, and Katherine detested her. There was a haughtiness in her manner, as though the cottage were hers, and her tone was insulting – it smacked of the worst kind of upper-class accent, drawling and affected. 'Let's have complete introductions, shall we?'

But how pretty she was with her fragile charm! How her dark eyes shone as she looked at Gareth!

'Surely you know I'm Katherine Hanson? After all, you are in my home.'

'Indeed I know you're Katherine Hanson. And my surname is Williams. An unremarkable name in Wales but remarkable as far as we three are concerned . . . I'm his wife,' she added.

Katherine looked at Gareth. His face was drawn and his expression hard.

'I want to talk to you on your own, Katherine,' he said, but nobody moved.

A clock was ticking away the moments – Katherine could hear it like a racing heartbeat. It was their clock, the old-fashioned time-piece they'd bought at Christmas, and it was their time that it was marking; she could feel it slipping away from her, like cherished silk between numb fingers, and panic swept her features.

Gareth saw it; his eyes flickered with compassion, and – for the first time since she'd known him – with absolute uncertainty.

'Didn't you know he had a wife?'

'Look, Miranda.' Katherine was prepared for battle; her words were brisk and she forced a smile to her lips. 'I knew full well he had a wife but we've scarcely discussed you and that's why I'm so surprised to see you here now.'

'Really? Despite the fact that this is where my husband lives. Sometimes. When he's working in Wales . . . Because he is my husband – not *ex*-husband, if that's what he's told you.'

'But it's not quite as simple as that, is it, Miranda? And it's not strictly true, either.' Gareth's voice was cutting.

'It bloody well is strictly true. In what way isn't it true? In your Celtic imagination? Or when you feel you can make it without my family's influence? Gareth and I, Katherine, are man and wife and not even *he* can deny that. Now shall we sit down and discuss the rest of his deceptions?'

There was a polite rap at the door.

'Come in,' Katherine called.

'Feeling better?' Hugo asked, as he crossed the room and sat down in the chair facing her desk. Her eyes were on a typewritten sheet; its edges were crumpled as though she had been creasing and uncreasing them for some time.

'Fine, thanks. I had a touch of some virus yesterday – it was probably one of those twenty-four-hour things.'

Hugo looked dubious.

'Is there something I can do for you?' she added.

'There's something I can do for you,' he replied.

'Oh? And what might that be?'

'Give you advice, which is what I'm paid to do. I was perturbed by the way you treated that girl this morning, and doubly perturbed because in all the time I've known you you've never behaved like that before. You've always been restrained even in the most testing circumstances, and you've always been professional. Your behaviour a few hours ago was not worthy of you.'

'I won't have that girl in my office.'

Hugo shook his head.

'I personally have heard nothing to Jennie's detriment. On the contrary people have always spoken well of her. I'd better tell Richard to have a word with her – I'd do it myself but it would look better coming from him – tell him to smooth things over with her, to say that you're not happy with her for various reasons, but that everybody regrets the error that was made today over those confidential papers. Because it was an error, to put it kindly, wasn't it?'

'It may not have been.'

He tutted, then said: 'The other advice I'm going to give you is not the kind I'm employed to give.'

'Then thank you, but please don't bother to give it at all.'

'I intend to advise you,' he continued regardless, 'because I told you when you were first made chairman that you had my support and loyalty. In your position—' he leaned forward to emphasize the importance of what he was saying – 'you cannot afford, as you well know, to behave in anything but the most rational manner. I have no wish to mention things that are personal to you – they're your own business – but if you're truly as distressed as I think you are at the moment, then you're going to have to do something about it.'

'Oh, Hugo—'

'Could it be that your judgement's at fault?'

'I don't think so. I'm pretty sure about what I know.'

'Katherine, do you also know that trouble is brewing

for you here? I'm not a leader and I've never joined in
the mêlée, but I see an awful lot from the sidelines.
There's gossip, and—' he shrugged – 'other things I can't
put my finger on as yet. Excuse my saying so, but you
have this strange combination in your character of
emotion and logic, and in your present circumstances it's
like an incendiary device. Do try and get back to
normality, or you won't be aware of what your enemies
are doing until it's too late.'

'Thank you,' she said. 'I will take your advice if I
possibly can. I only wish I could be certain who those
enemies are – I could hazard a few guesses, but that's all.'

'If I knew who they were I'd tell you, but I'm not
certain either.'

Jo Cleary was angry. He'd wanted to sit on the fence over
the strike decision, certainly he'd wanted a free hand in
manipulating his own union, but trouble was escalating
and slipping out of control.

Whether the information about Katherine's financial
plans was true or false, he had had no intention of letting
it go beyond himself. Not merely because of the risk of
slandering her, but because it was more useful to him that
way.

But somebody, some bloody trouble-making bastard,
had spread the word amongst the rank and file of his
union.

It would have been easily done: a word or two here and
there amongst his members and a rumour could spread
like wildfire. The tale had been both oversimplified and
distorted in the telling, and one of his members – a
belligerent Scotsman – had said to him only today:
'What's all this about Borjex overspending? Is it true
they're not going to be able to meet our claim this year?
I hear tell they're in trouble.'

Jo had argued that that was not the case, that Borjex
was reinvesting fairly heavily, but that in no way affected

any wage claim. He had assured the man – untruthfully – that he knew exactly what the board was up to, and that there was no need for union members to meddle in things best left to their representatives.

The damage was done, however, and there was both resentment and concern, particularly amongst the men who had the dangerous and dirty jobs on the mining sites.

As far as Jo knew, only Skerrett or Rykwert could be responsible for stirring up his members. In which case that sickening pair were more determined than he'd given them credit for, and they'd also sunk pretty low. If it was them, he was bloody well going to make them pay, sooner or later. The other possibility, just as worrying to Jo, was that the larger union of Associated Mining and Technical Workers was responsible: for years now they'd been wanting to swallow up his little union, MATEX, and if they did Jo would become just another member of the union executive, rather than top dog. With his change of status would go influence, which he enjoyed, and a whole load of perquisites which he enjoyed still more . . . Volvo car – a new one supplied every two years – expenses, and endless entertainment in the pursuit of duty.

Jo coughed, lit a cigarette, and trudged across the spewed-up earth of the Tylowe opencast site. When he got to his favourite hillock, from where he could see as much as possible without having to move, he spat.

The next few weeks would be like walking on egg shells. If he went along with Skerrett and Rykwert, and manoeuvred Katherine out, it would be at the cost of a strike. However, he would then have Borjex's head of industrial relations and its company secretary eating out of his hand: he would have far too much on them for them ever to risk crossing him. He would never be able to manipulate Katherine in that way, and her replacement would inherit two treacherous senior men, and be totally unaware of the fact. It would be a good situation for Jo.

At one time he would have been glad to stick by

Katherine, because he'd always been able to rely on her fair dealings, and that knowledge was worth any number of corrupt board members. Now, unfortunately, he just couldn't be sure about her.

He didn't want a strike: too many people could get hurt, and if it went badly, MATEX members would almost certainly opt for being amalgamated to a stronger union. But if he didn't go for a huge claim and its consequent rejection followed by a strike, then his members might still desert MATEX – because some bloody idiot had had the bloody nerve to interfere with his men and spread the bloody rumours.

Whichever way he looked at it, a strike now seemed inevitable. Somebody's head would have to roll: he only hoped it wouldn't be his, and if Katherine wasn't crossing him, he hoped she'd be able to save hers, too.

His cigarette spluttered, and he glanced up at the sky.

Rain clouds were forming, and opening themselves above the porous Tylowe earth.

That was all he needed, a downpour on top of a strike.

Skerrett thought he was in heaven.

He was sitting in Helen's enormous brocade armchair, listening to her playing some old romantic tune on the grand piano and watching her elegant head as it bowed to the music.

Lady Helen . . . Why, he thought, she was probably one of the most graceful women he had ever seen. And the word 'dowager' had such a ring to it, lent an air of dignity to her otherwise rather abrupt title. Of course he knew all about titles now, because the first time she'd invited him to Tylowe he'd taken the precaution of rushing off to Hatchard's and buying a reference book. He could now address anyone from a baronet's son's wife to a marquess's daughter, both face to face and in writing.

How different the dowager Lady Helen was to pushy, upstart women like Katherine Hanson, how unconcerned and refreshingly naïve about money and business matters. Or, if you looked at the thing from a different angle, how stupid.

The familiar spasm of pain tweaked at some place that he thought was his liver, then edged towards his heart. He'd give it another minute, then kill it with a tablet.

It was the unfairness of everything that caused it – unfairness on all sides. He seemed to have been beset by iniquity for years, and now he'd got the gross unjustness of Katherine Hanson to cope with as well as having all this rubbed in his face. This house with its paintings and antiques, its beautiful rooms and the way of life that went on inside them . . . Naturally Helen was unconcerned and charming. Who wouldn't be if they had all this, and hadn't had to work even a single day to get it?

Helen had asked him once if he knew the Renbeighs. Of course he didn't know the Marquis and Marchioness of Renbeigh! What sort of circles did she think he moved in? Didn't she realize that he'd spent thirty years in offices and factories, tramping around mining sites and talking to men like Jo Cleary, having so much per month stopped from his salary so that one day in the dismal future he could have a pension? Those were the kinds of things that made up his life. A pension! A pathetic bit of an income – and even that would be taxed – to mark the end of a long, wearing and often boring career. And that end had been ruined, thanks to Katherine Hanson. She was another one – selling her own business to Borjex at such a profit, coming onto the board and trying to push him around, being made chairman and, as if to demonstrate how brazen she could be, sleeping with Edward Arlingham and getting in with this crowd. But she'd gone too far, and was in for a rude awakening.

He'd rather have a woman like Helen any day: she at least had listened to all his advice and opinions, even sought his help over her hopelessly muddled financial affairs. Then laughed, as though the odd few thousand here and there didn't matter.

'William—' she stopped playing.

'Yes, Helen?' He half got to his feet, partly out of politeness and partly because he was still a little overawed by her. He hated himself for that, too.

'When is your friend Mr Rykwert coming to see us?' She stood up, and rested one arm on the grand piano.

Skerrett wasn't sure whether to sit down again, or rise completely to his feet. He thought the latter might be a bit much, but he couldn't bear to sit while she was standing. On the other hand, he could hardly remain in this awkward position, with his hands clutching the sides of his chair, his knees bent and his torso leaning forwards at an angle of about twenty degrees. A renewed onslaught of pain decided him: he sat down again.

'Tomorrow, at five o'clock. If that's all right with you.'

'Perfectly,' she smiled at him, an encouraging smile as though she liked him a lot. 'I was wondering if you'd like to stay and have lunch with me? Unless you feel you ought to get back to Borjex?'

'Oh, there's no reason for me to rush back. My deputy's there and he can keep an eye on things. I've got everything very well organized at that end.'

'Marvellous. There were one or two points I wanted to discuss with you before we meet Mr Rykwert. It's rather difficult for me, you see, to grasp all this – I don't really have the brain for it, never have had. And then it's upsetting, too, having to try and raise money like this. I'm not so young any more.'

'Nor are any of us.' He attempted a smile similar to hers, happy and reassuring. 'But don't worry, it'll all be as clear as day when I've explained it to you.'

Rykwert was happy too. He circled 17.00 hours in his diary, then stretched his thick-set frame and yawned.

He'd always been rather afraid of Jo Cleary, and he

was glad that Skerrett's new plans obviated the need for using the man. It was encouraging, too, that Jo would soon be coming to a sticky end and would be out of harm's reach.

The spreading of a few well-timed rumours, by both himself and Skerrett, had ensured that. Jo would be in dire trouble as union leader no matter which way he turned, because the strike was bound to go ahead now, much more quickly than Jo could ever have anticipated. And it was going to be a lovely strike: everybody knew it was Katherine who negotiated with Jo, rather than Skerrett, so the blame would fall fair and square on her mishandling of industrial problems. Add to that her current low standing in Irv's eyes, and she was in it up to her neck.

The *coup de grâce* would be delivered by Skerrett, through Katherine's precious statel scheme. That was a nice touch, he thought, like destroying someone with their own weapon.

Skerrett, poor sod, was entirely deluded in believing he would then be in the running for the deputy chairmanship under a new leader. No matter how dull-witted Katherine's replacement might be, Skerrett would not be promoted. It was true that Bill had been first rate in the past, and New York would certainly be pleased when they received the news about his brilliant and unexpected deal, but Bill Skerrett was finished. An ex-gratia payment plus a golden handshake was all he could expect.

He, Rykwert, was a different matter entirely. With his experience, sound track record, comparative youth and unflawed reputation, he would be in the running for a senior board appointment at least. Maybe even the chairmanship, if New York opted for a steady leadership after Katherine's rather flamboyant style.

If all else should fail, he would still have the pleasure of seeing Katherine flung out ignominiously. He disliked her almost as much as Skerrett did: she'd done nothing for him, not even moved him up that small but important step from company secretary to board member. He wished, when he thought about women like Katherine, that he had a wife. If he had, he'd go home and batter her, and pretend her face was the chairman's.

Katherine worked at a furious pace that afternoon, dispatching letter after letter and sending people scurrying from one end of the building to the other. It was the only way she knew to keep her thoughts from straying to Gareth.

A harassed lady from personnel came to discuss Jennie Corrin, and Katherine gave her a non-committal reference then passed the woman back to Richard. Thirty seconds later she decided to stir up some of the time-wasting administrators in personnel, and summoned a senior director to discuss next year's recruitment figures, as well as a graduated retirement policy. Then she sent for the home-based specialists of the statel team and asked to see their plans for the Rome *palazzo*. The architect was preparing some ingenious designs for the ballroom, which would ensure the retention of most of the original features while turning the body of the chamber into a conference theatre: there would be audio-visual aids concealed behind panelling, closed-circuit television cameras so that people in other rooms could switch in to whatever debate was in progress, and chairs you could sit in for hours at a time without discomfort. They would even recline, like aeroplane seats. Katherine vetoed the last suggestion.

At six-thirty, she tidied away the various papers that littered her desk, and went through to the outer office. Mrs Egerton had left an hour before, and the place was deserted, as was the rest of the penthouse suite and the corridor beyond. Pressing the button for the lift, she waited patiently till the doors glided open.

Gareth stepped out.

'Bastard,' she said as she brushed past him. 'Screw you and Jennie Corrin as well, and next time take her somewhere further afield than Borgia's.'

She was in the lift by this time, and jabbing repeatedly at the 'Down' button. The doors refused to close because Gareth had his foot in the way, and would have pushed inside except that she gave him a violent thump in the chest.

The unexpectedness of the blow, rather than its force, made him stagger, and as his shocked expression deepened he said, 'Katherine—' in a correspondingly shocked voice.

There was a thud on the doors as they closed and the lift hummed meekly downwards.

As Katherine crossed the foyer towards the revolving doors, she thought she heard a clatter of footsteps a floor or two above, descending the marble staircase. She quickened her pace, the commissionaire nodded a 'good-night' to her and opened an adjacent door, saving her the effort of having to rotate herself, then she was out in the street and flagging down – rather than hailing – a passing taxi.

It was forty minutes later, while she was throwing away the meal that the housekeeper had prepared for her, that she remembered where she'd been heading when she encountered Gareth: to the underground car park at Borjex. The chauffeur would still be waiting to drive her home, sitting there patiently, hour after hour all on his own, and her eyes filled with tears for the pity of it all. When she telephoned to let him know he would no longer be needed, she had to swallow to keep the distress from her voice. After putting down the receiver, she looked through the mail that had arrived in the second post. The first letter she opened was from Marius, and consisted mainly of news about his rugby team. It then went on to mention his father and to say he hoped all was still going well. Katherine presumed this meant he hoped all was still going well between his father and her. She resolved to scribble him a jolly but uninformative reply the next day. She chucked the rest of the post onto the hall table, without bothering to open it. Then she filled herself a brandy and – something she rarely did – opened the cigarette box, took out a filter-tipped cigarette, and lit it. Then she took the phone off the hook, settled herself in her favourite chair and wondered how, at her age and with her experience of life, she could have been so foolish.

Gareth was walking the Knightsbridge streets, insulted and furious about Katherine's behaviour this evening – and thinking about her reactions fifteen years ago, on the night they'd split up.

Trying to shake the memories from his mind, he walked on and on through the noise and bustle of Knightsbridge, into Beauchamp Place then out again – not even noticing where he was going till the lights of a pub attracted his attention. He went inside and tried to phone her, but the line was engaged. He had a drink then tried again, but it was still engaged, so he went back into the night to walk, calm down and collect his thoughts.

It was impossible. Katherine's display of temper at the office had brought it all back, his brain couldn't leave it alone – the fifteen-year-old memory, those last scenes in Abertawe that would be etched for ever and ever on his heart.

He remembered Miranda, arriving so unexpectedly at Gwilym Cottage; then Katherine had turned up, come face to face with her – and that gruelling night of truth had started. Politely, at first, as mistress and wife went into feminine battle.

Miranda's revelations were delivered skilfully, so as to have maximum impact on Katherine. First came the announcement that she and Gareth were married, which – legally – was true.

The shock and the pain on Katherine's face when she

heard the news! He was mortified, and her quick recovery humiliated him still further.

Having made her announcement Miranda sat down at the table, and Katherine – cunningly, in Gareth's opinion – joined her and suggested that he do the same.

He did, though all he really wanted to do was to separate these two women, because he knew that worse by far was to come.

It came just after he'd filled drinks for them all. Filled them drinks! He'd hoped that by being civilized he would somehow be able to control the situation, but he hadn't been prepared for Miranda's next thrust – it took him so completely by surprise that his reaction was unchecked fury.

She contrived, politely, to let Katherine know that her family were not only influential but also wealthy. And then she intimated that it was their money that was paying for Gwilym Cottage.

'You bitch!' he exclaimed. 'You lying bitch! And what's more your family's *influence* as you call it means fuck-all to me. The less I have to do with that crowd of wets and half-wits the better.'

But Miranda had scored a bigger triumph than she knew: she had inadvertently hit on one of Katherine's weakest points – this throwback from her childhood, her lifelong fear of insecurity.

There was a terrible pause, then Katherine said: 'You shouldn't speak to Miranda like that, Gareth. It would appear that you have much to thank her for.'

'You scheming bitch,' he rounded on Miranda. 'When did you think this one up?'

Then he looked at Katherine and saw utter scorn in her face.

'I've never really had a home, anyway,' she said. 'I've spent years benefiting from the kindness of others – as you know – so it doesn't surprise me to learn that I've been wrong in looking on this as my home. *Our* home, Gareth.'

But her face was flushed and her hands were trembling. She moved them swiftly from the table to let them rest on her lap.

'Don't believe her!' he said. 'That's sheer invention,' and things that Katherine had confided in him flitted across his mind – her father leaving, her Aunt Joan giving the family a home, the institution Katherine and her brother had lived in while their mother was having a cure for alcoholism. He'd had so much sympathy for her, and now Miranda had had to make such a poignant allegation.

Then he'd really rounded on this wife of his, called her things that made her mouth gape and her eyes fill with tears. His words hurt, all the more so because she knew the truth in them – and then as Katherine intervened Miranda got to her feet, put her hands to her ears as though she would hear no more.

'Bastard!' she shrieked. 'How dare you accuse me of such things? You who've caused this terrible situation.'

Silence fell, and he knew exactly what she was referring to, knew she'd caused it at least as much as he had, but that Katherine would never believe it. The moment had come at last, the crux of the whole problem, the moment he'd striven for weeks to avoid – searching for a way round it, trying to be fair to Miranda and fair to Katherine, too.

He'd caught sight of his own reflection sometimes during these past weeks, seen grim lines about his mouth, and knew now he was beyond trying to be clever, beyond trying in any way to ease this hopeless tangle of unhappiness. He felt that his despair must be written on his face for all to see.

Katherine saw it, anyway, for she suddenly rallied to his defence, speaking to Miranda in words that so rang with loyalty that his heart leaped – and he prayed in that instant, prayed that he might never lose her.

'But, Katherine,' Miranda said, 'I'm pregnant. Gareth and I are going to have a child.'

Fifteen years later Gareth could still hear those soft-spoken words, each one falling like an act of betrayal; and he remembered the fiery words that were spoken during the months that followed, culminating in the insult that astonished even the hospital nurse before she closed the door in Gareth's face.

'It'll be a girl!' Miranda found the strength to sob. 'And I hope I don't see one trace of you in her face! I hope she has brown eyes like mine and I shall call her Elizabeth after *my* mother!'

But it was a boy, with blue eyes just like his father's, and they called him Marius.

TEN

How bloodily the sun begins to peer
Above yon dusky hill! the day looks pale
At his distemperature.

– KING HENRY; *Henry the Fourth*, Part One

Katherine swirled her brandy round her glass and thought she ought to go to bed soon: she'd scarcely slept at all the night before and doubtless tomorrow would be a typically busy day. There was to be a confrontation with MATEX at nine-thirty, followed by the vetting of a list of English property in the afternoon. One of the houses on the list was a Georgian manor house in Buckinghamshire and sounded exactly what she'd been hoping for; she would look at it herself next week, and all being well the purchase could be completed and the architects moved in before Christmas. Then there were arrangements to be made for the forthcoming visit to France: there would only be Richard to accompany her this time.

That bastard hadn't even bothered to follow her home. If she'd needed proof of his guilt, this was it. Not that she would even bother to argue with him; she would merely treat him with disdain when they met in the board room tomorrow. Contempt and disdain – that was all he was worth, and whatever happened she must not lose her temper.

She'd lost her temper with him once before – though 'temper' was a tame word to describe the violence of their row fifteen years ago. That last night in Abertawe had been the scene of a lifetime – and it had done nothing except make matters worse.

How bitterly they'd clashed! It was Miranda who'd brought Katherine to explosion point, telling her not only that she was Gareth's wife – but that she was going to have his child.

Katherine could see her haughty face even now – hear the words that, at first, she'd been quite unable to believe . . . 'Gareth and I are going to have a child.'

And then she was back there again, back in her early twenties, in Gwilym Cottage with the youthful Gareth and the lovely Miranda.

'Gareth and I are going to have a child.'

A child! Gareth – Gareth and this woman with her night-dark eyes.

For a second it didn't even hurt, scarcely registered. Then she looked at Gareth. His face was drained of colour.

'Hypocrite,' she said softly. 'Liar.'

She got slowly to her feet, and he rose, too. They faced each other, not more than a foot apart. Instinctively, and without saying a further word, Miranda pushed back her chair and edged towards the door.

'Or are you going to deny it?'

'No,' he said quietly. 'It's the truth.'

It was then that Katherine went white; she felt her limbs tremble, heard the blood rush to her ears and it roared in her head like the sea.

'But it's not as simple as that,' he went on. 'You must let me talk to you.'

'It's simple enough,' she said, and hit him with all the strength she had.

He didn't move.

She flew at him, scarcely able to see him for pain, hurled herself against him as though to obliterate them both.

He caught her, pinning her arms tightly, and his eyes were blazing in his sheet-white face.

'I'll be back another time,' Katherine heard Miranda's voice from the doorway, caught a glimpse of her retreating figure and felt little more than jealousy and enmity.

It was nothing to what she felt for Gareth at that moment. Hatred and distress tore through her with a force that made her cry out; it was an inarticulate, animal sound, frightening in its intensity. Its only counterpart was the joy she had voiced, long ago, when he had first taken her in his arms and loved her.

He let her go; she clutched at the back of a chair.

'Will you listen to me?' he said.

But she heard the mechanism of the clock whirring, adjusting itself to strike the hour; and then the first chime rang out, clear and definite across the twilight of the room.

That night Gwilym Cottage had resounded with accusations and tears.

They argued for hours.

Round and round in circles they went, covering the same ground time after time. Sometimes Katherine cried and sometimes she raved, and Gareth shouted and cursed and they got nowhere.

Four or five times they called a truce; she would listen, talk calmly, ask him questions – then it would hurt all over again and she was shouting.

He *had* left Miranda, he protested. Not as long ago as he'd led Katherine to believe, but still long before last summer. They were getting a divorce but then she'd changed her mind – she was neurotic, spoiled, suddenly lonely and wanted him back. She'd contacted him in London and they'd met a few times to discuss the divorce.

When? Katherine wanted to know. When? And why didn't you tell me?

He'd hoped they could have sorted out the divorce first, then he would have said something. He went to bed with her again by mistake.

By *mistake*?

No no, not mistake. On impulse. She got pregnant by mistake.

Then Katherine was crying again, and he was swearing and running his hands through his hair.

It was only once or twice, he said. They'd gone out to dinner to – anyway, she got pregnant deliberately. Couldn't Katherine understand how he felt? He was at his wits' end. He didn't love Miranda – he had loved her once but that was a long time ago.

She's so affected, Katherine said, so false. How could you?

No she's not affected – he defended her – not always. She was nervous. She always gets like that when she's nervous.

Katherine screamed and swore and he poured himself the remains of the scotch.

At midnight he cooked them omelettes and they got drunk on cheap wine. By four in the morning they were sober again.

'Katherine,' he said, 'I did wrong not to be honest with you from the very beginning. I know that and I'm truly ashamed. You must believe me.'

'But you saw her again!' She was walking up and down, twisting a handkerchief between her fingers.

'She was my wife, there were things to sort out. It had to be done. I shouldn't have gone to bed with her again, but I did.'

'Oh Gareth—' suddenly exhausted, she flopped down in an armchair.

'But I didn't love her and had no intention of any kind of reconciliation. I thought we could go to bed as old friends, and it wouldn't matter. It's the only time I've been unfaithful to you. I was planning my life to include you.'

'And now? What are we going to do now?'

He sighed, threw his hands up in the air and paced the room.

'It's complicated,' he said at last.

'That's the understatement of the year, isn't it?'

'I have to make some arrangements for her. Help her or do something.'

'Have to go on seeing her, you mean?'

'Just see her from time to time. I must – she's pregnant—'

'And what's all this about her paying for Gwilym Cottage?'

'That's a *total* lie!' he yelled. 'It's the kind of thing Miranda *would* say to try to emasculate me in your eyes. Like this family influence thing.'

'I don't know. You and your big masculine bit – making such a thing out of not letting me pay any of the rent—'

'I did not make a thing out of it. I wanted to be the one to pay.'

'Why?'

'I like it that way. If you don't believe me—' he went across to the bureau and pulled open a drawer.

'I wouldn't lower myself to look at any of your personal correspondence. I'm not interested. If this cottage is yours and hers rather than yours and mine, then I hope you both enjoy it.'

'Katherine, this cottage and our lives have nothing whatsoever to do with Miranda.'

She laughed.

'Not much they haven't! . . . And you took her joy-riding in our jeep. I know you did because I noticed it was parked differently when I came home.'

'I did not take her joy-riding. She found out my address here and came to make a scene – I took her for a drive to try and calm her down. I don't want her; you shouldn't have screamed like that in front of her. What we needed to maintain was a united front—'

'A *united front*?'

'I'm going to make us some coffee.'

She heard him moving about the kitchen, and when he returned she noticed how exhausted and dreadful he looked.

'I love you,' he said. 'I loved her once. But life isn't just black and white, it's shades of grey. Pieces overlap here and there – emotions get muddled, interact. Try and understand.'

He held out his arms to her, but she covered her face with her hands and sat bunched up in the easy chair.

'You still feel something for her, don't you?'

'Katherine – I know what you're going through now, but I've been through hell these past weeks, too. Guilt about her, guilt about the baby, guilt about you . . . We've got to work out some sensible compromise.'

'Please never see her again.'

'It's not that simple! I wish to God I never had laid eyes on her again – all this misery, because of half a dozen brief encounters—'

'Don't see her again!'

'Be sensible, Katherine. Be adult.'

'Free and easy Gareth. I can't imagine you with a child. Christ – a child that you've fathered. And a woman who isn't me sharing your bed and so many other intimate things. All the little things. I just can't imagine you in this situation – not you of all people.'

'Well I am.'

'We can't talk any more tonight,' she said. 'I'm going to a hotel.'

'Don't be ridiculous. Not at this hour.'

'I need some sleep, and I'd rather sleep alone.'

'All right,' he sighed. 'If that's the way you want it. I'll take the jeep and drive along the peninsula; I'll get out and walk when I find a big enough beach.'

'It hurts,' she said quietly. 'It hurts so much.'

For a moment he didn't move, then he put his arms round her and cradled her to him.

'I wouldn't have hurt you for the world,' he said, and his voice was soft as a kiss.

Oh she loved him in that instant! That fraction of time when all the tenderness she'd ever craved was here in his arms.

'I'm sorry,' she muttered. 'I can't talk rationally.'

'Perhaps neither of us can. We'll try again tomorrow.'

'I didn't want anything from you, you know. I wasn't planning on possessing you for ever, I wasn't planning anything except being with you for a while longer. Marriage and formal ties had never crossed my mind. I thought I had no use for them, couldn't see the point in them. Truly. I just loved you.'

'Oh Kate, Kate.'

She swallowed hard, then said: 'If we'd agreed from the beginning that we'd both—' she shrugged – 'that we'd both have others, then it might have been different . . . But *this*—'

'I never wanted anybody but you.'

'Nor I.'

She closed her eyes to fight back the tears.

'Katherine—'

'I wish you'd leave me for a while.'

He sighed, a slow, worn-out sigh, then muttered, 'If that's what you really want,' and got to his feet. 'I'll be back later on this morning, before I go to work.'

'Oh yes,' she said. 'Work. I'd forgotten about that.'

She didn't even see him go. She heard the door close behind him, a sudden burst of power as he revved up the jeep, and then there was nothing but the crash of the waves and the ticking of the clock, and the gulls crying in that grey Celtic dawn:

LIAR HYPOCRITE BETRAYER

When he got back to Gwilym Cottage, he felt the first stirrings of optimism. He'd walked for miles through the dawn on the misty beach, and had made up his mind: he was ready to do anything – anything at all save leaving Miranda to fend entirely for herself – anything that was necessary to hold on to Katherine.

But as he pushed open the door of the cottage and called her name, he got the worst shock of all.

She was gone. And a glance in the tiny rooms told him that she'd gone for ever, for she'd taken everything she possessed.

He searched everywhere, even in the kitchen cupboards, to find some small thing that was personal to her. On the sitting room floor he discovered a screwed-up, sodden handkerchief, and in the bathroom an empty make-up bottle.

The clock was still there.

He took it down, wrapped it in a clean towel, and put it away.

Overhead the gulls were wheeling, screaming, and at last the sun was up.

He sat down in an easy chair, the one she'd sat in, covered his face with his hands, as she had done, and wept.

It seemed like only yesterday, those tears he'd shed. But it was rain that was coursing down his cheeks now – a dirty, London rain that streamed down his middle-aged wrinkles and steadied his temper, reminding him of the passing years.

He'd tried so hard to trace Katherine when she'd walked out on him in Abertawe, but without success. There'd been no reconciliation with Miranda at first, they'd just seen each other once a week and made plans for the baby's future. Her family would have welcomed him with open arms, because they too were tired of Miranda and longing to be rid of her. They were rich, it was true, but he'd never taken a penny from them – he'd valued his independence too highly.

He had loved Miranda once – long, long before he'd

first met Katherine: he'd been amused by the way she'd chased after him, thrilled by her dark good looks and frigid attitude that he could turn, with lazy movements of his hands and lips, to wild excitability. But their infatuation and their marriage had lasted only months; after that it had been marriage in name only, a separation and a divorce to be arranged – until she'd contacted him again, and by so doing put his relationship with Katherine at risk, and finally destroyed it and altered the course of his life.

He was certain she'd become pregnant deliberately, out of spite because he'd met and fallen in love with Kate, though of course she always denied it.

True to his word, he stood by Miranda throughout the time she was carrying Marius, went on seeing her regularly and tried never to reproach her – for he blamed himself at least as much as her.

For four or five months she delighted in the idea of becoming a mother, then – when it was too late – she changed her mind, swore she didn't want the baby after all. Her mother tried to cheer her up and help her, and Gareth did, too – right up until the moment that he realized she wasn't putting on an act. She did not want this child. It was going to ruin her life, she declared, ruin her looks and – of course – it hadn't won Gareth back, except as a shoulder to lean on.

In the eighth month of her pregnancy, she began making arrangements to have the baby adopted. Gareth stormed and raged at her, then quite suddenly, he checked himself.

That was when he redoubled his efforts to contact Katherine, because he knew that if he could only get hold of her and explain everything, calmly and rationally, she would understand and help him. He knew how sympathetic she could be in situations such as this – the unhappy start in life his child was going to have. He'd seen how kind she could be to students at the university, the ones

who were somehow in difficulty or struggling. She had a
weak spot, a sensitive streak that she would deny but
which was nevertheless there.

This baby had separated them, but in the end it would
bring them together – and then, perhaps, they would have
children of their own as well.

He and Katherine would start all over again! As soon
as this child was born they would bring it up together –
because they loved each other, and she would never reject
what was his.

All his letters were returned, unopened. All his telephone calls were cut off within seconds – even Miriam
and Aunt Joan refused to talk to him. How he cursed his
own foolishness for having allowed this terrible state of
affairs to come about, cursed Katherine for her stubbornness and grieved because it could all have been avoided.
But then Miranda was finalizing her plans and there was
only one decision left to be made.

So when Marius was born it was Gareth who took over,
determined to bring up his son despite all opposition. The
first two years of Marius's life were spent with his father
and a Spanish *au pair* – the nearest equivalent to a nanny
Gareth could afford at that time.

When he pressed once more for a divorce, he never
dreamed that Miranda would contest the custody of the
child. But she did, with tears and lamentations that finally
made his heart bleed, and their reconciliation began. It
started as just a week together with Marius. Then the
week rolled into two, and the weeks into months while
Miranda swore that she'd turned over a new leaf, that she
would always be a good wife and mother, and that it was
only depression and Gareth's lack of understanding that
had made her reject the child in the first place. She did
seem different, more considerate to him as well as to
Marius, and she tried so hard at first that he almost began
to love her again.

'We've got to work at this, Miranda,' he used to say. 'Ours isn't the kind of marriage that was made in heaven.'

'I know,' she would agree. 'But we are working at it, aren't we? And I am different now, and it's better for us to be together for Marius's sake, isn't it?'

'Yes, I think so. Provided we can be happy together as well.'

'But you do love me, don't you?'

'Of course, I've told you so.'

'You never—' she hesitated – 'you never tried to contact that woman, did you?'

'Which one?'

'Gareth—!'

'I've never seen her since that day in Wales.'

Yet once, in the middle of that ice-cold January when Marius was just a year old, he'd fancied he'd heard her voice. It was in an underground station, of all places, with the rush hour noise all around. Still, he'd paused, half turning his head before moving on again, reproaching himself for such useless sentimentality.

Miranda's good resolutions didn't last long, and within a year both she and Gareth were starting to have regrets about having patched up their relationship.

He was ruthlessly ambitious in those days – ambitious and hard-working to the exclusion of all else. Miranda resented the ever-diminishing amounts of time he spent at home, and then created scenes that made him wish he hadn't come back at all. There was the problem of keeping Marius well away during those arguments, and the difficulties of trying to run a business while tied to a wife who was a hindrance rather than an asset.

Gareth was in his early thirties by the time he and Miranda and their son made the move to America. It was good for Gareth's expanding business but no help at all to his disastrous marriage, and when he finally told Miranda that he would divorce her come what may, she was as relieved as he was. She was awarded custody of the boy, but quickly remarried and went to live in Florida which meant Gareth could go on seeing Marius at regular intervals.

As he grew up Marius chose to spend more and more time with his father, and one thing both Gareth and Miranda were agreed on was his education. If things had been different Gareth wouldn't have wanted him to go away to school, but in view of his unstable family background it had seemed the best idea.

He went to schools in the States at first and then, when he was old enough, to that English public school that was only a stone's throw from Tylowe Castle.

As Gareth made his way through the damp Knightsbridge streets, heading towards South Kensington, he was thinking about his son who would be fifteen next birthday, and Katherine who'd had no share in his upbringing.

He thought, too, that his choice of England for Marius's education had turned out to be a fortuitous one. It was going to be convenient in the future, much more so than America.

A taxi approached and he hailed it, gave the driver Katherine's address and felt his temper shorten.

Katherine Hanson and that stubborn expression of hers! Obviously she hadn't changed at all with the years! Katherine – the forty-year-old, mature Katherine – was still hot-headed and obstinate, still wouldn't trust him.

What a way for her to have behaved this evening, when he'd bumped into her at the office! Accusing him and swearing at him before he'd even had the chance to speak!

Her stubbornness had caused more than enough problems in the past, and he resolved that this time – whether she liked it or not – he was going to make her listen to him.

*

In her house in South Kensington, Katherine was peeling off her clothes and regretting that she'd ever – statels or no statels – agreed to let Gareth join the board. It hurt too much, that was all: it had opened scars that she thought had long since healed, and – worse still – was inflicting new ones. These would never heal. Nobody's skin was that tough.

Tying a long, white bathrobe round her, she went back to the sitting room and switched off all the lamps except the one by the record player. She was going to listen to an album before she went to bed, and perhaps by the time it had finished she would be tranquil enough to sleep.

She put on soothing music by Debussy then sat down in an easy chair. The melody was so subtle, so evocative, that she leaned back and closed her eyes. The tears stayed trapped behind the lids.

The doorbell rang, and she ignored it. But it went on ringing, loud and clear.

She got to her feet, padded through to the hall, then slipped on the safety chain before opening the door.

'Yes?' she said.

'Would you mind letting me in, Katherine?'

'Very much, Gareth. Unless you have anything to say that relates to work, please go away.'

'I need to talk to you, so let's both be sensible and talk inside instead of allowing me to shout from the street.'

'You can shout from the rooftops for all I care,' she said, and tried to slam the door shut but his foot was in the way again. 'Go away, Gareth.'

'I've had a phone call from Galeotti,' he said. 'That was what delayed me earlier. The Rome deal's off.'

'It can't be, it's already signed.'

'There's a clause on—'

Then she couldn't hear what he said; it came through the woodwork as a muffled noise with consonants and vowels all blurred together.

'Speak up, Gareth,' she said. 'Speak through the gap.'

'I said an option clause.'

'Whose option? Oh all right, just a minute,' and she slipped off the chain and opened the door.

He slammed it back against the wall, grabbed her by the shoulder, shook her as he dragged her into the sitting room.

His face was set and hard and they were fighting immediately, she clutching at his hair and shrieking and kicking while he made abortive attempts to pinion her arms. She pulled away, hit him across the cheek then side-stepped, while he lunged towards her, grabbed her round the waist and they toppled to the floor.

A table overturned, ornaments crashed against the wall and tumbled to the carpet: Debussy's sweet notes played on regardless.

He was on top of her, fastening her arms across her chest as she swore at him; he held her with one hand, let go with the other and slapped her – slapped her quite hard though she scarcely noticed it, just spat at him in answer.

They froze, stared at each other, then he covered her mouth with his, wound his fingers into her hair and their love flared up in the midst of their hatred.

They lay there damp and spent; there were fragments of glass and broken pottery everywhere, and the smooth, polished surface of the table bore an ugly scar.

'I couldn't bear to lose you a second time,' she said. 'It would be too cruel.'

'I don't want to lose you, either,' he retorted, but his voice was hard. 'How could you have believed that of me? Do you still have so little trust?'

'You'd have believed it, too, if you'd been in my place. She was infatuated with you, wasn't she?'

'Infatuated, yes, in a way. But she's only twenty. Surely you know I'm not the kind of man who takes up with girls

of her age? She has a boyfriend, someone she's in love
with and not merely infatuated by, and that's what the
trouble was. When I came back yesterday she wandered
into my office on the pretext of wanting to help out, but
in point of fact she wanted someone to talk to – and I can
only presume she feels I'm someone she can trust. Which
is more than can be said for you . . . Anyway, my secretary
had the day off because she wasn't expecting me back
until today, and—' he shrugged – 'to cut a long story
short, Jennie was in tears within about two minutes, and
obviously desperate to unburden herself on me. So I took
her to lunch, sympathized and cheered her up and gave
her some advice. I didn't even know you were in the
country – not until I stepped out of the lift and you swore
at me.'

Katherine bit her lip.

'What's the matter?' he said. 'Suddenly at a loss for
words? That's just how I felt when you called me a
bastard. That's why I walked the streets to try and cool
down before I came here.'

'You weren't very successful, were you?'

'What man would be with a woman like you? But I was
successful enough. Except that—' he grinned suddenly,
his face lighting up as if he were a boy again – 'I hadn't
intended to—'

'Well nor had I. Far from it.'

Then his smile faded.

'The trouble is, Katherine,' he said, 'I don't know how
to make you see reason at times. What if I had been
civilized tonight? What good would it have done? You're
only listening to me now because you've had to . . . You
were just as stubborn fifteen years ago over Miranda.'

'I wasn't stubborn. I acted for the best for us all at that
time.'

'You didn't, but I don't want to rake all that up again.'

'Hey – don't you start accusing me! Just remember how
you behaved—'

'Don't,' he said. 'Or we'll argue all night again . . . You weren't really bitchy to Jennie, were you?'

'I was, as a matter of fact.'

'Poor kid,' he muttered.

Katherine wasn't sure whether this remark irritated her or if she agreed with it; the former, she thought, and hoped it was purely irritation and not some recurring doubt about Gareth himself that had always – and always would – disturb her.

'I'll do something about her tomorrow,' she assured him. 'Personnel will find her a nice job, so there's no need for you to worry . . . In fact,' she added with a bright smile, 'I'll look after her myself. Make amends.'

'How?' he said doubtfully.

'I'll promote her.'

'Oh. That's very big of you.'

'Not in the circumstances, because I was in the wrong. Wasn't I?'

'Yes. And now listen to this for the last time and listen properly – I don't have the remotest interest in Jennie Corrin.'

'I believe you.'

He watched her closely.

'I do believe you,' she promised. 'I shall fix her up with a job as principal secretary to a board member. That's better than being an assistant in the chairman's office, isn't it?'

'Which board member?'

'Bill Skerrett.'

'Christ – sounds more like a form of punishment to me.'

'Nonsense, she'll soon get used to Bill's little ways. And he's always moaning about the lack of secretarial help on the statel team.'

'Hasn't he already got a secretary?'

Katherine shook her head.

'He did have – but the lady has to work for Hal

Maitland as well, the guy who's in effect taken over Bill's industrial relations job. I couldn't see the point in giving Bill full-time help for his statel work.'

Gareth groaned.

'Bad move on your part, Katherine. Bill's the very person you should be giving lots of sweeteners to.'

'Maybe,' she shrugged. 'I'm usually careful with things like that, but quite honestly I don't think Bill's bothered one way or the other anymore. He's too concerned with his stomach pains and his pension. My guess is that he'll ask for an ill-health retirement within the next few months. He hasn't done his job properly for ages – I do work that he should be doing or else I have to give it to somebody else – and now he looks so sickly as well . . . Finally, Gareth, I think I feel sorry for him.'

'So do I. I've had a drink with him once or twice, tried to get to know him a bit better and see if he would open up – but no luck.'

'You drink with Skerrett?' she asked, surprised.

'I've had the odd drink with him – that's all. He's not a friend of mine, if that's what you're implying.'

'I never thought he was,' she retorted. 'Why should he be?'

But a casual remark of Irv's sprang to her mind. It was when they had been discussing Gareth's joining the board, and Irv had told her that he'd already had a look round Borjex. He'd called in purely on the off chance, Irv had reassured her, talked to one of the board members – Bill Skerrett, as far as Irv had been able to recall.

Skerrett did not want Jennie. Rather than being pleased at Katherine's suggestion, he professed himself to be insulted, saying that the girl was too young and inexperienced to work for a board member.

Katherine retorted that Jennie had experience in the chairman's office, and had proved herself to such an extent that she already deserved promotion. She then anticipated his next question: why – if Jennie was so good – did Katherine want to let her go? But the question never came, and Skerrett grumbled on about the responsibilities of working for a senior board member, and how truly first rate she would have to be in order to help a man in his position.

Katherine said that if, after all his complaints about insufficient secretarial help, he would not accept somebody who had worked for the chairman, then she couldn't promise letting him have anybody at all.

'In fact,' she concluded, 'I shall speak to personnel myself – tell them that your requirements are so excessively high that they needn't bother sending you any candidates.'

A bubble of saliva appeared at the corner of Skerrett's mouth; it frothed over his lower lip and headed towards his chin.

Disgusted, Katherine looked away.

'I'll have her,' Skerrett muttered.

'I'll suggest she comes and sees you,' Katherine said, 'so that she can find out if she'll be happy working for you. She may not, of course, want the job.'

Skerrett's entire being seemed to shrivel up to dwarflike proportions. His eyes and mouth disappeared almost entirely, and he clutched at his diaphragm.

Katherine was alarmed: distaste was suddenly overtaken by pity.

'Bill!' she said, getting to her feet and rushing round the desk towards him. Fighting down a wave of revulsion, she put a hand on his shoulder.

He knocked it off.

'You make me sick,' he said, with such sincerity that it would have been impossible to doubt him.

'My sentiments entirely,' was what she would have liked to have said.

'How unfortunate,' was what she did say.

'That's all that's wrong with me,' he added, as he

tottered unsteadily to his feet. 'But don't think I shall leave this company because of you. I shall leave here when I'm good and ready, and not before.'

'Naturally,' she said. 'There's no rush; you take your time.'

'Tell the girl to come and see me.'

'All right,' she agreed, and did genuinely feel sorry for him as his sick and ageing steps carried him uncertainly towards the door.

The next problem was Jennie. Personnel had already told her about the job and she was keen, but Katherine wanted to speak to her herself.

She looked uneasy, Katherine thought, as she crossed the office and sat down very straight-backed in a cushioned chair. Then her sharp little brown eyes met Katherine's, and there was nothing there except apprehension – not one trace of guilt, unless she was experienced enough to know how to hide it, and Katherine doubted that very much. In fact, as they talked she decided she liked her and that Bill was going to get a first-class deal out of this upset.

'By the way,' Katherine said, as Jennie was preparing to leave after their interview. 'I'm not sure how much you'll enjoy working for Bill Skerrett. He can be difficult and exacting, but that's just his method of trying to get results. If you can manage to, look on the job as merely a step in the right direction.'

'Oh, I'll cope with Mr Skerrett,' she said happily.

'That's the spirit,' Katherine grinned.

'I know,' Jennie retorted cheekily. 'I learned it from you.'

The wage claim from MATEX was unjustifiably high. Deadlock was reached after only three hours of bargaining, and both the board side and the union side left the negotiations in solemn mood.

Katherine was too preoccupied afterwards to deal with

her own affairs, apart from making time to pen a hasty letter to Marius. Then it was back to the board room to deal with the statels.

She spoke briefly about the renovations that were being carried out on the Rome *palazzo*, then handed over to Gareth who would explain in more technical detail.

He talked for about ten minutes, dwelling largely on the architects' plans and the structural assets of the building, then moved on to its drawbacks – from an antiquated plumbing system that would have to be entirely replaced to an equally poor sanitation network in the surrounding area. Next he mentioned the paintings that had been bought along with the *palazzo*, and informed the board of the value of the three originals that had been discovered amongst the dozens of copies. This news went down well, and interest was increasing.

Katherine looked up uneasily at his next remark: it was on much broader policy issues which, strictly speaking, he should have discussed with her before mentioning to the board. He was talking about sales and purchases of property in England, and this was the first she had heard of the stance he was now taking. His comments were excellent, but phrased in such a way that they could have been taken to be suggestions rather than merely informative remarks.

He was delivering his talk fluently, as usual, with his unhurried manner that was pleasant to both watch and listen to. Katherine fidgeted: his next point, on land valuation, was rather obscure, and when she glanced round the board table she realized something was amiss. Exactly what, she wasn't sure, but some vital element had gone awry.

Dr Beloff interjected with a comment of his own, and that, too, was obscure – in typical Dr Beloff style.

Katherine automatically straightened her shoulders a little, preparatory to clarifying the situation for the other board members.

That was when it registered: the entire board were looking to Gareth for guidance, not herself.

'D'you think it's necessary for you to come to France with me?'

They were sitting in Katherine's office at the end of the day, and Gareth had flopped down in the chair behind her desk. She was perched on the edge of the desk, long legs crossed over each other and one foot tapping out a rhythm in the air.

'It's essential,' he replied. 'In fact since you've got so many problems at the moment with MATEX, it might be better if I went alone and you stayed here.'

'No,' she said. 'I must go.'

'At least leave the English side of things to me. I'll look at this Georgian manor house in Buckinghamshire, and deal with the councils for planning permission. If we do buy it, we'll have to build extensively in the grounds—'

'I'll come with you to Buckinghamshire.'

'That's crazy,' he said. 'I've told you, you can leave the English side to me.'

She cleared her throat, uncrossed her legs, then crossed them again.

'Er – Gareth?'

'Mm?'

'Why did you hold forth about policy issues in the board meeting today?'

He frowned at her, as though unable to understand what she was getting at.

'Whatever subjects I covered today,' he replied, 'were strictly related to the statels.'

'Yes, but they weren't just technical details, were they?'

'I didn't accept a board membership in order to give technical details – we employ practising architects and surveyors and people for that. I was invited to join Borjex because of my business knowledge, my experience in property.'

'But there was no need to touch on questions of *policy*, not without discussing them with me first.'

He raised his eyebrows, then lowered them and frowned again, and finally laughed.

'Here,' he said, getting to his feet. 'Have your chair back. You seem to be getting worried.'

Helen poured tea into bone china tea cups, handed one to Skerrett and one to Rykwert, then lowered her violet blue eyes and wept.

'Helen!'

'Don't worry, William. I shall be all right in a moment. Really.'

Skerrett wavered on the faded old rug, and she raised her eyes to his. He was flabbergasted: even in distress she was beautiful. Every other woman he'd known – including his niggardly wife who'd died some ten years earlier – looked dreadful when they cried. The skin around their eyes swelled up, the eyes themselves turned red, their make-up smudged and even their noses became discoloured. Helen, however, bore no trace of disfigurement. The whites of her eyes were still clear and shining, her make-up was exquisite and her glistening lips were parted in a sigh.

He adored her.

The only way you'd have known she'd been crying was that heart-rending sob she'd been unable to conceal, and one huge tear oozing slowly down her velvet-soft cheek.

'We'll – uhm – we'll get the surveyors in tomorrow,' Rykwert said.

'Don't be so heartless,' he hissed, and yet he was glad things were moving quickly now. He was certain that Helen respected him and was fond of him, and when all was said and done it was she – not he – who had instigated this relationship. The thought made him strangely uneasy . . . He had no doubts about her lack of brain, nor her sentimental ways that must cloud her judgement; nor did he have doubts about the fact that he would come off best from all this. It was simply that, now and then, he would be aware of how charmingly but relentlessly she'd cultivated his friendship. What he wanted to know was: was he worth it?

He supposed he was. He was older, it was true, but then so was Helen – considerably older than him, in fact. And he did have a lot to offer a mature woman. Helen had told him in graphic detail all the things he had to offer, and quite frankly he tended to agree with her.

'Perhaps, Mr Rykwert,' Helen was saying, 'you would like me to show you over the castle?'

'There's no need for that,' Skerrett interrupted. 'I've seen all that we need to see.'

'I would like to look round,' Rykwert said, levering himself determinedly to his feet and knocking over one of the delicate, bone china cups. 'Uhm – sorry,' he added.

'It doesn't matter. A broken tea cup's neither here nor there in the circumstances.'

'My dear Helen—' Skerrett stepped forward and put a hand on her shoulder.

She knocked it off: the gesture seemed familiar, and it pained him.

'I wouldn't want you to be upset, too, William,' she said, and her voice held a note of concern.

He cheered up.

'You can rely on me,' he assured her, 'to see you through this most distressing time.'

And he couldn't help thinking that she really deserved a bit of distress. It certainly distressed him to think of any one person owning a place like Tylowe.

'Thank you,' she muttered.

Rykwert was looking impatient, probably – Skerrett thought – because success was so close now.

Skerrett himself was equally excited, not only because the deal was going to ferment his relationship with Helen, but because it was going to make him respected once more in the eyes of the New York board – and destroy Katherine at the same time. He would buy Tylowe and have the ideal site for the English statel. Irv would be delighted and full of praise, particularly since Katherine had been unable to find suitable property and was already behind schedule. He, Skerrett, would save the day . . . It was Katherine's own fault, because if she hadn't let Helen's son down so disgracefully, then Helen would have approached her rather than one of her board members. Skerrett chuckled to himself, savouring Helen's malicious streak.

'Before we look round,' Helen said, 'is Mr Rykwert quite clear about Katherine Hanson? He knows that she isn't to be told, doesn't he?'

'Oh yes,' Skerrett reassured her. 'Nobody will be any the wiser until the purchase has been completed. It suits us as much as it suits you, Helen. And the surveyors won't be a problem; they're not Borjex employees so there's no chance of them coming into contact with Katherine at all.'

How foolish and inefficient Katherine would look, when one of her team brought off a brilliant deal beneath her very nose, a deal that should have been hers. There was no time to lose, though, because Gareth Williams already had his sights on some Georgian property in Buckinghamshire.

'There's nothing for you to bother about now, Helen,' he told her. 'We'll hurry it all through as quickly as possible.'

'I'm sure you will – I was convinced from the first that I would be able to depend on you, William. Come along, then,' she heaved an enormous sigh, 'We'll start by showing Mr Rykwert my splendid underground creation. There's even a gymnasium and a jacuzzi, so your renovations are going to be minimal.'

They followed her down to the ground floor, then across the hall towards a wooden door concealed in the panelling. As they descended the first steep flight of stone steps that led to the cellars, Skerrett reflected on his ultimate triumph in this deal: money. The price he was offering Helen was about half the correct market value . . . he could just imagine the board members' faces when they received that piece of information.

He had no conscience about this whatsoever: Helen was too scatty and feminine ever to be aware of the true value of money, so she would continue in ignorance to be grateful for the sum he was offering – and in any case, that was quite large enough for her to live on in comfort for some time to come. And at her age she couldn't be expected to last much longer. Then the money would revert to her son or, if she married again, to her husband. He hoped she wouldn't change her mind at the last minute and demand an independent valuation. In a sudden tremor of panic, he almost knocked her down the cellar steps.

'Goodness,' she said, clutching at the wall to support herself. 'You are in a hurry, aren't you? Take care, Mr Rykwert, not to trip. William almost has, and these old steps can be deceptive.'

The dispute at the Tylowe site was bitter and sudden. For a while it seemed probable that a twenty-four hour lightning strike would be called, and Katherine was standing by every minute of the day. She told Hal Maitland, Skerrett's industrial relations deputy, to stand by as well, and for form's sake arranged for Skerrett to be kept in constant touch with events.

The disagreement was over trivia, which made it even more worrying, because it meant there was serious discontent amongst the union members and they were simply waiting for an excuse to come out.

A foreman had asked a man to move a piece of machinery during his lunch break; the man had agreed, then complained to a union representative, who had in turn complained to Jo Cleary. From then on the unrest had escalated, but Jo had managed to avert an all-out stoppage and work continued.

Katherine decided to visit the site herself, along with Hal and Richard Stempel. As the party were about to leave, Mrs Egerton called Katherine back to take a telephone call.

'Tell them I'm in a meeting,' she said. 'I'll call them back tomorrow – or you could put them through to Dr Beloff.'

'It's Lord Arlingham,' Mrs Egerton mouthed the words as though they had some fearful implication.

'Oh – very well, I'll come.'

Picking up the receiver, she said: 'Edward?' with a note of disbelief.

'Katherine, how are you?'

'I'm fine, thank you, Edward. And you?'

'Missing you,' he said, with all his old charm, 'but bumbling along.'

'I'm sure you are, you old rogue.'

Then they laughed and the ice was broken.

'I know we agreed not to contact each other for a few months,' he said, 'but I'm in a spot of bother.'

'What's that, Edward?'

'This strike at the Tylowe site – what's the news on it?'

'As a matter of fact I've just heard that it's all blown over – for the time being. I'm on my way there now to try and suss out the scene. But how does it affect you?'

'The drift mine,' he said. 'You remember that most of the men are in MATEX?'

She groaned. 'Of course they are. Oh dear, it would cost you heavily if they pulled out.'

'Without the maintenance shift working,' he said, 'the place would be unsafe within hours.'

'Well there's nothing for you to worry about at the moment, but if the tide should look like turning again I'll make sure you're warned.'

'Won't do much good, though, will it? Once they're out, that's it . . . What d'you think the odds are on a full-scale strike?'

'If I knew that,' she replied, 'the problem would be halved. As it is, I'm afraid that we're in for a difficult autumn.'

'Ten lives were lost in the last strike at this mine.'

'And more than a dozen families were left homeless last year,' she said, 'when there was a landslide on an opencast site.'

Hyde Park in the early morning was fresh and damp. Clusters of greenery still lingered on the trees, but another summer was over and they were about to fall.

Katherine was beginning to think she'd made a mistake in deciding to walk to work; it was only seven a.m. and the air was invigorating, but a light drizzle made her shiver and turn up the collar of her jacket. She quickened her pace: she wanted to be in the office no later than seven-fifteen, otherwise there would be no chance of clearing all the routine correspondence before she made yet another – and possibly final – attempt to forestall disaster.

Crossing Rotten Row and approaching the Kensington Road, she felt her heart sink: the skies were opening and the rain beginning to teem down, silently and resolutely. She looked up at the thin, grey clouds above her, and realized that the weather was set for a long, long time.

It was going to be a wet autumn, just as forecasts had promised.

With the possibility of a crisis looming on the horizon, priorities had had to be switched. The decision on the Georgian manor house in Buckinghamshire had been left to Gareth, and his verdict, after receiving the surveyors' and architects' reports, was that the property should be bought. Katherine had also left the problem of planning permission entirely in his hands, and he had informed the board that as soon as he could be certain of obtaining it from the local authorities, he would finalize the purchase.

Katherine went ahead with her plans to visit France, but altered the arrangements so that she would be there for only four days instead of a week. She had a private meeting with Jo Cleary before leaving the country, but to her dismay their five-hour discussion did nothing to ease the strained industrial situation. She was convinced that Jo had doubts he would not – or could not – voice: she'd had the same impression when she saw him at the Tylowe site, and knew that unless he had enough faith in her to open up and explain what the root of the problem was, they would never be able to work together as they had in the past.

MATEX's claim was now down to twenty per cent from twenty-five, but it was still unjustifiably high and there was no way the European board or, ultimately, the New York board would sanction such a rise. There was to be a vote by MATEX members on Borjex's latest offer the day after Katherine returned from France, but Jo was gloomy about the outcome.

The atmosphere was tense when Katherine, Gareth and Richard Stempel flew to Paris; it would have been even worse except that Gareth tried to lighten their mood by talking of other things, and was so kind and considerate to Katherine that – almost without realizing it – she began to lean on him.

Château Fernand, which was situated just outside Paris and only an hour's journey from Orly Airport, made the prospect of four days out of England seem worthwhile. With help from Borjex's office in Paris, the property short list had been whittled down to two estates, and the château was by far the better of the two. It was a dreamy looking building whose foundations dated from the twelfth century, but whose interior echoed the influence of the seventeenth century – the golden age in France's artistic achievements.

Katherine saw it first in the early morning, and was spellbound by its charm: the sky behind its turrets and spires made a pink-tinged backcloth for the pale grey stone, and all around was rich, harvested farmland and even a small vineyard which still belonged to the Fernand family.

The wine cellars were limited but very fine, and were for sale along with the rest of the estate. There was no time, however, to do more than make a precursory tour of them before inspecting the main body of the château, and this was even larger than the *palazzo* in Italy.

Towards the end of the afternoon, Gareth suggested that they return the following morning rather than hurrying their assessment through in one day, and they agreed to meet the Fernand's agent at nine o'clock tomorrow, in his office in the 16e arrondissement in Paris.

The three of them drove with their hired car and chauffeur across the outskirts of Paris to the Bois de Boulogne, where they had arranged to have dinner and meet Dominique Lefèvre, Borjex's director in Paris.

It was an autumnal scene in the Bois, with luke-warm shafts of sunlight falling onto the rough-cropped turf, and a light breeze whisking at the leaves.

'Let's try,' Gareth said, 'to spend a little time out here over the next few days. A few hours off duty wouldn't hurt, would it?'

'I'm sure it wouldn't, but in view of the rumours that have been circulating about us I think we ought to be seen to be as busy as we really are.'

'There's only Richard here. And I don't see that one evening would matter.'

'Nevertheless,' she shook her head, 'let's be cautious.'

'Has anything else been said?'

'No, but I still don't know who was responsible in the first place. My guess, though, would be a woman – or someone who daren't cross me in any sizeable kind of way. The whole thing reeked of spite and vindictiveness, and there are a couple of women managers at Borjex who detest the very sight of me. I know for a fact that one of them started some rumours about me and Irv when I first joined Borjex, though I was never able to prove it. There are plenty of men who dislike me, too, and they're probably just as capable of starting rumours.'

'Bill Skerrett isn't over-fond of you.'

'Yes, but he's a board member—' she shrugged. 'And much as he may dislike me, he's never seriously tried to cross me. What's more, my efforts to inch him out will soon be needless. From things he's been saying recently I gather he'll be glad to leave the company.'

'Don't bank on it,' Gareth recommended.

'Oh yes—' she commented, 'I was forgetting. He's a friend of yours, isn't he? So you probably know rather more than most of us about his plans.'

'One day, Katherine Hanson,' he warned, and this time there was no glimmer of amusement in his eyes, 'you'll come screaming to me for forgiveness and help and by then it may well be too late.'

'What's that supposed to mean?'

'You've got a sharp tongue and a sharp brain, only the two don't always work together. I'd advise you to watch your tongue to start with.'

'Would you now?'

Her voice was scathing, but the coldness in Gareth's words had hurt. The same coldness was in his face, too, as if to make it plain that he had no intention of retracting what he'd said.

He had the power to hurt her that easily. She'd allowed him that power, the power to upset her with one rebuff.

'I think,' she said, and kept her voice low for fear of betraying some tremor in it, 'that I'd better ring the hotel before we have dinner, find out if there are any messages.'

'Stop worrying, Katherine,' and his face softened and

her heart lifted. 'There's no point in ringing them again. You rang them this morning and you rang them at lunchtime. Even if something had gone wrong, you'd have to have dinner before you did anything about it.'

'It would depend on what it was.'

'Come on, let's go and see if Dominique's arrived.'

Dominique had, but his first question after greeting them was about the likelihood of MATEX striking, and even when Gareth changed the subject to the statels, Katherine's mind wandered back to the watery ground at Tylowe.

'Why don't you join us at the château tomorrow?' Gareth asked Dominique. 'After all, you're the one who found it in the first place.'

Katherine backed up Gareth's invitation, and made a point of thanking Dominique for all the hours he had put in, vetting property and drawing up such an excellent short list. But she was momentarily surprised. The invitation to join them should have come from her rather than Gareth . . . for all Gareth knew, she might have had any number of good reasons for excluding the Paris director at this stage.

'I'm afraid we must leave you early tonight,' she told Dominique. 'I have a telephone call booked to England at eleven, and in the circumstances it could be disastrous to miss it.'

They went their separate ways soon after ten o'clock, Dominique driving himself back to his flat off the Boulevard St Michel, and the English party being driven back to their hotel, the George V.

As they approached the reception desk for their keys, one of the assistant managers hurried towards them.

'Madame Hanson?' he said.

'Yes, I'm Katherine Hanson.'

'Madame, there is an urgent telephone message for you from England.'

He handed her a folded piece of paper. She opened it,

scanned its contents briefly, then asked the receptionist to book her a seat on the next available flight to England.

Gareth was the only part-time board member in the emergency meeting. His presence was needed because MATEX had raised the issue of Borjex's heavy investment in property, and it was hoped that Gareth would be able to help give them a satisfactory explanation of what was actually happening.

Richard Stempel had returned to England with Katherine on a 2.00 a.m. flight, and Gareth had followed the next evening. The negotiations with MATEX, after hasty briefings on both sides, had begun several hours before Gareth took his place at the board table.

The twenty-four-hour stoppage at Tylowe had been called over an unnecessary accident: machinery had been left blocking the exit, a man had categorically refused to move it outside working hours and the site manager had moved it instead. Unused to handling such heavy equipment, the supervisor had reversed into a coal lorry, causing minor injuries to its driver – superficial bruising and a broken finger. The driver of the lorry, a MATEX member like all the rest on the site, had had the immediate – though perhaps unlooked-for – sympathy of his colleagues, and a lightning strike had taken place.

News was now filtering in about the results of the ballot on Borjex's latest wage offer, and the atmosphere in the board room was electric. The accident and the lightning strike couldn't have come at a worse moment: if the men now elected to turn down the offer, then a full-scale strike – which could last for days or even weeks – would be inevitable.

So far, the results were pessimistic. Jo Cleary and his executive looked as tense as did Katherine and her board members.

'Gareth Williams,' Katherine said, 'the person who – apart from myself – is most closely connected with our property schemes, is now going to explain to you some of the reasons behind our choice of reinvestment areas, and our projected expenditure and returns over the next five years.'

Gareth did exactly what she'd prayed he would not do: he launched straight into a detailed breakdown of facts and figures, rather than giving a reassuring outline, and had the riveted attention of the entire board and union executive.

Silently cursing the fact that she hadn't had time to talk to him beforehand, she realized that his approach was nevertheless working. She could see Jo's expression change; he scribbled a note to his deputy who was sitting on his right, and the man scribbled one back. Two or three board members exchanged glances, then looked at Gareth again.

He wasn't lying, but he was discussing hypothetical benefits as though they were certain results. If they didn't materialize, then next year or the year after Borjex would have an even worse industrial problem on its hands.

It was an approach that eased an immediate crisis but ran the risk of causing a much greater one later. She had refused to use such an approach during all her years of dealing with unions, and the facts Gareth was purporting to give now were the self-same facts she had refused to give Jo Cleary only weeks before: more than that, she had told him she was unable to give them.

Jo looked across the table at her now, and there was unveiled distrust in his eyes.

The doors opened and one of MATEX's more junior representatives came in, crossed the room and handed Jo an envelope.

Silence fell as he tore it open, extracted a piece of paper, read it then looked up again.

'They've turned it down,' he said. 'And opted to strike.'

Katherine strode into her office with Hal Maitland, Hugo

Palfreyman and Richard Stempel only a step behind her. Gareth followed a moment later.

'Excuse me, gentlemen,' she said. 'I must have a quick word in private with Gareth.'

As soon as they were alone she turned on him.

'How dare you?' she said, her eyes flashing with anger. 'How dare you take it upon yourself to alter the whole course of how Borjex deals with its union problems? I don't know whether you realize this or not, but you've made me look a liar and a complete fool as chairman, and stored up a whole load of trouble for this company in the near future.'

His eyes hardened and there were tired lines etched deep from his nose to his mouth.

'A strike is inevitable,' he said, so quietly that his voice was almost menacing. 'But I might have limited it from weeks to only days – weeks that might save lives, to say nothing of millions of pounds.'

'You're wrong!' she retorted. 'It was too late for a stance like yours – a stance that doesn't work in the long run, anyway. You've entirely exceeded the terms of your membership on this board, and I'd like to know just what the hell you think you're up to?'

'If you can't see that without asking the question,' he replied, 'then I suggest you hand over these negotiations to somebody who has clearer vision.'

'Get out of here,' she said. 'And when we meet again after this adjournment, make sure you bear one important fact in mind before you speak – *I'm* the chairman.'

ELEVEN

The southern wind
Doth play the trumpet to his purposes,
And by his hollow whistling in the leaves
Foretells a tempest and a blustering day.

                – PRINCE; *Henry the Fourth*, Part One

He watched the chairman's buttocks swing round the corner. They were good buttocks, a little on the large side but none the worse for that. He could have happily slapped them, there and then.

'They're going back in, Gareth,' Richard said. 'Are you ready?'

'Fighting fit,' Gareth said. 'Any more news through yet?'

'One of Jo's people has just had a phone call – my guess is that it looks bad.'

Gareth grunted.

'Come on,' he said. 'Got your note pad at the ready?'

'Doesn't seem to be much of a contribution, does it?' Richard said. 'Sitting there making notes.'

'It's more than I was doing at your age. I'd just been sacked for punching my boss on the nose – I had to take a labouring job after that to try and get some money together. I worked on a site not unlike Tylowe for over three months.'

Richard's face brightened.

'Really?' he said. 'Imagine, you actually hit your boss. Hard to believe in this civilized atmosphere, isn't it?'

'Oh I don't know,' Gareth shook his head. 'The boss I had then wasn't a patch on your chairman.'

'I say,' Richard said, 'I thought she looked a bit annoyed before the adjournment. You've altered the course of her argument, you see.'

'I do see,' Gareth replied, and as he stepped into the board room with Richard by his side, he was just in time to hear Katherine's shattering announcement.

The nightmares Jo Cleary had been suffering from were less than half as bad as reality. Not only did the MATEX members strike immediately, withdrawing their labour from over a third of the country's opencast sites and drift mines, but two other unions came out in sympathy. The next stage, should agreement be impossible, would be a nationwide pit strike.

If that happened, then even the government could topple – and whether it did or not, the entire country would grind to a standstill: it was early autumn, the long winter months lay ahead – power stations would use up their reserves of fuel during the next six months, there would be electricity shortages and perhaps a three-day week. Lay-offs, company closures and bankruptcies of the smaller firms would be a few of the symptoms of the sickness: it had happened before, and there was no reason why it shouldn't happen again.

The whole thing had escalated at a frightening rate and would soon be out of Jo's control – indeed it had largely slipped away already. He tried to get hold of Skerrett and Rykwert privately, but neither seemed terribly concerned – but then again, neither was directly responsible, because it was obvious now that Skerrett was being replaced by Hal Maitland in the industrial relations hot seat, and Rykwert was one step removed in his capacity as company secretary.

Jo didn't even know what purpose would be served by speaking to them now, but since they'd been the instigators he couldn't bear to watch them slip through unscathed and so complacent.

He'd tried and tried again to act as a moderator with his union, but now the larger unions had moved in and were stirring up more discontent, he was fighting a losing battle.

Skerrett and Rykwert . . . he wasn't going to let them get away with what they'd caused. They'd probably never intended that events should get so out of hand, but they were still to blame – with their rumours and trouble-making and 'agent provocateur' work amongst his own men. And now they wanted to disassociate themselves from Jo. Small wonder, but knowing them they probably had other and better schemes in mind now. Whatever they were up to, they'd made it perfectly plain they no longer needed Jo Cleary, and had dropped him as abruptly as a red-hot iron.

It was against Jo's nature to give in, even when he knew that failure was assured, and so he tried to prepare himself mentally for the weeks and perhaps months of battle ahead. Soul-destroying days stretched out before him: Hal Maitland, whom he scarcely knew, would soon replace Skerrett; if the deadlock continued, Katherine would or would not resign, and in any case their working relationship was finished – particularly after the doubts that Gareth Williams's talk had raised; there was a ninety per cent chance that MATEX would decide to amalga-mate with one of the largest unions after this strike, or even during it, and then there were the consequences of the strike itself.

He felt sick when he thought about them – not the bigger consequences that could bring the country to a halt, but the smaller ones that he'd seen so many times before: subsidence caused by untended pits, the earth rupturing and cracking houses on the ground above; water pouring into workings because pumps had been left standing idle; men returning to work after the strike, dying during the first maintenance shift, in a roof fall or in flooding.

As he left Borjex's headquarters that evening, Jo noticed that it was raining for the third day in succession.

At ten p.m., Katherine, Hal Maitland and Hugo Palfreyman were still sitting round the desk in Katherine's office. The rest of the board had left only half an hour earlier, and – without a word to anyone – Gareth had gone with them. Richard was holding the fort in Mrs Egerton's room, answering the telephone and making pots of coffee.

Katherine had just put the receiver down from a conversation with Irv, when Richard rang through.

'The Secretary of State on the line,' he announced, and after a soft click there came the sound of Henry Bentinck's voice.

His tone, as always, gave nothing away – but he contrived to make it clear that if she didn't bring matters to a satisfactory head before any more unions gave MATEX their support, then it would be her head that would roll.

Henry Bentinck might have been instrumental in putting her where she was, but he would have no qualms about having her removed: his power worked both ways.

When Katherine arrived home at midnight, there was only one person she wanted to talk to, and lean on – and that was the person she both mistrusted and loved.

Partly to stop herself thinking about him, and partly out of politeness, she telephoned Edward instead – but he'd already heard the news and there was nothing she could say to reassure him.

Then a thought crossed her mind: it wouldn't matter now, but it would later when the strike was over and the first maintenance shift moved in.

'By the way,' she said, 'could I or one of my people speak to the drift manager tomorrow?'

'Why should that be necessary?' he asked.

'I'm only trying to help you, Edward,' she replied.

'Perhaps the manager would be glad of some outside advice.'

'He's quite competent.'

'His competence isn't in question, but managing a drift mine is a lonely job; he might find it helpful to talk to other engineers.'

'Leave it, Katherine,' he said. 'He won't want to talk to any outsiders.'

Then she was suddenly wide awake again.

'You know the mine's going to be unsafe when work starts again, don't you? . . . Edward?'

'Yes, of course.'

A picture of the mine flashed across her mind – of the anthracite and of the lie of the seams – and it was followed swiftly by the memory of a conversation she'd had years ago with Edward, when Borjex had tried to buy the Tylowe Drift.

'The mine must soon be worked out, mustn't it?' she said. 'At least, all workable anthracite must almost have been removed. If conditions are bad after the strike, perhaps it won't be worth your while to continue?'

'I have no intention of closing down the Tylowe Drift,' he said, quite snappishly. 'Any more questions?'

'Yes, a very important one. If you say it's not worked out, then you must have driven a fresh face – and there's only one direction you can go in that mine to get at the last reserves of anthracite.'

'What are you implying, Katherine?'

'I'm saying,' she told him, 'that you would have had to endanger men's lives to get your anthracite, that you would have had to have driven the new face beneath the walls of the castle itself.'

There was a pause, then he said: 'The men in the Tylowe Drift work in conditions that are just as well regulated as those in any other mine. But yes, a face has been driven quite close to the castle. And what do you intend to do about it?'

Katherine sat at the foot of her bed and stared at the floor.

There was nothing she could do about it. Neither Helen nor anybody else had applied to have Tylowe listed as an ancient monument: few owners would have done, because of the restrictions that would have come into force under a government order, and the effects on the value of the property. It meant that the owners of the drift had every right to mine coal beneath the very body of the castle, provided the owners of the castle put up no objection. And since Helen had occupied Tylowe for several decades, naturally no objection would be forthcoming.

There was a chance that it would not matter: Tylowe was solidly built – it should be able to withstand even the most violent subsidence, and its cellars were deep enough to take the brunt of any radical movement in the earth below. But it was a risk, and if Edward was so greedy to extract every ounce of highly profitable anthracite, who knew what other risks he might not encourage his manager to take. There was a thin line between what the law laid down and what was a dangerous contravention . . . but all mining was dangerous, even the most safeguarded operations, because you were working in the bowels of the earth and God alone knew what the earth might do.

She jumped when the doorbell rang, then made herself stand still for a second before hurrying down the spiral staircase.

Slipping on the safety chain, she opened the door.

'Gareth!' she exclaimed, having expected some urgent, hand-delivered message about the strike. 'What on earth are you doing here? It's nearly one o'clock.'

'I tried to ring you,' he said, 'but your phone was engaged. Could I come in?'

'After today,' she said, 'I'd rather not. Not just now, anyway. I don't know what to think and I'd rather not talk about it at the moment.'

'I haven't come to discuss work – I've come because of you.'

'Well you can't stand in the street, you'd better come inside.' She pushed the door to, unfastened the chain and let him in. 'Only for a few minutes though.'

She led the way into the sitting room and felt too exhausted to discuss anything at all.

'Pour yourself a drink,' she said. 'And I think I'll have one, too – a small brandy.'

He poured them and handed her one.

'Listen, Gareth,' she said. 'I feel just as angry with you as I did earlier today, only I'm too weary to show it. I don't know what you were up to, or what your intentions are, but I don't like it. The only thing is, I want to spare my energy right now and try to get some sleep.'

He sat down in the chair opposite hers, drank his brandy, then said: 'I understand that you can find neither the time nor the clear-headedness to rethink the course you're on, and that you can't see what I'm trying to do in the middle of a crisis. But I do wish you would believe that I'm attempting to salvage something from a situation that's blowing up in our faces. Your face in particular.'

'What you did today merely aggravated matters. You—'

'Stop it,' he said. 'Or we'll be doing exactly what I'd hoped to avoid. I said I'd come here because of you, and that is the sole reason I'm here. To help you if I can.'

She looked at him warily.

'You're on your own with mammoth problems and that's not a good situation to be in.'

'What are you proposing to do about it?' she asked. 'Have another word with Jo Cleary? Fetch him over to hold my hand?'

'I thought you might like to talk.'

She smiled.

'I'll just bet you did,' she retorted.

'Well then don't talk. Or else talk about anything you like except work. I'll stay with you and I won't even touch you.'

'You're bloody well right you won't touch me! You've caused me enough problems as it is with your lies and hypocrisy and double-dealing, to say nothing of—'

'Shut up.'

And his tone so startled her that she did.

'One more insult,' he said, 'and I'll lose my temper in a way I haven't lost it for years. Then I shall leave and I shan't come back. Not this time.'

'Oh Gareth —' and an indescribable sadness swept over her.

He got up and went over to her chair, drew her to her feet and put his arms around her.

'You shouldn't stay here with me tonight,' she muttered. 'It would be better not to. If we have anything to sort out between ourselves we'll have to do it later.'

'*If* we have anything to sort out? Katherine Hanson!'

'What am I supposed to think? I get angry with you because I'm hurt. Nobody can hurt me like you can, you know that. The thought that you who I've trusted again, you who I—' she shrugged. 'I couldn't bear it. And then at Borjex today—'

'Fuck Borjex,' he advised, and grinned.

She grinned, too, and for a minute felt a lightening of every load she carried.

'Let's have a bath and go to bed, Katherine. We won't talk about us or work or anything at all. OK?'

'OK. But it is going to get worse, the strike. I feel as though I'm getting ready for the battle of my life. I'm nervous.'

'That's why I came.'

'D'you think—?'

'Fuck it!' he said definitively. 'How many more times? Borjex, Borjex twenty-four hours a day. We'll drive ourselves mad, Kate,' and he started undoing his shirt as he headed for the door.

*

Peeping through the curtains next morning, the first thing she saw was the press: there was quite a crowd of them, journalists and photographers chatting together and glancing every now and then at her front door.

'Gareth,' she whispered. 'Are you awake?'

'More or less,' he said, and ran a hand through his hair as he struggled into a sitting position.

He'd been true to his word last night and done nothing but sleep with her in that huge double bed; nothing, in fact, except letting her talk for a while before tiredness overcame them. At three o'clock, when she'd woken briefly from a shallow sleep, she'd heard his steady breathing and thought he must be in the deepest of sleeps, but he'd reached out and drawn her to him. She'd closed her eyes and must have slept again with his arms around her, and when she'd woken at seven-thirty he'd had his back to her but she was pressed up close against him.

It had, after all, been good to have him there and she felt stronger again this morning.

'The press are out there.'

'Don't worry,' he said. 'I'll make some coffee while you get dressed, then you can leave by the front door and I'll leave an hour or so later through the back door.'

'There's no way out, the garden's enclosed.'

'I'll find a way.'

'Mm,' she commented.

He folded his arms across his chest and sat looking at her.

'Weren't you glad of me last night?'

'Mm.'

'Aren't you going to thank me?'

'Cheeky bastard!' she smiled.

'When we meet at that unmentionable place, you needn't have any worries. I shall have forgotten last night.'

'How can you?'

'I think we ought,' he said. 'I wouldn't want you to

have any fears about having betrayed some weakness. Or said something indiscreet.'

'I haven't got any fears.'

'Ah,' he said. 'So now who's the liar? Go on – you'd better go now. And remember –' he added solemnly, shaking his head – 'not to trust a single soul. That's one of your mottoes, isn't it? "Beware of the Greeks when they come bearing gifts".'

'That's a fine thing to say to me right now, isn't it?'

And she didn't know whether the glint in his eyes was laughter or cruelty.

Rykwert was sitting on a chair with spindly arms and legs: Skerrett guessed it to be a Chippendale, and contemplated asking Rykwert to remove himself.

Three-quarters of the man's perimeter overlapped the delicate and costly woodwork, while his central mass was putting heavy plebian strain on the basic structure. One arm, clad in garishly checked tweed, dangled below his thigh like lagged piping come loose from its weldings; the other was close against his chest, the stubby fingers curled tightly round a piece of gleaming Waterford crystal.

'More scotch, Mr Rykwert?'

'Thank you.' He proffered Helen his glass, despite the fact that it was still half full.

'What about you, William?'

Skerrett shook his head and simultaneously put his hand over the top of his cut-glass tumbler.

'No, thank you,' he said, and allowed his head to swing disapprovingly from side to side for a few moments longer.

Helen filled Rykwert's glass to the brim, handed it back to him, then glanced lovingly round her drawing room and sighed.

'I've seen to all the arrangements,' she said. 'The documents are in the safe in the library – so if you'll excuse me I'll go and fetch them.'

'It's only a formality,' Skerrett said.

'But we do need them,' Rykwert added, 'to make the transference of the property legal.'

'Please don't apologize. I understand perfectly.'

When the door had closed behind her, Skerrett said: 'We'll wait until she's gone before we decide on the antiques. Her flight's at nine-thirty tomorrow morning, so she'll have to leave here by eight-thirty at the latest – that should give us plenty of time to make a preliminary selection before we have to be back at Borjex. It's a nuisance, having to sit in on this business with poor old Jo, but never mind. We can always come down again over the next couple of days – it won't hurt to hold back breaking the news to Irv for forty-eight hours.'

'I made notes,' Rykwert told him, 'while I looked round. My impression is that a lot of the stuff is good fake or of little value. She must have disposed of a small fortune – piecemeal – over the years. Some of it's original, though – but I don't think we ought to take more than, say, one painting each plus a couple of the smaller antiques.'

'They'd never be missed,' Skerrett agreed. 'And if we choose wisely, we could make a packet. Besides, we deserve our commission.'

'You don't know if she's got an inventory of the contents, do you?'

'She says not. We'll make our own, as soon as we've told Borjex about the purchase. And at the price we're paying, we're getting the contents free in any case.'

'Lucky she didn't ask for an independent valuation, isn't it? There was a moment when I thought she was going to.'

'That's why I upped the offer, but we're still getting it dirt cheap. It's the time element, as well. I gather Williams is on the brink of getting planning permission for that place in Buckinghamshire. Still,' Skerrett laughed out loud, 'he's too late now.'

Rykwert made a low, rumbling noise, which could have been either a sign of agreement or excessive wind.

'You reckon she likes you?'

'My dear chap –' this was a new phrase of Skerrett's, brought into use since his last visit to Tylowe – 'I've got her eating out of my hand. I know how to treat her, you see, and that's why she's so fond of me, I'm the one she looks to for advice, general guidance in her business affairs – and that is the sole reason we're in the happy position of bringing off this deal. She is, I'll admit, reasonably astute in her own way –' and even as he spoke the old pain started up, the warning signal to accompany anxiety and frustration. 'Anyway, it'll be a good thing when all this is over.'

'It will.' Rykwert stared into his scotch. 'She wouldn't actually marry you, would she?'

'What makes you think that I would want to marry again? Though she's a fine woman for her age –' Skerrett shrugged. 'I can understand her wanting a holiday after all this upheaval – I suppose it must be upsetting, selling the home you've lived in for years – but when she gets back, I think we may well be seeing more of each other. I wish,' he added rapidly, 'that she'd hurry up with those papers.'

Suddenly nervous, he wandered over to the grand piano and lifted the lid.

'Going to give us a tune, William?'

'Ah – Helen—'

'I have the documents here,' she was holding an enormous stack of papers. 'They date back so far –' her eyes misted over, and she sat down unsteadily on an upright chair.

'Don't think about it,' Skerrett suggested.

'Just give them to me,' Rykwert held out his hand.

'Let's sit at this table,' Helen indicated a small, oval table by her side, 'and go through them. Though I suppose you'll want to show them to your legal department before we finalize the deal?'

'Oh no,' Skerrett said. 'That won't be necessary in these circumstances.'

'I suppose it might come to Katherine's ears?'

'She'll hear about it after it's all been settled, not before. Most probably she'll hear about it from her boss, because he's the person I'm going to inform.'

Helen gave him a tender smile.

'Sweet William,' she whispered.

Rykwert rolled his bovine eyes and took a gulp of his scotch.

'And since we're dealing with you, Helen,' Skerrett added, 'we're not going to have to double check things with lawyers. Distasteful goings-on at the best of times, doing business with friends – no need to make it worse. Tony here is a company secretary, he's quite capable of reading over a few bits and pieces on conveyancing.'

'There's no reason why Katherine should get any credit for all this, is there?' Helen said, as she pushed the documents across the table to Rykwert.

'No,' he grumbled, and began wading through the sheaf of papers.

The earlier ones had little or no relevance, but he tried to read the later ones with more care. And all the time he was trying to concentrate, he was aware of Skerrett – muttering and squawking and saying again and again that it was only a formality. Helen, the stupid bitch, was encouraging him.

'That'll do, Tony,' Skerrett nudged his elbow. 'We don't need to take a magnifying glass to the things. Just have a quick glance and see that the essential piece is there.'

'It's here.'

'Cheque, then – come on.'

Papers were exchanged, a cheque was produced and signed by Skerrett – as board member and full-time executive of the statel team – then countersigned by Rykwert as company secretary.

Gareth and Jo Cleary stood shoulder to shoulder on Jo's favourite hillock.

The Tylowe site looked like a graveyard: grey, upturned earth and machinery embedded in mud. The solitary tree was still standing at the far boundary: its roots had been destroyed during the mining operations and it had refused to come into bud this year. Its darkened branches stuck out sharply against the dismal sky. Soon, it would have to be felled: a few swift blows would suffice.

'See them houses over there?' Jo nodded in the direction of a small cluster of dwellings. 'The occupants have lodged a complaint already, and I can't say I blame them. Dust all summer from the opencast workings, followed by subsidence from the Tylowe Drift.'

'What are the chances of looking round the mine?'

'The manager's none too friendly, but the MATEX blokes will let you in – so long as you're with me. Give it another day or two, though, and I'm not sure that I'd risk it.'

'Bloody awful land, isn't it?' Gareth said.

'You're telling me. Mind you, the anthracite's worth a packet.'

The rich, water-logged land was all around them: dirt and jagged boulders, then the trees and park of Tylowe – and in the centre rose the turrets of the castle itself. In front of it, encircled by marshy ground and reeds, lay the stagnant water of the lake. At the very edge of the park, partly concealed by a dip in the land, was the drift mine. The massive headgear needed for deep mining was absent, but there was a pit yard with a few huts, a couple of brick buildings, a weighbridge and a coal lorry that had been stopped by pickets.

'D'you know anything about mining?' Jo asked.

'A bit. I come from a Welsh mining village.'

'Well you won't like what you're going to see now,' Jo told him. 'It's what I call greedy mining – driving faces where they shouldn't be driven, and doing it too quickly. Not enough spent on roof supports, either. The manager and a few of his men are going down every day while the strike lasts, trying to keep it as safe as they can, but I've told them they'd better not bother.'

'Have they listened to you?'

Jo shook his head.

'It'd be better for them if MATEX banned them completely. There's not enough of them to keep it safe – it's difficult enough at the best of times, with full maintenance shifts working.'

'From what you and I have been talking about, Jo,' Gareth said, 'd'you reckon you've got enough material to make them change their minds?'

'Not now. It'd take more than persuasion to break this deadlock. It'd take –' he shrugged. 'I hardly dare think . . . It'll be the same as always. Someone will get hurt before people start to see sense.'

Over the past forty-eight hours, there had been no progress whatsoever.

Katherine knew that Irv was itching to come over, but apart from the fact that such a move would take the responsibility out of Katherine's hands – something Irv had no cause to do as yet – there was nothing further he would be able to achieve even if he did arrive in England. He would merely have to sit in on the frustrating negotiations.

Finishing her sandwich and cup of coffee – a belated and hasty snack to take the place of lunch – she was about to leave her office and return to the board room when the intercom buzzed.

'Yes, Mrs Egerton?'

'I have a message from Mr Williams – he sends his apologies for this afternoon's meeting.'

'I see. Thank you.'

From a work point of view, this was irritating. The meeting was to be with Borjex's industrial relations staff, rather than with MATEX, and new tactics were to be decided on. Personally, it was both infuriating and perplexing, because she'd neither seen nor heard from him since that morning in her bedroom.

The intercom buzzed again.

'Yes?'

'Mr McKenzie on the line.'

Having spoken to Irv only an hour previously, Katherine was surprised. When Irv's opening gambit was to mention the statels, she was even more amazed: all was going well in that area, and this was hardly the moment to discuss an issue that was not a problem.

His news that Skerrett had concluded a brilliant deal over Tylowe was stunning. At first she thought there had been some terrible error, then she realized Irv meant exactly what he had said: that Skerrett had handed over to Helen a considerable portion of Borjex's reinvestment funds.

'Helen Arlingham,' she told Irv, 'had no right to sell Tylowe.'

'But that's just what the lady has done.'

'No she hasn't. She's committed fraud.'

Jennie Corrin was rifling through Skerrett's desk.

It had been a practice of hers with every person she'd ever worked for, and she found it was very instructive. As a relatively junior secretary, nobody ever bothered to tell her anything, and unless she read each confidential document that passed through her bosses' offices, she would never know anything worth knowing and – consequently – would never get on.

She'd read almost everything that had passed through Katherine's office, but had never removed anything: that would have been foolish, and that was one of the reasons she'd been so distressed when Katherine had accused her of tampering with those highly confidential notes relating to the statels. There were other things that Katherine had accused her of, but those were just lies – forgivable lies, in the circumstances, but still lies – whereas there was an element of truth in that fraught denunciation over the statels. It had seemed ironic at the time that she'd almost got the sack for something she did regularly but never got found out over – because somebody else had been doing exactly the same thing, but carelessly. How unfair it had seemed that she should carry the blame: some reckless person had removed the notes, then returned them to the wrong place.

Jennie sat down in Skerrett's swivel chair and read those same notes now, except that these were photocopies. She wondered why he'd wanted them and why he'd needed to have copies made – probably to show to somebody else – and then he'd kept them tucked away in the bottom drawer of his desk either to produce again, should the occasion arise, or because he was a silly old fart. Either solution seemed likely.

These were Katherine's own notes, for her talks with the New York board. If read out of context, they would give the most misleading impression: astronomical sums of money were mentioned, and unless you were familiar with the related papers, it would seem that Borjex was actually proposing to spend that kind of money on property over the next eighteen months. But that wasn't the case at all, these were just hypothetical figures about what the statels could cost, should Borjex's actual policy not be followed.

Replacing them exactly where she found them, Jennie went over to the cupboard that Skerrett always kept locked. Having removed the key from its secret hiding place in the portable medicine cabinet, Jennie had no difficulty in opening it.

She gave a long, low whistle when she saw the contents:

only three days ago, when she'd last checked, there'd been nothing here except several drafts of a sickening love letter, addressed to a woman called Helen. Although not posted, it had served some purpose, since it had given Jennie the best lunch break she'd had since her rather drunken outing with Gareth. She'd read the sheets three times, and in the end had doubled up with the pain of laughter. There were phrases like 'Darling heart', and 'Since I am still an extremely vigorous man . . .' and even 'Little one, you must know you can depend absolutely on the selfless devotion of your adoring Sweet William'. Had it not been against Jennie's adamant resolutions, she would have taken the sheets down to the photocopying room, had them duplicated and distributed them amongst her friends.

Today, however, the cupboard was nothing short of a treasure trove. There was a framed oil painting of a Victorian lady, a marble bust of what looked like a Grecian soldier, and half a dozen ornaments in some green substance which might have been jade.

There was another sheet of paper, too; it appeared to be an inventory that Skerrett was in the process of compiling.

Sitting back on her haunches, Jennie had a think.

All things considered, it might be wise to mention the photocopied statel notes to Katherine – just in case Katherine still harboured any doubts about Jennie. Also, the knowledge of who was responsible for the disappearing notes might be useful to Katherine, it might save her from – or get her out of – whatever trouble Skerrett was brewing, and then Jennie would really be back in favour.

It would be an added bonus if Skerrett got the push, because then Borjex would have to find Jennie another – and maybe even better – job.

She thought she might mention the treasure trove as well. The antiques were probably Skerrett's own, but then why had he locked them away like that in his office at

Borjex, and why was there this inventory listing even Chippendale furniture . . . She would make some excuse to Katherine as to why she'd been rifling through the cupboard – say she'd found it already opened, and was hunting for a letter: anything would do.

Sitting down in Skerrett's chair again, she tapped out Mrs Egerton's number on the telephone and waited.

When Mrs Egerton told her that Katherine would be tied up for the rest of the afternoon, Jennie had a rethink: she'd talk to Gareth, instead, and he could tell Katherine if he thought it worthwhile.

Jennie was still a little nervous of Katherine, whereas she felt perfectly at ease with Gareth. Besides, she'd told him so much about herself already, that if she made a fool of herself now it wouldn't matter. He would pass on the important details to Katherine, and the rest could be discreetly forgotten.

Having made up her mind, she called Gareth's secretary, discovered that he had just this minute walked into the office and would be leaving again within the hour, but that he would see her now if she hurried.

Relocking the cupboard and returning the key to its hiding place, she scurried off down the corridor.

'The sale of Tylowe Castle –' Katherine looked first into the dismayed face of Tony Rykwert, then into the contorted face of Bill Skerrett – 'is completely fraudulent. What's more, Helen Arlingham cannot be found – but the cheque you gave her has been cleared. Not long ago, but it has gone through.'

'I saw the deeds, I read the—'

'I'm afraid, Tony,' she said, in a voice that was pure ice, 'that they are forged. Not the earlier documents – that wouldn't have been necessary – just the essential pieces of paper. They wouldn't have been terribly difficult things to forge, or to arrange to have forged. Our lawyers might have spotted some flaw, or you might if you'd vetted them very carefully. They're being vetted now, of course, but that's rather a useless exercise at this point – unless there should be a criminal prosecution.'

'How could she have done such a thing?' Skerrett looked at Katherine beseechingly.

'That's the question I'm asking myself about you two. Why didn't you keep me informed about what you were doing? Especially since you knew Gareth Williams was on the brink of getting planning permission for the place in Buckinghamshire. It can only be that you were trying to outsmart me – make me look a failure as far as New York was concerned. Well? Isn't that so?'

Neither man spoke.

'Helen's outsmarted you both, and I don't know what New York will decide to do with you as a consequence. I know what I'd do, if it was left to me.'

'Will we get the money back?' Rykwert muttered.

'I don't know yet . . . Why do you think she was prepared to accept so little? The dowager Lady Arlingham has always spent heavily, but she has *always* had her eye on the main chance. She started life as one of a family of seven girls and at the age of ten had already left school and was working in a factory. Then she worked in a shop, and then as a lady's maid – and after that as a manicurist in a salon in a London hotel. It would probably be best to draw a veil over the next few years, but by the time she was twenty-four she was on the stage. I understand that she was a reasonably accomplished actress – at any rate she was celebrated and fêted. She once told me the most amusing little story, Bill – about how one man had tried to buy her from another, and she'd discovered what they were plotting and said that that was all right, provided they gave her fifty per cent of the price. Each. Otherwise she'd disgrace them publicly. How she laughed when she told me that story! Of course they paid. One can only presume that she's been a pretty good lay in her time.'

Skerrett made a whimpering noise.

'Her second husband,' Katherine went on, 'was Lord Robert Arlingham. I gather he loved her very much. She'd had a son by him – their only child – many years previous to their marriage, before she even went on the stage. He wasn't in a position to marry her at the time, so the child remained a bastard until his parents were middle-aged . . . Strange –' Katherine suddenly smiled to herself, as though the thought had temporarily distracted her from current problems of fraud and finances. Then she sighed, a brisk exhalation of breath.

'But her first besotted husband,' and her voice was scathing again, 'was a man called Howard Cleave, an industrialist who was later knighted for his services to Britain – exports in particular. He was besotted enough to accept both Helen and the child, though doubtless she'd have fobbed him off with some tale about the boy being an orphaned nephew or something equally dramatic. She's always been highly skilled at making hearts bleed for her. Well our problem, Bill – and Tony – is this: Howard Cleave had been married before he met Helen and had a son and a daughter by that marriage. I know nothing of their whereabouts, except that the son may be living in New Zealand. We shall have to find out, because the son is the owner of Tylowe. The bulk of Howard Cleave's wealth, including the Tylowe Drift, was bequeathed to Helen – and the castle was left to her in trust. On her death, it would revert to Cleave's son. Helen had no right to sell it, nor even to raise a mortgage on the property.'

'I didn't know.' Skerrett's voice was the lowest whine Katherine had ever heard.

'If you'd discussed your plans with me,' she said, 'I would have been able to tell you. There's something else I would like to ask you – why did you wait so long before telling Irv about your splendid deal? If we'd found out sooner, we'd have been able to stop the cheque.'

'I—' Skerrett began. 'We—'

'Yes?'

'There didn't seem to be any rush.'

'That's a lie. In view of what's happened, you ought to have been bursting to spread the word. That was the idea behind it all, wasn't it? To cover yourselves in glory?'

'Not entirely,' Rykwert said. 'We were doing it for the general good of the company, too. It's not our fault that documents were forged.'

'Oh, I see,' Katherine said. 'You merely wanted to upstage me in the grandest possible manner, and in the process were duped by yet another businesswoman. One should have a certain amount of sympathy for you, even. Is that what you're saying?'

'Sympathy might be too strong a word,' Rykwert said. 'Understanding, perhaps, that we made a terrible mistake – a mistake anybody could have made – but apart from the way you must feel about all this, it's quite clear that we were pushing ahead with the investment work. You – we were falling behind schedule with the pilot run—'

'Save your excuses for the board. It's the time gap that concerns me today. You weren't, by any chance, making little trips to Tylowe? Possibly removing some of the contents before Borjex could make a proper inventory?'

'That's a scandalous allegation!' Skerrett exclaimed. 'A dreadful thing has happened and I'm not trying to shirk the blame for it, but you can't go around making slanderous accusations like that.'

'Can't I?'

'She was your friend!' he persisted. 'You probably set her up to it – you were falling behind on your schedule – you—'

'Bill,' Katherine said quietly. 'You'll make yourself even sicker than you are already.'

Then she sighed, and thought for a moment. She knew that Helen had kept no such thing as an inventory, and if there had been one she would have conveniently mislaid it years ago. She had no right to sell the contents of Tylowe – many of them were heirlooms – but Katherine guessed that was what she had been doing, bit by bit ever since she'd lived in the place, in order to maintain her lavish life-style.

'You two –' she spoke very slowly – 'are in dire trouble as it is. But if I find out that you've been trying to feather your own nests through Borjex – on top of what you've attempted to do to me – then I'm going to make certain your heads roll like heads have never rolled before. You'll never work again in any country where Borjex has any influence whatsoever. Can you name me a civilized country where it doesn't?'

Even as she spoke, she knew that the chances of obtaining the decisive proof were negligible. The other thing she knew was that only one member of Borjex's senior management had outside interests in property: Gareth.

She tried to quash the thought as soon as it had been conceived, but it stayed, along with the distress his recent behaviour had caused her. Much as she may not want to face facts about Gareth, she was going to have to now. The time for fooling herself was over, and it did hurt. Gareth manipulated people: he had manipulated Irv with the result that he had been offered this board appointment; he could easily have manipulated Skerrett and was certainly attempting to influence Jo Cleary. He was a past master at that sort of thing. Even the European board were looking to him more and more for guidance. It followed that he would also try to use the chairman . . . She wanted to say to Skerrett, 'Just what part does Gareth Williams have in all this treachery?', but she had no intention of showing her hand too soon. If Gareth was cunning, then she, too, would be equally subtle and bide her time.

'You're dangerous,' she said, and saw only Gareth's face, and thought that if she'd loved him less there would have been no place for all this pain. 'It would be an excellent thing if you could be prevented from holding responsible positions. Meanwhile, you're suspended from your duties with this company until we have time to investigate your dealings further – and that, I suppose, will be after the strike.'

The disaster happened in those eerie moments just before total darkness. The skies had clouded over early that day, filling themselves with swollen grey clouds that massed and rumbled ominously.

Katherine was in her office at the time, and Mrs Egerton had popped her head round the door to say that Gareth had left a message for her: he'd gone out shortly after lunch and wouldn't be back for the rest of the day, but needed to see her urgently either tonight or first thing tomorrow morning. Would she contact him at his home number after 7.00 p.m.?

'All right,' Katherine nodded. 'Did he say what it was about?'

'I'm afraid not – all he said was that it was important.'

'I'll contact him. And could you get me New York on the line?'

There was a flash of lightning, followed a moment later by a loud clap of thunder.

'The storm's coming this way,' Mrs Egerton commented. 'Blowing over from the west,' and before she had time to return to her own office, there was a prolonged bleep on the external phone.

She hurried away to answer it, and was back within the minute. Her face was drained of colour.

'There's been a landslide at Tylowe,' she said. 'People are buried – the rescue teams are on their way.'

TWELVE

Swear me, Kate, like a lady as thou art
A good mouth-filling oath.

> – HOTSPUR; *Henry the Fourth*, Part One.

Katherine stared at Mrs Egerton. For a split second, while she took in the full import of her words, she froze. Then she snapped into action.

'Get me a driver,' she said. 'Any that's available so long as he's good and fast. Tell Hal Maitland to meet me at Tylowe – unless he can be in the basement car park in the next five minutes. Fetch me my overalls, helmet, gum boots – I'll change into them here and take these clothes to put on later. And make sure Irv's kept informed.'

They drove through torrential rain, and the further west they headed from London the heavier it fell. By the time they reached the Tylowe site, the windscreen wipers were unable to cope and water was streaming in rivulets down the front of the car.

All seemed confusion at first, but it took only the briefest of inquiries to discover what had happened: a slurry tip, which had been inadequately inspected since the strike, had become more precarious by the hour over the last few days. Built on porous land which – so one engineer suggested to Katherine – could contain underground springs concealed amongst the faults in the strata, the tip had been unable to withstand the sustained onslaught of the ferocious weather. Part of it had moved, and the rest had followed automatically in an avalanche of mud and boulders.

The number of casualties was uncertain as yet: when

the disaster occurred, a man had been driving his car along the country lane that skirted the site, and both he and the car had been instantaneously engulfed; half a dozen houses nearby had also been partially covered, but nobody knew if there had been any trespassers near the tip when it had given way – and that was what the rescue team was trying to find out. If there had been trespassers, the chances were that they would have been children, playing on what was to them merely disused land.

Hopefully, the bad weather would have acted as a deterrent, but it required brute force and digging to find out.

One blessing was that the site was in the middle of the country, with only a poor road and a scattering of houses in the vicinity; otherwise the toll of injured or dead could have been in the hundreds.

There was nothing for Katherine to do at first, and inactivity coupled with dread made the frustration almost unbearable. She had Hal Maitland with her, and Jo Cleary was there, too, talking to a group of men at the far end of the site; Dr Beloff and a senior PR man from Borjex joined them around six-thirty. It had been completely dark for the past half hour; the rain had eased off a little, but was continuing to slough across the landscape in an almost solid sheet, hampering the rescuers and turning the ground into a network of thin, muddy streams.

The arrival of television cameras and journalists caused further confusion, until Hal and the PR man organized them into an area just outside the site's exit; a helicopter flying low overhead indicated that one TV company at least was getting aerial shots, and soon after it had passed from view an almost audible sigh of relief went up from the team: the rain was stopping. It blew in chilly gusts for a further quarter of an hour or so, then ceased completely.

The sky was suddenly black and starlit, and a pale moon appeared. Arc lights were being set up as well, and their powerful beams illuminated the gruesome scene:

the tip looked like a huge cake that had been splayed across the undulating land; when it had moved it had taken with it the hillock that had been Jo's lookout post, and the solitary old tree that used to stand spectrelike against the horizon, then carried the whole lot on towards the road and the houses.

Digging operations were concentrated in a section about two hundred yards from where Katherine was standing, and it was when a huge arc light swung across the place that Gareth was caught in its glare. He was talking to the man who was in charge of the operations, and Katherine disobeyed the instructions she'd been given and waded through the slurry towards him.

They exchanged the briefest of words. Loves, hates, disagreements and doubts were of no consequence now: all that mattered was the injured.

'How long have you been here?' she asked.

'I was here when it happened,' he said. 'So was Jo Cleary. We were just leaving.'

'*What?* What the hell were you doing here with Jo Cleary? . . . Oh – save it for later. Where did you get the clothes from?'

'Jo had spare overalls and a helmet in his car. You'd better get back and help with the inquiries.'

Information was being relayed from the site by field telephone, but there was a large crowd of people behind the cordoned-off disaster area, and apart from the press who wanted news there were frantic people who'd lost relatives or friends and were desperate for fresh details. There were also the usual sick people who'd come only as spectators and were getting in the way: Katherine, Hal and the PR man took charge and sorted them out, then offered what reassurances they could to those who had genuine inquiries.

A van arrived containing a load of blankets, and another one with tea and coffee that was distributed amongst those in greatest need. Katherine was consoling a woman who was near hysterics because she hadn't seen her son all day: he was twelve, she said, and his name was Peter. He'd been going onto the site ever since the strike – and perhaps before – with other boys of his age. Two of his friends had already been brought out from the mud alive, and had been taken to hospital, but there was still no news of Peter.

Katherine thought of Marius: he was older but just as reckless for adventure, and it could easily have been him. Offering this woman bland assurances and cups of tea seemed so pathetic, and as she was racking her brains for something else to say that might calm her temporarily, Gareth appeared by her side.

He advised Katherine to go back to London: she could do nothing here and might as well await developments at headquarters. A list of names of the missing had been drawn up, and all but one had now been discovered. The occupants of the worst-hit houses had been given temporary shelter in a village hall a mile away, and although the list of the injured had reached fifteen, none was in a critical condition and only the last name on the list had still to be crossed off.

The woman whose arm Katherine was holding let out a terrible wail, and her face crumpled up with tears.

'It's her son,' Katherine said. Then, as she heard one of the rescuers call for more volunteers to be organized, she signalled to a girl wearing the uniform of a nursing auxiliary. Handing the woman over to her, she sought out Jim Beloff and told him to get back to London and deputize, and to take Hal Maitland with him to make an official announcement to the press. The PR man could stay to cope with inquiries here.

Glancing at the crowd behind the cordons, she saw white, strained faces – a few softening now with relief but others drawn and watchful. Peter's mother had pushed the nurse away from her, and she was standing alone:

there were no tears on her face now, but her expression of desperate hope was pitiful.

Katherine turned away to join Gareth at a mound of rubble.

'Get back,' he said. 'This is no job for you.'

'I'm staying,' she replied. 'So you might as well tell me what to do.'

'We don't need any women here – go and console somebody.'

'Plenty of people are doing that already, people better at the job than I could ever be. Nobody will know I'm a woman in these overalls, and with my hair in this helmet.'

'Somebody will recognize you.'

'They're too busy. Where do I start?'

Gareth had been digging for nearly five hours . . . despite the cold of the night his face was drenched in sweat. The job was a delicate one, he explained to her, because although the earth had to be moved, it had to be done with extreme care so as not to injure whoever might be beneath it.

They dug without speaking for hours, he doing the heaviest of the work and she helping him by taking over the lighter, and working side by side they made an effective team. Katherine scrabbled through silt and stones with her bare hands, and it was her hand that closed over another still smaller one, shortly after eleven p.m.

Tearing at the remaining earth, Gareth uncovered the body and lifted it gently free.

Peter's ribcage was still rising and falling, but erratically. One leg was badly twisted and he must have been unconscious for a long time. What had saved his life was the boulders: they had been responsible for his fractured bones, but had deflected the mud and silt and allowed him vital breathing space.

Ambulancemen and a stretcher arrived within seconds, and only minutes later Peter and his mother were being sped through the countryside to hospital. Katherine had accompanied the stretcher as far as the cordons, and found herself surrounded by pressmen. Still more were trying to talk to Gareth; he looked across at her but lights were flashing and people were jostling and they were being forced further and further apart.

Borjex's PR man took hold of Katherine's arm and suggested he drive her back to London. She was about to agree, when it crossed her mind that it would be easier and more convenient to stay down here for what remained of the night. First thing tomorrow morning she would want to join the inspection team to look at the site in daylight, and it would be good to be on hand in case there were any further developments before daybreak.

'Don't bother,' she said. 'If my car and driver are still here, it means I've got a change of clothing so I'll spend the night at Tylowe. You can reach me there – at the castle – if you need me, and you'd better tell the site engineers where I am. Have you got a pen handy? I'll give you the number. Make sure the press don't know where I am, won't you?'

The staff were awake, listening to news bulletins on the radio. They were agog for first-hand information; Katherine told them what she knew and asked them to give her driver a cup of coffee before he returned to London. She herself wanted nothing but a bath and hot drink, so they were free to return to their quarters.

She soaked in Helen's bath for twenty minutes, put on clean clothes and went down to the deserted kitchens. Hot, milky coffee cheered her momentarily, then her spirits flagged again. Exhaustion hit her suddenly, now that she had the time to notice it. The depression she felt was probably a symptom of fatigue, but it seemed very real. There were sixteen casualties from the landslide and the strike was still on – quite enough to make anybody depressed.

Tylowe was yet another worry, and despite the lateness of the hour she decided that Edward could be woken.

His telephone rang only twice before he answered it: he, too, was still awake and listening to the news.

'I thought you ought to know that I'm staying here for the night,' she told him. 'I hope you don't mind.'

'You're most welcome to the place,' he said. 'I'm only too glad it can be put to some use. You say there were no deaths?'

'No, thank God. But if I were you, I'd keep clear of the Tylowe Drift – the land's in a terrible condition.'

'The manager and his men go down regularly to check, but that's all.'

'I don't think it's safe, Edward – there's been no proper maintenance shift for days.'

'They're doing their best.'

'There aren't enough of them . . . but I'll talk to you again about it tomorrow. By the way, any news on Helen?'

'Nothing, I'm afraid. I can't tell you how sorry I am about what she's done – if I hear anything at all from her I'll let you know immediately.'

'We're trying to trace her, as well, but that's something else we'll have to talk about tomorrow. I'm going to go and get some rest now.'

'D'you need anything?'

'No, thanks. I've told the staff to go to bed, and all I want to do is the same.'

'Goodnight, then.'

'Goodnight.'

Katherine went upstairs to Helen's bedroom – the only one with a telephone – pulled back the quilt of the four-poster and lay down.

She was glad she'd come to Tylowe – the press wouldn't find her here and she could be back on the site within a quarter of an hour if need be. She was glad in another way, too: she'd spent so many happy hours here over the past few years, and would probably never have the chance to stay in the place again. It was like a second home to her; she knew the staff so well, from the butler to the man who cleaned out the pool, just as she knew every room in the lovely old house. Tylowe was in a kind of limbo now, with Helen absconded and the heir still to be located. She felt that she had as much right as anybody to be here, because Borjex would have to assume responsibility for the castle until either Helen returned or Howard Cleave's son could be found. She supposed Edward had a moral responsibility, too, since Helen was his mother, but he was unlikely to look on it that way. She wished she hadn't been so abrupt with Edward the other day about his work in the Tylowe Drift: he had a tendency to be greedy but he was basically a kind man and meant well. That outburst of his when they'd split up was so uncharacteristic of him – and yet there'd been an element of truth in it. She should have heeded his warning to 'watch out for yourself', kept her wits about her and never slackened in her hostility towards Gareth. He *was* unscrupulous, and he *had* caused problems. A rogue and a charlatan, who must surely have bewitched her . . . It was the classic set-up – a forty-year-old chairman, dazzled and besotted because of sex or love or passion or whatever else you chose to call it. Perhaps there was a grain of truth in other things Edward had said. She did have regrets – not to the extent he'd implied, but they were there nevertheless. She'd worked with such determination, against such odds and – for many years – in such dismal surroundings that she hadn't even seen the roses on the way. Maybe that was why she was susceptible to them now. Yet she didn't think she'd do anything differently, if she could turn the clock back. Winning was a prize in itself – and it was very, very sweet.

She'd done a lot with her life, but she thought she was going to be awfully lonely in the future. Loneliness . . . She was familiar with it. How lucky Gareth was to have Marius – he could have wished for no finer son. How

Katherine would have loved a son like that! Marius! She supposed she would never see him again now, which seemed typically unfair of life. One more person that she'd loved but had to be separated from.

Katherine groaned and stretched her legs. Every muscle in her body was aching, making sleep impossible despite exhaustion.

Flinging back the cover, she got up and walked over to the window. The curtains were open and she could see the park out there, shining ghostly in the pale moonlight.

That, too, brought a lump to her throat – the sheer breathtaking beauty that lay just beyond arm's reach. Everything was gone, finished, spoiled. It was too late to win Edward back, and she didn't really want him – not in the way she'd wanted Gareth. But she didn't want Gareth, either, not now that he'd deceived her and let her down yet again. He should have stayed hidden in the past, not come back to torment her and remind her that she had never, in all her life, loved any man as she had loved him.

Bitterness, that was what she felt now. It was a new and unpleasant emotion, and she hoped it would pass. If this was how Bill Skerrett felt all the time, it was no wonder he was ill.

When the nastiness should finally disappear, the next thing would be numbness – a total hardness, a real hardening of the arteries so that she would never feel again the heartache she felt over Gareth.

Something inside her was dead already, and that was an excellent thing. She would go on working now – surviving rather than living – until she was no longer physically capable of dragging herself into an office. Then, she supposed, she would fizzle out somewhere as people did. She would go on alone, and it wouldn't hurt because she didn't want anybody. It seemed a futile existence, but it was the best she was capable of. Apparently, it was what she'd been created for.

Improving working conditions for others, doing her bit

towards the country's economy – they were tedious enough reasons to go on living, but better than many. Some women, and men, had no reasons at all.

No matter from which angle the situation was viewed, it was evident that Gareth had used her. The facts were all there: his acceptance of the board membership, his own company's interests, his destruction of her arguments during the union negotiations – and then all the other indications, from fraught phone calls while they were in Italy to his trips to Cardiff where he obviously had severe business problems. She didn't know enough as yet to piece the whole thing together and come up with the perfect answer, but she knew enough to make her loathe Gareth Williams. He'd been unnecessarily friendly with Skerrett behind Katherine's back, and today – by his own admission – had been fraternizing with Jo Cleary while her own negotiations had reached deadlock.

How useful he must have found it to be part of the statel team . . . He was a trouble-maker, using both her and Borjex for his own ends, and if guilt had to be apportioned then a great deal would surely come to rest on Gareth Williams's shoulders – because he was the only board member whose private business interests were in property. Opencast sites, stately homes . . . Skerrett and Cleary . . . Gareth had manoeuvred himself into the ideal position for making a vast amount of money.

Charming and handsome and clever and deceitful: that was what he'd always been – from the heartbreak in Abertawe to the destruction of his ex-partner, Ellis McKay – and that was what he would continue to be. On reflection, she realized he'd achieved an admirable amount during his few months on the board – he was wielding as much power as the chairman in every area that mattered to him, and now he was manipulating a union as well, a union concerned with land. And everybody respected him, from Irv to little Jennie Corrin.

She hoped she would be able to find the energy and

intelligence to stop him. Both Skerrett and Jo Cleary would have to be persuaded to give some answers, then she would discover the full extent of what he was attempting to do.

She sighed, rubbed her arms because they ached, then rubbed her head because that ached, too. Then she opened the window and drew in a lungful of deliciously cold air.

The night was perfectly still, and the black sky was sprinkled with stars. A frosty moon was sailing above the treetops of Tylowe, reflecting dully on the swollen lake – just as the lamps of the Ponte Vecchio had shone on the Arno, an age ago, when a dream had come true and she'd found him again. After all those years.

Edward was frightened. Katherine's words about the drift had troubled him, and he'd telephoned the manager to check that all was well.

The manager's wife had told him that her husband, disturbed by the news of the landslide, had gone to the site to see if he could help. She had heard nothing further for over four hours. Perhaps, she suggested, he'd gone on to the drift to see if that had been affected.

Thanking her, Edward rang off. He poured himself a scotch, thought for a few moments, then put a call through to the office in the pit yard. Nobody answered, and he found himself praying that it was simply because nobody was there.

He finished his scotch, was on the point of pouring himself another one then changed his mind. Snatching up his car keys, he hurried out to the Rolls and drove as if his life depended on it towards the Tylowe Drift.

A light was on in the office, and the silhouette of a man was pacing the room.

The door was flung open before he even reached it.

'What's happening?' he said.

'I don't know,' the man looked worried, but not frantic.

He was an old man, an ex-miner who did clerical and light surface jobs at the drift. 'Nothing, I hope, but something's gone wrong with the phone.'

'Is that all?' Edward heaved a sigh of relief. 'I rang you just now—'

'No,' the man said. 'I mean with the pit phone. Boss decided he ought to do a maintenance check – he went down about three hours ago with a couple of deputies. They should be coming back from the face by now, but they're not answering.'

'Let me try,' Edward said, brushing past him into the office and snatching up the phone. He rapped at it, shouted into it, but the line was completely dead.

Roy Davis, the manager, was also worried. He was a youngish man, a graduate in mining engineering with several years' experience in deep mining, plus another eighteen months in drift mines. As far as he could tell, there was nothing seriously wrong, and one of his deputies agreed with him. The other, Vince Dickson, was adamant that something was seriously wrong.

Vince was a man in his late fifties; he had worked in pits as a collier since he was a boy, and taken qualifications later at night school. Roy depended heavily on his judgement, because during Vince's long years in all types of mines – some, like this drift, with appalling conditions – he had acquired a rare facility: the hardened miner's sixth sense for disaster. It was a talent possessed only by such men as Vince – older men who had spent the greater part of their lives below ground, working physically at the getting of coal.

'I told you before,' Vince said, 'we drove this face too quickly.'

They were on the new face, the one that had been driven within a hair's breadth of the castle walls.

'But it's perfectly safe,' Roy's words belied the doubts that nagged at him. 'Can you tell me what's wrong?'

Vince shook his head, but thoughtfully rather than to imply a negative answer.

Behind the hydraulic supports that kept up the roof, another section of the roof – from where coal had already been mined – had fallen away, exactly as it ought and easing the strain on the face itself. The pumps, which the men had just checked, were working and there was no sign of water.

Roy and the other deputy moved on, tapping the roof and heading towards the tailgate which gave onto an underground roadway and, ultimately, out. But 'out' was half a mile away, up a steep incline.

Vince stayed on the coal face: it was high, nearly five foot, and since he was a short, wiry man he only had to stoop a little.

'It's not gas, anyway,' Roy called to him, glancing down at his lamp. The words echoed, reverberating from the black, shiny walls that gleamed gently in the electric light beams.

'Sh,' Vince said. Then, more quietly, he added: 'We're not worried about gas in this pit, are we? It's water – and this roof—'

His words carried along the tunnels, almost to the fresh air outside.

Then total, eerie silence fell.

'Out!' Vince yelled, and nobody hesitated.

Roy and the other man ran, they were out of the tailgate and onto roadway before they even heard the crack.

When the noise came, they paused, turned back to grab Vince's shoulders and pull him forward. He was hurt and his face was bloody: he pushed the other two men in front of him but they grabbed him and ran with him, half dragging him along.

The roof had gone. The fracture ran the length of the face, and the fall followed the men up the tunnel. It was the moment every miner dreads, and the half mile to fresh air was the longest imaginable journey.

Cracking and rumbling, the earth split apart then caved in with a deafening, triumphant roar. In its wake came the water – a whole sheet of it fell down, flooding the pumps and forming itself into a black and grimy stream. Pieces of the costly anthracite danced on its surface, like flotsam from a wrecked ship – and as the men stumbled up the incline, it snarled at their heels.

Katherine moved from room to room, saying her farewells. Later, when she no longer ached so much, she might try and sleep – but at the moment the pain was too great.

She went into the ballroom, switched on the chandeliers and saw all her friends again – Edward, Helen, Irv, Richard, her mother, Barbara Spencer . . . and of course Marius, with that giveaway tilt of the head. She could hear some old favourite of Helen's – 'Blue Moon', perhaps – and she hummed it softly, as she extinguished the lights and closed her eyes against the tears.

The library was the next room she visited, with its faded old rugs and shelves of well-thumbed books. She traced her finger along them lightly, and when she reached the window rested her forehead against chilly, mullioned panes.

It was frosted over out there: an early autumn whiteness covered the gardens, and the dark shape of some animal was picked out clearly by the moon. A fox, that was what it was, slinking across the lawns with its head stuck forward and its brush trailing like a banner behind. The dog in the stable yard must have scented it, for it howled suddenly and rattled its chain.

Katherine supposed she had better not be away from the telephone too long, but an hour wouldn't hurt – and in any case it was unlikely by now that they would need her.

Tomorrow morning, that was when it would all start again.

That wretched dog was still howling, baying at the moon like some soul in torment. Katherine shivered, and headed towards the great hall, and the cellar steps, and Helen's underground creation where she hoped to find respite from physical, if not from mental, pain.

The whirlpool of the jacuzzi was marvellous: all her aches began to disappear and, as they faded, her thoughts became quieter, too.

She opened her eyes, and looked through the archway to the vaulted chamber beyond. How grand and rather spooky it was, with Helen's 1920's decor and the sheen of the ceramic tiles reflecting the blueness of the pool. Beyond that was the first chamber, the one that had been turned into a gymnasium, and there was the door that led to the stairway, and beside it were her clothes.

It was a weird sensation, being on your own and naked down here in the middle of the night. Behind her was a locked door, and although she'd never been through it she knew where it led: to the dungeons, where centuries before people must have lain frightened and alone, night after night. . .

How he must have laughed at her, when she told him she loved him . . .

Reaching out to adjust the controls, she turned the whirlpool up to 'full': its force rammed her against the side of the tub.

Her first assumption was that the controls were faulty, but then she was caught in the most violent current. It felt as though her muscles were being torn apart; she was buffeted from side to side, smashed against the rim of the tub then plunged down to its depths. She came up gasping for breath, clutched at thin air, was dragged down again. This time she touched rough earth – the ceramic tiles were gone.

She came up for the second time, screamed, reached for the controls. There was a bang – something broke, tiles coming away – more tiles . . . She fought through the maelstrom, reached the controls and hung on to them: she switched the handle back and forth – again and again but nothing happened. Gripping it fiercely, her body whipped by the water, she struggled to lever herself free.

The whirlpool pulled her back twice, then with an effort of will that blinded her to the searing pain in her shoulders, she heaved herself up and out, and lay panting on the wet floor. As she scrambled onto her hands and knees, she realized that the water was blue no longer – it was dark grey and filled with grit; the same substance coated her body from head to foot. It was in her hair that hung bedraggled across her face, and in her eyes that smarted and wept.

She stumbled through the archway into the central chamber, and screamed again. Her voice bounced back at her from the high ceiling, and she covered her ears with her fists. Her eyes were fixed on the pool: its floor had been rent by subsidence, as though some giant mole had burrowed beneath it. It had risen three feet, split open as the jacuzzi had done, and was spilling water over its sides.

Paddling through it towards the door, she realized the pool was being topped up from some external source – a gap in the ruptured tiling that was letting in a powerful jet of slime.

Then something cold touched her shoulder. She flinched, looked up at the ceiling, but out of the corner of her eye she saw a long, thin, vertical fissure in the outer wall – the wall that kept the earth from tumbling into the cellars. It was a hairline fracture as yet, but drops of water were squeezing through it, falling one by one onto the flooded tiles.

She rushed to the door, wrenched at the knob, but she could see it was useless even now. It was impacted, moved inches and bludgeoned into place from the tremor. She heard a noise, sharp like the report from a rifle, spun round and saw that the fracture was longer, and that the drops of water were falling faster now.

They were drops from the bowels of the earth, from the rich seam of coal. But of course! What an appropriate punishment after a life like hers – from Jack Bartley and Langston to Edward and Tylowe, from Max Holman to her ruthless treatment of Skerrett – all the people she'd crossed or hurt. The mine! It was dying – they'd killed it with their greed. It would be roaring now, folding in on itself with a terrible, primaeval sound, then it would burst through the walls of Tylowe and take her with it.

She flung her body at the door but the woodwork was fixed and jammed. Like this entire underground world it had moved with the subsidence, and she crashed her shoulder against it half a dozen times before, through her panic, she realized that it opened inwards not outwards.

She yelled and cried but there was no one to hear; then she ran towards the dungeon door, falling into the water and picking herself up again, trembling as she hurled herself against the solid oak panels.

There was no way out; only the outer wall was keeping her alive and God alone knew if it would hold.

An hour ago she hadn't cared whether she'd lived or died, but now there seemed to be no choice – she wanted desperately to live.

Then she heard the outer wall crack open; heard, then saw, the torrent of black water as it tore into the vaulted chamber. It carried with it fragments of anthracite, and jettisoned itself towards the glittering ceiling like some monstrous black fountain.

Gareth was the nearest he'd been to panic since that morning in Wales when she'd left him, when he'd returned to Gwilym Cottage to find it deserted, and had searched everywhere – even in kitchen cupboards – to find some small thing that was personal to her. He remembered his frantic efforts now, how he'd tried for months to trace her, and how he'd failed.

Tonight, after the injured boy had been taken to hospital and Katherine had been lost in the crowd of journalists, he'd stayed on at the site. He'd helped with the basic organizing that was required in the aftermath of the landslide, and talked to the rescue team. Then, just as he was beginning to feel exhausted and was wondering where Katherine could have got to, the news came through of the roof fall at Tylowe Drift. He'd gone there with the rescuers but – mercifully – no volunteers were needed because the men had already been helped free by Edward and some old man that Edward had with him.

It was Edward who was muttering about Katherine; he looked harrowed and weary, and was saying that she'd warned him and ought to be told.

'If anybody round here has any brandy,' Gareth put a comradely hand on his shoulder, 'I should ask them if you can have a swig of it. There's no point in blaming yourself now, and thank God nobody's been badly hurt. I'll phone Katherine.'

'She's at Tylowe,' Edward said, and Gareth went into the office and put through a call to the castle.

When nobody answered, he decided to drive over there; he was only vaguely worried at this stage, but wanted to be with her, and in any case had no intention of driving back to London tonight.

His own car was at the opencast site, so on the spur of the moment he helped himself to Edward's Rolls, telling himself that since the man looked so shaky he was probably doing him a favour.

He drove quickly through the moonlit countryside, through the park gates and up to the castle entrance. The doors were unlocked; whoever had been the last to go to bed was either forgetful or careless, so Gareth walked straight into the main hall and called out Katherine's name. He was met by silence: the servants were presumably in bed, so rather than wake them he headed for the stairs to look through the main bedrooms. He guessed she would be sleeping in one of these, so his hunt shouldn't take long.

His body ached; he would have loved a bath and to lie down between white linen sheets with Katherine beside him. Not that he was particularly pleased with her at the moment, but as soon as he got her on her own for a few hours he would sort all that out.

After a quarter of an hour's search he still hadn't found her, so he returned to the main hall. That was when he noticed a gap in the panelling: it was a door, open a few inches and with a light shining behind it. He opened it still further, looked down at a twisting flight of stone steps and began to descend them.

As he rounded the last bend in the staircase and came to a tiny vestibule, his foot met with water.

He heard a woman's voice that might have been Katherine's, and it was screaming at the door. Then he knew it was her, for she was cursing and swearing and the words he could make out were alarming. For a second he paused, laughed to himself; then he called out to her, took a deep breath, tensed his muscles and rammed his shoulder against the door with all his might.

Nothing gave, and he felt himself swept by panic.

The water was rising; it was up to her calves now and she clawed frantically at the woodwork. A couple of her nails were torn back to the quick, but she didn't even notice.

She screamed and swore, at the door and at the thought of Gareth and at life that was slipping away. Then she hammered at the panels; they were solid, just as the door to the dungeons had been.

For a while she'd waded through the dark water, going back and forth through the chambers in panic, choking on the stench of air that had been trapped long underground – air that was now released; she'd wrenched first at one door then at the other – pounded on them – flung herself against them – but now all her efforts were concentrated on this one spot where, just possibly, the warped old hinges might yield.

She was going to die and she wanted to live, wanted some God-given moment with him again. She didn't care what wrong he'd done or why, she only cared that she loved him and that this parting would be the last. Now the end was so near it was the joy they'd known that made her weep – the splendid moments. Everything else was insignificant, paltry, transitory.

An hour would do, even a minute with him. One minute so that he could convince her – not of rights and wrongs, but that she was a foolish woman who didn't know when she was well loved.

She scrabbled at the door, looked about her desperately for some implement but only an axe would have done; she sweated, tried to force the hinges with her fingers as though her very bones might make them shift, then she screamed for help and when none came she screamed for forgiveness.

The roar of the black fountain was deafening, but she yelled above it, mingling oaths with curses in her terror. Then she slipped to her knees in the water and sobbed.

When his answering shout came she didn't believe it. She thought it was the kind of false hope people have when they are about to die. But Gareth was real, because a second after he'd called to her he rammed himself against the door and she heard the thud of his body.

She got to her feet and stood back, listened to blow after blow that crashed against the wood, listened to the grinding protest from the twisted hinges and saw the door break open: he shoved hard against the water, opened it still further and a moment later he was there in front of her.

'Gareth—'

Then the vestibule behind him was splitting and crumbling, filling quickly with water and grey stone.

He glanced over his shoulder, saw the staircase covered with silt and the first half dozen steps already gone, swallowed into some yawning hole that was growing by the second.

'Christ – is there another way out?'

'There's a door over there – but I can't open it.'

He slammed the door to the vestibule shut. It burst open again immediately. Water, earth, stone and anthracite flooded in.

Putting his arm about her, he waded with her across the chamber – beneath the fountain where jet-black splinters shot into the air, whipped at their skin, tore at their faces – on to the jacuzzi, fighting through the rising water.

He flung himself against the dungeon door, swore as nothing gave.

'I can't get enough leverage! The water's holding me back!'

From the vaulted chamber came the shocking, inhuman bellow of the mine as it burst through stone, intensified its onslaught and rent a gorge so wide in the outer wall that there could be only minutes now, perhaps only seconds before the whole base of Tylowe was gone.

'God Almighty!' Gareth breathed, then looked down at the dark foaming waters and suddenly plunged in his hand.

'We'll try this!' he yelled, holding up a jagged piece of anthracite. Then he leaned back, raised his fist and smashed it in a giant blow against the ancient woodwork. It took two more wedges – the last so huge that he could scarcely grip it in both hands – and a dozen blows before it worked: a whole panel splintered. Blood gushed from his hand as he thrust it through the gap, yanked at the bolts on the far side, then pushed open the door.

The water had already seeped through to the dungeons,

but now it surged forward in a sickening wave. Gareth gripped Katherine's hand, pulled her into the darkness.

They stumbled against pieces of iron, against foul, nameless things and against steps. Katherine fell head-long; Gareth lifted her out of the water, flung her across his shoulder, and as the final, victorious thunder of the mine came rumbling through the earth, he began climb-ing, up and up . . .

The flood followed them – swelled all the way up to the second big landing – then fell back, frothed in one last grimy wave, licked tamely at the worn, stone platform.

'Where the hell are we?' he said, and put her down. 'Can you stand?'

'Yes.' But her voice was unsteady and she was shivering and trembling.

He peeled off his shirt and put it round her shoulders.

'It's not much,' he said, 'but it's better than nothing. There's a passageway down here—'

'It must be – let's see, if we're as high as I think we are – then it's a corridor that skirts the game cellars, and they open up in the dairy.'

'Right, come on. Are you going to walk or shall I carry you?'

'I shall walk,' she said, and heard his laugh in the darkness.

But as he stepped forward she clung to his arm; he stopped, put it round her, then helped her along, rubbing at her to keep her warm, saying things that cheered her heart as they made their way down that cold, winding passageway.

Ahead of them was a pinpoint of light, and it was growing. They came to a half-open door and Gareth shoved at it. There was a crash, the sound of something solid overturning and the shattering of pottery and glass. He pushed the door wider and they saw the first glim-merings of dawn: it filtered through high, gridded windows to light up the dairy with the palest of morning lights.

'Dawn's breaking,' she whispered.

'Yes,' he said. 'All over again,' and swept her up in his arms.

'Oh!'

'The next few steps could be tricky,' he grinned, 'but I shall put you down again in a moment. After you've sworn one more oath to add to that list you came out with earlier.'

'I was panic-stricken.'

'But now you're not. Swear, Kate, that our next parting will be the kind that's not of our choosing. And that until then you'll keep to your vows.'

'Vows? What vows?'

'The "love" one's easy – I reckon we can handle that. But then comes "to honour"—'

'Stop there,' she smiled at him. 'There could be a bone of contention already.'

THIRTEEN

A peace is of the nature of a conquest;
For then both parties nobly are subdu'd,
And neither party loser.

ARCHBISHOP; *Henry the Fourth*, Part Two

He was sitting in front of his French windows, and the chair next to his was empty.

'Hurry up, Katherine!' he called.

'Just one more person to ring!' she called back.

He waited, listening to the tick of that funny little clock, thinking it was a good thing he and Katherine had managed to get at least a couple of hours' rest, because the past eighteen hours had been exhausting and neither of them was as young as they used to be.

It had been mid-morning by the time they'd got back to London, both of them dressed in clothes lent to them by the anxious servants at Tylowe. They were ill-fitting garments, but as welcome in the circumstances as ermine robes. Katherine had been as relieved as Gareth when they'd finally limped into his flat in Hampstead, and it wasn't until they were about to lie down on that invitingly soft bed that she'd blurted out something odd – something about him and Skerrett and Tylowe Castle, and how quickly his own property company was growing.

He'd got the point immediately – had felt an enormous surge of anger, then shelved it. Normally he would have shouted and stormed, but quite frankly he'd been too weary by then and the moment for showdowns wasn't now. Later, he'd promised himself, when we're both thinking more clearly, that's when I'll tackle her.

So instead of shouting he'd done nothing at all, and the look of resignation that had crossed his face had been genuine enough.

'Oh well,' he'd said, and shrugged in a gesture of absolute hopelessness. 'What else could I have expected from you? So that's that, I suppose.'

To his surprise her face had gone ashen, and suddenly she didn't look like a lioness anymore: her freshly washed hair was plastered down flat against her head, and those slanting hazel eyes were round with dismay.

Then he remembered! It was his warning of a few nights ago, that if he had one more insult from her he would leave, and he would not come back. Not this time.

Obviously she'd believed him. But then she'd always believed the worst things about him, and skipped so carelessly over the best. He was not a good man, not entirely, but he wasn't entirely bad either – and in his opinion Katherine had treated him most unfairly on so many occasions.

Her lower lip had begun to tremble and she'd drawn nearer to him, moving with hesitant, wary steps as though she might even be a little afraid of him. He couldn't think why, just as he couldn't think why he should feel this mild sense of shame that made him put his arms around her, cradle her to him and then kiss her lightly on the forehead, smile at her in a gentle way that held neither guile nor mischief nor even lust. Just love, and comrade-ship, and goodwill.

She'd put her arms round his neck, kissed him on the cheek – and then of all things she'd rushed off to the kitchen and started clattering about in there.

She made him a hot drink – in case he'd caught a cold, she said – and then of course he'd had to try not to look amused, to accept the foul-looking concoction with appropriate thanks. It was hot milk and whisky, but he drank it all the same, and in fact it didn't seem so foul after the first sip or two. She'd made one for herself, as well, and they sat up in bed together drinking their evil-looking mixtures, subdued and tired but perfectly content.

They'd got up only half an hour ago, about one-ish, and while she was making her phone calls he'd taken his turn at acts of kindness and brewed them a pot of coffee. It wasn't much of an effort, he realized, but it was the best he was capable of in the domestic realm: at least it showed willing and he'd have plenty of time to learn more, in what remained of his life. And a pretty fair whack still remained.

'Coffee's going cold!' he shouted, because she'd already been on the phone twenty-five minutes, and that was all Borjex were going to get of Katherine Hanson on this glorious autumn day. Also, before any more of it ticked by, he'd got one or two things to sort out with her.

'I've taken the phone off the hook,' she declared, as she breezed into the room and sat down beside him. 'As far as I'm concerned it's close of business for today.'

'Not as far as I'm concerned!' He put more anger into his voice than he actually felt, but it paid to be on the safe side in dealing with Kate. 'I've got a couple of things to say to you that I don't think you'll care for too much – and I don't want us to be interrupted.'

Her face fell.

'What's the matter with you?' she said.

'What was that you were saying to me this morning about Bill Skerrett – and me and my property company?'

'It's not important. I understand and I forgive you. I'd rather accept you the way you are than not have you at all. When I was in the cellars at Tylowe, I realized that – well,' she shrugged, 'I thought I was going to die. Then I knew that nothing was terribly important compared to—'

She stopped.

Gareth had risen slowly to his feet, and his anger was sincere as well as obvious now.

'You must be mad,' he said. 'I tried to excuse you

earlier on grounds of exhaustion, but it's a different matter entirely now.'

'Don't bother to explain. Let's leave it.'

'We most certainly will not leave it!' he retorted. 'What – and have our married life blighted with your suspicions? Do you really doubt me so much? How could you, Katherine, how could you?'

'It was a possibility, wasn't it?' She, too, rose to her feet. 'Look, for instance, at what you did to Ellis McKay.'

He froze, then smiled – very, very slowly.

'And what—' he asked her – 'about you and Jack Bartley?'

'How do you know about that?'

'And how do you know about Ellis McKay?'

They stared at one another – then said, within a split second of each other: 'Irv.'

'The bastard's broken my confidence!' Gareth added.

'I didn't even realize,' Katherine said, 'that he knew about Jack Bartley, though it was common knowledge in the North – and Irv must have made enough inquiries about me before he offered me a seat on the board . . . Bloody hell, and he's the one who's always complaining about gossip!'

'He did say that he admired you, especially since you were a woman, for managing to do down Jack Bartley. He told me that was one of the reasons that decided him to offer you a board membership.'

'And he told me he respected you for the way you dealt with Ellis – and considered you honourable for the way you tried to save his wife.'

Gareth's eyes narrowed, then he smiled again.

'Finally,' he said, 'I'm glad Irv put his foot in it. Because do you know what those two incidents tell me?'

'What?'

'That you've got everything wrong, Kate. I might be a rogue – that's my particular way of doing things – but the person who's been coolly and determinedly ambitious is you, not me! You walked all over Jack Bartley – and whether he was a likeable man or not is beside the point – simply because it helped you claw your way upwards. No other reason! I've never done that kind of thing in my life. What I did to Ellis McKay is only what any other self-respecting man with an ounce of guts would have done. Likewise with the drama at Abertawe – what kind of a man would turn his back on his wife when she was pregnant? What would you have said if you'd been pregnant, and I'd refused to even see you?'

He waited for the holocaust, but she said nothing. In fact she didn't seem to take his words as insults at all: she looked – almost pleased. He found it hard to believe.

'Well?' he prompted.

'Yes,' she said. 'You're quite right.'

'Oh.'

'Shall we sit down again?'

'For the rest of our lives,' he went on, ignoring her, 'I shall remind you about Ellis McKay and Jack Bartley – and Skerrett and Rykwert. When I think that those two bastards tried to ruin your reputation, and engineered the strike, by all accounts – and you linked my name with theirs! Me – who loves you! *I* was the one that Jennie Corrin confided in about those papers and antiques she found in Skerrett's office. *I* was the one who made sure that at least one board member was on good terms with Jo Cieary. *I* was the one who was trying to help both you and Borjex. *I* was the—'

'All right, all right! I'm sorry. Truly. I didn't want to believe the worst about you. It's only because I love you so much that sometimes I get – sort of frightened. I'm suspicious of our happiness, worried that it might go away again. Please believe me. I am sorry.'

'I know I'm not perfect, and I do manipulate a bit at times—'

She smiled.

'I'm only trying to be honest, Kate.'

She moved up close to him, kissed him.

For a moment he didn't respond, but as she was on the point of drawing away he put his arms around her, held her tightly and kissed her in return – long and hard and searchingly until he felt her body grow weak against his. Then he stood looking down at her: she really ought to have been pale after the traumas of yesterday, but there was a tinge of pink about her cheeks and a brightness in her eyes that cheered his heart.

'You're forgiven,' he told her. 'Temporarily.'

'So can we sit down now?'

'Hm.'

They sat down again side by side, and as the minutes rolled by he began to feel curious: Katherine really was unusually silent.

'Uhm—' he began – 'How did your phone calls go?'

'Fine.'

'Well tell me about them!'

'I rang Edward first,' she said.

'How was he?'

'Quite distraught to think that those men in the drift almost lost their lives. The mine, though, is dead and buried forever. It'll never be reopened. And the first estimates on Tylowe are that three-quarters of the sub-structure is gone, and that sections of the castle itself are going to need very attentive surveying and possibly reinforcing in places. I've told Edward to stop thinking about what might have been and just be glad we've all come through this nightmare safe and relatively sound. He said he'd try . . . He wants the four of us to get together one evening, and perhaps spend a weekend at Arlingham.'

'Who's the fourth?'

'This woman of his. He says she's lovely.'

'Then I'm sure she is – his taste in women is impeccable. We have a lot in common, Edward and I.'

'I hope,' she retorted, 'that you're not going to come

out with remarks like that every time I mention Edward's name.'

He glanced at her curiously, because despite her words her voice was casual and unconcerned, and there seemed to be a softening of that mouth that could appear so hard and so determined. It was an illusion, he presumed, something to do with the muted afternoon sunlight that caused her to look – just for a moment – like the Kate of fifteen years ago. Illusion or not, it was nice. It made him feel boyish, and he grinned and ruffled her hair.

'Don't!' she ducked, and laughed. 'Could I have some coffee?'

'I've poured you some, but I suppose it's a bit cold by now.'

He topped up her cup with hot coffee from the percolator, then poured another cupful for himself and sipped it gratefully, aware of total contentment for what seemed like the first time in years. There was peace on all fronts, and he prayed it would last for as long as possible.

Jennie Corrin had unwittingly played a major part: her antiques find had been sufficient to settle Skerrett and Rykwert, but the papers that had been discovered had proved even more useful. If Katherine hadn't been busy interrogating that treacherous pair, Gareth would have got the information through to her before the landslide, and instead of taking it upon himself to let Jo Cleary be the first one to know . . . Gareth was disgusted – but not entirely surprised – that Borjex's company secretary and its head of industrial relations should have been so instrumental in provoking this appalling strike. But they would also be the ones to end it. The near-tragedies had shocked everybody, not least the main body of the unions who had been unhappy about striking in the first place. They would have an excuse to return to work now without losing face, because public blame would be directed towards the two Borjex people who had instigated the unrest. Skerrett and Rykwert would be more than scapegoats, they would be fully deserving of the disgrace that was coming their way. If he was in their shoes he'd opt for the first available flight to Buenos Aires.

No wonder Jo Cleary had mistrusted Katherine after the lies he'd been told and the misleading papers he'd been shown. Had Gareth not been on such good terms with Jo, then the complete details might still be submerged in a mass of half-truths and suppositions. Gareth was well aware that he himself was a bigger rogue than Katherine could ever be, yet it was Gareth – and not Katherine – Jo had really warmed to. He was the one who'd managed to inspire Jo with confidence. Happily. But then, he was a past master at that sort of thing.

Maybe his approach with the MATEX leader had been rather unscrupulous, and it was undoubtedly storing up trouble for next year, but he'd won him over and gained his trust so that Jo would have added assurance when he urged his men back to work. But they would need little persuading, and next year could take care of itself. It was too soon to worry about it now, and in another sense it was too late – the seeds were already sown.

He hoped Jo would not lose out to the more powerful unions: there was a fair chance that he wouldn't; the MATEX members respected him and he'd run that union for many years. Gareth wouldn't object to doing a little wheeling and dealing and public speaking on Jo's behalf, should the need arise – and if he could find time with all his other commitments: his own business was expanding rapidly in England, and he would have to keep a very watchful eye on it.

'Did Edward mention Helen?' he asked.

'Mm?'

Goodness, she did look peaceful.

'What were you thinking about?'

'Nothing in particular. Sorry, what did you ask me?'

'What's the latest on Helen?'

'They can't trace her. Cosmetic surgeons in Florida or

Los Angeles would be at the top of my list, if I was looking for her.'

'I suppose you've told Borjex that?'

'As a matter of fact, I suggested Sweden or Brazil. Who knows, she may well have gone to either.'

'You should know, she was your friend.'

'That's what the board said.'

Gareth was conscious of having received some minor shock. He looked at Katherine closely, felt a conspiratorial smile touch his features, then felt it change almost instantly into a puzzled frown. He was uneasy, mildly alarmed. He hoped she wasn't starting to get up to his tricks. That would take some living with, two of them at it.

'Katherine?'

'Yes?'

'You do know where she is, don't you?'

There was a stony silence.

'Katherine – where is she? . . . If we're going to be man and wife, we have to trust each other – we can't have secrets like this.'

'Why not?'

'Katherine—'

'If I tell you,' she said, 'you must promise not to play one of Irv's tricks on me.'

'Of course! I've got a sense of honour, remember.'

'Oh yes, sorry. As a matter of fact, she was one of the people I was speaking to just now.'

'You're joking?'

She raised her eyebrows, then smiled.

'It wasn't too difficult to find her – or at least, it wasn't for me. I had an idea – just a long shot, really. I contacted an acquaintance of mine in the States, arguably one of the finest cosmetic surgeons over there. I'd once told Helen about him, and she'd seemed rather interested. Well, he's got clinics in New York, L.A. and Florida – and Helen was booked into his Florida one. Not as Lady

Arlingham, but as Mrs Roxana Cleave. Roxana used to be one of her stage names, and Cleave was her first husband's name. God alone knows what she's done about passports, but she certainly isn't bored anymore.'

'Christ! But she must have known you'd find her!'

'She knew there was a chance, but she obviously thought it worth the risk. And she also knew that I was her friend, and that although I might try to persuade her to come back and hand over the money, I'd never betray her. You're not the only one with a sense of honour, Gareth Williams. Do you really think I'd lay a friend of mine – an elderly woman, at that – open to the possibility of prosecution, maybe even a prison sentence?'

'No.'

'I did ask her to come back, and she may do eventually, but not until there's some kind of promise of a pardon. In the meantime she's spending money hand over fist and planning a cruise. I think I shall have to talk to Irv – a guarantee of no prosecution, so long as she handed back at least seventy-five per cent of the money, would be the best solution all round. Borjex will have to put the remainder down as a tax loss.'

Gareth frowned, thought for a minute, then decided it might be politic to change the subject.

'How's Richard coping?' he asked.

'Calmly and efficiently, as far as I can gather. I told him I'd be back at work tomorrow and if anything he sounded disappointed. I don't know what he's getting up to in that office. D'you know the first thing he said to me when I told him the strike would be ending?'

'That he'd go ahead and book his Christmas holiday.'

'How did you know?'

'Ah – I even know where he's going.'

'Where?'

'Italy.'

'To the Alps?'

'To Rome.'

'At Christmas?'

'Uh – huh.'

'Ohh –' she drew the word out slowly, letting her voice rise at the end. 'So we weren't the only ones who were preoccupied this summer.'

'He's a smart lad, Richard. Improving by the hour.'

'Yes, I think he is . . . This coffee's tepid and awful. Shall I make some more?'

'In a minute. Let's just sit still for a while. Shall we open the french windows or will you be cold?'

'No, open them. The sun's out and it's quite warm now.'

He opened the windows, sniffed contentedly at the greenness of the lawn, then returned to his easy chair.

'What a battered-looking couple we are,' he commented, glancing at his own hand swathed in bandages and her fingers covered in gashes and cuts, to say nothing of the painful bruises that marked their legs, arms and shoulders. 'Like a pair of old warhorses.'

'Oh I don't know – slightly injured racehorses, maybe.'

'You've got a hefty pair of thighs on you, Kate, for a racehorse.'

'Then it's a good thing you like some substance to your women, isn't it?'

'When shall we get married? Next week? Next month? Tomorrow?'

'We don't want to do it on the spur of the moment, do we?'

Again, he was aware of mild alarm.

'For Christ's sake, Katherine, it's been fifteen years! There's nothing to hold us back. Just tell the board you're having a holiday and that's that. Besides, you don't intend to do this job for ever, do you?'

'No,' she said, with abrupt decisiveness. 'There are other things I want to do, and I can do them equally well married or single. There's a book I'd like to write, for one thing, about women in business. Not geared solely to women, though, but dealing with the whole issue of current trends in—'

'All right, Katherine.' He was about to pat her hand, but checked himself. 'I've got the general idea. But when will you stop?'

'When my term of office comes to an end. I shan't ask for my contract to be renewed, even if they want me to stay on. Though I'd like us to see the statels through together.'

'If you stopped now,' he pointed out, 'there's a chance we could have a child. Of course you may consider it to be a foolish risk at forty, trying to start a family of our own.'

'Having a baby at my age—' She shook her head, but more as if weighing up the pros and cons than in a gesture of refusal. 'What a beautiful thought.'

'My trips to Cardiff weren't entirely for business,' he said. 'I've bought a house near the English border. A lovely place, only a few miles from the sea. It's built of beige-coloured stone, and it stands on a mountainside. The view from our bedroom window is magnificent.'

She turned her head to look at him, and though she smiled there was a touch of something enigmatic in her eyes. This was a new and unexplored side to Kate, and he was going to have to approach it with plenty of fore-thought.

He began calculating his next move, staring out at the trees that were shedding the summer like confetti now.

How happy he felt. More than happy. His hand pained him and he'd probably acquired an extra strand or two of grey hair since yesterday, but still he felt happy as a lark, watching that garden where the leaves were fading quickly to gold. He tried to think what it was that made him feel this good, and as a breeze sang through the dying foliage, he realized what it was: he felt as though he'd come home.

He smiled, and his eyes as they met Katherine's were very blue and warm.

Then he played his winning card.

'We shouldn't put the wedding off too long,' he said, 'because apart from anything else I need your help. As a wife.'

'Oh? Help in what way?'

He allowed his smile to disappear, let a sad, troubled look flit across his features.

'With Marius,' he said wistfully. 'The boy's a terrible worry to me.'

Her face lit up, just as he'd known it would.

'Walk out onto the lawn with me,' he said, 'and I'll tell you what's been going through my mind. He's coming to stay with us in Wales at Christmas, and I want your advice.'

She slipped her arm through his, and they stepped out into the garden side by side, just as the clock behind them adjusted itself to strike the hour.

The day was already well spent, but that patched-up old clock must have been losing: it was the noonday chimes that rang out, clear and joyful across the sunshiny room.